Indebted

A Novel

Braxton DeGarmo

Christen Haus Publishing

COPYRIGHT

E-Book and Paperback Editions Publication Date: January, 2013

ISBN-13: 978-1481857192
ISBN-10: 1481857193

Cover design by Brianna Lock of Word+Design, LLC

For more information, go to **www.braxtondegarmo.com** or **www.facebook.com/Braxton.DeGarmo.Author**

DEDICATION

For my children, Braxton Jr. and Stacey.
You both continue to make me proud.

TABLE OF CONTENTS

ACKNOWLEDGEMENTS

As always, I again want to acknowledge and thank my loving wife, Paula, for giving up time that we might have spent together and for her valuable proofreading skills, help and encouragement. She even added a new notation to the proofreader's lexicon: yuk! Fortunately, I only got a few of those red marks. (As always, any typos or errors are mine alone.)

Similarly, my son, Braxton, and our friend Kendra Duffield contributed with their comments and proofreading. Thank you both. In addition, many thanks to Susanne Lakin for her in-depth critique. Her valuable suggestions helped raise this book to the level needed for publication.

I'd also like to thank Sam(Nadara) and Jeff Feldman of the Bridgeford House B&B in Eureka Springs, AR for their warm hospitality and fount of information on their delightful city. Crescent Dragonwagon, formerly of Eureka Springs and "founder" of the city's B&B industry, was the inspiration for one character. Thank you, Crescent.

And ... a final note of appreciation to Sgt. Emory Albritton, who retired at the end of 2011 after 30-plus years in law enforcement. Now, you get to be the "bad guy."

One
(Spring 1969)
❧✦✦☙

Alice Cummings awakened early, her maternal instincts calling. "Time to eat, Jimmy Bob." As she sat up in bed, her head swooned as with a major league hangover. She rolled toward the cradle at the side of her bed. Her baby was gone.

Eight hours earlier, she had laid two-week old James Robert II, named after her maternal grandfather, in the secondhand crib that nestled the side of her old brass bed. She had anticipated a middle-of-the-night feeding, but had either slept through his fussing or been blessed with his sleeping a full night. Now, alert in a flash, she found not only Jimmy Bob AWOL, but also his crib and meager collection of hand-me-down clothes, baby pictures, and assorted accessories.

She jumped from bed, rushed out of the room and ran to the adjacent spare bedroom. Empty. With hesitation, she eased open the door to her pa's bedroom and peeked in. He, too, was missing and a sense of relief mingled with her anxiety. She cleared the stairs to the first floor in three leaps, almost missing the step on her second jump, and charged into the kitchen. Nothing but the dark and the colicky hum of a refrigerator in its death throes. She flipped on an overhead light bulb that flickered with the threat of failing, and headed toward the front door. She nearly stumbled on her old man's work boots and that's when his sonorous breathing identified him as the dark lump on the ragged couch. That's also when she realized he had made good his threat.

"Wake up, you stinkin', drunk son of a sow! Where is he?" Alice threw all of her one hundred and sixty pound frame behind the punches she launched into her pa as he slept on the

1

couch.

"Where is my son? Wake up, you drunk bastard! What did you do?" she screamed.

Her initial blows seemed ineffective, but soon her pa emerged from his stupor and growled as he sat up. Scowling, he caught her next punch with an iron grip and her hand froze in mid-air. She winced at the squeezing pain.

As he twisted her wrist, she began to cry in agony. She gave him a fierce kick in the shin, but that only fueled his anger and strength.

She tried to pull away, but he used that as leverage to begin to stand. Fearing her wrist about to break, and even more fearful of what he would do once on his feet, she grabbed the side table lamp with her free hand and smacked it into the side of his head, but refused to put it down.

He released her and sagged back onto the couch.

"Did what I told ya I'd do, ya little slut. Think you could bring shame on this family without consequence? You should be on your knees prayin' forgiveness."

He stood to his full six foot, three inch frame holding nearly three hundred pounds and Alice backed off. She'd felt the back of his hand too many times to remain in easy reach. Yet, like a mama bear, she refused to back down.

"Forgiveness? You're talkin' about me needin' forgiveness? You drunken, old fool. Ain't ever seen you on your knees, or in any church for that matter. Don't you get preachy to me. Now, where's Jimmy Bob?"

He smiled a half-toothed smile. "Sold 'im. Like I told ya I would. I'm not keepin' no bastard child under my roof."

"Then why you livin' here?"

A sudden surge of fear mingled with her anger. He had threatened to take her baby. She hadn't believed him. She hadn't believed him capable of "selling" his own grandchild. Now her baby, the only person in the world who would love her without fail, was gone.

"Where is he? Where'd you take him?"

He snarled and moved toward her. Drunk, sober, half in between, the man could move. She'd seen him cover the length of the room in a split second and she wasn't about to underestimate him now. She threw the lamp as hard as she could at his forehead, and turned to run for the stairs. She heard the heavy ceramic shatter, followed by a sinking groan and a thud as he fell to the floor. She knew better than to go back and check on him. The man had suffered blows from two-by-fours and survived to win the fight. That lamp might daze him, but not for long.

She ran to her room and hastily dressed. She threw a couple of changes of clothes into a nylon backpack; grabbed her wallet, a small purse, an envelope with her "important" papers, and a few toiletries and dumped them into the pack as well. She had planned to leave when Jimmy Bob was a little older to forge out a new life beyond the reach of her pa and his destructive ways. She wanted a better life, a happy life with a husband and family to love properly, and Jimmy Bob was her motivation. With plans to leave, she'd already prepared a small suitcase of clothing and hidden it in the tool shed. She would reclaim it from behind the broken washing machine and flee to town.

More problematic was recovering her papers and the inheritance her grandfather had left her. She would need that money to find Jimmy Bob. She had retrieved the small, locked chest a few days earlier, placed a photo of her and Jimmy in it along with her copy of the papers given to her by the midwife, and rewrapped it in rubberized canvas. She would need those papers to convince the sheriff. She had reburied it next to the foundation of the shed. Ten paces along the western wall, at a spot where she'd be able to locate and dig it up in complete darkness if necessary. She regretted not having simply hid it somewhere nearby. She had no time to dig it up now. She needed to leave. Now. She already heard movement downstairs.

At that moment, she hated her father more than she ever had since her mother had died and left her to his abuse. His moonshiner friends and alcohol-fueled rages, along with the verbal and emotional abuse, had convinced her years earlier that she would leave home as soon as possible. Having graduated from high school and turned eighteen a few months earlier, she was old enough to pursue her own life, even if she hadn't become a legal adult yet. She would hate him forever for what he had done this time.

Through the door, she could hear the stairs groan under the weight of her father's step. Despite his drunken rages and repeated bouts of abuse, he'd never entered her room. As if it was her sanctuary, her home base where she couldn't be tagged "It," her room had always been sacrosanct. She realized he had violated that unwritten rule during the night, to take Jimmy Bob. She also realized by her headache that he must have slipped her a Mickey to make sure she didn't wake up. To exit that door right now tagged her as fair game in an inequitable contest. She had but one option if she wanted to escape to find her son, to give them both the good life she'd never had.

She quietly raised the lower sash of the old wooden window and laid her pack on the roof of the front porch to the side of the window. A mid-April frost on the shingles confirmed the early morning chill that nipped into her flesh, the cold made worse by a relentless wind whipping up the side

4

of the mountain. Spring came late to the Appalachians of western North Carolina. Daylight had yet to display itself on their western side of the mountain, except for a few shafts of light highlighting the fog at the far end of the valley.

She zipped her jacket tight to her neck and followed her backpack. In a moment, the pack was hanging from her shoulders and she eased down the side post of the porch. In the instant when her feet touched ground, she heard the door to her bedroom splinter under the weight of the man and crash onto the floor of her bedroom, the room no longer a safe haven. She heard his growl from the front window, but waited no longer.

With an adrenaline surge fueled by both anger and fear, she ran down the gravel drive to High Mountain Road, turned downhill, and a hundred yards later moved off the pavement onto an old dirt logging road now overgrown to the point of being more of an infrequently traveled path than a passable road. She had played on and walked this trail so many times throughout her childhood that she could traverse it without fear in the dark, blindfolded. She knew when to expect each exposed tree root, every eroded wash, all of the side paths and even how to cross safely the old creek bridge with its rotted, condemned planking.

Fifteen minutes later, she attempted to shimmy up a small tree that led to her perch on the rocky promontory jutting up from the hillside. Her post-partum body didn't cooperate, but with more effort, she made it and sat down to rest. The lights of Frampton Corner speckled the valley below her.

She had come here often throughout her teens, to think, to cry, and to escape the slow death of living at home with an unloving alcoholic father. She had shared her spot with Jimmy Bob's father, JT, and suspected she had conceived their baby at that very spot. Why in the world JT had volunteered for Viet Nam, when they had a child on the way, baffled her. He could have had a stateside assignment for a year before going overseas. His death one month into entering that foreign war had devastated her. Yet, many happy memories existed from that very spot overlooking the valley and she tried to focus on those.

The spectacular sunsets, as well as spring and fall foliage vistas here, could be surpassed by only one place, her front porch and front bedroom window. The peacefulness of Nathan's Rock far outweighed anything resembling quiet at home. After learning "the rabbit had died," she had sought this spot alone as her refuge to contemplate her future. Yet, none of her deliberations had ever conjured up the future that had now become her present. She would miss these views, the beauty of the valley, and the peacefulness of 'her spot', but staying was not an option.

She looked out over the basin and cried. The aching in her breasts did not match that in her heart. Where was Jimmy Bob? How would she ever be able to find him? When she started to show, her pa had taken her to the home of a distant cousin in the middle of the night. She might as well have been a captive in chains with the lack of freedom she had there. The same had been true after she delivered. Dropped off at her home after dark, she'd not been allowed outside with the baby, much less given access to town or to any of her few friends. Her pa was too smart to use that same cousin for the baby. Jimmy Bob could be anywhere. That thought made her heart sink.

The sun's rays touched the top of the mountain across the valley, illuminating the white dogwoods and pink redbuds that claimed their glory amidst the green mixture of emerging leaves. As the sun rose, its steepening angle would quickly ease the light down that slope. She had but thirty more minutes before the valley saw full light and she needed to reach town unseen. She glanced around and touched the granite thumb, hoping to imprint its feel into her memory. She'd never see it, or its panoramas, again.

Sliding down a side of the rock, she touched down and worked her way toward town. With time to spare, she entered town behind Shorty's Used Car lot. The 1966 orange Mustang 2+2 she coveted shone under the single floodlight securing the lot. Not yet two years old, only 11,000 miles. With no job or income, all she could afford was to admire it on the lot, but not this morning. No time. She worked her way around the hardware store, passed several old homes and the courthouse, and eased around the corner of the Post Office.

She looked both ways down Main Street. No traffic. No sign of Pa's truck. Had he followed her? She suspected he probably downed another beer to assuage his anger and then reclaimed his spot on the couch, working his body back into the permanent indentations in the deteriorating cushions. He'd stopped caring about her or her whereabouts long ago. That realization made her recognize that he would care even less about a grandchild. Both were simply burdens to him. Both were commodities eligible for sale, just like his precious moonshine.

With no sign of the old drunk, she walked past the Post Office headed for the Sheriff's sub-station. Outside the building, she saw Sheriff Connelly's sedan and immediately began to have reservations about being there. She could talk with the deputy, Jake Fischer. She trusted him. The Sheriff, on the other hand, had let her old man and his "activities" slide so many times that she suspected he was a regular customer of her pa's. Upon entering the office, she found him sitting at the desk, conferring with Jake. They turned in unison to acknowledge her as the door squealed closed.

"Alice, it's good to see you up and about," Sheriff Connelly said as he stood to greet her. "Your pa said you'd been having a rough time of it."

"Yeah," added Jake. "We're real sorry about the baby."

Klaxons of alarm blared in her brain. Her pa? Jimmy Bob?

"So, what can we —"

"Y-you know about my baby?"

"Look, Alice, we're not here to pass judgment. Mistakes like that happen to young girls all the time. Most folks 'round here knew you were pregnant. Can't hide it very well in a small place like this. We're real sorry he was stillborn. That's gotta be tough to deal with. Your dad —"

"Wait a m-minute. He wasn't stillborn. I brought him home just a week ago. I breastfed him just last night. M-my pa took him. Sold him. I-I came here to ask you to help me find him." Tears burst from her eyes.

The two men looked at each other, concern etched on both faces. The deputy slid a chair in her direction and motioned for her to sit.

"Alice, again, we're sorry about the baby. Why don't you sit down and rest?" said Jake.

"Alice," said Sheriff Connelly, "your pa showed us the birth certificate that said stillbirth on it. I'm so sorry."

Alice's legs turned to putty and she grabbed hold of the chair. What sort of nightmare was this? She hadn't imagined it. Her engorged breasts were proof, weren't they? But then, she wasn't sure if a woman's breasts filled with milk after a stillbirth. Maybe they weren't proof. How could she convince these men when her father had already played his hand and won that round? She heard the two men whispering and heard her father's name.

"What about my pa?" she cried.

The Sheriff turned back to her. "Look, your old man said you'd been taking this hard, imagining things, not taking the medicines the doctors prescribed for you. We just want to help. Let me call Amos and have him come get you."

"No!" She tried to think. She had underestimated him once again. No wonder he had insisted she and the baby stay home until he was a little older. No one in town could ever claim to have seen Jimmy. No one could support her claims. He had staged his revenge well. Who would believe her against him? "No. He stole my baby. Told me he sold him. I got …"

She'd started to say she had proof that Jimmy wasn't stillborn, but she had buried the photo and papers with her inheritance. At that moment, she realized the papers given to her by the midwife held no legal birth certificate. What exactly were those papers? What good were they against the legal certificate held by her father? She needed the photo. Unless she could get that photo, no one would believe her.

As the deputy dialed the black rotary phone and handed the receiver to the Sheriff, her adrenaline took charge yet again. Alice bolted from the chair and charged out the door. She was near to a block away before she looked back and saw the deputy standing on the sidewalk outside the office, watching her. The Sheriff joined him and Jake moved toward the patrol car parked nearby, but the Sheriff put a hand on the younger man's arm and stopped him. She could only imagine what they were saying.

Alice ducked behind the hardware store and made a beeline for the trailhead back to Nathan's Rock. Where should she go? How? What? When? Her mind flooded with questions. She mentally considered and tossed aside a dozen action plans. One concern overrode all of her thoughts, what her father would do to her if he ever again caught up to her. Only one plan could save her. She needed to get her suitcase and her inheritance, and leave. Once safe, she could send the Sheriff a letter and copy of her proof, and then hope he believed her enough to act on her accusations. In the meantime, she would find some way to begin her own search. Somehow.

The trek uphill took a lot longer, but a little over an hour later, she positioned herself at a point in the woods uphill from her house where she could observe the buildings and driveway. She had arrived in time to watch the Sheriff shake her pa's hand, climb into his car, and drive off. Her old man, now forewarned, would be on the lookout. Her hope of success dwindled.

A sense of despair pushed her deeper into the soft forest floor. If only it would engulf her and she could emerge in late spring as a new person, unaffected by the past eight years of abuse. Instead, the emotional fatigue swallowed her up and she drifted off to sleep.

Two
ɔ❖✦❖ɔ

Alice awoke with a start, unsure whether the renewed chill of dusk or the grumblings of her stomach had awakened her. She had no food in her pack, but she had an extra jacket, so she pulled it out and put it on. She stared at the house. Her pa's truck sat rooted in the same place. The lights in the kitchen, front room, and her pa's bedroom added to the single gooseneck light illuminating the drive. He seemed to be continuing life as usual, with or without her.

She checked her watch to discover the day had progressed further than she'd thought. The last bus came through town at 7:30 and, after stops in four other small communities, arrived in Asheville at 10 pm. She had to be on that bus, preferably unnoticed. She had only an hour to retrieve her goods and hoof it back to town. Whether awake, asleep, drunk or sober, her pa, inside the house, would be only fifty feet away from the shed and there were scant shadows to hide her as she dug up her cache next to the foundation.

She had no choice. Now or never.

She slid her arms into the straps of the backpack and stood. After one step, she froze. An all too familiar van, followed by a pickup she hoped never to see again, pulled into the drive and parked by the house. Three men climbed out of the van along with two more from the pickup. The first three opened the rear door of the van and pulled a young man and woman, their wrists bound behind them, out onto the gravel. The man looked to be twenty-something, thin and ragged. He appeared to have been beaten, his face bruised and swollen, several teeth missing. The woman was Alice's size, with similar hair color, but she couldn't see her face to determine her age.

Her father walked around from the front of the house. "What the hell you bringing them here for? You crazy?"

"Them's the ones told your damn neighbor about our stills on his property. Feds busted 'em up, plus we lost two month's worth of product 'cause of them."

Alice knew the owner of that voice and trembled at being so close.

"Don't you think I know that? Idiots! What if someone sees them here or with you driving through town? I told ya to deal with 'em. Somewhere else."

"What do you want done?"

Her pa laughed. "Your choice, Dewey. You know what to do. Don't bother me with it." He started to turn back toward the house.

"Hey, where's that fool girl of yours? She have that bastard yet? She ready for a real man?"

The smile on Dewey Hasting's face made the scar along its left side crinkle and flush. She'd given him that scar a year earlier when he tried to rape her in her own bedroom. She had inflicted the damage with his own switchblade. Her pa had saved her from his hand that time. She doubted he would do so now.

"Probably down at Nathan's Rock. She'll be back. Gots nowhere else to go. Go take care of these two." He walked back to the van, pulled a jug of white lightning from the back, and carried it into the house.

Dewey walked up to the girl and put his hand on her chin to force her to look at him. Alice couldn't hear any crying, but could see her chest heave with sobs. Or maybe it was fear.

"You're not bad looking, girl. How about we have a date in the woods?"

With the young man restrained by two of the other men,

Dewey began to fondle her breasts. She responded with a knee to his groin. Alice knew better than to make a sound, but for one brief instant she enjoyed watching Dewey fall to the ground. A second later, however, he shot up, that switchblade in hand, and sliced one forearm and then the other. He sliced open her shirt and gave each breast its own bloody mark.

Why didn't she scream?

The woman started to kick out at Dewey again, but he seemed to expect it and quickly gave one thrust of his knife into her chest just under her breastbone. She fell to the ground and Alice saw that her mouth had been stuffed with a rag.

"Too bad, we coulda had such a good time."

The young man fell next to her, placing his forehead on hers, tears running down his cheeks. Fear caused his eyes to blaze. He knew he was next, and he bolted up and lunged headfirst at Dewey. A second man caught him and with a quick jerk of the man's head, broke his neck.

Dewey nodded to the others to load the bodies into the van and followed up by kicking gravel and dirt over the blood evidence. The next rain, likely only a day ahead, would wash it away.

"Let's dump 'em in the lake. I got some chain and blocks. Meet you at our usual spot in half an hour. Gotta take a quick trip to Nathan's Rock." He grinned. He pulled away in his pickup while the others loaded into the van and pulled away.

With little time left, Alice headed for the shed, watching each footfall and wishing she could float. She slid close to the outer wall and maneuvered her way toward the front door. Peering around the corner of the outbuilding, she saw a shadow moving back and forth in the kitchen, but no face at the window. *The old man's actually fixing something to eat?* she wondered. Did that mean he was sober? Her heart raced and her breathing picked up. She would have to be extra careful.

As the shadow moved to the far end of the wall, she darted to the shed's front door and sighed in relief to find it open. *One less noise to worry about*, she thought.

Once inside, she worked her way through the piles of trash and old machinery to the old washing machine, the rollers of its topside clothes ringer cracked with age and the exposed metal parts sat rusted but movable. She reached back and found her suitcase, lifting it with ease. She'd forgotten how she had packed it and was glad now to find it less of a burden to carry downhill under her time constraints. She parked it next to the front door and moved to the back to find a shovel.

In the waning light, she discovered the shovel she'd used earlier was no longer where she'd left it. That, in itself, was not suspicious. Her pa used it regularly. She moved further into the deep of the building, groping for similar handles, looking for the same or another digging implement. Reaching behind yet another household relic, she suddenly felt a sheering pain in her forearm and cried out in pain.

She pulled her arm back and held it up for inspection. She couldn't see it in the dark but felt a warm fluid trickling down to her elbow. The coppery aroma of blood caught her. The pain was nothing like labor, but matched nothing else in her experience. She moved to the front door for a better look. The gash was three, maybe four inches long, deep, and bleeding profusely. She forced her forearm against her blouse to provide clean compression. That's when she heard his voice.

"Who's out there? Who's in m'shed?"

Her scream had alerted her pa, but it had also scared something else. Two old barn cats scampered around her and bolted from the door.

Blaamm!

The old man's shotgun echoed across the valley.

"Damn cats! Git outta here!"

Another retort followed.

Alice froze just inside the door, unable to make herself peek through the opening. All she could hear was her heart and her breathing. She tried to hold her breath, to stop hyperventilating before she passed out, but fear commandeered her brain for the next few minutes. Finally, she focused on noise outside the shed and realized she heard no approaching footsteps. She forced a quick peek out the door and saw no one.

"Damn it!" she whispered to herself. She grabbed her suitcase with the good arm, held her injured arm tight to her abdomen, took a deep breath, and bolted from the door. She had no options. No way could she reclaim her inheritance now, but under no circumstance would she even contemplate waiting another day. It was time to leave … forever.

As she rounded the corner of the building, her pa's voice rang out. "Alice, you come back here. You need your medicine." She heard him huff. "You got nowheres to go, girl! Damn! What'd you see? Get back here, girl!"

Fear turbocharged her legs. Just what kind of medicine did he have in mind? Something lead-based? She wasn't about to find out as she raced into the woods.

Again, she found her mind deluged with "what ifs." He no doubt had seen the suitcase in her hand. The only logical way out was down the mountain, so she would head up. She would climb to the very top and walk down the other side if that's what it took.

Only one other residence stood between her and the top of the mountain. Curt Umfleet, his wife, Mary, and their two children lived in a home more decrepit than her own. He worked as a janitor at the area high school, while she tried selling Avon, and baked goods, and anything else she could do from her home. Their youngest, the son, had some sort of mental retardation, or learning problem, or something. She knew for a fact that Mary disliked and mistrusted her pa. Maybe her motherly intuition had clued her into the reality that nothing good happened in the house below them. Plus, the whole town knew of the bad blood between Curt and her pa after Curt caught him poaching on Umfleet land. Now, after what she'd overheard, if Curt knew about her pa heading up the moonshiners, there'd be hell to pay. She didn't want to involve them in this, but did she have any other choice?

Alice found her breathing getting hard and her head getting light as she neared the Umfleet home. She began to wonder if she could make it to their house, much less over the mountain. She struggled to carry the suitcase and her pack without the benefit of her one arm for balance, but every time she pulled her arm away from her belly, the bleeding resumed. The front of her blouse and a good portion of her jeans seemed soaked in that vital fluid.

She could see the building now. Lights were on in the front room and a single, bare bulb lit up the front porch. She stopped to catch her breath and gazed at the house. Could she trust them to help her, and not turn her back over to her pa? Did she have any other option but to try?

With reservation, she moved to the front porch and heaved her suitcase onto the bare planks making up the floor before climbing its three wobbly steps. The noise must have alerted the occupants because before she could knock on the door, it opened and Curt Umfleet stood there looking down at her broken body as she sat on the top step, breathing deeply.

"Somethin' wrong?" His voice held no pleasure in seeing

her.

"I-I need some help," pleaded Alice.

"Who is it, Curt?" Mary Umfleet's voice floated from inside, sounding as feeble as Alice felt.

"Alice."

"Well, for God's sake, ask her in. Where's your manners, man?"

Curt nodded his head toward the door as his invitation, but as Alice stood his eyes widened at the sight of her blood covering the front of her clothes. "Omigosh. Here, here, let me help. What happened? I heard gunshots. What ..."

He assisted her to the nearest chair, a hard-backed, handcrafted Windsor of hard maple, and eased her down. Alice watched as he rushed back to the porch, took a quick look toward the road, and retrieved her bags. Only then did she glance about the room. The children's bedroom door stood closed and Mary lie in a small bed near the hearth, a fire blazing for the room's only warmth, her head and back propped up by pillows. The woman looked pale and anorectic. Alice's injury seemed minor compared to whatever that poor woman was going through. She wondered if the woman would even make it through the night.

"Lord in heaven, child, what happened?" asked Mary. "Where'd all that blood come from?"

Alice slid her forearm away from her belly and displayed the laceration, which again began to drip. "I-I cut myself in our shed." She saw no sense in wasting these peoples' time. "I need to get away. I was trying ... I c-cut it on something sharp. The last bus leaves at 7:30. Do you have some Band-aids? I think I can still make it."

Mary shook her head. "Needs more than that." She gave Alice a stern, quizzical look. "Where's the baby?"

At that, Alice broke down. "H-he ..." She started to repeat the story she gave the Sheriff but remembered his response and changed her tack. "What do you know about my baby?"

She saw Curt re-enter the room carrying what looked to be an old military ammo box. He motioned for her to join him at their dining table. As she hesitated, Mary nodded and said, "Go on. He was a medic in Nam. He can either fix it, or patch it up to get you to a doctor ASAP."

At the table, Curt opened the metal box and pulled out gauze, sutures, and more. To Alice, the tabletop soon looked like a mini-hospital. He handed her a pad of gauze. "Here. Hold this tight to the wound." He went to the kitchen and washed his hands for what seemed like forever, and then returned and gently took her arm, more gauze ready should the bleeding resume.

"As for your baby, Alice, I know what I heard in the market and I know what I hear at home. The gossipmongers say your baby were stillborn, but I know a baby's cry when it drifts up the mountain on the wind currents. Sure don't sound stillborn to me; so what happened?"

Alice winced at the pain from the man's strong hand compressing her wound as he prepared to cleanse her forearm.

"Sorry. Some good direct pressure should stop the bleedin'," said Curt.

As Alice told the Umfleets everything about the baby, the death of Jimmy's father, and her own father's claim of selling her son, she saw anger energize Mary. She told of her flight from the house and her encounter with the Sheriff. She ended with her rushed departure from the shed. The only aspect of the story she held back was that of her "treasure" chest and the proof within. Despite the help they offered now, she didn't trust these neighbors enough to divulge that information. Anyone digging up the "proof" she needed would also reveal her inheritance, money left to her by her grandfather.

Mary rose up and sat on the edge of her bed. "I don't like admitting this to you, Alice, but I never have liked or trusted your father. I-I don't think I can physically help much myself, but we, uh, Curt can help somehow, I'm sure. If it'd help, I can tell the Sheriff that I've heard your baby crying and he sure didn't sound stillborn."

"First things first," he said. "This needs stitches, but I don't have any numbin' medicine. Think you can put up with six, seven stitches?"

Alice shut her eyes and gulped in a big breath, before nodding. She fought back the tears every time the needle went through her skin, arguing with herself that altogether they didn't hurt as much as the initial laceration did.

"All done," announced Curt.

Alice opened her eyes and gathered the courage to inspect her forearm. She was amazed at the man's workmanship. She'd seen no better by the doctor in town and she'd had plenty of friends requiring such services over the years. She held it up for Mary to see.

"Told ya he could fix it." The woman smiled, but briefly. "The clock there tells me there's no way you'll make it to the bus on time, even if Curt drives you down there. Plus, that'll be the first place your father might be waitin'." The woman paused in thought. "The bus stops next in Cashiers, right? Curt will drive you there. You should be able to beat the bus."

"I can't ask you to –"

"You didn't ask. We're offerin'. No, tellin' you. But first, you need some clean clothes. One look at you and the driver'll be calling the Highway Patrol in Brevard." She looked at her husband. "Curt, get that big box marked for the church. She should find some things that fit. Lord knows I won't be getting back up to her size again."

Alice started to weep. "I-I don't know how to thank you."

"No need. The Lord is our provider. He always sees fit to meet our needs." Mary reached behind her bed and pulled up a purse. She removed an envelope and handed it toward Alice. "Here, take this, too. You'll need it."

Alice took the packet and opened it. Five hundred dollars in twenties and fifties stared back at her. "I can't take this," she declared.

"Surely you can," answered Curt as he returned to the room. "If'n it helps, consider it a loan, no interest." He opened the box and pulled some things out. "Take a look and take what you need. You can change in there." He pointed to a door to his right.

"How ... how could I ever repay you?" She sat there, incredulous. This family had less to spare than her "family," yet they gave everything to help her.

A few minutes later, Alice emerged from the bathroom in clean clothes. Nothing stylish, but they fit well, were in great condition and would serve her purpose. She held the bloody clothes daintily from one hand, and Curt took them and walked toward the back of the house. To the trash, Alice presumed.

While she'd been changing, Curt had given Mary the box and she had spread several items across the bedcover in front of her. "Don't know what you have packed in that case of yours, but take these, too. You might need something like them for job interviews."

Alice picked up a princess seamed short-sleeved, floral dress, a couple of simple A-line skirts and half a dozen complimentary tops. A quick check confirmed they would fit and she placed them, neatly folded, into her suitcase. She scurried back to Mary and gave her a gentle hug, unsure whether the woman could hold up to anything heartier.

She stood erect and, with Curt again present, addressed both of her benefactors. "I don't know what to say or how to thank you. I'm going to get settled in Asheville and then I'm going to start looking for my son. And if you'd talk to the sheriff, that'd be a great help."

"When you find him, let us know. Please. It would mean the world to us to know we helped reunite you somehow. In the meantime, I'll call the sheriff in the mornin' and keep my ear to the grapevine here. Any number of ladies from church just love to come by and keep me posted on the town's comings and goings. The busybodies. And you know for sure if a new baby just shows up out of the blue in a home around here, everybody's gonna hear about it. Doubt that'll be the case, but you never know. Anyway, make sure you get us a way to contact you."

Alice nodded, but for the first time that evening, she noticed Mary grimace in pain. The gesture was subtle, but undeniable. Alice wanted to understand, but was afraid to ask what the problem was. Mary must have seen the question on Alice's lips.

"Breast cancer. It's already spread to several places. The doctors don't offer any hope." Then Mary smiled more brightly than Alice had seen all night. "But Jesus is my hope. If He sees fit to heal me then I will continue to serve him here, and if I go home to be with Him, I know and trust He will take care of my family. Now, get going you two, or Curt might well have to drive you to Asheville."

Alice hugged Mary once again, more vigorously this time,

and gave her a kiss on the cheek. The woman in turn handed her a slip of paper with a phone number written on it in a terse block style. Curt had already gone outside and poked his head back in the door.

"Coast is clear. Let's go."

He picked up her suitcase, and Alice followed to the old Ford pickup at the side of the house. A minute later, they were driving down the road. Well before passing her driveway and house, she ducked down to avoid any chance of discovery.

"Don't see anyone outside," said Curt. "… but your pa's truck is there. That be a good sign, yes?"

Alice shrugged. She wasn't so sure. Once down the hillside, they still had to drive through town and past the reservoir to get to the road that would shortcut them to Cashiers. She wouldn't breathe easily until they were well out of town. They passed Shorty's and the hardware store. As they passed the Sheriff's office, the other deputy, Mike Albritton, emerged from the building. She ducked – her heart racing and her mind unsure whether she'd been seen. A minute passed. Then two. Then five. No car in pursuit. Maybe, just maybe, she would make it. Escape. Freedom. A new life. Hope. She would find her son, and they would succeed together.

They traveled on for another fifteen minutes in silence. Curt broke the quiet. "Alice, I know once you get to Asheville, you're gonna start to think 'bout how to repay us. Please don't worry about it. I got some family land we rent out, so we're not hurtin' financially as much as it might look. Been our choice to live frugally and use our money for God's work. As a single woman, you're gonna face enough hurdles. I know; my sister's been there. We helped her, too. Focus on your goal. Find your son and create a good life for the both of you."

Alice mulled over his words. In her heart, she knew his

advice to be sound. Yet, no matter what money they had, she would repay them. Somehow. She would be indebted to them forever.

Ten minutes later, they entered the town limits of Cashiers and saw the bus as it came to a halt at the covered bench of the bus stop. The bus would wait ten minutes before departing, so Alice relaxed. They had made it. She had made it.

She leaned across the seat and kissed Curt on the cheek. "Thank you. Thank you. Thank you."

He smiled and nodded. As she opened the door, he placed his hand on her shoulder. "Got one more piece of advice, if you'll take it." She looked him in the eyes. "I've seen your writin' and your artwork, on the display boards at the school. It's a God-given talent. Don't waste it."

Alice was surprised at this comment. No one had ever complimented her on her work before. "I, uh … thank you. I'll keep that in mind."

She stepped out of the truck, paid her fare, watched the driver load her suitcase, and climbed aboard the bus. At the driver's suggestion, she took the seat right behind him.

Ten minutes later, the bus pulled out of the stop and she caught a glimpse of the Umfleet pickup in the driver's side mirror as it shrank from view. She'd never forget them. Her new life started right then. Only Jimmy could bring her back to Frampton Corner. Otherwise, to the people there she might as well be dead.

Three
(Present day)
 భ◆◆ఏ

Myra Mitchell tore off another sheet of paper from the yellow legal pad on her lap, wadded it up, and tossed it toward the already overflowing trashcan. Her muse had abandoned her, disappeared, left her behind, vamoosed. She struggled for ideas and that bothered her. She never struggled to come up with ideas.

She doodled on the next clean sheet, trying to relax her mind, to let her usual creativity flow. Yet, Myra could barely keep her eyes open. Where had her stamina disappeared to over the past six months? Had it eloped with her muse? She closed her laptop to put it to sleep, so she could do the same. The clock informed her it was only 9 p.m. Once upon a time, just a year earlier in fact, she could have stayed up all night writing. She had the first several chapters of this story worked out in her mind, but the middle wasn't just sagging, it hadn't left the floor. And her body felt just like the story.

She took her glass of wine to the deck overlooking the waters off Carmel. The shorebirds had retired to their nests. A raft of sea lions looked like rocks dotting the sand as they collected in the dusk, preparing to sleep under the protection of the group. The surf pounded the shoreline in its usual rhythm. A soft breeze lifted off the water, bringing with it that distinctive smell of the ocean.

As she sipped the last of her wine, she mentally listed her upcoming calendar. Four more days at home, then she would drive to Beverly Hills for three events. Unlike most A-list authors, she loved the limelight. She had attended all four previous movie premiers based on her books, insisting on walking the red carpet, even if no one paid attention to her.

She enjoyed the coverage she received in People magazine and US Weekly, even if it did highlight her more rambunctious side. She was after all, the "Diva of Disaster." And the coverage helped book sales, sales that made her the number-one selling author in the English-speaking world. Well, number-one now that J.K. Rowling and her pesky boy wizard no longer competed for the title.

The day prior to the premiere, she had a book-signing event scheduled. After the premiere, she had to attend a Meet'n Greet for the new Ph.D. students selected to the Creative Writing Program at the University of Southern California. Myra sat on the program's Board of Advisors and was one of the visiting faculty members. The group would be small, as the program was small, but she always enjoyed the annual gathering.

She finished her drink and turned to enter her home. A glimpse of her reflection in the glass of the sliding door caught her off-guard. Was she a little yellow? No, she decided it was the light cast by the fading sunset. She looked just fine, for a woman in her early sixties. A little time worn, perhaps, but well preserved for her age. Why did the term "pickled" come to mind?

Alexia Hamilton stretched her shoulders and rolled her head to stay awake. The drive from Asheville back to her apartment near the University of North Carolina in Chapel Hill was just a tad over three hours, but the hour was late. Her visit to her parents' home had been brief and bittersweet. She still found it hard to think of it as *her* home, but it had been bequeathed to her after her mother's death several months earlier. Six months before that, her father had died from a massive myocardial infarct. The year had not been good to her.

She had wandered the house remembering the good times, in particular the day she received her letter of acceptance into UNC's Masters Program in Mass Communications. Her father had called her a "professional student" and spent the day ribbing her about getting a real job, finding the right guy, and giving him grandkids. None of that had happened, but she continued as that professional student.

The purpose of her trip had been to store her furniture and extra belongings at the house in preparation of moving to Los Angeles. She had been accepted into the doctoral program at USC to earn her Ph.D. in Literature and Creative Writing. She had been honored by their acceptance. Maybe the next two years would turn her life around.

She wanted nothing more than to be a writer. Maybe even the next Myra Mitchell, but that was just a dream. She knew she had the work ethic to put in the hours and do the hard work. Did she have the ability?

One longtime dream would be fulfilled. She would actually get to meet Ms. Mitchell, provided she showed up at the reception next week. She hoped to use that meeting to gain access to the author because she had decided that her thesis would be on modern female fiction authors. She had to get Ms. Mitchell's attention somehow. To achieve that, one idea kept flitting through her mind, an idea straight out of a Mitchell novel.

She yawned for the hundredth time that night as she pulled off I-40 onto Durham-Chapel Hill Road. A quarter mile to home. Five minutes to a good night's sleep.

Alexia found a parking spot near her apartment and pulled in. She grabbed her purse and a small box of family photos she had collected from the house, and climbed the steps to her apartment. The deadbolt on her door appeared broken and the door stood slightly ajar. Hesitantly, she opened the door and nearly dropped the box.

Her place lay in shambles. Ransacked. Boxes opened and dumped.

She stumbled over a pile of books and placed the box on an open spot on the floor. She moved into the bedroom and kitchenette. Only the kitchen appeared untouched, but then she discovered each box had been opened, just not dumped out.

She pulled out her cell phone and called 911. Fifteen minutes later, a patrol car appeared on the road below and she watched the officer climb to her doorway.

"Mornin', Miss. I'm Officer Doane. What happened?"

Alexia nodded her acknowledgement to his greeting. "Thanks for coming. My name's Alexia Hamilton. I took some things home to Asheville and just returned twenty minutes ago to find this." She backed away from the door to allow the officer inside, but he stopped at the doorway and simply glanced around. "Have you touched anything?"

"Just a little, while I was waiting. I didn't want to disturb things until you guys saw it."

"Thanks. Could you tell if anything is missing?" The officer took out a small pad of paper and jotted some notes.

"Nothing obvious. I didn't have any cash or jewelry here. My laptop and other electronics were with me and I gave my old TV to a friend because I didn't want to move it."

"Someone from EFIS will be here in a moment."

"EFIS?"

"Our Evidence, Forensics and Identification Service. Could I get some information from you?"

Alexia nodded and replied, "Sure." They stood in the

breezeway outside her door as he took her name and other basic information. She was glad it was early morning. The heat and humidity of the day would have made that outside wait miserable. Five minutes later, another police car pulled up and a young woman with a rectangular satchel walked up to her place. After introductions, Alexia watched the woman take photos, first of the door and then of the room as she moved toward the bedroom door and kitchen.

Officer Doane regained her attention. "Where you headed?"

"I've been accepted into a doctoral program in Los Angeles. I'm supposed to leave day after next." She continued to watch the evidence technician take photos. "Will she dust for fingerprints? I'm a writer and always interested in procedures."

"Yes, and she'll probably want yours, to rule out your prints here. Give me a couple more minutes of your time and I'll finish up the police report."

Alexia answered his questions, but wanted to see firsthand how the evidence tech did her work. A moment later, the woman retrieved fingerprinting dust and what looked like a make-up brush from her kit. She started at the door and methodically worked her way through the apartment. She scanned a handful of prints into a small palm-sized scanner and returned to Alexia. The patrolman took that opportunity to return to his car.

"I need your prints so we'll know which ones are yours."

"Sure. Hey, this is fascinating. So you found some different prints?" She paused. "Um, I had two friends help me pack. Will you need their prints, too?"

"That would help," replied the tech.

"Okay, so how do we do this?" The woman used the

scanner to record Alexia's prints directly. "Do you think you'll find out who did this?"

"Maybe, but I gotta be honest. If nothing's missing, this isn't going to be high on the service's priority list. Plus, with you moving, well, I can't say much will come of this. I don't make that final decision, but that's been my experience with these kinds of break-ins. Sorry."

Alexia frowned, but she understood her response. "Thanks for the honesty. You know, I did find one thing unusual, to my thinking anyway."

Officer Doane returned in time to hear her comment.

"What's that?" asked the tech.

"Well, if someone was looking for valuables, why would they seem to focus on boxes that were obviously packed with books and papers? Every one of those boxes was dumped but a lot of the boxes with personal items were just opened and barely rifled through."

The technician appeared contemplative. "Don't know that I can answer that one. Could be just teens wanting to make a mess. Maybe whoever was pissed off they didn't find anything. Maybe they're literature buffs."

Alexia didn't smile at the attempted joke. The tech gave her a subtle shrug, as if to say, "Sorry," and picked up her satchel. "Good luck with the move." She turned and headed for her car.

Officer Doane said, "I called this in and they told me to let you go ahead and start cleaning up. If you find anything missing, call this number …" He handed her a card. "… and ask for Investigative Services. Use this police report number." He pointed to the number at the top of the paper he gave Alexia.

"Okay. Thanks."

The officer nodded and returned to his car. Alexia turned back into her apartment, closed the door and secured it with the secondary sliding bolt. At 2 a.m. she wasn't about to call any friends to help. Yet, she wouldn't fall asleep under the circumstances, so she made herself busy by starting to pick up her things and repack her boxes. She would need a new roll of packing tape to secure them, but at least she could make a dent in the task ahead. So much for a leisurely day visiting friends and saying good-byes.

Myra awoke to bright sunshine flooding her bedroom. She glanced at the clock and felt shocked to see she had slept a full twelve hours. She couldn't recall the last time she'd slept that long. She also had no recollection of the last time she'd felt rested, truly rested, upon waking. Today, she did. She stretched and smiled as she looked out the picture window overlooking the ocean. It would be a good day, a productive day.

As she prepared for that day, she studied herself in the mirror while brushing her hair and applying a light dusting of make-up. Had something happened to her powdered foundation? It cast an orangish pall to her skin. Maybe it was the bright sun reflecting off the ocher wall nearby.

Myra walked to her kitchen where she prepared a light plate of fresh fruit and a bagel. She sliced the bagel and placed it in the toaster. Returning to the refrigerator, she pulled out the cream cheese and tomato juice. While waiting on the toaster, she added a shot of vodka to a glass, then a dash of Worcestershire sauce and pepper, and filled it with tomato juice. She hadn't found a commercial Bloody Mary mix that she liked more than her own recipe. After preparing the bagel, she took food and drink to the deck and enjoyed the sunshine while she ate.

Half an hour later, she entered her study, sat down and picked up her legal pad. An idea had come to her in that twilight sleep just before fully waking. She would run with that and see if it had the legs to reach the finish line.

Four
(Spring 1969)
❧❖◆❖❧

"Good evening there, young lady. Watch yer step." The bus driver took Alice's suitcase as she tried to hand him her ticket and board the bus. "We'll just put this in the luggage compartment. No room inside."

Alice reluctantly gave up the worn hard-shell suitcase but clutched her backpack tightly in her arms. With her valuables in the pack, she would not allow it out of her sight for even a minute.

"Backpack's okay to go on board with you," the driver added. "But you'll find more room for it in the first seat right behind me."

She watched where he placed her suitcase and then climbed the steps into the old bus. She wrinkled her nose at the smell of diesel and stale food. Her shoes stuck slightly to the floor as if walking through spilled soda pop partially dried on the rubber mat. She swung her body into the aisle seat behind the driver and tucked her pack onto the adjacent window seat, keeping her body between it and anyone with wrong intentions.

She gazed around the old bus, its seats half-full. Placards advertising stores and restaurants in Brevard and Asheville formed a static marquee over the windows on both sides. The people were of various ages, but generally, all appeared older than she was. Some slept, despite the earliness of the evening, while others occupied their time with various distractions. All seemed pre-occupied and focused on themselves.

Only one additional passenger boarded after her, and the driver quickly hopped into the bus and stood surveying his

32

freight, making sure the final passenger found seating before taking his own seat behind the wheel. A minute later, the bus pulled away. She would never forget the Umfleet's kindness and generosity.

A sense of excitement mixed with trepidation filled her. The farthest she'd ever been from Frampton Corner was Brevard. She had been eight years old then, accompanying her parents on a visit to a doctor there. That was the day her mom learned she had cancer, a disease she fought heroically for two years before passing away and leaving Alice to the moods of her father. After that, her father's drinking problem no longer felt the restraint of her mom and he dove deeper into the bottle to fight his own emotional fallen angels. He had no preparation for raising a daughter, much less a teenage daughter, by himself and the alcohol deprived him of any motivation to perform that duty well. Emotionally isolated and rejected by him, Alice raised herself.

Lost in reflection, Alice started when the driver asked her a question.

"So, headin' to Asheville to visit kin?"

She shook her head, watching him watch her in the inside rearview mirror. "No, Sir. Moving there, hoping to find a job."

"Got a place to stay?"

Anxiety wormed into her mind, as she again shook her head. She had planned to get organized and research her options before leaving with Jimmy Bob. Her sudden departure from home had given her no time to do that and, in fact, she hadn't given a thought to where she would go, what she would do when she reached the city, or just how she would go about searching for her son. She just would. Somehow.

The driver just nodded and launched into a history of the bus and of how he came to buy it directly from the Chicago

Motor Coach Company a few years earlier. He gave a spirited, detailed account of how he had restored it just for the rural trips he made. The 1947 Ford Transit 9B was twenty-five feet, nine inches long, and ran on normal gasoline instead of diesel. It carried ...

She tuned him out but kept nodding and saying "uh-huh" at various points in his monologue. She didn't want to seem rude but her mind raced with worry over what awaited her at the end of the trip. She pulled a Hershey bar, which she'd bought from a vending machine at the bus stop, from her pocket. Where would she stay? She felt sure she could find a motel room, but for how much and would they rent a room if she answered honestly about her age. How long would her funds hold out? What kind of work could she find? How would she be able to get back and forth while trying to find Jimmy Bob?

About half way to Asheville, the driver stopped talking about his bus and how hard it was to build a new business and asked her a question, which shook her out of her mental state.

"So, what kind of work you lookin' fer?"

"Don't know. Whatever I can find to get started and I'll take it from there, I guess."

"What can you do? Any particular skills or training?"

"I can write. Maybe I could try the newspaper."

He nodded. "Might work out. I had an army friend did that for a while here but soon found it boring. He wanted something more exciting but all the bigger city papers called for a college degree. Ever consider going to college?"

Alice shook her head. "Don't know how I could ever afford it."

She suddenly felt like a guppy leaving the estuary for open water. She'd never thought that having a high school degree would be inadequate. Her list of worries overflowed onto a new page. She wished the driver would stop talking and focus on his job. Every time he asked a question, she learned she had no answer and soon a third page of worries sat before her. She needed time to sort out answers for the issues he had already raised, not more of them.

The man finally stopped his inquisition and Alice turned to the window of the bus. By the lights and storefronts lining the road, she knew they were close to, if not already inside, the Asheville city limits. She had never seen so many shops, gas stations, and small businesses in one location before. She could scarcely imagine the likes of New York, Chicago, or Los Angeles.

The driver announced they would be arriving at the final stop in five minutes and Alice's heart fluttered. Ready or not, here she was. She paid close attention to the places they passed, hoping to spot a place to stay. Within a minute, she noted two motels, but neither looked like a place she wanted to use. By the time they arrived at the small depot, she counted five motels within walking distance, but only one that appeared halfway clean.

The driver stood to open the door and assist elderly patrons down. He turned to address her as he opened the door.

"Young lady, could you wait until last? I have something to ask you."

Alice wanted to get started. She needed to find a room and didn't feel comfortable wandering a strange town after dark for one second longer than she had to. Still, she deferred to the man by sitting back in her seat while the other passengers disembarked. When the others had cleared the bus, she stood and emerged to the pavement below. She watched him move all of the luggage from the storage compartment to the sidewalk except her suitcase.

As the driver approached, she asked, "May I have my suitcase, please?"

"In just a minute, Miss." He assisted another passenger and gazed around the area in a final sweep looking for anyone else needing help. He then turned back to Alice.

"Miss, can I ask you a question? It's none a my business, I know, but are you runnin' away from home? I just get this feelin' in ma gut you're runnin' and you're gonna need help."

"I, uh ..."

"How old are you? Seventeen? Maybe eighteen?"

"I turned eighteen six months ago, and I'm not running away from home 'cause I don't have one anymore." She realized that her answer was partially the truth.

"I see. Got folks somewhere?"

"No, Sir. Ma died when I was ten. Pa's gone now, too. Got some cousins but I don't even know where they live now."

"Sorry, family's 'bout the best thing I got going for me." He paused and scrutinized her. "Look, you seem like a nice kid. Let me do somethin' for you. Get back on the bus and I'll drop you off at a clean little motel near my bus yard and shop. The owners are good folks, in their own way. Known 'em for years, in fact. There's also a little café across the street with decent food at a good price. And, if you want, I'll pay you six dollars a night to clean this thing. Takes a couple hours to do right, but that gives you the chance to find a day job, too."

Alice was too stunned to say anything. She'd read about this thing called karma. She seemed to be reaping the good side of it. First the Umfleets, and now this guy.

"What's your name?"

She paused a moment. If this marked the start of a new life, she needed a new name as well. Nothing that could connect her to her old man, or to Frampton Corner. "Betsy, Betsy Weston."

"Well, Betsy Weston, I'm Lester Eaton. My wife goes by Hilda, but don't ever ask her real name, 'less you want a glare that'll turn you to ice. Let's get goin'."

With that, he put one hand on the side of the door and with the other motioned for her to climb aboard. A minute later, the old Ford lurched forward and they moved along several back roads until Lester stopped in front of the J & S Rest Stop.

"J & S. That's for Jim and Sally Fleming." He tooted the horn and a silver-haired lady, a bit heavyset, poked her head out the door where a small, red neon sign announced the "Office." She waved and stepped onto the stoop as Lester opened the door.

As Alice got off the bus, she overheard him tell her, "Got another stray, Sally. Name's Betsy. Told her you'd take real good care of her." The woman, Sally, responded with a broad smile and nodded. She leaned toward the driver and whispered something Alice couldn't hear, but she did hear the man answer with a "Thanks." Sally motioned for him to follow and they walked a little further away. The conversation turned a bit heated, but both turned back to Alice with smiles on their faces.

"Thank you again, Les. Got a nice room right close to us here."

Sally walked over to Alice and extended her hand. "Evenin'. I'm Sally. Let's get you settled in."

Despite what appeared to be a minor argument between Sally and Lester, Alice's first impression of the woman was of a warm and generous grandmother. She'd never watched much television, only the rare occasion at a friend's home. "The Andy Griffith Show" was one of her favorites and Sally reminded her of Aunt Bea, down to the tonal inflections in her voice.

Lester opened the luggage compartment and pulled out Alice's suitcase. Alice grabbed the handle and hoisted it to her side. She caught the woman sizing her up from head to toe with something of a malicious gleam in her eye. Suddenly, Alice felt self-conscious and noted a tingle of awareness run down her spine. The image of Aunt Bea morphing into Cruella DeVille sizing her up for her pelt jumped into her head. A moment later, Sally's beatific smile returned and she walked to the office door and leaned in.

"Hey, Jim, we got a new guest! Come carry her bag to room two."

An elderly male voice echoed back. "Coming, honeybuns."

Sally sighed and turned back to Alice. "Love him dearly, but the old fart can't hear worth a dime and sometimes I think he requires more work than the motel."

A boney old man came to the door and joined them. He had a full white mane of fine hair and poorly fitting dentures that he flicked back into place every few seconds with his tongue. He was half the size of his wife, but despite the frail demeanor, had a spring in his step that seemed to defy gravity and a man-made smile any dentist would claim to his credit, as long as it stayed in his mouth.

He walked right up to Alice and gave her a curt bow. "I'm Jim. Welcome to the Rest Stop." He reached out for her suitcase. "Here, please let me take that."

Alice didn't know what to do. He certainly did not look

any more capable of carrying the case than she. Yet, he seemed so eager to please.

She relinquished her suitcase and watched as he nearly toppled over with it. Sally steadied him and once stable, he carried it toward the first in a row of twelve small motel rooms, each door separated by long narrow front window and each facing a single parking slot in a crumbling asphalt drive. Cars filled all but two slots, which Alice thought to be a good sign. She felt that the good karma was following.

A light emanated through the window of Room 2 and Alice glanced in as they neared it. The space appeared to be clean and functional. Jim set the suitcase down and opened the door. He ushered Alice inside after turning on a second light. The room held a double bed, nightstand, a cozy cushioned chair, and a small wooden table with two matching chairs. The bathroom seemed an afterthought, appearing retrofitted into a corner of the room, and held a toilet, shower stall, and small pedestal sink. All appeared spotless.

She turned to find Sally in the doorway. "Okay, here's the deal, sweetie. Nightly stays are fifteen dollars. We have a weekly rate of a seventy-five dollars, up front, but I don't clean up after you. You make your own bed and if you need a fresh towel, you can come to the office and trade in the dirty one. I catch you stealing towels or linens; you're out on your ear even if your week ain't over."

Alice had no idea what motels cost. She did some mental calculations, but math had never been her favorite subject. She had a hundred and fifty dollars of her own, plus the loan from the Umfleets. With the six dollars a day that Lester offered for cleaning the bus, she covered over half the weekly rate. Still, she'd have to find a second job real fast or her savings wouldn't last but a few weeks, maybe four or five if she only ate once or twice a day. That would, of course, depend on what the meals cost at the cafe. Maybe there was a cheaper motel or boarding room she could tolerate. Still, it had to be within walking distance of Lester's bus yard. Maybe she could keep some simple things like bread, peanut butter, and cereal in her room. She'd have to find a grocery nearby. She knew she was tired and answers didn't come quickly. Should she just pay for one night and start looking around tomorrow? Or, take the weekly rate and have more time to investigate housing and transportation?

Sally noted her hesitation and spoke up. "Look, you ain't gonna find a cheaper place nearby and ... Tell you what, I'll make it sixty dollars a week if you keep the parking area and yard clean. Jim sure ain't doing a grand job of it."

"Okay, if I can keep some food in the room."

"Sure, sweetie. Got nothing against that, 'cept no hotplates, no cooking. Don't want the place burning down out a someone's carelessness."

That cinched it for Alice, now Betsy. Boy, she was going to have to get used to the new name. Betsy, Betsy, Betsy. Weston. She faced away from Sally and rummaged through her purse. She turned back and presented three twenty dollar bills to the proprietress. "Here, one week up front."

Sally glanced at Betsy's forearm as she extended the money toward her. "What happened to your arm?"

"Cut it on some broken glass. It's nothing." She wished she could have said that just a few hours earlier. If it had been nothing, she'd have her inheritance and Jimmy's birth documents. She wouldn't be worrying about her money holding out.

Sally nodded. "Well, goodnight, sweetie."

As the woman left the room, Betsy, formerly Alice,

surveyed the room more closely and sat on the bed. *Seems comfortable enough.* Her mind raced ahead to the next day and all the things she had to do, first of which was to call the Umfleets. She double checked her purse and found the slip of paper on which Mary had written their phone number. Unlike her pa, who had no hesitation in sharing news over a party line, Curt had arranged for a private phone line because of his wife's illness. Few in Frampton Corner shared that luxury.

Betsy knew the hour was closing in on midnight but having slept most of the day, her exhaustion was more emotional than physical. She had lost her baby, lost her home, and was close to losing everything she needed to prove her baby still lived and to fund her search. She felt overwhelmed and tears welled up in her eyes. Where they came from, she had no idea. She thought she'd cried them all earlier that day.

Sally had failed to close the door fully and it drifted open a crack as a slight breeze filled the room. Betsy walked over to close it, while perseverating, "I'm Betsy, I'm Betsy, I'm Betsy" so her mind would respond by rote. She glanced outside and noticed the car in front of the room next door had changed. A red Ford pickup had been there minutes ago, but now a white Chevy Impala occupied the space. Farther up the line of rooms, the two previously empty spots each now held a vehicle.

She drifted away from her door a few steps for a better look at the doors and windows of the rooms. Subtle lighting emerged from around the edges of the curtains. Suddenly the door to one room opened up and a man walked out, slipping on a coat as he crossed the walkway to his car. A young woman, her dark brown hair slightly disheveled and wearing only a light, lacy white chemise, struck a seductive pose in the open doorway. She blew a kiss to the man as he looked back before opening his car door. When she looked up and noticed Betsy, her affect flattened and she quickly turned back into the room.

Betsy stood there for a moment, unsure what she had witnessed. Yet, before she could return to her room, the scene recurred at the room two doors down from the first woman, with a different young woman wearing lingerie Betsy had only seen once before in a magazine she had found under her pa's mattress while cleaning the house. She glanced around and caught a stern-faced Sally peering from the office window. Pretty sure she now understood what she'd seen, she rushed back to her room and upon reaching for the doorknob her heart quickened. Why was there a hardened steel hasp fastened to the outside of the door, minus a padlock? Had she just been "sold" into bondage at a brothel?

Five
❧◆◆◆❧

Emory Albritton repositioned his great-great-grandfather's oak desk in front of the picture window overlooking Cashiers Lake. The small frame building on Canoe Point needed more remodeling than he could afford, but was structurally sound and came with two acres, acreage he hoped to sell for a nice profit in years to come. Cashiers, North Carolina was a sleepy little town in Jackson County in the western tip of the state and just a moonshiner's midnight run from the South Carolina state line. However, he knew that was about to change. The scenic beauty of the area, which now included the Nantahala National Forest along with man-made lakes like Thorpe Reservoir eight miles north of Cashiers, had attracted visitors for nearly a century.

Albritton finished unpacking his legal books, stacking them into two second-hand bookcases filling one wall of the office. The next box he opened held his diplomas. He was a Tarheel through and through. A "Carolina blue" blood. Magna Cum Laude from the University of North Carolina at Chapel Hill, followed by a law degree from the same institution. Filled with enthusiasm upon graduating, he had found a position as an Assistant District Attorney for District Court 30A in Macon County. His older brother, Mike, was a deputy sheriff in the adjacent county and they got together frequently for good times. More importantly, the job allowed him to live in his childhood home, now his family's vacation home, in Highlands while working in Franklin, the county seat, just thirty minutes away. Living rent-free had enabled him to save for this building, his first office, which he had purchased with the "help" of an old elementary school classmate, Dewey Hastings.

Dewey certainly knew the area and its people. And they knew him, not always in a positive way. Albritton would be counting on that in the future.

His year in Franklin had confirmed what he'd believed for years. The area was ripe for development. After a year of prosecuting small-time criminals, the county's staff attorney position opened up and he jumped the ship of criminal law for the more genteel ways of land management, zoning disputes, and the like. During that two-year stint, he witnessed the growing presence of moneyed businessmen and retirees and positioned himself for the coming land boom. Now, at age twenty-eight, he felt ready to strike out on his own.

He inspected the glass in each frame for smudges and cleaned them yet again with an ammonia-based cleaner before hanging the diplomas on the wall behind his desk with care. He glanced at his watch. Almost midnight. He hustled to repeat the cleaning and hanging of numerous other framed awards and honors, photos with the governor and various state and federal officials, and finally a large map of Jackson County showing land plats of one hundred acres and more. He took a moment to inspect the map after hanging it and then walked to the picture window. The small lake appeared as smooth obsidian under a starless sky. Yes, the growth occurring now in Lake Toxaway after the town rebuilt the lake would extend west to Cashiers in no time. Land prices around Cashiers had increased ten percent over the past two years and Albritton expected his nearly $75,000 in school debt to be erased within seven years. Less if he lived frugally. Then, after he'd made his fortune, maybe a career in public service.

He walked over to his desk and picked up one more item to hang. He checked his watch again. Five minutes into the new day. He carried the one-by-two-foot sign to the front door and stepped outside. A bracket extended out from the wall at one side with two chains hanging down. He held up the sign, slipped its two slightly opened eyebolts into their respective chains, and let go. The chains jingled a bit as the sign wobbled and came to rest. He stood on his stoop and looked down Valley Road toward town. To the empty night sky he announced, "It's official, Cashiers. My shingle's hung and I'm open for business. Emory Albritton, Attorney-at-Law."

Six

Betsy rushed into the room, slamming the door closed. She crawled onto the bed and pulled her knees up to her chest, crying, wondering what in the world she had gotten into. House of ill repute. Brothel. Cathouse. Whorehouse. Bordello. The names flooded her mind. How could this day have gotten any worse?

Then, with a glance at the door, she realized she couldn't leave it closed. The simple click of a padlock would make her a prisoner, force her into a life of prostitution. She'd never be able to sleep knowing it was open. The dilemma seemed a no-win situation, an impasse she was ill prepared to face, even without the emotional drain of the day.

She jumped up and raced back to the door, afraid that Sally or Jim or some unknown person had already caged her. To her relief, the door opened without resistance. She looked about the room for something she could place between the door and the jamb that would make it impossible to padlock without leaving the door open wide. She found an old wire hanger, which she wrapped around the bottom corner of the door in a way that it stayed in place but stopped the door at the frame. She nestled the door to the frame and moved the table behind it so no one could come in without some effort and a lot of noise. She took hold of the knob and pulled. The table kept it from freely moving. Then she pushed the door and saw with satisfaction that the door would not close tight into the frame. She stepped back and sighed, her pulse and breathing easing toward normal.

She moved back onto the bed, pulled her knees tight to her chest again and stared at the door, willing it to stay put. In what seemed like no time, her eyelids became heavy. She fought the fatigue by changing position and when that became too comfortable, she moved to one of the straight, hard-backed chairs. For the first time that night, she noticed her breasts aching, but this time she welcomed the discomfort that helped her stay awake.

After a while, she noted she was leaking and the heaviness of her breasts made sitting in the hard chair more uncomfortable. She walked to the bathroom, picked up one of the stiff, worn towels and returned to the bed. She raised her top, pulling her arms from its sleeves, removed her bra, and wrapped the towel around her chest. Its scratchiness irritated her, but she wanted to minimize the laundry she would have to do. She pulled the top back down and shifted to her left side. The aching and irritation only helped her stay awake for a short time.

"Hey, Sleeping Beauty, wake up! What's with the door?"

The voice and rattling at the door started Betsy awake. She sat up and instantly wrapped her left arm around her chest to hold the towel in place and provide support. She blinked a number of times to clear the sleep from her eyes and saw bright daylight outside. Two eyes framed in long, light brown hair peeked through the crack in the doorway.

"What's with the door? You might want to get this stuff off it before Sally sees it. She don't take kindly to anyone messing with the room."

"Who's there?" Betsy asked, her voice cracking from dryness.

"I'm Jennie, Jennie Mae. Room six."

"Room six?"

"Yeah. I saw you last night and I guess you saw me, too."

Room six. The lady in the lingerie. Betsy recalled the image of the man leaving the room, but the room number hadn't registered. Only now did the position of the room jive with the number as she thought about it.

"Okay. Yeah, I, uh, remember. Just a minute."

She sat up on the edge of the bed and glanced around until she found her bra. She picked it up and walked to the door where she pulled back the table and pulled off her wire contraption. She opened the door and saw a young woman not much older than her, dressed in jeans and T-shirt, her long chestnut hair combed nicely, her face holding just a touch of makeup. She looked no different from some of Betsy's high school friends, which made it difficult for Betsy to reconcile what she had seen last night with the person standing before her.

"C'mon in. I, uh … Give me a minute." Betsy walked to the bathroom where she removed the towel and redressed. She returned to the room and saw the woman standing in the door. "Hi. I'm, uh, Betsy."

"So, what's with the door?"

Betsy shook her head. "Did you see the door? There's a hasp on it. I'm not about to let myself get locked in."

Jennie laughed. "Silly. No one's gonna lock you in. Besides, even if someone put a lock on there, all you have to do is use the window. Look for yourself." The woman pointed to the window.

Betsy walked to the window and pulled back the curtain. There was a sliding window with a standard interior catch, plus a small metal rod in the track. Betsy tried to open the window but it wouldn't budge. She pulled harder and managed to rock it open a bit at the top, but the pane fell back into place.

"Take the metal bar out, girl. That's there for your security, not to lock you in."

Betsy saw it now. She removed the bar and the window slid open. She'd never seen sliding windows before. She peered out the window and saw no way to lock it from the outside. *What a dummy*, she thought. *Gettin' all upset over nothing.*

"So, why the lock?"

"Jim and Sally go to Florida for January. We all do actually, and they had someone breaking in using a duplicate key. So, she put these on to secure the rooms while they're gone. Cheaper than changing all the locks and keys."

Betsy crossed her arms in front of her and scrutinized the young woman. Silence reigned for a minute as Betsy floundered with what to say. "Umm, about last night …"

"Yeah, life's a bitch. What can I say? I am a working girl as we say, in the world's oldest profession. Sally's been runnin' this place for years. I ended up here as a runaway two years ago. No money. They took me in and one thing led to another. Do I like what I do? No. Do I like the money I make? You bet. It's putting me through South College. Once I get my B.S. in Legal Studies I can quit this and become a paralegal, and not a day too soon."

Betsy didn't know what to say.

"So, you here to join the stable?"

Betsy's eyes widened. "What? Me? I-I …"

"Hey, you're not going to offend me. Trust me. I've heard all the names and taken a few licks from some of the johns. If you can get away without getting involved, more power to you."

"Hey, Jennie."

Betsy heard a new voice from outside. Two more girls peeked around the door into the room. The dark haired girl in the chemise last night stood on the left dressed casually like Jennie now.

"Who's this?"

"Sally's gonna hafta work on this one. Got some weight to lose. But she's got the tits for the work."

"Hey, be nice, Billie. Her name's Betsy and she's not here to work."

"Yet."

Betsy frowned at the dark haired girl named Billie and stood erect, riled and ready to prove her mettle.

"Don't pay her no mind, Betsy. She's just jealous of girls with better curves."

Billie put her hands on her hips and her lips formed a pout. "Dammit, Jennie, you know I'm not like that."

She stared at Billie for a minute. "You're really pretty. Why be jealous?" Betsy made the compliment in naïve honesty but saw in an instant how it changed the mood of the moment. Billie's hostility vanished and Betsy realized she had learned an important method of dealing with people.

"Thanks. Have you had breakfast? We're going out to get some and you can join us... if you want," replied Billie.

The third girl stepped into the room. "I'm Joan. C'mon and join us. My treat. But, you ought need to change your top. You're all wet."

Jennie looked closer at Betsy. "Wet? Hell, that's ... you're nursing? Oh man, where's the baby? Don't tell us Sally let you stay here with a baby."

"Baby?" Billie spurted out. "Don't you let Sally —"

"Don't let Sally what?" The three girls' eyes bugged at the voice of their madam and they stepped back to let her enter the room.

Betsy heard Billie take an audible breath. Her heart started to race at the uncertainty of what was about to happen?

Sally faced Billie and said, "Go ahead. Finish what you were about to say."

Billie swallowed hard and nodded toward Betsy. "Ask h-her," she stammered.

Sally turned back to Betsy, brow raised and started to speak but pulled up short as her gaze caught Betsy's predicament. She sighed.

"Okay. Do you have the baby with you? It's obvious you're leaking milk and there's only one reason for that."

Fear caught Betsy in its swell for the third time in just over twenty-four hours. "I … yes, um no … I …" Betsy's shoulders sagged and she plopped down onto the bed behind her, crying. "H-he's not with me. I-I …" Deep sobs filled her being.

Sally's demeanor changed to one of concern as she sat next to Betsy. "Hey, hey. Calm down. Tell me what's going on."

Betsy looked at Sally and then at the three young women standing to one side. Sally followed her gaze and spoke to the others. "Why don't you go on and get some breakfast. Bring it back here." She held her arm out and flipped her hand up and toward the door three times to shoo them out. "Go on. Get."

How much did she want to share with this woman, a total stranger? And the owner of a whorehouse at that. Jennie and Billie seemed friendly enough, but could she trust any of them? Whom could she trust? She realized she knew no one in this city. She had limited resources. These women were likely to have connections she could never make on her own. If she had any hope of finding her son, she had to start by trusting someone.

Betsy watched them inch out the door, but heard only

one pair of feet leaving. She suspected one left to get food while the remaining duo lingered by the door to hear whatever she had to say. A fleeting shadow across the opening confirmed the presence of at least one individual outside. She took a deep breath and exhaled forcefully. "Y'all might as well come in and have a seat. It's okay. Really."

Sally put her hand under Betsy's chin and turned Betsy's face toward her. "You sure?"

Betsy pulled away and nodded.

"Okay, girls. C'mon back in, like she said."

Jennie and Joan eased back into the room, pulled the wooden chairs away from the table, and sat down.

Betsy once again launched into her story, but this time she started at the beginning with her boyfriend, JT. After a brief introduction, she stated, "JT joined the army and was about to head off for basic training. It was his last time at home and he begged me to share my body with him. You know, in case something happened to him, he'd always remember our last night together."

Joan huffed. "Like we haven't heard that one a million times. Oldest line in the book."

Betsy offered a sheepish nod in reply. "So, I've been told. But, with JT, I'll never know. He shipped off to Viet Nam soon as basic was over and was killed just over a month after arriving there. I received one letter from him, from Nam. Said it was rememberin' that night and knowin' he had a baby on the way what kept him going."

She told the women of her father's reaction to learning she was pregnant, of how he shipped her off to a distant cousin of his as soon as she started to show, and of the way he'd treated her after she'd had Jimmy and brought him home. She finished with the details of the previous day and of how she came to arrive at the Rest Stop. The tears resumed as she described waking up to find her baby missing and the awful encounter with her father. By then, the two young women had joined Sally on the bed next to Betsy, trying to console her.

Sally gave up a grunt of disgust. "Wretched man. Your father or not, he needs a good …" She inhaled sharply. "I'll be back in a minute." She stood and left the room.

The others huddled closer to Betsy and peppered her with questions about the infant. Betsy answered honestly, and felt her heart lighten as she recalled her son. She found the girls encouraging and knew in her soul that she'd find her son.

"Look," she said. "Is there a pay phone around here somewhere? One with a little privacy? I need to call those folks what helped me last night. I told 'em I'd give them a way to contact me."

Jennie fished out a business card from one of her pockets and handed it to Betsy. "That's got the motel office number on it. Sally don't mind you taking short calls there, but don't ask her to let you make any calls out."

"Best pay phone for private calls is a couple blocks away. That way." She pointed right. "There's a phone booth on the corner by the bank."

Betsy nodded. "Thanks."

She stood up just as Sally returned.

"Here. Call this guy and tell him I sent you. He's a lawyer, and he'll be able to tell you what actions you can take … and tell him his advice better be on the house 'cause I pay him a big enough retainer." She handed Betsy another business card.

Betsy felt a rush of excitement at this positive turn in events. A lawyer. He'd get on her old man's case and help her find Jimmy Bob. She walked to the head of the bed and grabbed her purse from under the pillow where she'd hidden it all night. She thought through her plan of attack. She'd walk to the bank, get change for the phone as well as break one of her larger bills into smaller ones, and then make her phone calls. With any luck, the lawyer could see her today and she'd be back in time to find her way to Lester's work yard to clean his bus that evening. Oh, and she'd find a hardware store to get a padlock of her own. She didn't like carrying all of her money and important papers with her everywhere.

She was about to leave when Billie arrived with four bags containing the same number of carryout breakfasts. "What'd I miss?"

Betsy didn't want to wait a second longer, but her grumbling gut won out. She ate while the two girls gave Billie an abbreviated rendition of Betsy's story. In between bites, she offered her own colorful opinions, finally saying, "Guys can be such assholes. Don't worry. We're gonna help. Aren't we, Jennie?"

After wolfing down breakfast, she ushered the others from her room, changed tops, closed the door and locked it with the door key Sally had given her the night before. She hurried out to the street where she turned right toward the bank. Within minutes, she entered the limestone structure and stood in line behind a dozen patrons. Fifteen minutes later, she pulled the door of the phone booth closed behind her and retrieved both business cards, as well as the Umfleet's number, from her purse. She first dialed zero to get the operator and then changed her mind, deciding to try the lawyer first.

"Lessing, Costello, and Mathews."

"My name is, uh, Betsy Weston. I'd like to make an appointment with Mr. Mathews. Um, Mizz Sally, Sally Fleming, gave me his name."

"I see." The receptionist's tone of voice frosted the walls of the phone booth. "Well, Mr. Mathews is in court all day today and tomorrow. How much time do you think you might need?"

"Gee, I don't know. Half an hour, maybe."

"The first slot I have is next Tuesday at one o'clock."

"Next Tuesday?" Betsy echoed. That was a week away. "Nothing sooner?"

"I'm sorry. That's the soonest I can give you that much time. I can ask Mr. Mathews and get back with you."

Betsy knew enough to work with the system. "Would you please? I'll take that appointment for next week, but if I can get in sooner, it's real important, Ma'am."

"May I ask what this is about?"

"It's about getting my baby back. My pa stole him from me and sold him."

"Excuse me? Is this a joke? We don't have time for —"

"Please, Ma'am. I'm not joking." Her voice began to crack. "I had a baby two and a half weeks ago and my pa threatened that if I come home with him, he'd take him and sell him ... and that's just what he up and did ... yesterday."

"How old are you?"

"Eighteen, Ma'am."

"Where did this occur and did you notify the police?"

"Frampton Corner ... that's in Jackson county, and I tried to tell the Sheriff but he don't believe me. I ran away from home last night and I need help getting my baby back."

"Miss, I'm not sure —"

"Please! I need the help of someone who knows this legal stuff."

"And you say Rest Stop Sally referred you?"

Condescension oozed through the receiver. "Are you working for her?"

"No, Ma'am. Please, I need help." Silence commandeered the phone line. "I, uh … the bus driver took me there. Told me I'd be safe there and the rooms were cheap but clean. Last night I witnessed what goes on there, but, honest, I'm not a working girl."

"Look, can I reach you at the Rest Stop number?"

"Yes, Ma'am. They'll let me take a short call there."

"Okay. I'll talk with Mr. Mathews and get back with you. In the meantime, I've penciled you in for next Tuesday, and if by chance the bus driver's name was Lester, be real careful. Let me just say his reputation is not a good one. You hear me?"

Betsy listened to the empty buzz of the phone line long after the law firm's secretary hung up, and stared at the traffic passing through the intersection. What did the woman mean? What kind of reputation? This new quandary settled in as the latest in the growing list of obstacles facing her. She needed the money. His offer represented a job she could do easily and start right away. But now? Could she trust him to pay her? Or worse … could she trust him not to assault her?

She felt her emotions roiling and forced her mind to end its ruminations. She had another task immediately before her and then she could tackle this new problem. She dialed "0" for the long distance operator and held up the Umfleet number for easy viewing. After a brief conversation and depositing a dollar-fifty into the phone, she heard the line ringing at the other end.

A vaguely familiar voice answered, "Umfleet residence," but Betsy couldn't quite place its owner.

"Is Mary there, please?"

"I'm sorry. Can I ask who is calling?"

Betsy felt a sting of anxious fear. "Um, I'm a cousin. Is Curt available?"

"No, sorry."

"Who is this?" Betsy asked.

"Deputy Albritton, Ma'am. May I have your name please?"

Betsy started to hang up in panic, but from somewhere deep inside she got the courage to continue, praying, fingers crossed, that the deputy did not recognize her voice. She added a bit more drawl to her speech. "I'm Mary's cousin Sarah. I got word she weren't doin' well and thought to call and see what I could do to help."

"Well, Ma'am, Curt is with the Sheriff about a serious matter, and, well, I'm not supposed to say … but since you're family … I'm sorry to inform you that Mary died in her sleep early this morning."

Betsy slumped against the side of the phone booth, her heart fallen. Mary was going to talk with the sheriff about her baby and now she would never have the chance. Would Curt remember? Under the circumstances, she couldn't blame him if he forgot.

Seven
(Present Day)
❧ ✦ ✦ ❧

Myra closed the lid on her laptop, putting it to sleep. This day had been no more productive than the previous two, and she again felt drained. Her idea of three days ago had gained no traction. She had run out of legal pads, and her recycling bin was full of scrap paper wads. Her twelve-hour sleep of the dead of three nights earlier had also been a fluke, but one she wished she would repeat tonight. She could use such a night's rest before driving to L.A. in the morning.

She walked to the dry bar across the room and claimed a glass from the overhead rack. The merlot, just a taste, beckoned. She poured the wine and took it outside onto the deck. The weather appeared to be changing, earlier than forecasted, and she could see a front approaching from the west across the water. The wind had picked up and shafts of rain were visible in the distance. That rain would be on her within the hour.

She watched the horizon and pondered her dilemma. She needed a book idea. She considered the options and decided her brainstorming could continue as she drove the next day. Plenty of time to think then. Already, the wind carried scattered, cold, wet droplets to her face.

She entered her home, prepared a light supper, and retired to her bed where she picked up her latest Rizzoli & Isles story by her friend, Tess Gerritsen. She preferred not to read other authors while actively writing, but on occasion she made an exception. Two pages later, the book dropped to her chest and a sonorous snore echoed within the bedroom.

*　　*　　*

Myra glanced out the window of the limousine at the Village Theater Westwood and the cordoned area for the red carpet. After driving from Carmel to Beverly Hills, she had checked into her garden suite at the Beverly Hills Hotel and napped. The next day's book signing went well but again she felt exhausted by the end of the day. This morning she did some shopping and had lunch with a friend who hemmed and hawed and tread softly around her concern for Myra's health. Myra reassured her that she felt fine, but then she again had to nap for an hour before preparing to come to the premiere of "Sisterhood of Terror." Maybe she would see her doctor after getting home.

At that moment, she sat there thinking, "What the hell am I doing here?" She didn't feel up to it and that thought surprised her. When hadn't she felt up to a party before? Never. Yet, this was beginning to feel like some form of personal masochism.

She glanced about to see aerial spotlights combing the sky, a live jazz band playing something indistinguishable over the din of the crowds, and heavy gold braid ropes cordoning off the red carpet stage where she now disembarked. She moved into 'diva' mode as a tuxedoed escort one-third her age approached and offered his arm, but she declined. Not that she disliked cavorting with the younger studs. She refused to let him hurry her past the crowds into the theater. She wanted to relish the experience.

Plus, this young man didn't even know who she was, and called her "Ma'am." Not by her name or even by "Madam," although that resounded too much of a southern brothel. Nope. Simply "Ma'am" with a Texas twang, like uninspired dialogue right out of a grade B western. The old mood ring dimmed from red-hot to sleepy blue. Mood ring? Gawd, even her thoughts betrayed her age.

Too bad, too. He smelled great and looked even better. Probably gay.

She waved to the crowd, but got few return gestures. The previous four premieres she had attended had been the same. She always hoped someone would be polite enough to wave back, but in reality, she would be surprised if she was actually recognized and her waves returned. Nobody ever recognized the author behind the book behind the movie. She had often wondered if anyone even knew, or cared, that someone's book formed the basis of most movies.

She smiled her best smile, one she thought might challenge the spotlight, but she suspected her eyes showed no thrill at being on the red carpet for her fifth time. Her fifth bestseller to become an expectant blockbuster. Her third time having sour grapes with a producer. Despite a contract that gave her final approval over the screenplay, this producer had found a loophole and bypassed her. The result? A mediocre interpretation of her bestselling novel yet. Sixteen weeks at the pinnacle of the New York Times list. Sixteen! This movie had an even chance of going straight to DVD the following week.

Sure, it had great action scenes. Fantastic special effects went without saying. But, the steamy sex scene hit the cutting floor to extract a PG-13 rating, which was too bad because that was the strongest part of the whole, lame script. And character development? What was that? All in all, anyone who'd never read the book wouldn't know the difference … and that's what the producers counted on. That, and a casting coup already worth tens of millions in free publicity. Oh, the tabloid press saw a wormhole open to heaven with this one. Myra thought *she* wrote great fiction. Imagine the bold headlines and the phony stories when word leaked out that Jennifer Anniston had been cast opposite Brad Pitt. Rumors on the set said they never crossed paths during filming and all scenes of them together had been digitally spliced in the editing room. One gossipmonger went so far as to suggest they weren't even aware they were in the film together until after final production.

Myra began to walk toward the theater when a security agent approached her, his hand cupping the ear with his earpiece. *What now?* she thought.

He nodded to no one in particular, lowered his hand and held up a clipboard to scan it as he asked, "May I have your name please?"

Myra about choked. What would Sweetie say? She would say… For some reason, Myra went blank. Sweetie never went blank. "Sweetie … and George" was her favorite cartoon and Sweetie always had just the right comeback.

"Myra Mitchell." *You know, the author who wrote this book. The we-wouldn't-be-here-tonight-without-her Myra Mitchell. That Myra Mitchell.*

"Thank you, Ms. Mitchell. They'd like you to move along the carpet a bit faster. Mr. Pitt is arriving."

She took two steps forward as he moved away, and then slowed down. "Like hell I'm getting out of their way," she muttered. At that moment, the crowd erupted and camera flashes outshone the spotlights now aimed at the arriving limo.

A devious smile crossed Myra's lips. She hadn't earned her "Diva of Disaster's" tiara for simply great writing. In an instant, she did a one-eighty turn and swept across the carpet directly to Brad Pitt. They'd met on more than one occasion during the filming and had hit it off well. She'd even had dinner on the set with him and Angelina, whom she discovered was a great fan of Myra's books. She had no doubt they could ad lib this move without effort.

She arrived at his side before any security could move in and kissed him on the cheek. Angelina was by his side and Myra moved on to give her a sisterly hug while whispering, "I hope you don't mind sharing him. I absolutely hate walking into these things alone."

Angelina laughed and squeezed her hand. "Only if your next book has a role specifically for me," she replied.

"It's a deal," Myra answered.

"Myra, it's a pleasure to see you again, and a pleasure to escort you in," said Brad.

Brad offered Myra his left arm, while Angelina took his right and together they moved along the red carpet. The two women waved in proxy for Brad and Myra's mood brightened again, until she reflected on the promise she'd just made. Her next book? Again, she saw a yawning black hole sucking away all of her creativity, and with it, that next book.

They reached an area where security was tight and the concourse narrowed. Myra noticed one security man nod at them and Brad gestured back. He leaned toward Myra and said, "Thought we might actually get to walk straight in. Sorry, but it's time to go to work." He lowered her arm and squeezed her hand. In an instant, he and Angelina began working the lucky crowd next to the cordon, signing autographs and posing for snapshots. Myra wondered how long those fans had camped there to secure those precious spots near the rope. She did know that security had already screened all of them and granted them leave to remain where they were.

Suddenly, Myra felt all alone. She watched the two stars interact with their fans and realized, yet again, how lonely and isolated the life of a writer could be. Still, she wouldn't change a thing. Authors had stories to tell. Actors could only animate what an author created. Which required the most creativity?

"Ms. Mitchell!"

Shocked, Myra heard her name over the commotion about her, but couldn't quite pinpoint it. She turned her head and slowly started to walk along the carpet.

"Ms. Mitchell! Please!"

The young female voice came from her left. Myra turned and saw a young woman, a girl really, maybe late teens, waving a book at her. Myra smiled and approached her, noticing what looked to be a personal journal in the girl's hand. "Hi. Nice to meet you. You are?"

The girl looked at her askance. "Hi, I'm Desiree. Hey, do you think you could get Brad and Angelina's autographs for me? They aren't even looking this way."

Myra did choke this time. She raised one eyebrow and tried to contain the steam rising within. She wasn't some autograph gofer. Inwardly, she sighed, feeling more like the Diva of Deflated Ego now. "I'm sorry. I have no influence over that. Keep trying." She encouraged the girl despite knowing that the actors would work just the one area of the crowd.

As she turned back toward the theater entrance, she heard her name again. The same voice, further down the line. She turned her smile back on and walked along, closer to the barricade. About ten feet ahead, she saw a young woman, brunette, tall and slim, holding Myra's book and waving a pen at her. She walked directly to the gal, beaming.

"Good evening. Nice to meet you. You are?"

"Alexia. Alexia Hamilton. It's really an honor to meet you. I adore your books. Really. I have them all ... in hardcover."

Myra chuckled, eased the pen from the woman's nervous grip, and opened the book to the title page. "To Alexia, Best wishes and may you live your dreams to the fullest." Myra signed off with a flourish and handed the book back. "Let me guess, your accent tells me the Carolinas, the western end, and you hope to be a writer."

"Yes'm. Near Asheville to be precise ... and I love writing."

"Asheville. Lovely town. And Biltmore? What a place. I've been there once."

"Yes'm. I'm out here now to start work next month on my PhD in Literature and Creative Writing at USC."

"Wow. I'm impressed. That's a highly selective program. It has what, four slots and over eighty applicants each year? Congratulations and good luck." Myra mentally debated whether or not to mention her position with the program.

"Thanks. I, uh ... Will you be attending the reception tomorrow evening?"

Myra smiled, thinking, *Guess she already knows.* "Why, in fact, yes, I will be there. I suppose we might see each other there."

"Great. I really hope I get a chance to talk with you."

The first tuxedoed escort came up to Myra. "Ma'am, they'd like everyone to move toward the theater. Thank you."

"Well, I need to move along. Perhaps tomorrow night."

Alexia nodded. As Myra began to turn away, she blurted, "Ms. Mitchell, I, um, have one more thing to ask of you."

Myra turned her head just enough to see the woman. "What's that?" asked Myra.

The young woman handed her a business card, and then leaned forward to speak into Myra's ear, "Please make time for me tomorrow. I know your secret."

Eight

The movie hadn't yet started when Myra arose from her seat and worked her way past the short row of minor celebrities lining her path to the aisle. Something was off. She was off. She neither looked forward to the film, knowing it was a hatchet job of her book, nor to the party afterward. That wasn't like her.

"Going so soon," asked a minor player in the movie. They had been photographed sharing a drink at the last premiere Myra had attended.

Myra sighed. "Afraid so. Something's come up." She didn't want to add that it felt like dinner was about to come up. Or was it simply her nerves?

"Will we see you at the Hilton?"

Myra gave no answer, but moved on and approached the valet director to ask for her car and driver. The woman seemed surprised. Myra doubted many people left *before* a screening.

She returned straightaway to her hotel, and her suite. By that time, her nausea had eased but not her thirst. She needed a drink and room service obliged her request.

The clock had eased toward midnight and Myra draped herself over the chaise on the patio of her garden bungalow suite at the Beverly Hills Hotel, "The Pink Palace," and watched the moonrise over the Hills. She imagined herself at home in Carmel watching the surf hammer the rocky shoreline below her and etch the sand with foamy frown lines. She could hear the pounding surf, until she realized the beating was a jackhammer giving her a headache the size of the Pacific and the sand was the gummy, yet gritty, dryness in her mouth. Both were the customary results of a night filled with too much

Merlot and a scarcity of sleep.

The allure of Beverly Hills, the second wealthiest zip code in the country, "90210," stretched all around her. The jubilant opening night party after the screening was likely in full swing at the Beverly Hilton, where a number of hangers-on no doubt would haunt the Lobby Bar to await breakfast at the Circa 55 restaurant. Once upon a time, Myra had been part of that group – just two years ago, in fact, the year Beverly Hills' finest hauled her to the main police station and almost booked her for a wardrobe malfunction while frolicking in the fountain in the Beverly Gardens Park across from the Hilton. That was a story the tabloids had loved.

How many glasses had she consumed? She'd stopped counting at six. She arose, re-entered her suite for a refill and frowned at the blinking light on her phone. She had already taken one message from her agent, Samuel DeMoss. He wanted an emergency meeting with her for brunch. Myra still wondered what "emergency" existed, but he had come to town for opening night and insisted on meeting with her. Perhaps Samuel had used the term to force a sense of importance on Myra, who had partied a bit too much when last in New York and had totally forgotten the scheduled meeting with both her agent and editor, a meeting that had been her primary reason for visiting New York. As Sweetie would say, "Get over it."

She pressed the button on the phone to retrieve the message.

"Myra, call me whenever you get in. I heard you left before the premiere. I want to make sure we're still on for breakfast. Call me. Please."

Well, he said please, she thought. She placed the call.

"Bout time. You okay?" asked Samuel.

"Well, howdy-do to you, too, Sam. Yes, I'm fine." She

lied.

"Okay. We're still on for breakfast, right?"

"Yes, Sam. Let's do brunch at ten-thirty."

"No can do, Myra. Got a plane to catch. See you at nine on the patio."

"Alright. See you then."

"Myra, do me a favor. Put the glass down and go to bed."

"Goodnight, Sam." She hung up, hoping she didn't seem too irritated at his comment. He knew her too well.

She wandered back to the patio and sat down on the chaise. She sighed … and took another sip of wine to rinse the foamy frown lines from her tongue. She wondered if soaking her face in it would ease the lines there as well.

She thought back to her incident at the theater. In fact, that's all she'd thought about since leaving the premiere early. The girl had made no mention of what secret she knew, so why was the comment bothering Myra so much? Guilt? Fear? Which one could be considered the strongest reason behind a secret? For Myra, that was an easy question. Both.

Her mind seemed like an old, scratched, vinyl record with a jumpy needle playing over and over and over, as she contemplated her situation. Which secret had that girl discovered? The one about her first husband? Maybe the shame inflicted by her second husband. Those were personal but manageable if revealed. The money she took from her almost third husband could possibly get her in trouble. There were others.

The problem with secrets? They bred like rabbits. At least, that had been her experience. One lie led to yet another. One secret, formed with only good intentions, led to another rationalized by a maybe so-so purpose, but whose real intent was to hide the first secret. Like a character in one of her novels, she knew the truth to be the easiest path. Yet, now she found herself entrenched in a sinkhole of questionable motives without a ladder to help her climb out of the hole she had so expertly excavated for herself.

She stood up, empty glass in hand, and returned to the bar inside her suite. She picked up the vintage Merlot and discovered the bottle empty. She tipped it upside down, hoping her eyes had deceived her, but nothing dripped into her glass. Not just empty, dry. She empathized with the bottle.

Her trademark ebullience. Cocky comebacks. Her "*joie de vivre.*" All had been drained from her by four stupid words from a stranger. "I know your secret." Her Diva's tiara looked like the empty wine glass she now turned upside down and sat next to the bottle -- frail and empty. But was it just those four words? She had faced worse situations. She acknowledged that she hadn't been herself for several weeks now. There was definitely something else wrong.

Myra picked up the business card for the umpteenth time and inspected it. Nothing fancy. Eighty-pound matte stock with standard black ink. No embossing. Probably a quick order from a big box office supply store. Less than a dime to produce. How much did the woman want in return?

State Senator Emory Albritton sat at his antique oak desk, a family heirloom passed down from a great-great-grandfather who had captained a merchant clipper ship in the grand days of sail. State budget shortfalls, funding for pet projects in jeopardy, and a crisis of trust in public office holders should have commanded his constructive attention, but he sat there, staring out the window of his state office in Raleigh, twiddling a pen in his fingers. He had come to the office early, and the capitol was just beginning to buzz with worker bees. The weather outside matched his mood, somber and gray. He hoped the approaching tropical storm held no forecast for his personal future.

He had come so far from that first office in Cashiers. He had made his fortune, moved into state politics and now appeared to be the frontrunner for a U.S. Senate seat. The mid-August primary was but a week away. His manager had said more than once that the race was his to lose.

Only he, and Dewey Hastings, knew how close he was to losing not just the Senate race but everything. His life teetered on the edge of an abyss. A month earlier he had gotten word that the Hamilton girl was looking into a murder case for Project Innocence and that she'd started digging into property records, records that could upend everything he'd accomplished in life. Her acceptance into the doctoral program had stopped her work, but had that young girl discovered anything and why had she run off to California now, at this particular time? Her doctoral program wouldn't start for another month or so.

"He should have called by now," he complained to the empty room. The minute hand of the nearby walnut Regulator wall clock had scarcely moved since he'd last looked at it.

He turned back to the desk and slipped a key into a retrofitted lock on the bottom drawer. He rifled through several folders until he found the one he wanted, background on that young woman from his district, that Hamilton girl. He'd added nothing new to the file since the woman gained acceptance to USC, until last night.

The ringing phone startled him. His private line's Caller ID displayed the number he'd been expecting. Dewey.

"Yes?" he answered.

"Yes, Sir. I, um, got nothin' substantial to report. I almost lost our friend at the movie premiere. Too much security and too big a crowd. But, I managed to catch a glimpse of her getting an autograph from some woman on the red carpet. Afterwards, the Hamilton girl left the premiere, walked south on Westwood and took the Metro 720 bus south. I couldn't get to it in time to join her, but I assume she was going home."

"Assume?"

"I know, I know. Dangerous to make assumptions, but that's all I can say. All she's done is unpack and settle into her new place for the past two days. Groceries. Books. Tonight was her first venture out. We took the Metro 550 to the 720 to get here and that's the way she'll go back to USC. You know, it's damn hard to tail someone on public transit. She's gonna make me sooner or later."

"Who was the woman she met?"

"Myra Mitchell, that author you like. I figured you might want to know, so I went back to the theater to find out. I was asking around when all of sudden she's back out front getting into her limo. Don't think the movie had even started yet. Anyway, she seemed agitated and it got my gut tingling. Maybe our friend said something. Or maybe passed something to her in that book. Anyway, I grabbed a cab and followed her back to the Beverly Hills Hotel. Once I knew she was staying there, I realized the Metro passed by less than a mile away. Our friend could easily have gotten off to come here and maybe that's why the Mitchell lady left early. So, I watched her until I was satisfied the girl wasn't meeting her there and, quite frankly, she's boring."

"Trust me, Dewey, from what the tabloids say about her, she's anything but that. Usually. What'd you see?"

"Nothing basically. She returned to the hotel, went

straight to her room, and showed up on the patio with a glass of wine, which she refilled, let's see ... I tallied up eight glasses in just a couple hours and she didn't even sway when she walked in and out of the suite. I sure wouldn't want to face her in a drinking contest."

"No visitors?"

"None. No phone calls either, at least while I was there. I can't prove otherwise, but I still think something happened at the theater."

"Why do you say that?" replied the Senator.

"Because she didn't stick around for the movie or join the party. I did some checking and, you're right, that's not her reputation. She's never missed a party at one of these things. Not that anyone has ever reported, anyway."

"So?"

"So, something upset her enough to leave early. Never even attempted to go to the party."

Albritton thought about that. The logic was sound. Had she felt ill, she wouldn't have turned to two bottles of wine as a cure. However, had it been their "friend" who foiled the author's night?

The senator glanced at his bookcase. Nestled among the requisite state tomes were numerous titles of fiction, including hardcover copies of every Myra Mitchell novel. She held her own on his top-five list of personal favorite authors.

"Get back to our young grad student. I need to be certain she's just out there to get that PhD and nothing more. Let me know if she contacts the Mitchell woman again."

"Yes, Sir."

Dewey Hastings could be trusted only so far, but Albritton held his chain in a chokehold. He would do anything the legislator requested. He *had* done everything Albritton had asked. Therein lay the rub. Hastings held the senator's chain mutually tight. They were joined at the neck. A noose around one meant a noose around the other. Albritton's only advantage: he held the purse strings.

Whether she knew it or not, young Miss Hamilton had almost stumbled onto what could have been the biggest story of her short journalistic writing career. His problem was two-fold. He couldn't simply have Dewey remove her as a threat. He was guilty of much, but never murder. Plus, her unexpected demise might draw scrutiny by the professional investigators at Project Innocence. They wouldn't fail where she left off.

So, his second problem? He didn't know exactly what she knew and what she didn't, or whether she'd connected any of the dots she had uncovered. Had she turned over her work to the professionals? Dewey had not found any notes or reports in her apartment. On the flip side, he'd found correspondence with a PI and it made no mention of her research. Now that she was out of state, what Albritton didn't need was her piquing the interest of someone like Myra Mitchell, someone whose experience could form a high-def, three-dimensional picture from those dots, someone with the resources to dig deeper, someone who could cause trouble for him, his twenty-plus-year career in public service, and his bid for the U.S. Senate.

Nine
❧✦✦❧

Myra awoke to the UCLA Marching Band strutting across her bedroom, the clamorous snare drums competing with the thunderous bass drum for her attention. She rolled over and missed the snooze button three times before falling out of bed onto the plush carpeted floor.

"Owww," she moaned, rubbing the shoulder that became the focus of her one-point landing. "Damn, it can't be nine o'clock already."

She stood up only to promptly fall back onto her butt as her head performed a dreidel imitation and her eyes channeled John Lennon's "Lucy in the Sky with Diamonds." Back on the floor, Myra waited for the kaleidoscopic merry-go-round to end and then sat up slowly, moving to use the bed as back support.

"I'm never going to make that brunch meeting on time at this rate," she muttered. "Damn, why do I do this to myself?" She refused to answer.

She eased up onto the edge of the bed and, with eyes closed, turned on the lamp. One among the many advantages of luxury hotels was their excellent ability to darken a room at any time of day. Her eyes weren't yet ready for the explosion of light she knew existed beyond the heavy drapes. As she opened her lids to slits, she realized they weren't quite ready for the lamp either, but she pushed ahead.

With improved visual orientation to the dimly lit room, she stood up and waited for the spin to recur. It didn't and she took baby steps to the bathroom where she found another advantage of luxury hotels … complimentary ibuprofen. She gulped down two of the over-the-counter strength tablets with

73

a full glass of Evian, also "free." Her tongue thanked her for that and soon her head would show its gratitude as well.

She looked up and found a stranger, an alien of sorts, staring back at her from "Alice's mirror." This alien from beyond the looking glass bore a vague resemblance to her, but its eyes were matte orange in color, its hair outdid Medusa on a windy day, and the skin of its face looked oddly bulldog-like with a strange pumpkin coloring. *Should have soaked in the wine after all*, she thought, *instead of drinking it*. Her mind filled with the image of the Queen of Hearts crowing, "Off with her head. Off with her head."

She thought also about calling to postpone the meeting until lunch to give her time to "tone up" at the spa first. Unfortunately, she did not recollect the spa's brochure mentioning "miracles" in its service listing. She also vaguely recalled her agent, Samuel DeMoss, saying he had a mid-afternoon flight to catch.

Myra grabbed the coffeepot and a small filter pack containing some foreign brand that promised "all the richness of the Ethiopian countryside where coffee was first discovered." Somehow, the idea of Ethiopia producing fine coffee didn't jive with her mental image of Juan Valdez and his donkey carrying the world's richest coffee beans. The label said "medium roast" and she wondered if that would be enough. A lighter roast would contain more caffeine and a stronger taste. She picked up another filter pack to find a dark roast. The medium would have to do.

Forty-five minutes later, buttressed with two cups of coffee, her skin steamed back into shape by a hot shower, and her hair unbelievably tamed, she inspected her reflection in the cheval mirror and pronounced herself ready for the day … as soon as she found the right pair of shoes.

*　　*　　*

Myra stumbled a bit along the garden path to the main building, in pumps that weren't quite a match to her outfit, but gained strength and walked into the "Pink Palace's" lobby with her regal head up. Her plan? To meet Samuel as he entered the building and surprise him with newfound punctuality. She glanced at a clock behind the reception desk. Ten-twenty. He would arrive at any moment.

She meandered around the lush room filled with potted palms among the broad golden peach pillars and admired a magnificent floral piece on the round table under the central crystal chandelier. She kept her eye on the entrance and took deep breaths whenever her body shouted, "Sit down!" Impatient, she walked to the main door to look down the red carpet entrance. The porter tipped his cap and greeted her by name, another advantage of a five-star establishment like the Beverly Hills Hotel. She smiled back as she looked outside. No Sam.

As she turned, she heard a flurry of footsteps behind her and saw three twenty-something gals rushing toward her, waving. Her smile brightened … and then extinguished as they rushed past her. She sighed and shrugged her shoulders, and then returned to the lobby where she saw the women mob a young man who she recognized from his supporting role in "her" movie. Yes, she created and the actors only animated … but they got all the glory. *Just once*, she thought. Maybe someone could start some kind of "red carpet" event for book releases.

The concierge approached her. "Ms. Mitchell, I'm sorry to interrupt, but Mr. DeMoss asked us to tell you he's waiting on the Polo Patio for you. He asked us to hurry you along if we saw you." He ended with a subtle bow of the head.

She turned and hurried along to the Polo Lounge patio, a garden spot of red brick terraces surrounded by colorful flowerbeds and shaded by trees and mushroom-shaped canopies of trailing fuchsia bougainvillea. The white wrought iron bistro tables and chairs lent an old English air to an otherwise Mediterranean atmosphere. As she walked through the doors to the patio, she found Samuel sitting in the shade of the lounge's famous Brazilian pepper tree, a tree that had seen the likes of Bogart and Hepburn and was older than the hotel itself. He wiped his mouth and stood as she neared.

She noted that his plate was nearly empty. "Wow. Thanks for waiting." Her irritation dripped from her tone.

"Whadayou mean?" Sam replied in a thick Brooklynese. "I should say 'bout time. We were supposed to meet at nine o'clock. It's after ten-thirty and I've got a plane to catch in just over two hours." His irritation out-dripped hers. "I just figured you'd stood me up again."

"No, I clearly remember our agreeing to ten-thirty."

"Hell, Myra. When was the last time you clearly remembered anything?"

She raised a hand and started to answer, and then stopped. He had a point. Her shoulders sagged. "Sorry, Sam. I …"

"C'mon, c'mon. Have a seat."

He pulled the chair out for her and she eased down, hoping he wasn't going to pull it out from under her as she deserved. In an instant, the waiter was at her side with a menu, but she already knew what she wanted. "I'd like to start with a screwdriver, then the sliced pink grapefruit, a Dutch apple pancake and an espresso. Thank you."

The waiter moved off and she looked up to see Sam staring at her, one eyebrow raised.

"What?"

"A screwdriver?" he asked.

"A little hair of the dog never hurt."

"Myra, when ya gonna learn? My Elizabeth, she's got me eating so healthy my blood's clear. From the looks of you, that would do you some good, too. Geez, you look like a pumpkin. You need to see a doctor."

"Thanks. Love you, too, Sam. You know my motto, eat like a Goddess, drink like a fish."

"You got that last part down pat," Sam muttered.

"What?"

"Nothing. Look, I don't have much time. I wanted to let you know that Lizbeth is leaving Penguin and you'll be getting a new editor there. Ever worked with Donna LaPorte? I don't think you have."

Myra looked up at the waiter, who had arrived with her drink, and took the glass. "Thank you." She took a sip and looked back at Sam. "Never heard of her. She okay?"

"Sure, I guess. But she's already asking if you'll have something for her next month as promised. You know, Myra, it's been over a year since your last release—"

Myra, her hand poised over breakfast to snatch her first bite, held up her hand, fork and all, to stop him. "Sam, Sam, please. I've been pumping out a book a year for what, fifteen years? Maybe I just need a break."

She couldn't let Sam in on her current project. It was so far removed from her genre bestsellers that she knew without a doubt he'd think she'd lost it, needed commitment on a 96-hour hold and psychiatric assessment. As she thought about it, maybe he'd be right.

Sam sighed. "Fine, Myra. I understand that. I really do. But you signed a contract with them that commits you to one more book and you promised a rough outline, at the least, by the end of next month." He paused, watched her slather her meal with maple syrup, and start to eat. After one bite, she put down her fork and looked up. "You do have an idea, don't you … for the new book?"

Myra felt conflict in her gut unlike anything inflicted on her by previous indulgences. She stared toward the bougainvillea, trying to find that happy place, any happy place, hoping the sensation would disappear in a puff of mist.

"Myra? You okay?" He paused. "Look, maybe I can stall them a bit without risking a breach of contract. I mean, they don't want to lose an author who outsells Brad Thor, Steve Berry, and James Patterson combined. Right?" He paused and waved his hand in front of her face. "Myra? You still with me?"

Myra's gut became a wave pool rolling out nauseous whitecaps and her head regained its earlier psychedelic swirl. She saw Sam wave his hand, but couldn't seem to react. This incident would seem surreal if only she didn't feel so awful.

"Myra?"

Myra knew she was about to pass out and feared making a scene, but had not the strength to leave the patio or even to ask for help. She had no need to worry. The thud as her body hit the brick pavers caught no one's immediate attention but that of one couple at the nearest table, who resumed talking fifteen seconds later.

Ten
(Spring – 1969)
ও◆◆ও

Counselor Albritton paced the wide planked pine floors of his new office and gazed out at Cashiers Lake more than once. He hadn't expected business to flood through the door on his first day in practice, but he had anticipated at least a few inquiries. He hadn't settled on Cashiers lightly. In fact, after discussions with several fellow county attorneys and more than a dozen area lawyers, he had become convinced that Cashiers was the right place to open shop. Yet, as the clock's hands converged on noon, the phone had not rung once and the front door's hinges produced nary a squeak.

Albritton left his office and walked down a short hall past the two small offices he hoped might one day hold junior associates and entered a small kitchenette equipped with a porcelain sink, a third-hand refrigerator, hot plate, electric percolator for coffee, and a small wooden table with four chairs. From a cabinet adjacent to the sink, he produced a small plate, a loaf of white bread and a jar of peanut butter. From the refrigerator, he claimed a half-full jar of Welch's grape jelly. In due order, he assembled his lunch with potato chips and a Royal Crown Cola accompanying his sandwich.

He stood at the small window on the back wall of the room and watched the lake as he ate the sandwich and chips. A grey heron worked the eastern shallows looking for its own lunch. Albritton liked PB&J well enough, but today, lunch was more a means to break the monotony than something to savor. His custom as county attorney had been to lunch at the Franklin Golf Course clubhouse or Maggie's Café, before a kitchen fire leveled the building. Now, until he had a steady income, frugality ruled his palate.

With the sandwich half-eaten, he turned back to the table and picked up his bottle of pop. He heard the front door open and prepared to greet whoever was there, when he heard a familiar voice.

"Hey, Counselor! You here?"

"Back here, Dewey."

The man entered the break area and smiled.

"Another gourmet lunch, I see."

Albritton nodded. "Help yourself."

The pair went back to elementary school on through high school, where Albritton was a stellar student and Hastings, not so much. At least, not when it came to books. The man was street-smart and had shown Albritton how to skirt the rules when necessary. Now, although Dewey had his less-than-savory side businesses, he continued to help Albritton get an edge on the competition, so to speak.

Albritton resumed eating as Dewey made his own sandwich of PB&J plus potato chips. As the lip of the glass bottle neared his own lips, he heard his phone ring down the hall. Bottle in hand, he rushed back to his office and caught the caller on the fifth ring.

"Albritton Law Office."

He watched Dewey enter the office and make himself at home.

"Hey little brother, how's the day going? Beating off the hordes of real estate speculators with their multi-million dollar deals?"

Albritton's adrenalin level dropped and he sighed as he placed the soda pop on his desk. "Well, big brother, they're about as common as a first degree murder in Tuckasegee."

"Man, that'd cut the population there by what, ten, fifteen

percent? So, slow day, huh?"

"Didn't expect throngs of needy clients, but slow is a hyperbole."

"Look, you didn't hear this from me, but ..."

Albritton heard a sense of giddiness in his brother's tone

"... we got this young girl missing from Frampton Corner. She was last seen with a neighbor. That man's wife died early this morning ... that was kinda expected, cancer ... Jake Fischer took the call and went to meet the coroner there. They had to wheel the body out the back, and ends up, he saw a pile of bloody clothes in the trash pit, ready for burnin'. Wasn't the wife's. The guy admits to them being the girl's and says he stitched up her arm before taking her to the bus. He says he don't know where the girl is, just that he drove her to Cashiers last night."

"You saying he did something to the girl?"

"Mebbe. Need more than bloody clothes to go on, though. You know that. We did ask the bus driver and he said several young women were on that bus. Since we don't have a picture of the girl, we couldn't confirm she was one of them."

"So, clue me in. You thought I'd be interested in this because ..."

"Because, Emory, I think you've mentioned the guy's name to me a hundred times if you've said it once."

"Curt Umfleet?"

"You got it, little brother. You do the math."

The neurons in Albritton's mind began firing like a turbocharged GTO. The Umfleet Family Trust owned nearly two thousand acres of real estate bordering the southwest shores of the reservoir. Curt remained the sole trustee and his family the last remaining beneficiaries. His children were minors and his wife gone. Should he be charged and convicted of a felony, the courts would be moved to name a new trustee. If that happened, Emory Albritton would do whatever it took to make sure he would be the one, the only one, to answer the court's call.

"Umfleet?" asked Dewey as the attorney hung up the phone. "What's up? Heard the wife finally died."

Albritton repeated what his older brother had told him.

"Want me to just make him disappear? Believe me, nothin' better I'd like to do after what he done to my boys and me, gettin' the feds to bust up our stills and all. And I kinda favored Alice Cummings. If he helped her get away, I look at that as a second strike."

"Don't say any more, Dewey. I'm an officer of the court and I won't be a party to your schemes." Dewey grinned at the "officer of the court" bit. "Seriously."

Albritton used Dewey and "his boys" on occasion to play bad guy to his good guy, but they were ordered to stop short of anything physical, and he certainly wanted no part of a murder. That's all he needed to derail his career.

"You can't just kill the man, Dewey. That's not the right way to settle anything. Besides, if he dies, then the kids go into state custody and folks from Asheville to Raleigh get involved. The trust's custodianship would likely go to someone appointed out of Raleigh. I need the case to stay local, in the district court."

Dewey finished his sandwich with one final bite and rose from the chair. "Whatever you say, Counselor. Whatever you say." He paused. "So, just stopped by to see if you had any work for us." Albritton shook his head. "Well, just let me know when you do."

Albritton watched the man leave the building and felt uncertain. The thug had a certain look whenever he came up with an idea, particularly ideas Albritton didn't want any part of. Hastings had that look now.

Dewey Hastings drove straight to the Cummings residence, where he found Amos working in his shed.

"Hey, just got word your neighbor up the hill was the one helped Alice escape."

The big man looked none too pleased at the message, but Dewey didn't fear his role as messenger. They were partners, of sorts.

"Figured that out myself. So?"

Dewey shrugged, to look nonchalant. "Just sayin'. Figured we could get some revenge."

"How's that?"

"Well, you know. I got a body in the reservoir. Kinda looked like Alice last time we saw her. I could arrange for the body to float ashore. You could, you know, testify that it's your girl's body. The DA's up for re-election and might like a big case to handle. Might be enough to put the man away … for a long time. Just sayin'."

Amos stopped working, looked at Dewey, grinned and nodded. "It just might at that."

Eleven

❧◆◆❧

The following morning, Betsy wandered down the main street, afraid to take any side roads until she had a better lay of the land. She took the opportunity to stop at two small motels, inquire about rooms, and confirmed Sally's statement that she'd find no cheaper room. At the second inn, she asked for and received directions to a hardware store and twenty minutes later, she placed a new padlock, a blank journal, and a map of the city onto the clerk's counter.

"Can I help you with anything else?" the clerk asked.

Betsy thought for a moment, and then unfolded the map. "Could you show me exactly where I am on this map?"

The middle-aged man quickly pointed to an intersection of two roads.

"Thanks. And if I wanted to get groceries, or get police help?"

He smiled. "New in town, I take it." He took his pen and made a few marks, "G" for grocery, "P" for a police substation, "H" for his store, and "C" for a small clothing store. "Anything else?"

"A library maybe."

He chuckled. "Didn't expect that one. It's not too close, though." He marked it with a small star. "Are we done now?"

She didn't want to ask him to mark the Rest Stop. She'd figure that one out on her own. She grabbed a new pen from a display at the counter and added it to her items. "Yes, Sir. I think. You don't know anyone with a job opening, do ya?"

He sized her up. "Think you can lift fifty, sixty pounds on a regular basis?"

She held out her arm and showed him the laceration. "I

probably can, but not for a couple of weeks. Gotta let this heal."

"Well, if you think you can do it, when you're ready, stop back. We need part-timers, but a good worker might get hired on full." He paused. "Mind if I ask? You here alone? If so, this ain't the best part a town and you might want a can of that mace o'er there ... for protection."

Betsy turned toward where he was pointing. The canister was too big for a pocket, but would fit into her purse. She thought about his comment and a knife display down the aisle drew her eye. By the time she left, the clerk had sold her on not only the mace but also a pocketknife that bordered on being too large for any typical woman's pocket. The four-inch spear blade had a spring to assist opening, so she could flip it open one-handed if necessary, and a latch lock to keep the blade open, so it wouldn't fold closed in a fight.

Betsy's gut grumbled as she examined the receipt. Her first shopping trip had made a larger dent in her funds than she liked, but she felt more secure and that peace of mind was worth the cost. She made straight toward the nearest grocery and, with one paper bag of food items in tow, she returned to the Rest Stop. A clock in a store window she passed told her it was after two in the afternoon already.

She noticed the wind-scattered debris across the front of the "motel" as she crossed its parking lot. She decided to park her belongings in her room and then make good on her bargain with Sally, a deal which amounted to yet another part-time job at fifteen dollars a week.

She set the grocery bag on the ground and retrieved her key. She unlocked the door, swung it open and gasped. The bed linens lay on the floor and the mattress sat askew on top of the box spring. The small dresser's drawers sat upended on the floor and her clothes lay scattered across the room. She quickly slid the paper bag inside the doorway, closed the door, and ran to the office.

"Mizz Sally! Mr. Jim!" No quick reply came forth. "Anybody here?" Did she dare to venture beyond the desk? She started toward the gap between the desk and wall when the proprietress appeared in the back door.

"Yes?"

"Please call the police. Someone ransacked my room."

At the mention of police, Sally moved quickly toward Betsy. "Whoa there, girl. Let's take a look-see first, okay. We don't 'xactly like the police nosin' around here."

Sally exited the office first and hustled toward Room 2, Betsy rushing to keep up. Sally inspected the door and jamb first, and then flung open the door. She put both hands and her hips and surveyed the room. Betsy joined her inside the room.

"I went out to get some things and came back to this. Why would —"

"Anything missing?"

Betsy paused and scanned the room, thankful she had everything of worth with her. "I, uh, don't know. I found it like this and came to you right away."

Sally moved past the table, up righting it first, and walked into the little bathroom. After a second, she turned back toward Betsy. "Here's your problem. You didn't have the security bar in the window. Someone jimmied it open and climbed in."

"I-I didn't know it had one of those things, too. Jennie showed me the one in the front window. I'm sorry."

"Doesn't look like the window's damaged so I won't have to charge you for repairs."

"What?" protested Betsy. "Charge *me* for repairs. I'm not the one who did this." Her second thoughts about staying there became third thoughts. As soon as the week was up …

"You didn't leave the room secured."

"I didn't know I had to do anything more than lock the door. You never mentioned any of this last night."

"Okay, okay. I'm mentioning it now … and soon as you clean this place up, get started on the parking lot and grounds. They're as much a mess as this room."

"Hey, wait a minute …" Betsy started to protest. She didn't like the woman's bossy attitude or tone of voice. Yet, Sally yielded nothing and walked out of the room.

No sooner was she gone then Jennie and an older blond appeared at the door. "Hey, Betsy, this is … wow, what happened here?"

Betsy sat down on the bed, her shoulders sagging. "This is how I found it."

The blond picked up a drawer and slid it into the dresser. "Hi, I'm Sue Ellen. Anything taken?"

Jennie helped Sue Ellen clean up the drawers and then straightened the mattress and piled the linens on top. Betsy stood up and began to pick up clothes. She refolded each piece and laid them on the table or top of the dresser. It took but a minute to see that everything was still there and no damage done. The would-be thief had spared her in that sense. Her clothes could have been ripped apart or stolen, not just thrown about.

"Looks like everything's still here. What little I have."

"More than I had when I got here," replied Sue Ellen. Jennie nodded in agreement. "'course, now I can afford 'bout anything I want in clothes. Just can't find anything stylish in Asheville."

Betsy stared at the woman whose attire matched anything she'd ever seen in a fashion magazine. She made Jennie look homespun and Betsy held Jennie high up on the style gauge. Betsy watched Sue Ellen for a moment and then glanced in the nearby wall mirror. Her reflection said "hick" and Betsy resolved right there that she'd work as hard as it took to move beyond the hills and backwaters of her youth with a sense of style ... short of selling her body, not that she looked down on the two woman in front of her for using that route.

As Betsy put away the last of her belongings, Jennie spoke up. "We stopped by to see if you wanted to join us. We got a color television and kind of a communal living area where we hang out together, when we want. It's behind the office. Kinda hidden, for our safety."

Betsy's stomach growled loud enough for the others to hear and she flushed red. The two women laughed.

Jennie added. "We have a kitchen and all that stuff in there as well. It's like our home."

"Thanks, but I have a few things to do first." Betsy didn't want to feel beholden to Sally or her "girls." She appreciated their friendliness, but something inside told her to be wary, that to get too comfortable might snare her into their lifestyle.

"Suit yourself, but we'll be there 'til after supper ... if you want to stop in. It's right through there, that gate in the fence." Jennie pointed to a gate in the tall wooden fence just outside Betsy's door, a fence that ran from the back corner of the office to the near corner of the long structure holding the rooms.

Betsy nodded and shrugged a bit. "Okay, maybe in a while. I'm also trying to figure out how to start lookin' for my boy."

Jennie gave Betsy a curious look and then the two women

left the room and Betsy closed the door. She walked into the bathroom and checked the window. *Curious*, she thought. The security bar in the window lay right where it should have been. She tested the window and could not open it. Had Sally closed the window and replaced the bar in the brief moment she stood in the bathroom? Betsy removed the bar, opened the window, closed it, and replaced the bar. Now she felt certain Sally could not have done that. The window made too much noise as it slid along its rusty track and Betsy would have heard her close the window if that had been the case.

She returned to the main room and began making the bed. How could she go about searching for Jimmy Bob? She had little money and no transportation. She had never traveled any further from home than she had the day before. More importantly, where would she start? The only thing she could be certain of was that wherever her pa had gone with the boy had to involve a short trip. He'd been at home sleeping when she discovered Jimmy's absence. However, her pa could have delivered the baby to someone from out-of-state just as easily as to someone local. He could have arranged a meeting spot in town. Heck, they could have come directly to the house and she wouldn't have known it. Her heart sank at the realization of how daunting the task ahead would be.

Betsy's gut complained again, so with her bed remade and her hands freshly washed, she emptied the grocery bag and stashed most of its contents on the shelf above the clothing rod outside the bathroom door. She took the loaf of white bread and small jar of peanut butter and laid them on the table. She retrieved her knife, but thought better of using it for peanut butter and slipped it into a pocket in her jeans. Without another suitable utensil, she used her finger to spread the oily paste onto a slice of bread and then sucked her finger clean.

She topped the sandwich with a second piece of bread. As she eagerly consumed it to satisfy her hunger, she wrote her first entry on the first page of the blank journal. She finished her sandwich long before completing her diary entry. She wished she had more to eat, but until she secured steady work, it would have to do. *Besides*, she thought as she scrutinized her reflection in the mirror one more time, *after seeing these gals, I'm gonna have to lose some weight if I want to become fashionable.*

Betsy inspected her room, looking for a suitable hiding place for her valuables. No good place jumped out at her, so she stuffed her purse into a bottom drawer of the dresser, where it wouldn't be easily seen, and with the windows secure, her knife in her pocket, and her key and the empty grocery bag in hand, she left the room and added her own padlock to the hasp on the door. She worked to memorize the combination but slid the tag holding those numbers into her other pocket.

She worked her way along the front of the rooms and back along the opposite side of the gravel drive, picking up paper, empty soda bottles, and more, and dumping them into the bag. She discovered a few nasty discards she preferred not to pick up by hand but managed to use a small stick to snag these and drop them in with the rest of the trash. She didn't take long to fill the grocery bag and found herself wondering where to put it. Back home folks threw all the trash into a pit where they burned it once a week. A few of her old friends' families made routine trips to the community dump.

She looked around outside the office and found a large metal can marked "trash" but it appeared near to overflowing. She realized Jennie would know, so she walked to the gate and hesitantly pushed it open. The other side of the fence held a courtyard unlike anything she'd ever seen. The building that held the office and what she assumed were Jim and Sally's living quarters extended back into an "L" that enclosed two sides of a large brick patio holding a black metal kettle-like thing marked "Weber" and numerous chairs and chaises. Large sliding glass doors opened into the back of the "L" and revealed the most beautiful furniture Betsy had ever seen, along with a console television in color. She stood mesmerized. Jennie stood up from a suede leather couch and noticed her, waving for her to join them. She walked to the sliding glass and opened it.

"C'mon in."

Betsy held up the paper bag. "Uh, where should I dump this?"

Jennie nodded and pointed toward the back of the building. "There's another gate back there. Go through it and hang a left. You'll see a green dumpster. C'mon back when you're done and I'll show you around."

Betsy had no idea what a "dumpster" was but figured she'd learn soon enough. Walking toward the back she again stopped in amazement. An extensive flower garden, showing its early spring growth, extended for at least half an acre. She wondered what it looked like in bloom. Jim and Sally were discussing something near the middle of the plot. Jim waved first, but Sally followed his gesture and saw Betsy. She said something to her husband and walked toward Betsy. Jim bent over, and with his rear facing them, began to dig, an ample slice of his crack displayed to the sky.

"This must be beautiful in bloom," Betsy stated.

"My little slice of heaven," replied Sally as she waved toward the garden. She noticed Jim and huffed. "For God's sake, man, pull up those pants!"

Jim stood erect, tugged on his trousers. Yes, honeybuns."
He waved at them before bending over again with the same display resulting.

"Goodness, I ask for hemerocallis and all I see is hemorrhoids." She turned away from him and continued, "But he does go out of his way to please me. Lord knows why." Sally pointed to the bag. "I see you're keeping up your end of the deal. Dumpster's through that gate and to the left."

"What's hemero ...?"

"Callis. The botanical name for daylilies."

Betsy wasn't sure what a daylily looked like, but figured it would be beautiful with a name like that.

"Honeybuns, where do you want this one?" Jim yelled as he held up another bare-root plant.

"To the left and behind the first one, like I told you." Sally shook her head. "Better get back over there or I'll go hoarse giving the ol' fart directions." She left Betsy and returned to the center of the garden.

Betsy walked through the gate and found a large, grass green metal bin with hinged lids. "So that's a dumpster," she thought. Empty-handed, she returned to the courtyard and tapped on the glass door. Jennie, holding a partially unwrapped chocolate bar, waved her inside.

Betsy stared at the candy in Jennie's hand, unfamiliar with the elegant wrapper.

Jennie followed her gaze. "It's Belgian chocolate ... from Belgium, in Europe. It's called Godiva. You can only get it from Wanamaker's Department Store in Philadelphia. Want some?"

Betsy nodded and took a small square from Jennie. She felt like she'd died and gone to heaven. Never had she tasted such exquisite chocolate.

Jennie laughed and said, "I know. Perfect, huh? I think I'm addicted to it." She paused to let a square begin to dissolve in her own mouth. "Here, let me show you around. This is where we live. Nice, huh?" Jennie showed her their kitchen, the main living area with the color television and two luxurious bathrooms. Adjacent to the baths she saw a room that looked like a small school gym.

"We use the weights and stuff to stay in shape. It's a whole lot easier to do it here than travel halfway 'cross town to a gym," explained Jennie.

Betsy noted hesitancy in Jennie's statement and wondered if that was the only reason.

"We're going to fix dinner soon. Then we got to get ready for our clients." She stressed the word "client." "Want to join us."

"Thanks, but not tonight. I, uh, want to rest a bit before going to clean Lester's bus. Plus, I gotta figure out how to get there."

Jennie's face contorted and she looked uncomfortable. "It's just a few blocks that way, but you sure you want to do that?"

This was Betsy's second warning about Lester.

"I need the money ... so until I find something else ..."

"He calls himself Sally's handyman when he comes around here, and he sure gets handy, if you catch my drift. We call him Lester the Letch." She paused. "You know, it's real nice here and the work, well, that has its risks but the money's good, really good, and your days are mostly yours to do what you want. In January, we can head south with Sally or stay here. Look, I know we just met, but I kinda like you. I'd like to see you stick around."

Betsy didn't know what to say. She had no desire to sell

her body, but she didn't want to insult Jennie. On first impressions, she liked the young woman, too, and realized she might be the only one she could call on for help.

"I like you, too, Jennie, but I don't know I'm cut out for this. It's, uh, well, I ..."

Jennie hung her head as she said, "I understand." Then she held her head high and continued, "You know, we're not bad people. The girls here, we all got into a bind, some were livin' on the street; none of us knew where our next meal might come from. We did what we had to, to survive ... and then Sally found us and here we are, maximizing our assets as she always tells us. There's lot of pimps who'll run you into the ground, who don't give a shit about you except you make them money. Others'll get you hooked on drugs and control the supply so you get trapped there."

"Sally watches over us. Makes sure we're healthy. Teaches us basic business practices and how to invest our money. She's got accounts for each of us with our money and we're free to leave whenever we want. No one forces us to do this. Like I said, soon as I graduate, I'm out of here." A tear fell from each eye. "So, don't judge us."

Betsy placed her hand on Jennie's shoulder. "I'm not judging anyone. This is all new to me, but I just don't believe I'm up to doing this. Only thing I know I'm good at is writin' short stories and drawin'."

"Can you make money doing that? You need money to survive, you know."

Betsy didn't know the answer to that question. She'd never tried to sell a story, but she knew that magazines had to get their articles from somewhere and surely they paid the authors something.

"What kind of writing can you start with that'll make

some money?"

Betsy still had no confirmed answer.

"You could do this while writing all day. Think about it. I really, really want you to stay."

With that, Jennie turned and marched off to the kitchen leaving Betsy alone in the main room. Jennie's tone, as well as her final statement caught Betsy as unusual. They'd just met. Why would she feel so strongly about Betsy staying on? Why was she pushing so hard? There had to be something else, some other reason.

Nevertheless, Betsy wouldn't be there long. She would find Jimmy quickly and they would move on. How could she tell her son that she supported herself as a hooker while searching for him? Her pa had already called her a slut for sleeping one time with a boy she had loved. She didn't want to earn the title legitimately. Not that her pa's opinion mattered to her. He was as good as dead to her, and she hoped he felt the same way about her because she didn't want to run into him ever again.

Still, this place sure looked nice. She gazed around the room and walked toward a wall of photos. Most showed Sally with a variety of young women over a number of years. Some showed Sally with prominent looking men in suits. Most curious were photos of what appeared to be a younger Jim, some dancing, some of him on stage, some of him in a variety of costumes. He had obviously been a performer of some type when younger.

Betsy retreated to her room, happy to see it undisturbed when she opened the door. She grabbed her map and the address of Lester's bus yard. As Jennie had stated, it was less than half a mile away. She opened a box of Ritz crackers and her peanut butter, and realizing she had again forgotten to get a knife she could use to spread the PB, dipped each cracker into the jar. Her hunger abated with less than a dozen pieces and she stopped, dreaming of another piece of that chocolate. Maybe Jennie would sell her a couple of bars.

She wrote in her diary and had time for a brief nap before setting off for her first day at work, so she lay down on the bed and thought about the day. What a curious cast of characters she had met. There had to be some short stories she could write mixed in there somewhere.

She also thought about Jennie's comment about earning money with her writing. Magazine articles were a possibility, as were newspaper articles. Maybe she could write for the newspaper as she had mentioned to Lester on the ride to town. If she liked it and wanted to move up, maybe college wasn't so far a reach as she once thought. That thought birthed a new realization: she would have to provide high school grades and a diploma. That meant going back to Frampton Corner. She would have to come up with some other means.

She thought about other types of writing. Businesses had to have someone write their brochures and flyers, didn't they? Maybe there was an opportunity there. A scene from the grocery store flashed through her mind. A rotating rack of greeting cards. Yes, that was something she could definitely do. She could write that kind of stuff for hours on end, and draw the art, too.

Betsy woke up to discover she had slept longer than planned. Lester had told her to be at the yard no later than ten fifteen that night so she'd be ready to work when he pulled into the yard. Her watch told her she had but ten minutes to get there on time.

She jumped up from bed and rushed to the bathroom. On her way back out, she grabbed an apple from the bag on the shelf. Her biggest dilemma was what to do with her valuables. She didn't want to leave them behind while she was off the property, yet she didn't want to become a target for some robber in this "not so good" neighborhood, as the guy at the hardware store called it. She decided to trust in her new lock and hid her papers and most of her money between the pad and mattress. Someone would have to tear apart the bed to find her cache, not just lift up the mattress. She confirmed that the mace sat in a convenient location in her purse and placed the knife into the right pocket of her bell-bottoms.

She did a quick recheck of the map and picked up her purse. As was to become her ritual, she rechecked the windows, closed the door tight, locked it, and added the padlock to the hasp. She rushed along the strange streets keeping her eyes open and mind alert to her surroundings, much of it hidden in deep darkness now. Two left turns, four barking dogs, and ten minutes later, she approached a tall, chain-link fenced yard surrounding a taller barn-like building in the middle and a modest home to one side. A weathered sign of red block letters on a dirty white background announced, "West Mountain Motor Coach Co."

Betsy walked through the open gate and approached the barn but made it no closer than thirty feet from the building when a large German shepherd confronted her, snarling with teeth bared and ears alert.

She knew to stop and make no provoking moves. "Nice dog. It's okay. I'm supposed to be here. Nice dog." She moved her hand slowly into her purse and wrapped her fingers around the can of mace. The guard dog eased toward her, sniffing the air. Betsy's grip tightened around the can and she eased her hand to the opening of the purse. "Good dog." She lowered her other hand, displaying the back of it toward the dog in a non-threatening manner at a level where the animal could choose to sniff it. She noticed its ears relaxing a bit. "I'm not here to hurt you. Good dog," she said softly.

The shepherd came closer and smelled her hand. Betsy didn't want to make any sudden move but the dog's nose tickled and her hand jerked subtly. The dog jumped back and growled. "I won't hurt you. Nice dog," she repeated. *How long will this standoff last?* she wondered. She took a small step backward, but the dog responded by crouching in preparation to jump.

"Roscoe!" The shrill voice came from Betsy's rear right, near the house. The dog immediately sat, alert to movement behind Betsy. She turned slowly and saw a giant of a woman bearing down on them. The grey-haired woman with strong Germanic features appeared over six-foot tall and heavyset even for her large frame. The image of a Wagnerian opera entered her mind. Had the woman been wearing a helmet with upswept horns and a dark velvet cape, and started to sing, Betsy knew it would be all over for her.

The woman pointed to the dog and waved it back into the barn. "Inside, Roscoe!" The dog obeyed in an instant. By then the woman was next to Betsy. "Who are you and what do you want?"

Betsy felt a nervous tingle quiver through her body. "I-I'm Betsy, Betsy Weston. Are you Hilda? Your husband offered m-me a temporary job cleaning the bus. I came into town on it last night. I-I'm supposed to meet him here as the bus returns tonight."

The woman scrutinized Betsy from head to toe. "He take you to that whorehouse he think I know nothing about? You one o' them?"

"Um, yes, ma'am, he took me to the Rest Stop but I just thought it was another motel, until … Oh! Oh, no, I'm no working girl. I-I paid rent on a room for one week, 'til I can find something else."

"Well, he not here yet. He not mention to me about hiring anyone. He can clean that bus all by himself."

"I'm sorry. I'm just doin' as he asked. My family's gone and I'm on my own. I think he felt sorry for me. I'll leave if you want." Betsy didn't want to make trouble. That seemed to be finding her well enough without encouraging such fate.

The woman's countenance softened and her shoulders relaxed as she eyed Betsy from head to toe again. "He be here soon enough. Then we discuss it. Might be okay to agree, long as you not one of them trollops he visit." The woman turned back toward the house.

"Thank you, Ma'am. Mind if I wait inside?"

The woman spoke over her shoulder without turning back. "Long as you don't mind Roscoe. Go ahead."

Betsy eased open the smaller man door and peeked inside the barn. The dog lay on a large dirty cushion off to one side of a half-windowed door that appeared to lead to a small separate office. It stood and faced her as she slipped quietly through the exterior doorway, but after a moment, he resumed his place. *Must think I'm okay if I made it this far past Hilda,* she thought.

She looked about and saw all kinds of mechanic's tools sitting organized along one wall, while spare tires and parts sat on shelves adjacent to the small office. The central area remained clear with large double doors on both ends that allowed the vehicle easy ingress and egress from the building. Betsy saw a couple of battered metal folding chairs next to the far set of doors, and slowly walked toward them, leery and watchful of the dog … which seemed equally distrustful of her.

She made it to the chairs without incident and sat down, placing her purse on her lap with one hand on the mace can just inside its leather throat. She scanned the building a few times and softly whistled to bide her time. She noticed the dog's ears perk up and watched it cock its head back and forth, as she unthinkingly whistled "You Ain't Nothin' but a Hound Dog." When she realized what the song was, she added a bit more vigor. The dog inched forward, off the cushion and onto the dirt floor, it forelegs extended forward while its hind legs remained cocked and poised to spring forward in a split second. Its tail started to wag slowly, almost in beat with her tune.

When she concluded the song, she launched into another Elvis Presley melody, "Heartbreak Hotel." The dog's wag became so energized, its rear end joined in and Betsy started to laugh.

"So, you're an Elvis fan, too, huh?"

She switched from whistling to humming and the dog stood up, seeming ready to dance. She stood up and began an emotional, and awful, Elvis impersonation of "All Shook Up" and dog began to jump and dance around her. As she finished, she sat down laughing and Roscoe's head was in her lap, licking her hands.

"Good thing you're not a critic. That was terrible." She fondled Roscoe's head and rubbed his ears. A moment later, those ears peaked and he let loose a "woof." Betsy heard the engine gear down a moment later. Roscoe ran to the opposite doors and danced as they opened. Betsy watched as Roscoe ran to his master and Lester bent over and gave the dog a welcoming rubdown and ear scratch. The man looked up, caught sight of Betsy, and looked surprised.

"Well now, wasn't sure I'd actually see you here tonight." He looked down at Roscoe and waved his finger at the dog. "Some guard dog you are." The dog ran to the door of the bus and wiggled in glee until Lester said, "Okay." Roscoe bound up the steps and sat down in the aisle right next to the driver's seat. Lester shook his head, climbed aboard, and pulled the bus into the barn. As he turned off the engine, Roscoe jumped from the top step to the dirt and ran to Betsy, pulling up and sitting next to her.

Lester chuckled as he dismounted his stead. "I see you've met my ferocious watchdog."

"Um, yes, Sir. He, uh … Actually, he did his job real well. Your wife came to my rescue and …"

"Uh-oh. Forgot to mention you to her."

"Um, yes, Sir. Once she let me by, I guess Roscoe figured I was allowed to be here. Then I discovered we're both Elvis fans and we've been friends since."

Lester's hearty laugh echoed off the walls. "I'll be. 'All Shook Up' is his favorite."

"So I learned," replied Betsy and Lester hooted and slapped his thigh.

"All my fault. Shoulda trained him better."

"Lester!" Hilda's yell pierced the barn walls and ricocheted through the rafters.

"Better go clear this up. There's a broom o'er there and that short metal bin. If'n you put it right under the bottom step, you can sweep the trash right into it. We need to sweep it out first, then clean windows and seats, and finally mop the floor. I wash the outside, luggage compartment, and wheels, too, if they need it. We can probably pass on that tonight."

"Lester!"

"Be right back."

Betsy retrieved a straw broom that had seen better days and the stout rectangular metal tub. She slid the tub in place and found she couldn't climb past it to enter the bus. So she slid one end askew, hopped aboard the first step, and used the broom handle to pull the tub back in place. Within minutes, she had the floor swept and the tub half-full of candy wrappers, napkins, empty potato chip bags, and the like. This trash was a whole lot easier to deal with than some of the things she found outside the rooms at the Rest Stop.

Lester returned and glanced into the bin. "Pretty typical. You can empty it into the dumpster just outside those doors there." He pointed to the exit doors. "If it's too heavy for ya, there's a dolly over there you can use to move it."

"It won't be. I can lift that."

Lester nodded. "Look, the old lady's not too happy 'bout my offerin' you this work, but I talked her into one week. If she sees a benefit, then we might be able to extend it. 'Course, I'm the one usually doin' all the work, so I'm not sure what she's gonna count as a benefit. Just so you know."

Betsy wasn't sure what to think. Despite the warnings, the man had been straightforward and pleasant, and the work didn't appear daunting. She'd done harder chores at home, things her pa should have done but never did. If the man remained businesslike, she hoped the work would continue. Of course, if he became the "handy" man of earlier warnings, her outlook would change.

Over the course of the next two hours, Lester showed her how he liked things done and when she finished, he gave her his nod of approval … and her ten dollars. So far, this job lived up to her expectations.

Betsy hurried back to the Rest Stop. She noticed cars

parked in only half the slots as she tried to slip past unseen. Already beer bottles and more littered the gravel drive. She arrived at her door to find a note from the front office taped to the outside. She grabbed it and rushed to unlock the padlock and door. Inside, the room appeared as she left it. She checked on her valuables and found them as she had left them. She sat on the bed and unfolded the note.

"Mr. Mathews will see you at ten o'clock sharp. Don't be late."

Twelve

❧✦✦✦☙

The morning presented Betsy with a dilemma. A front had moved into the area overnight and scattered showers fell across Asheville. Currently the sky was dry, but should she risk a sudden soaking in the rain or should she arrange for other transportation? She had no umbrella. To buy one would add yet one more modest expense to her growing chain of minor purchases. These everyday expenditures were adding up too fast, and the item would be something else she would have to carry when she moved on. Did Asheville have taxicabs? She wondered what that would cost.

At nine-twenty Betsy opened her door and scanned the sky. She decided to take a chance on the weather. Dressed in a straight skirt and blouse given to her by Mary, along with her only pair of nice shoes, she placed her important papers in her purse but left most of her cash in its hiding spot in the room. She performed her ritual of securing the room and scurried out to the street. A block down the road she picked up a newspaper left behind on a bench and figured it would provide some protection from the rain, if needed.

Fifteen minutes later, she started looking for the road where she'd have to turn right, but after two, three, four blocks down the road, she had not seen the street she needed. She stopped and retrieved her map. In her hurry, she had missed the turn and now backtracked six blocks. When she came to the right intersection, the name on the street did not correspond to the map. She stepped into a nearby dry cleaner's shop and stepped up to the counter.

"Excuse me. I'm looking for Wright Street. I figure this should be it, but the street sign says Wesley Boulevard."

"You're okay. Street name got changed to honor some politician but the maps don't have the switch yet. To make matters worser, soon as you leave the city limits, the name changes back to Wright Street. Leave it to politicians to muck up the simplest things."

Betsy noticed the clock on the rear wall and realized she needed to hurry. "Thanks." She rushed from the building and raced toward the law office. Breathless, at nine fifty-eight she entered the front door and presented herself to the receptionist. She had made it on time and dry.

Promptly at ten, a prim lady in her mid-forties appeared from a hallway to Betsy's left and called her name. The woman ushered Betsy to an office at the end of the corridor and opened the door. Betsy entered the walnut paneled room with bookshelves lining a long wall and fancy fringed carpets on the floor. A tall striking man who appeared to be in his early forties rose from behind an old oak desk and adjusted the rimless spectacles on his nose. He towered above Betsy wearing a well-tailored gray serge suit, dark maroon bow tie, and expensive looking shoes. His full head of short-cropped brown hair added to his military bearing.

"Miss Weston. I'm Thomas Mathews. Please have a seat. May we get you something to drink? Coffee, perhaps, or a soda."

Betsy hadn't had the luxury of a soda pop in as many weeks as she could remember. Though she normally wouldn't indulge in such before lunch, the thought of the sweet drink enticed her gut to purr in approval. "A Coca-cola would be nice. How much is it?"

The lawyer chuckled. "It's on me. Again, please have a seat." He returned to his chair behind the desk and sat down. "I made time to see you because the story you told my receptionist deeply worried me. I took the opportunity to make a few phone calls. The Sheriff in Jackson County appears to be involved in some big case and hasn't returned my call, but I checked several area hospitals and no one reports a recent birth to a mother named Betsy Weston."

The prim lady returned with a bottle of Coca-cola and a glass of ice, and handed them to Betsy.

"Care to start over?"

Betsy gulped down her mouthful of sugary drink, feeling cornered. If Sheriff Connelly did call this man back, her pa would locate her within hours. But, what choice did she have?

"My real name's Alice Cummings ... and I had my baby in a private home. There was a midwife by name of Sue Ellen there. She said she filled out several copies of the birth certificate and told me they'd be filed with the county."

"I see. Problem is ... I checked the counties as well. Jackson County has no records of any live births within the last three weeks. Macon County has a report of one stillbirth, mother's name not listed, and Transylvania County has two births, twins, to a thirty-year-old mother by the name of Dickson. I checked. Do you have a copy of the birth certificate? Or the full name of the midwife?"

"No Sir, I was a bit pre-occupied at the time, but I sorta have a copy of the papers she gave me. I, uh, I just don't have it with me, and now I'm wondering if what she gave me is really a copy of a legal birth certificate. I'm thinking now my pa paid her off." Had her pa bribed the midwife? Sue Ellen seemed so compassionate and nice.

The attorney shook his head. "Before I take up valuable time, I need proof you even had a baby and aren't sending me on some snipe hunt."

Betsy thought for a moment. "I-I'm not sure where I had

the baby. All I know is she said she was my pa's cousin and she lived in the mountains. I, uh, fell asleep on the rides to and from the house. When I went to the sheriff's station, the Sheriff was there with Deputy Jake. They commented on my baby being stillborn and seeing the birth certificate that my pa showed 'em, but I tell you, he weren't stillborn. I brought him home. I nursed him. I'm still making milk. I can show your secretary that much." Betsy slipped her purse to the floor, prepared to bare her breasts if necessary.

The man scrutinized her and then pressed a button on his phone. A moment later the neat woman appeared.

"Mrs. Johnson, I'm going to turn around for a minute. Would you please confirm whether or not this young woman is lactating?"

The lawyer swiveled in his chair toward the large picture window behind him and peered out toward the mountains. Betsy opened her blouse, proved her claim, and redressed.

"Yes, Sir, she is, uh, full, um, lactating." The woman raised her eyebrows as her boss turned back toward them, his brow furrowed and his countenance contemplative.

"See? That don't just happen for the heck of it ... or for a stillborn, for that matter," Betsy stated. She had learned that from Mizz Sally.

The attorney drew his hand across his jaw, and said, "I'll contact the sheriff again, but if you don't even know where you were at the time, well, that makes this hard."

Betsy grew agitated. "Sir, please don't call Sheriff Connelly in Jackson County. He'll just notify my pa, and that mean ol' bast ... I mean to say, he'll come lookin' for me and I might as well be dead."

Betsy thought and thought ... where had she been? There had to be some clue that she just didn't remember. That had to be the starting point of her search. She saw that now.

The man sat back in his chair, his fingers steepled in front of him and stared at Betsy. After a couple of minutes of silence, he said, "I'm going to assume you're telling me the truth, but I'm going to need something in the way of proof and this may require payment above and beyond what Sally gets in return for her retainer. I might have to hire an investigator. Can you afford that?"

"Sir, I'll do almost anything to get my son back."

"Anything?" He raised his eyebrows.

"I said *almost* anything. I'm not a working girl and don't want to end up there. If you know of any jobs, I'm willing to take a look."

He again watched her intently. "Actually, I believe you. I'll see what I can do. The fact that you're a parent isn't enough to get the court to grant you emancipation. You'll need a source of income."

Betsy gave him a quizzical look, thinking "*Emancipation? I'm nobody's slave.*"

He must have seen the question in her mind. "Emancipation is a legal term. The age of majority in this state is twenty-one, which means you can't enter into contracts or do anything as an adult until you reach that age. However, the court can declare you an adult if you meet certain requirements. If you're declared an emancipated minor, then your father would face much more serious charges of kidnapping, maybe more, provided we can prove the case."

Betsy nodded in understanding. "If'n I have to go to court, can I change my name, too?"

"I don't see why not. Give me two days to look into this more. I'll let you know what I've discovered and what it might cost you."

Betsy finished her Coca-cola and arose, not wanting to take up more of the man's time. "Thank you, sir. I greatly appreciate your help, and that of Mizz Sally."

Mr. Mathews nodded. "About Sally ... don't get the impression we approve of what she does, but take heart you're in good hands. Most of the gals working for her, she rescued from some rather nasty pimps. She's worked with every girl she's taken in, educated them, and let them leave whenever they want. She'll never force you into the business."

Thirteen
(Present Day)
℘✦✦℘

Myra initially noticed pressure on her upper arm, like the first time husband number one grabbed her to throw her against a wall. He'd been all charm, until he took to drinking. Then he sobered up, realized he was impotent and infertile, and blamed it all on her. After her second beating, she recognized the disturbing pattern and beat a quick retreat to safety. After several trial reconciliations, the divorce proceedings took almost a year. Myra didn't want to open her eyes, fearful of finding him standing over her.

Her mouth reminded her of an ancient piece of papyrus she once had the privilege to handle and examine while researching an earlier book … as dry as the Egyptian sands surrounding the tomb that had held it for thousands of years. She remembered the empty wine bottle in her room and decided to call room service for another magnum … until she noticed the sounds around her. Blip! Blip! Blip! A soft whirring noise seemed poised just to the right of her head. A television softly violated the air with its talk show banter. The squeaky wheel of some kind of cart competed with the other clatter.

The smells were not those of her room at the Pink Palace either. She sensed no clue of her own perfume or the floral scent used by the hotel. Instead, there was … what? Disinfectants? The subtle hint of blood. Blood? She knew its distinctive aroma, but why was there blood in her room? And whose blood was it?

Myra prepared to open her eyes to slits, waiting for the light to assault her as it had that morning before her breakfast meeting with Samuel. Her meeting! She now recalled meeting Samuel, starting to eat, and feeling ill. What happened after that?

In a flash, all the sounds and smells coalesced in her mind to answer that question. She was in a hospital. Which one? UCLA Medical Center would have been the closest.

She opened her eyes and gazed past her feet to see a partial wall and a curtained, large glass window. A doorway with a double glass sliding door filled the center of the wall and she saw a busy, wood-trimmed nurses' station beyond it. She began to turn her head to the right and felt a wave of imbalance. She allowed the sensation to subside and continued until she could see the source of the noise near her, an intravenous pump holding a plastic line filled with blood. She looked up and then down, from the bag of blood down the ribbon of tubing to where the crimson fluid entered into her forearm.

"Good morning."

The soft alto voice startled Myra. *Morning?* she thought. *How long have I been here?*

"I'm Christina, your nurse today. How are you feeling? Can I get you anything?"

The young woman of Hispanic heritage had long black hair that glistened like oil, tied back into a long ponytail. Her neon scrubs had a whimsical Disney theme, yet they did little to brighten Myra's improving recollection of events and the growing depression that resulted from those memories.

Myra tried to talk but her arid tongue could do little but chafe her hard palate. She attempted to point to her mouth. Her arms failed her.

"I'll get you some ice chips." The nurse left and returned moments later with a Styrofoam cup of crushed ice and a plastic spoon. She held a spoon of ice to Myra's lips and Myra sucked up the chips faster than she could pour a glass of zinfandel.

"More please," whispered Myra.

A few minutes later, her grateful mouth became articulate. "Where am I?"

"This is the medical intensive care unit at Ronald Reagan Medical Center. UCLA. You came here from the O.R. early, early this morning. They almost lost you on the table."

"Lost me? So, who found me? I should thank him," she whispered and noted the blank look on the woman's face. "Please, I hate euphemisms … and lord knows I've used them all. You're saying I almost died in surgery, right?" The nurse nodded. "Care to offer any details?" Her voice gave signs of strengthening.

"I can't, but I'll let your doctor know you're awake and he can fill in the details and answer your questions." She turned to leave the room and a young man, who looked little older than Richie Cunningham on "Happy Days," appeared in the doorway wearing institutional green scrubs under a knee-length white coat. "Oh, here he is now. This is Doctor Franklin." She nodded and smiled at the young doctor as she left the room.

"Good morning, Ms. Mitchell. I'm Michael Franklin, the critical care doctor today. I'm glad to see you awake. I'm a big fan of your books."

"Thank you," said Myra, her voice now evolved from faint rasp to croaky. "Christina tells me you're Doctor Answer Man. Would you kindly tell me what happened?"

The doctor kicked a wheeled stool in the direction of the bed and positioned it close to Myra's head before sitting down. Leaning toward her, he asked, "Can you tell me what you remember?"

Myra struggled to recall the chain of events. "I was having brunch with my agent and became ill."

He smiled. "Good, good. Do you know what day it is?"

Myra already tired of the drill. Her mind was sound. "Since I don't know how long I was unconscious, I can't say for sure, but my meeting was Saturday morning, after the premiere of 'Sisterhood of Terror.'"

"Excellent. Excellent."

"Doctor, my mind is fine, but you might want to see someone about your echolalia."

He laughed. "I might, I might." He gave her a grin. "Okay, you want answers. Here's the synopsis. EMS transported you to the Emergency Department yesterday, late morning. Your blood pressure was very low, so the paramedics gave you a liter of fluids in route, and by the time you arrived here, your pressure had improved but you still hadn't woken up. While the ED staff evaluated you, your pressure dropped again, and they pushed a second liter of fluids and added a medicine called dopamine to restore it. They told me you were in and out of consciousness at that point, so I'm not surprised you don't remember any of it. I don't suppose you've noticed the change in your skin color."

Myra shrank into the mattress. She had noticed … and denied it. Clearly, jaundice had infused its pumpkin color into her skin. She nodded meekly.

"You've got serious liver disease. Determining exactly what kind will require more tests. Anyway, the ED assessment suggested an upper gastrointestinal bleed and your blood count was critically low. You know what hemoglobin is, right? And how we use the value clinically?"

Myra nodded.

"Figured you did, 'cause your books have gotten it right.

Well, normal is roughly twelve to sixteen. We give people blood when it drops below eight. Your level was under five. I'm surprised you could function at all, but the fact that you could function, suggests your anemia came about through a very gradual change that allowed your body time to adjust. You passed out at the hotel because of the drop in your blood pressure and you might have had an episode of bleeding right before. They put a tube into your stomach in the ED and there was evidence of old blood, but no active bleeding. You were on your way here to the ICU last night when you started to bleed actively and they had to rush you to the OR. You have bad esophageal varices. That's like varicose veins in the lower esophagus. One or more of those veins broke open and with your low count to start with, you almost died. The surgeon succeeded in banding, or clamping, the veins and you've been receiving blood all night. That bag there …" He pointed to the unit of red blood cells hanging next to her. "… is your seventh unit. You'll get at least one more and if you remain stable, we'll move you to a regular bed later today."

Myra had no snappy comeback, nor an astute apothegm. This time she knew enough to remain serious and soak in all that he told her. She knew a little about liver disease and varices. She would have bled to death had she been alone at home. She sighed inwardly. She preferred seeing daisies from above, but the alternative would solve the dilemma of her next book and her potential breach of contract. The thought of continuing life sober distressed her. Too many skeletons in need of washing away. She wanted a drink *now*. Desperately.

"Your agent, Samuel, told me you're a heavy drinker. That makes cirrhosis the most likely candidate for your troubles. That also means you need to stop drinking. Totally. No excuses."

Samuel, Myra thought. The things she put him through over the years. Now this.

"Is Samuel still here? He had a flight back to New York yesterday."

"I believe so. I have a number and a request to call him when you woke up. Any family we need to contact? He didn't mention anyone."

Myra shook her head. Those people, family -- if you could call them that -- comprised a majority of the memories she had delegated to the dregs of the wine cask.

The doctor stood and faced Myra. "Well, I'll go give Samuel a call. I'll be in the unit for awhile ... so, if you have any questions, your nurse can get me."

"I have a question now."

The doctor stood silently, waiting.

"What's next? I mean, you said I'd go to a regular bed if I'm stable, but what's after that?"

The doctor nodded. 'I've consulted a hepatologist, a liver specialist, Doctor Wade Kennison. He'll be by to see you later today and will outline what needs to be done next. In a nutshell, a liver biopsy will be done to determine the type of liver disease, some other tests perhaps, and then he'll discuss your options." He paused. "Anything else?" At Myra's silence, he said, "Okay then," and turned to leave. At the door, he turned back.

"Oh, one more thing. You'll probably start having withdrawal symptoms, if you aren't noticing them already. The detox process isn't pleasant, but I have medications ordered to help. Just ask your nurse."

He left the room and Myra wondered if his mere mention of detox triggered her skin starting to crawl. For the first time, she noticed a drenching sweat of such magnitude as to produce

Flash Flood alerts from the U.S. Weather Service. Nausea escorted the jitters. Anxiety raced headache to the top of her symptom list. When she managed to raise her hand, the tremor threatened to destabilize the San Andreas Fault line. She needed that drink. She examined the IV line, wondering how to remove it so she could escape to her suite at the Beverly Hills Hotel and to the convenience of room service. Or better yet, how to get the alcohol directly into that bag of blood cells.

Myra recalled pushing one of her third book's characters into delirium tremens, that life-threatening extreme of alcohol withdrawal. The DTs. Illusory pink elephants dancing up the walls and along the ceiling. His had followed a week of binge drinking. Her imbibing outdid his on a logarithmic scale. What was she in store for? Striped and polka-dotted elephants?

She opened her eyes to find Samuel sitting in a chair next to her bed. No, there were two Samuels and one was green. She shook her head and closed her eyes, willing the green agent to disappear at the mental count of three.

"Well, well, well ... back to the land of the living, I see."

"Wh-where'd you come from?"

"Hey! I've been here for an hour while you keep drifting in and out. So, you gonna stay with me and be sociable for awhile? Or, maybe I should go home ...set up a conference call when you're ready."

Myra blinked several times to make sure Samuel's Martian twin had gone home. "Conference call?"

"Yeah. You, me, and the Betty Ford Clinic."

Myra shook her head, but stopped because she actually heard it rattling. "No way. Me and Betty, um, Betty *and I* didn't get along so well last time. Remember?"

"Like I could forget ... and I'd really *like* to forget that incident. Okay, look, here's the deal. You gotta stop the booze.

116

If the words alcohol or ethanol show up anywhere on the label, you avoid it … like you're avoiding writing this next book. Capiche?"

Myra said nothing.

"I mean it, Myra. You fall off the wagon and I'm history. You can find a new agent and pull his chains."

Myra stared at Samuel. He'd never threatened to leave before, no matter how bad she'd been. "Samuel, you really do care," she replied.

He leaned forward and took her hand in his. "Myra, don't ask me why, but I do. As foolish as it might be … and as painful as it has been at times, I care about you and hate to see you working so hard to fulfill some death wish. I don't know what haunts you 'cause you've told me squat about life before 'Rebecca's Bargain.' Hell, I don't even know where you were born, where you grew up, or where you went to school. Have you ever been married? Do you even like boys? Maybe you play for the other team. With that book, you suddenly materialized on planet Earth and still, fifteen years later, you've never shared anything private with me." He squeezed her hand. "Yet I still care. Enough that I don't want to be the first one called when someone discovers your lifeless body surrounded by a dozen empty wine bottles."

A tear formed in Myra's eye. A tear. She thought she'd been drained of those nearly a decade earlier when she discovered husband number two in bed with someone else … the delivery guy. Until then, the UPS slogan, "What can Brown do for you?" had carried a completely different meaning.

Two days later, Myra sat in a chair looking out her hospital room window toward the UCLA campus and the

Santa Monica Mountains beyond. She'd required assistance getting there, but for the first time since her arrival, she could sit up and the Richter scale shakes no longer threatened to propel the chair around the room like a child's wind-up toy. Even her skin color had improved, to something akin to a pastel ocher.

She turned at a knock at her door. "Good morning, Doctor Kennison. At least, I'm hoping for the good part."

He didn't smile. "Good to see you up in the chair. We'll try a little assisted walking later today. Eating okay? The green Jell-O is a favorite."

Myra's mood fell at his less-than-encouraging greeting. She pointed to an adjacent chair. "Please. Have a seat and give me the bad news."

He looked at her with a subtle tilt of his head and raised brow, as if saying "Bad news? Who said I have bad news?"

"You look like you downed a pint of sour milk," she continued. "So I assume …"

The doctor sat down next to her, knees together, holding her medical record in his lap. "Sorry I'm so obvious. Guile was not part of my medical training."

Myra watched his body language as confirmation of that statement. She'd spent several hours with this man over the previous 48 hours and liked him, despite his being frumpy, fidgety, and familiar to the point of being boring. What she liked in him was his compassion and integrity, and she discovered that she trusted his medical judgment.

"Okay then," he sighed. "The fair news is that some of your tests have improved with hydration and medication, as you've no doubt noticed by your skin color. However, any alcohol at all, or even some meds like acetaminophen will tilt things back the wrong way." He paused and watched her reaction, so she made a point of remaining as flat as possible. "Have you ever come across the MELD Score in researching a book?"

Myra shook her head.

"The acronym stands for Model for End-stage Liver Disease. The score ranks people for liver transplant. The score ranges from six to 40, and anyone having a score of 25 or higher gets ranked a level one priority for transplant."

Transplant? Myra wondered. *Did I hear him right?* The look on her face must have given her thoughts away.

"Yes, I said transplant. The bad news is … you have a score of 30. Your cirrhosis is so severe that statistics only give you a 20 percent chance of life three months from now without a transplant. However, the alcohol really worsens the problem. The worse news is that because this is alcoholic cirrhosis, and although you have no other medical problems, even with surgery, you have only a 50-50 chance of living one more year, and that year isn't likely to be pleasant. The worst news, however, is the catch-22. Many transplant centers won't consider you a candidate until you've been off alcohol at least six months."

Myra zoned out as the hepatologist droned on, hearing only smidgens and smatters. Weekly tests. Miss a test and your score drops. Living donors versus deceased donors. Then more about the transplant process itself. Her thoughts roiled along with her emotions. He said six months. That couldn't be right. She had too much to do. Her heart refused to accept his words, but her mind knew better. Six months was an educated guess. She could die any day, or live for years. She wasn't ready for the former.

When she came around and realized he was finished and sitting there staring at her, she responded, "Thanks for sugarcoating that news."

"I'll ask again, any questions?"

She hadn't heard him the first time. Questions. Surely she had some, but none teetered on the tip of her tongue at the moment. One thing rolled around in her head – Samuel's last request for her to write one more book, one for posterity. One to take its place among American classics. One that college students a century from now would find on their required reading list. He knew she had it in her.

She needed a life preserver to cling to, to avoid slipping beneath the chilly waters of Dr. Kennison's news. One more book. A book to occupy her mind, to take her focus away from the questions of eternal destiny. Yes, if she could focus on writing that book for Sam, she would prevail.

Her problem? That book might be in her, but she hadn't the foggiest idea where to look for it. Was it filed between broken, battered women and cheating husbands? Maybe it hid between psychopaths and serial killers. She was a genre writer – popular fiction, mysteries and thrillers, the books folks read on vacation or in front of a fire on a snowy evening – not a literary great. Such a story was as lost as she felt at this turn in her life. And the time frame for this beast? Three months at the worst, a year at best. Even if she found the hidden story, could she flesh it out in such a short time?

Probably not, but she had put dear Samuel through so much over her career she knew she owed him at least the effort of trying. The result might not pass his litmus test, but he'd have one more book of hers to sell. Maybe.

In her head, though, a still, small voice kept repeating that only one story might just be that book. It had the right elements – a cross-country epic of rags to riches, love abandoned, and more. The happy ending? That remained to be seen. She realized that until this story was told, she might find no other in the creative well of her mind.

"Can I travel? I mean, are there any limitations besides the alcohol? These tests, can they be done wherever I am at the time, or am I tethered to the medical center here?"

Questions poured forth until the doctor had to raise his hands to stop her.

"Whoa. How about one at a time."

Myra pieced together the idea forming in her mind and outlined her needs to the doctor.

"Look, Dr. Kennison, if I sit here, or at my home, with nothing to do but wait and wonder if I'll ever get a donor, I'll go crazy. I have to stay busy to keep my mind from dwelling on all of this, to keep my sanity. I have to start a new project and to do that I need to travel for research. Nothing major or out of the country, but it would take me to New Mexico and points east. Can I do that?"

The doctor appeared reflective. "I don't see why not, if you're up to it. You're not tied to the medical center here, but I hope we can continue to provide your care. I can set up testing just about anywhere in the country, I guess. Can't say as we've ever tried that before, but I can't see any reason we couldn't coordinate such a thing."

Myra smiled, for the first time in days. In her innermost being, she was a writer. Despite the potential death sentence she'd just been given, she was determined to keep writing, perhaps even literally to die writing.

"We would want you to keep a beeper or cell phone at all times because we could get a call about a donor at any time and have to be able to reach you 24/7. There's also the factor of transportation. You would have to be able to get back here within hours."

121

"I can do that. I could arrange a private jet at a moment's notice if I have to."

The doctor nodded. "You are fortunate that way. Most of our patients would never have that luxury."

"One last question. You mentioned living donors. I have no immediate family, so can a friend be a donor."

"Sure, if they pass the necessary tests for compatibility." He went on to give a brief summary of what that meant, and of the tests that friend would have to undergo.

Myra felt a surge of energy. Maybe her muse had returned. Ideas and memories galloped through her mind waiting only to be lassoed and corralled. For years, she had speculated on what should be her last story. She had approached each novel she wrote as if it was the second-to-last because one idea led the herd to claim the role of "alpha story." She had resisted previous urges to write it for a plethora of reasons, but largely the time wasn't right and its ending was so uncertain. No longer did that uncertainty surround her. "The Death of a Diva" would be her final book, classic-to-be or not. Whatever the case, she had only months to finish it.

Fourteen
(Spring – 1969)
❧✦◆✦❧

Betsy took heart from her meeting with Mr. Mathews, but the two days were up and she still hadn't heard from him. She had bought a local newspaper and scoured the want ads, circling potential jobs. She had taken on the chore of calling each employer starting first thing that previous morning, after securing a roll of quarters from the bank and staking her claim on the phone booth. She wondered when she might get a call from the lawyer's office and debated about calling him before the end of the day if not sooner.

While out, she'd also visited every store she came across that sold greeting cards. She scanned the displays and scrutinized dozens of cards from half a dozen companies. With the help of her map, she found the nearest library, where she investigated each company, its size, location, and annual sales. She bought a pad of drawing paper and some sketching pencils and made her first attempt to draw and write a card. By that morning she had three "cards" she thought were okay.

At noon, Jennie and Billie knocked on the door, encouraged her to join them for lunch again, and sealed the invitation with the enticement of Godiva chocolate. After Mr. Mathews' comments, she'd been more comfortable in accepting their invitations.

"What's that?" Billie asked, pointing to the papers on the small table.

"Somethin' I'm trying to learn. Mebbe a way of earnin' some money."

Billie picked up the "cards" and as she scanned each one,

a smile stretched across her face. "You're a fast learner. These are good." She showed them to Jennie, who quickly agreed.

"Hey, could you draw us? Make us into a card?" asked Jennie.

Betsy thought about that for a moment. She'd drawn a few cartoons in school and had made some money at the school fall fair doing character sketches. "Sure."

The two girls took up a funny pose, but Betsy frowned. "Not that. Here, try this." She posed the pair as two spies, back to back, pointing their fingers like guns as in one of those "James Bond 007" movies. She'd only seen "Thunderball" but had heard a new one was at the movie theaters. Fifteen minutes later, her sketch, complete with caption, was done. She showed the girls, who giggled with glee.

"Do another. So we both have one," said Jennie.

During lunch, she learned more about each one's backgrounds, as well as those of several of the other ladies. After lunch, she "entertained" the women by doing sketches of them and began to feel confident in her ability. Maybe the greeting card industry was her calling.

Later in the afternoon, the girls began to prepare for the evening. Jennie opened a small package that came in that day's mail and pulled out several small bottles.

"What's that?" asked Betsy.

"Some cosmetics from Elizabeth Arden. Can't get it locally."

"What's it for?"

"What's it for?" mimicked Billie. "Girl, don't you know anything about makeup?"

Betsy responded with a blank stare. "Had a couple of friends who used lipstick but we didn't need much else at home."

The other two looked at each other wide-eyed and grinned. Jennie grabbed Betsy by the elbow and led her to a room just off the living room opposite the kitchen. Together, Jennie and Billie pushed Betsy into a styling chair and started jabbering so that Betsy had difficulty following either one alone. Jennie started doing something to her face, while Billie began to attack her hair. Within thirty minutes, they announced their task complete.

"Ready?" asked Billie.

Betsy's heart raced in anticipation. The whole thing seemed to her like a fantasy. They spun the chair around so that Betsy could see her image in the large plate mirror.

"Omigod," she replied as she saw herself. "Th-that's really me?" The image in the mirror mouthed the words as she spoke. That had to be her, but it didn't look like her.

"Wow, you clean up nice," said a voice behind them. Sally walked into the room. "But I wouldn't walk out of here like that or some of my clients might get the wrong impression." She paused. "And I sure wouldn't walk to Lester's like that. If you survived the neighborhood bad boys, you probably wouldn't survive Hilda."

"I believe that," answered Betsy. "'Course, if'n I started singin' 'All Shook Up,' Roscoe might come to my aid."

Sally laughed. "You got that dog all figured out already, do you? Good for you." She looked at the other two. "You better get ready. Busy night scheduled, and don't forget, doctor's appointments tomorrow."

"Yes'm," replied the two girls.

Betsy examined herself in the mirror, not wanting to wash away the image she saw. "Can you show me how to do this myself?"

"Sure" said Jennie, as she worked on her own face. "Start

tomorrow if you got time in the afternoon."

Betsy sat in a nearby chair and watched the two primp and color. She realized in amazement that here she sat, in a brothel, watching two women prepare to sell their bodies, an action she'd always thought immoral, and yet she felt accepted and comfortable. In fact, she felt that these two young prostitutes had become, in a way, the best friends she'd ever had. Two days earlier, that thought would have been as foreign to her as thinking her dad would one day sober up and realize how wrong he had been.

Billie stood up first, walked up to Jennie and whispered something in the young woman's ear. Jennie nodded, and Billie approached Betsy.

"We weren't sure if we should do this, but now we are. We have a little secret we'd like to share with you."

Billie whispered into Betsy's ear and stepped away once done. Betsy's eyes widened and her heart felt the lightest it had felt since running from home. She was now not just a step closer, but a whole triple jump and pole vault closer to searching for her son.

"Really? You'd do that for me?"

"Yep, and Sally's cleared it for us if we're late getting back."

Mondays were always slow nights for the ladies, so Sally had given Jennie and Billie the night off. First thing that morning, they pulled Betsy from her room, literally.

"C'mon, we got a lot to do," said Jennie.

"I-I don't know if I can do this," replied Betsy. She felt sure the fear showed in her eyes. She hadn't realized that when the women had told her they were going to spend the day helping her look for her son, that they meant going back to Frampton Corner as the first step.

"Don't you worry. We got your back," answered Billie. "First things first. In here."

"What? Why in here?" Betsy was bewildered when they dragged her into the salon area.

"Girl, you can't go back there looking like you. When we're done, no one will ever suspect you're, well, you." Jennie giggled.

An hour later, Betsy's hair was cut, colored and styled. She loved the rich, new, deep auburn color they had chosen. The change from her dirty blond locks was amazing. Thirty minutes later, her make-up completed, they handed her new clothes as well.

"Here, go change into this outfit and meet us back here. We'll be ready in fifteen minutes."

Ten minutes later, Betsy stood in front of the large mirror in the salon and stared at the woman looking back at her. Had the image not followed her every move, she wouldn't have believed that was really her. Tears welled up in her eyes.

"Careful. You'll mess up your make-up," said Jennie as the two friends entered the room. "Ready?"

Betsy nodded hesitantly. Was she ready? Really? Her head ached at the thought of possibly running into her pa, or worse, Dewey Hastings. If that man saw her looking like this, and recognized her, she'd be in major trouble. Yet, her heart raced in giddy anticipation of reclaiming her inheritance and proof. On Monday, her pa spent most of the day away from home preparing his hooch for the upcoming weekend demand. With the three of them, they actually stood a chance of finally having something to show the authorities to verify her claim.

Of course, she hadn't yet told the women what she

needed to retrieve nor of the potential dangers. It was best they didn't know, in case she was recognized and they were stopped.

"Let's go," called out Billie.

Outside, they approached the driveway where the dumpster sat and Betsy stopped in her tracks. A bright yellow 1965 Mustang convertible sat outside the garage doors. The day was warm and the sun bright, so the top was down. Billie hopped into the back seat and motioned for Betsy to be navigator. Jennie always drove, or so Billie complained as Betsy took to the passenger seat.

Betsy directed Jennie along the route taken by the bus through Brevard, past Lake Toxaway, to Cashiers and then north to Frampton Corner. Over the course of the 90-minute drive, the girls got to know each other, superficially at first and more intimately as they neared their destination.

Finally, they entered the outskirts of the town and Betsy's anxiety ratcheted up ten levels. She was crazy to come back here, but at least there was some strength in numbers. The warm day had brought the townspeople outside and all of them watched the bright convertible with three stylish young women inside pass by. A few children waved, but Betsy's fears seemed to wane. She passed by school classmates and while they all watched the car go by, no one gave any sign of recognizing her. And, she realized, why should they? Her new look, new friends, and a classy car placed her so far out of the context in which they knew her that they could probably rent a room at the small no-tell motel and no one would ever suspect it was her.

She leaned toward Jennie and spoke so both could hear her. "Thanks for coming with me, for the moral support. I could never have done this by myself." Billie reached forward and rubbed her shoulder.

On the other side of town, Betsy directed Jennie to drive up High Mountain Road. Her bravado stayed at the bottom of the hill, and her heart rate rivaled the engine revolutions as they neared her old home.

"That it?" asked Jennie.

Betsy replied, "Yep," as she slunk low into the seat. She didn't want to be seen.

Billie, though, had other ideas and kept poking her in the back, saying, "Sit up. Sit up. You look suspicious that way. C'mon, sit up!"

Betsy complied, but not eagerly. "Drive past it slowly." She had been right that her father would be absent. His truck was nowhere to be seen, but as they passed the house, her hope deserted her. Adjacent to the shed sat a pile of rough-cut lumber, stick-stacked for air-drying. The edge of the stack appeared to be just far enough from the shed for a man to pass between them.

Tears welled up in her eyes and this time she didn't care about her makeup. She would not be able to retrieve her cache.

"Hey, what's wrong?" asked Billie. "No one's home. You're good to go."

Betsy shook her head. "Wh-what I need is buried under that lumber pile. We can't get to it."

Jennie pulled to the side of the road just out of sight of the house. "Hey, it's just our first attempt. We can do this again and again, if we have to. Cheer up. There's still hope. Maybe next week, that lumber will be gone. But for today, is there anything else we can do?"

Betsy sniffed and struggled to contain her emotions. "Y-yes, keep driving up to the next house. I need to see our neighbor there."

The Umfleet home was empty. In fact, it looked like no one had been there for days and there was nothing to indicate where they might be. Betsy speculated they had gone to stay with Mary's family for a spell, but that didn't dissuade disappointment from covering her like a shroud. The silent trip back to the Rest Stop was a stark contrast to the first leg of their journey.

Fifteen

Betsy's trial week at West Mountain Motor Coach had stretched into two and as week three began, Betsy seemed no closer to a full-time job and her funds diminished more quickly than she liked. Gasoline had become her major expense since she refused to let Jennie and Billie absorb that cost. They had been more than generous with the use of their car, going so far as to offer letting Betsy drive it on her own. That was too much stress, though. It had been one thing to drive her pa's battered pickup around Frampton Corner. Driving a classy Mustang, that wasn't hers, was quite another, especially without a legal driver's license. She'd never needed it for her pa's truck. Deputy Jake always looked the other way.

A second trip to Frampton Corner proved no more fruitful than the first. In fact, the lumber pile had been joined by debris from the moonshiners' broken stills. The Umfleet home looked even more abandoned.

Mr. Mathews had become an ally and made her case something of a personal cause célèbre. He had contacted every county records office in adjacent counties in three states and half a dozen hospitals within a day's drive of where Betsy thought she had delivered the baby. He looked for licensed and unlicensed midwives by the name of Sue Ellen. He checked for recent adoption records. As her pa had warned, no record existed anywhere that she could use to corroborate her claim.

A week earlier, at Sally's insistence, he also filed for her emancipation and a legal name change. Sally called a judge "friend" to expedite the requests, and lied about Betsy's income. Three days later, Betsy Weston was "official" and had a new driver's license to prove it.

The day following their recent trip to Frampton Corner, Mr. Mathews stopped by the Rest Stop to see her.

"Sally told me you drove back to Frampton Corner yesterday. Did you find anything?"

Betsy looked up at the man and saw compassion in his eyes. She had shared everything with this man, except the one thing she'd hoped to retrieve the day before, and the week before that. She hadn't entrusted Jennie and Billie with that information because of the danger. Could she trust him now? Did she have any other choice?

She quickly realized that with the law on his side, he was her one last hope. Hope that he could gain access to her pa's property, get the lumber pile moved, and regain what she had no chance of recovering on her own.

She sighed. "I went back to get the proof you need." She watched his face for a reaction and saw that she had his interest. In her heart, she knew she'd held his interest all along but that fear had held her back. "I haven't told you everything." She paused to gauge the look on his face.

"Go on."

"When my ma's dad passed on, he left me an inheritance of gold coins. My ma gave them to me before she died. Told me not to ever let my pa know about it, or that he'd drink it away. I'd lived with his drinking, so even as a ten-year-old I knew that was a secret I needed to keep. We got a strong metal chest, covered it in oilcloth, and buried it near the shed. It stayed there for ten years. After I came home with Jimmy, I dug it up and put the papers from the midwife in there."

"But you said those papers don't include a valid birth certificate."

"I know, but I'm not real sure."

"So, how is this proof?"

"There's something else in the chest." She filled him in on the additional item.

He took a deep breath and gently took her hand. "Why didn't you tell me this earlier? This would have spared me, us, a lot of time and grief."

"I-I'm sorry. I kept hoping for some other way, a way that wouldn't force me to confront my pa face-to-face. I was afraid the sheriff would label my papers fakes and that I'd lose them, too. They're my only concrete connection with my son. I didn't wanna give them up, to anybody. That, and I was afraid my pa would steal my inheritance, claim it as his, and rob me of my only chance to escape him and start a new life."

"So, that's what you went back to get."

"Yes, sir. Only, my pa has a stack of lumber sitting right on top of it now. I couldn't get to it, to dig it up."

"I'll get them, and you won't lose any of it. I promise."

Betsy gazed into his eyes and saw that he meant those words. Yet, she refused to let him buoy her spirits. She knew her pa too well.

"I'll have to get a court order, but I've got a favor owed me by Judge Daley. Day after tomorrow. My schedule is light and I can clear it easily enough. I'll have those items for you by nightfall." He gave her hand a reassuring squeeze.

She offered a wan smile. "Thank you, Sir, for everything you've done for me." She wanted to hope for the best. Her heart rose in anticipation, but her mind steeled her for disappointment.

That next day, she finally ate without coaxing from Jim and joined the girls in the living room to watch a little television. She slept that night without repeated awakenings and felt stronger the next day. By noon, she began to feel anxious. Had Mr. Mathews made it to Frampton Corner? Had he succeeded in getting the warrant, or court order, or whatever it was that would get him onto her pa's property with the sheriff's backing? Maybe he already held her small treasure chest, enclosed in its protective wrappings, in his arms, preparing to return to her with it. Maybe he had already inspected the papers inside and knew the next steps to take to force a reunion with Jimmy.

She reminded herself not to get her hopes up, to believe in his success only when she held the chest in her hands, and no sooner. Yet, she felt encouraged and excited that perhaps her ordeal was about to end.

She sat in the living room with two other women, watching "Guiding Light," when the door leading to the motel office opened with its distinctive squeak. She turned to see Sally and Jim enter the room, saw the looks on their faces, and felt her heart drop to the floor. She'd seen that look on people before. She didn't want to see that look again. Not today.

Sally turned to the two women and said, "Girls, we need to talk to Betsy. Can you give us a few minutes? Please."

The women stood up without a word and walked to the kitchen, and Betsy wanted to jump and run.

Jim spoke. "Betsy, dear, we just got word. Mr. Mathews has been in a serious accident. He went off the road near the reservoir and –"

Betsy began to sob. "I-is he dead?"

Sally put her arm around Betsy. "We don't know anything more. We do know that he was on his way there and not on his way back."

Betsy's heart lightened a bit. She worried for Mr. Mathews and felt sickened that this had happened to him on her behalf.

Yet, the fact that he had not been to her home meant two things. Her pa, and the sheriff, would not know where she was and her chest remained hidden in the ground, not spread across some hillside or stolen by someone at the accident scene.

Betsy left for Lester's that night with mixed feelings. She felt no desire to work, yet knew that sulking at the Rest Stop would solve nothing. Plus, she was now going to need the money even more. As she approached the fence gate, Hilda stood there waiting for her. Over those two weeks, Betsy had won over Hilda, Lester's German bride whom he met when stationed in Heidelberg with the Army. To Betsy's dismay, Hilda seemed intent on fattening her up with streusel, dumplings, sausages and more, while Betsy insisted on losing weight. At least the extra food had slowed her bleeding cash reserve. If Hilda had learned that Betsy was treating her friends, "Lester's trollops," with Hilda's fine food she might have discovered Hilda in that horned hat with trident in hand waiting for her at the bus yard gate, instead of the German chocolate cake she held on a covered plate.

"I hear what happen. You okay?" asked Hilda as she extended the comfort food offering to Betsy.

Betsy shrugged. "I'll be okay. I just wish we knew how Mr. Mathews was doing. That's the part what has me worried most right now."

"You want go back. I have Lester clean bus himself if you do."

Betsy stepped up to the woman and gave her a hug. Hilda seemed thrown off-guard at first, but then hugged back so vigorously Betsy nearly lost her breath.

Betsy stepped back and accepted the cake. "I'll be okay. I need to work, to keep my mind occupied. Thanks for the cake."

"You need anything, you come to house. I be there."

Betsy nodded and headed toward the garage, while Hilda returned to her home. She was about to enter the building when she heard the bus coming down the street. Betsy walked into the barn without garnering so much as a raised ear from Roscoe until she began whistling an Elvis tune. The dog eased up onto all four legs and rambled over to her, wagging his tail, and then he discovered she had a treat and wouldn't leave her alone. She put the plate on top of a tall file cabinet next to Lester's desk. By then Lester had turned off the engine and climbed down the steps to the ground.

"Evening," said Betsy.

Lester nodded but gave no reply. He held a stern, questioning look in his eyes that made Betsy a little uneasy. After a minute, he nodded toward the cleaning gear and grunted, "Get at it. Don't got all night."

Betsy started to ask if she'd done something wrong, but he marched out of the barn before she could make a sound. She shrugged, retrieved the tub and broom, and began her chores. A few minutes into sweeping, she heard sirens rile the night air. Not a single clarion, but several, from different directions. Obviously, something big had or was happening. She climbed down from the bus and walked to the door to step outside, but Lester had returned and blocked her way.

"C'mon, hurry up and get this done. I'm tired and ready for the sack. Just a buncha sirens." He waited until Betsy returned to the bus and then walked to his office. As Betsy began to mop the floor, she saw him leave the office and head back out the door. At that moment, she heard the brief burp of a siren and saw a spotlight scanning the ground outside the door. She heard a distant voice, followed by Lester's, "Nope, ain't seen nobody around here. Roscoe's calm, so must be okay." Then quiet again consumed the night.

Betsy figured Lester's conversation was with the police and thought nothing more of it as she mopped under and around the seats. The quiet became annoying. The previous few nights' rounds of Elvis songs had made the job go much more quickly.

Suddenly, she heard Roscoe growl. She glanced out a side window in time to see the shepherd bolt to the door where he met the firecracker snap of a gunshot. The animal yelped in pain but for a moment, and then silence. Tears filled Betsy's eyes as she processed what had just happened.

"On the ground, old man!"

The voice held a rough edge and South Carolina inflection, not a native to western Carolina. The voice was one she thought she'd heard before, but she didn't dare look. Betsy dropped to the floor and inched forward toward the door. She had a good idea this man was the target of the police search. What had he done? With a little luck, she could escape the bus and then the barn unseen and call for help.

"You shot m'dog! You sick bastard. You shot 'im."

No Lester, don't! Betsy thought as she imagined him going after the man with the gun. Did she dare to raise her head for a glimpse of the outside?

An instant later, a second shot echoed inside the building and she heard Lester groan. She had no time to lose, but she had to know where the attacker was. She lifted her head just high enough to see the assailant rifling through Lester's pockets and retrieve his cash and the keys to the bus. The man appeared intent on using the bus to escape the police search.

She had run out of time.

She crouched just behind the first seat, invisible from the ground level. The sound of the man's footfall showed him coming fast toward the door. The tub remained below the first step, still filled with trash mixed with water from her cleaning. If she wanted to escape, she would have to take the offensive. To do nothing would lead to her being his captive, or dead. She needed to get help for Lester. She planned to jump him as he moved the tub out of his way. Surprise was on her side, and the wooden mop handle could disable his gun hand ... if she moved quickly enough. Her time on the girls' softball team in high school had awarded her with a nasty swing of the bat. Tonight, it would be simply a different ball.

However, the man jumped over the tub and hit the first step with a thud. Betsy revised her plan and speared the man with the end of the handle just under the chin as he landed. He'd had no time to settle his balance and the blow thrust him backward. He landed with his back across the tub. Betsy hit him with both feet into his mid-gut as she jumped from the top step. She heard a sickening snap under her as a reward for her effort, and the man went limp.

As she hit the ground, she spun around to meet him again, mop handle at the ready, and saw him lying there, flaccid, the gun below his hand on the ground. He made no movements. He continued to breath but consciousness had left him. She kicked the gun under the bus and looked down upon the attacker. She lifted his gun hand and met no resistance. His hand dropped like a stone when she let go. She saw no need to waste time tying him up.

She took one look at the man's face and her heart accelerated. The voice. She had known it. The man was a moonshiner. Worse yet, he was Dewey Hasting's cousin. Had

Dewey sent him to find her? Panic filled her mind, until she heard Lester moan again.

She ran to the large open bay door and yelled, "Hilda!" She took a deep breath. "Hilda! We need help! We need an ambulance!"

She ran to Lester and found him bleeding from a bullet wound in the left shoulder. She ran to the cleaning supply cabinet and found a jumble of clean rags, which she applied with pressure to his wound. He moaned with pain, but he came to briefly and blinked at her.

"I'm gonna tie this tight against you. It'll likely hurt, but I have to get help."

He offered a subtle nod, so she completed the bandage and ran to his office. *Where is Hilda?* she thought. The phone there gave her no dial tone, so she reversed course and headed for the house. She stopped suddenly at the bay door. She began to hyperventilate. Was Dewey outside? Was her pa? Had they found her? She ran back to the bus and crawled under it to get the pistol. Only then did she dare to venture outside.

The back door of the house lay wide open, a sign that gave her pause. She stopped at the door and peeked in. *Is someone else in there?* she thought. *Is Dewey in there?* Her heart raced, but she had to get help. She eased into the kitchen and found Hilda, tied up and gagged on the floor. She saw no other signs of life.

"Lester's shot. He's alive but serious wounded. I gotta call an ambulance and the police, then I'll untie you," Betsy said. The woman nodded.

A minute later, her call completed, she freed the older woman.

"I-I hear two gunshots. Is ..."

"First one hit Roscoe. I didn't check him up close but I

saw him lying still on the dirt and suspect he's dead. Lester was shot in the shoulder."

Together they ran to the barn, where Hilda tended to her husband while Betsy watched over the attacker. His eyes were open, and his breathing seemed unsettled. He offered no sounds but a rare moan, and no movement of any limb. Betsy guessed she might have broken his back, or maybe his neck, by jumping on him as he stretched across the metal tub. *Serves him right*, she thought, at first without remorse. Then a nagging worry hit her. *Will I get in trouble for this?*

By the time the first police car arrived, Lester had regained consciousness. Hilda waved her over. Betsy breathed easier now. Had Dewey or her pa been with the man, they would have revealed themselves by now. Only now did she reflect on how the day had done. First, Mr. Mathews. Now Lester. Her ma had always said bad things came in threes. She didn't want to ponder that possibility.

"I-I owe you," stammered Lester.

Betsy tried to look brave, for him, and shrugged her shoulders. "I just got a lucky hit on the guy, that's all. Coulda turned out different."

"But ... but it didn't." Lester paused for a painful breath, his face grimacing as he tried to ease the air into his lungs. "I need to warn you. A man, surly and rough ... came to the bus stop ... in Frampton Corner tonight." He struggled for another breath. "Late forties, early fifties. By name of Amos."

Betsy could feel her throat constricting. Lester worked to continue.

"Lookin' for his girl, Alice."

Betsy wondered if the sweat she felt building actually

showed. 'Bad things in threes' echoed in her head. Her pa was waiting out there somewhere. She just knew it. Was Dewey with him? She felt her bravado plummet.

"Told him ... I don't usually get ... to know passengers' names." He looked as if he would pass out at any moment. "Offered me a hundred bucks ... if I could help him ... locate ..." He closed his eyes for a moment, his next breath appearing more laborious than the previous ones. "I took it. Told him a young girl ... took the bus ... from Cashiers ... a couple a weeks ago."

Betsy couldn't breathe any easier than Lester at that point. She held no doubt her fear was evident.

"Didn't give him your name ... but I mentioned ..." The agony in Lester's face magnified as his voice slurred over the last few words. "Shouldn't ... have ..."

"Mentioned what, Lester? What did you tell him?" Betsy pleaded.

"Rest ..." The man lost consciousness again as the ambulance driver and attendant approached.

"Lester, what? Please! Wake up! What did you tell him?" She gently prodded his good shoulder, but the ambulance attendant pushed her aside to set the stretcher next to the man.

"Will he make it?" she asked.

"Can't tell you, but the surgeon on call tonight's a good one. We gotta get him to the hospital fast."

A minute later, with Lester strapped into the stretcher in the back of the boxy vehicle, the ambulance left with lights ablaze and sirens disrupting the night's silence one more time. Betsy watched as the rig moved beyond sight, her gut twisting. Had he mentioned the Rest Stop to her pa? Or was he simply saying he needed rest? Could she return to her room with enough time to clear out? Where would she go?

"Can you go through it one more time," asked the detective.

She had already told her story to the man once, and turned over the pistol, although she would have preferred keeping it. Her pa was out there somewhere.

"Hilda met me at the gate and we talked. She offered me that piece of cake over there." She pointed to the file cabinet. "I was just getting ..." She continued in detail with what had happened.

"And why did you have the gun?"

"Like I said, I was afraid there was someone else out there. I didn't want to run to the house without some weapon. I didn't think I'd get so lucky with the mop again." The last phrase came out more sarcastically than she wanted, but she was exhausted, emotionally and physically.

"Do you know the man?"

That was a question she had hoped he wouldn't ask. What did she answer? The truth? That would lead to more questions. And if her pa wasn't in town, he would be soon if she told the truth because the authorities would be heading to Jackson County and her pa knew everything that happened there. He was already here though, wasn't he? Why else would Ned Hastings have been there, if not looking for her? But could she lie? She did know the man by name, nothing more. And if her pa was already in town looking for her, what would lying gain? Real trouble, with the law.

"I used to live in Jackson County. He looks like a moonshiner from down there. Ned Hastings. But I can't be totally certain."

"Why would he be up here? Was he known for whorin'?"

That one Betsy could honestly answer. "Beats me." She

had her suspicions and worries, but she honestly did not know why he was there. The second question actually gave her a glimmer of hope. Maybe that's why he was here. Maybe he wasn't looking for her. No, that would be too much to ask.

"Okay. Well, thank you, Miss Weston. We might need you to come into the station tomorrow, so please stay in town."

He said that with a gravity that Betsy could not ignore. She had told him they could contact her through Hilda and did not mention the Rest Stop. Lester's confession gnawed at her as Hilda walked up to her.

"Despite some flaws, Lester be a good man. I hope he not get you into any trouble."

"Maybe, maybe not, Hilda. If it's okay with you, can I come back in the morning to finish the bus? I need the income."

"It not going anywhere. Tomorrow, next day, next week, be fine, but will not need cleaning again until it used again. Sorry." She started to turn toward the house, but stopped. "You want maybe to stay here tonight?"

"I, uh, I don't know what to do, Ma'am. All my stuff's in my room. I gotta go back to get it, at least."

"I wait."

Betsy thought for a minute. Her pa could easily track her to the bus company. Would he find her here easier than finding her at the Rest Stop?

"Tell you what. If I'm not back in thirty minutes, I've decided to take my chances at the Rest Stop. Thirty minutes. Okay? If I'm not back, go ahead to bed."

"Not bed. I be headin' for the hospital, but I wait thirty minutes. There won't be news for me before that at the hospital."

"Ma'am, I wasn't thinking. Sorry. No, you just go on to the hospital. I'll manage. I can sleep on the bus if I need to come back here."

Betsy walked over to Roscoe's body. The Elvis fan never had a chance. Tears welled up again. She had grown to love that dog. She felt Hilda's hand on her shoulder.

"I miss, too."

Betsy walked over to some shelves and found a blanket. She lifted the dog's body onto it and then rolled it twice around the dog. She dragged the shroud over near the back door.

"I can bury him behind the barn, tomorrow, if you like," she said.

Hilda nodded, turned, and returned to the house, her head hanging low. Betsy grabbed her bag from the barn and broke into a run. Without a weapon, she refused to become an easy target for whoever was out there waiting for her. Halfway to the motel, she stopped, winded, and walked for a block before returning to a fast jog for the remaining distance. As she came into view of the Rest Stop, she stopped. Half a dozen police cars filled the lot and blocked its entrances. Undulating red lights swirled about the dark sky. Anguish filled Betsy's soul for the third time that day. "Threes. They come in threes," she could hear her ma saying.

Sixteen
(Present Day)

After a week in the Reagan Medical Center, Myra sat in the living room of her Carmel home overlooking the waves as they surged toward the rocky shoreline only to explode upon the plutonic granite outcroppings into a coarse spray. Had she been on the beach, she would have seen the sun cast prisms of light through the spray, but she wasn't yet up to such activity. After a total count of eight units of blood, she would do nothing to risk losing that precious commodity. She did find one thing curious about it. Had one or more of those units been donated by someone of oriental ancestry? She'd had cravings for Chinese food since leaving the medical center. She'd never been fond of Chinese before. It had to be the blood.

Her energy levels waxed and waned, but she awoke that morning to a good day. During the last two days in the hospital, she had developed a coarse outline for the new book. This morning, with the aid of her favorite travel agent, she had booked her next day flight via private charter to Albuquerque and made reservations at the Mabel Dodge Luhan House in Taos for what was to be the first leg of her final trip. She interrupted her packing to reheat and finish her chicken fried rice, while longing for General Tso's chicken despite knowing the risk such a spicy dish would have on her still-sensitive lower esophagus.

As she rinsed her plate, the doorbell rang for the third time that morning. *Who is it now?* she wondered. She checked her security video feed of the front door to find the third flower deliveryman of the morning. Make that delivery crew because she saw a small cargo van in the drive and two more men unloading floral arrangements. *Oh gawd,* she thought. Having collapsed at the Polo Lounge patio had one distinct disadvantage, her collapse and sudden hospitalization had made it to the gossip rags as well as Publishers Weekly, Time Magazine, People, and US Weekly. While the public might not recognize her, her fans made sure she felt appreciated. She had dispersed over five dozen floral pieces to patients throughout the medical floor and ICU upon discharge.

She opened the door to the head deliveryman, keeping her emergency alert button in hand should anything untoward happen. She'd never had to use it at home and never hoped to. Needless to say, it would be the one time she answered the door alone without it that some psychopath would be there. There was nothing like a writer's imagination to keep her on alert.

"Hi, Ms. Mitchell. Back again."

She recognized the young man as the same man who'd delivered the first gifts that morning. That time, he'd been alone and had only three pieces.

He laughed. "Got a whole truck load this time. Living room?"

Myra sighed, nodded, and looked again at the name on his uniform shirt. "You know where to go, Greg. Have at it." She opened the door wide to the men and fifteen minutes later, her living room looked like a conservatory during a holiday floral show. She couldn't very well refuse them and alert three strangers that the place would be vacant in twenty-four hours. Security system or not, why tempt fate?

As the last man exited her home, the phone rang. Caller ID listed a number she knew quite well.

"Myra. How are you doing?"

"Stephen, darling, it's so good to hear your voice." She cradled the phone on her shoulder as she signed the delivery receipt and then twiddled with her hair as she talked. "I've missed you, dear." Her latest beau, of sorts, was a plastic surgeon, not that she'd ever made use of his services. Well, not his professional ones anyway.

"Are you feeling well? I'm worried. I just got back in country yesterday and heard about your episode. Did you get my flowers? They promised delivery this morning."

She hesitated. Which was his? She started thumbing through gift cards, hoping for a quick discovery. "They're absolutely gorgeous, Stephen. But then, you've always had exquisite tastes." She still had not found his arrangement.

"Let's get together for dinner. You are up for that, aren't you? How about L'Escargot in Carmel. I'll pick you up at seven. Quiet dinner. Passionate night. Okay?"

"Stephen, dear, you should know better. I'm afraid it's bland foods, no wine, and no vigorous exercise for a while. Doctor's orders." Should she tell him the truth, the whole truth, and nothing but? Not on her life.

"Then how about a cozy evening of snuggling and watching the sunset from your deck?"

That was tempting, but she had no time.

"I'm afraid I'll have to take a rain check on that offer as well, dear. I'm leaving in the morning for Taos."

"I'll meet you there. Where would I find you?"

Can't this man take no for an answer? she thought. He was starting to sound a bit needy and that was one trait in a lover she found unappetizing. How might Sweetie put it? "Needy? If I want drama, I'll rent a movie." Still, he had performed well in satisfying her appetites in the past.

147

"Not this time. Please, I'll call you when I get back." Call waiting beeped on her phone. "Stephen, I've got another call coming in. I'll call. Promise. *Ciao.*"

Myra heard the beginning of his "Bye" as she pulled the handset away from her ear and glanced at the caller ID – "Mobile Caller" and a number she did not recognize. She ignored the call at first, thanking its timing for getting her away from Stephen. However, she noticed the number carried a New York area code. *Samuel?* she wondered. She hurried off to her study where the answering machine had picked up the call on the sixth ring.

"Myra? You there? Don't scare me like this. I don't wanna find you passed out or dead or something. Pick up the damn receiver. Myra?"

She picked up the phone. "Samuel, so nice of you to call." She heard a not-so-subtle sigh of relief on the other end.

"You okay? Don't do that to me."

"I feel great today. Thanks for asking." She chuckled. "And I didn't *do* anything to you. After all these years, you should know I let the machine answer, particularly if I don't recognize the caller or number."

"Okay, yeah, but ... Hey, look, I'm about ten minutes away and I've got someone you need to meet."

Samuel was in Carmel? "Oh? I didn't expect you back here. I-I'm flying out tomorrow and now's not really a good time to meet –"

"I know, I know. You emailed me about the trip, remember? But ..." He paused and Myra knew from his tone that she wasn't going to like what came next. "Look, I know what you're going to say, but I hired you an assistant. She's going to accompany you on your trip, and –"

"No, Samuel. I don't need ..." She realized what he was

doing. "This person isn't an assistant, is she, Samuel? You hired a babysitter, didn't you? You don't trust me to steer clear of the wine, do you?" From the blank air on the other end, she knew she'd caught him with his pants down. On second thought, that was a cliché she didn't want to visualize. She stopped pacing the room and plopped into the chair at her writing table. She didn't have the energy to get angry.

"Myra, hey, I know what this sounds like, but honest, she'll function as an assistant. She's capable, and understands the needs of a writer. Wants to be a writer herself. You'll like her; I just know it. I like her, and, hell, I don't like people as easily as you do. You know that. C'mon, be a sport. Do me this favor for once. *I'm* footin' the bill."

Myra realized he had her best interest at heart … and that the book project staring her in the face was all because of him. Plus, he had no reason to trust her. Not one, based on recent history. Samuel had preceded her to the house and emptied it of all adult beverages. He'd found every last bottle. How, she had no idea because she often found bottles tucked away that even she didn't recall hiding. He had even removed all traces of acetaminophen. Maybe, for this book, she could use an assistant … and a babysitter.

"Okay, Samuel, I'm willing to meet her on the condition that if we don't hit it off right away, she goes back with you."

"Thank you, Myra. I don't think we'll have a problem."

Myra placed the phone back in its charging cradle and started back toward the kitchen. She hadn't made it to the main hall when the doorbell rang. She huffed. "Guess he knows better than to give me much warning," she said to the empty hall.

She answered the door to find Samuel, flowers in hand, and a young woman whose back was turned toward her.

Something stirred in Myra's gut. The back of that head looked oddly familiar.

"We were closer than I thought. Myra, this is ..." The young woman turned to face her and Myra's color, jaundice and all, drained. "... Alexia Hamilton. She starts that doctorate program at USC in two months and has quite an impressive resume. We met at the USC reception, and, well, one thing led to another."

"Hi, Ms. Mitchell."

Myra stood there speechless. She had no doubts as to whose idea it was to become an assistant.

"Thanks, Samuel, but this won't work. You can take her home now."

Samuel's mouth dropped. "What? That's it? You're not even gonna talk with her?"

"We've met before, Samuel. It won't work."

This time Samuel eyed the young woman with a steely gaze that made the woman uneasy.

"Okay. Yes, we kind of met. I got her autograph at the movie premiere, but, we were going to meet at the USC reception and you couldn't make it."

Samuel's face reddened. He never had been one to accept being played, but all he said was, "Oh, really."

Myra hated putting Samuel in the middle of something she didn't understand yet herself. She touched Samuel's shoulder. "I didn't exactly promise we'd talk, but I did say I'd try." Myra stepped back through the doorway, and ushered a nervous girl and perplexed agent into her living room. Alexia gazed around the room, looking puzzled. Myra realized they had no place to sit.

"My god, Myra, you got a regular botanical garden going here." He started nosing around the flowers. "Geez, look at this one. Looks like a funeral director's award winner." He peeked at the card. "Stephen somebody. You sure he knows you're still alive?"

Myra ignored the comment and ushered them to a smaller parlor near the kitchen. She watched as Alexia studied the place, as if sizing up Myra's worth from the décor. Myra steeled herself for what was to come.

"Maybe I should step out," said Samuel.

"Nope, you're in this through thick and thin. Besides, you complained you know nothing about me. Maybe you'll learn something from this little blackmailer."

Alexia's eyes widened. "Blackmailer? Why, I never –"

"You did imply such. I believe your words at the movie premiere were, 'Please make time for me. I know your secret.'" Myra sat down in a plush, modernistic, cream upholstered chair and crossed her legs defensively, arms folded as well. "Well, just what secret might that be and how much did you think it was worth to keep quiet?" Myra tried to keep secret the fact that her heart was racing and her palms sweating.

"Zion's Revenge," replied Alexia.

"What about it?" asked Myra.

Samuel started chuckling. Myra gave him a steely look, which served to aggravate the man's amusement. He now laughed so hard tears formed in his eyes. Myra looked at him sternly.

"Attempted extortion isn't funny, Samuel. Whatever in the world are you …?"

The man could barely contain himself and struggled to answer. "'Zion's Revenge,' Myra." He wiped the tears from his cheek. "You wrote it. Think about it."

The man's laugh was contagious, at least to Alexia, who fought to contain herself. "You … you thought I was …" she said. Soon she, too, had tears running down both cheeks.

Myra glanced back and forth between the two, while she failed to get the joke. Then it hit her. Marcus Kolby, the book's protagonist, used the same phrase to throw people off guard and get their attention when he wasn't getting what he wanted from them. It never failed to reward him with a return phone call or a favor, even though he knew no secrets. He played on their petty paranoias and family skeletons to move along his own plan. Now, she, too, had been duped … by Marcus Kolby and her own imagination.

Myra reddened and slumped back into the chair, arms and legs relaxing. Her personal paranoia had been clearly on display, but the skeletons remained safely in their respective closets.

"I'm sorry. I don't really know anything. I figured you'd get it right away and realize I just really wanted to have some time to talk with you." Alexia looked truly apologetic for upsetting Myra.

"I-I don't know what to say," she uttered. She sat upright and addressed the young woman. "Ms. Hamilton, I must apologize for thinking the worst of you. You most certainly have my attention now. So, what can I do for you?"

"Well, now that we're getting off on the right foot, I –"

"Stop!" Myra shook her head. "Please, no clichés. You should know better if you made it into the USC program. I hate clichés."

The young woman composed herself and replied, "Okay. I have two requests. Actually, it's like one request with a part A and part B. I want to do my dissertation on the rise of women as authors of popular fiction and you are my favorite author. As part of my work, I'm hoping to have easy access to you, to learn how you think, how you became the writer you are, stuff like that. Part B came later, to become your assistant for this book, and that was Samuel's idea. It would help me accomplish the first part. I could help full-time until my coursework starts in September, and then part-time after that."

Myra didn't know whether to be flattered or terrified.

"Learning how I think might be scarier than you can imagine. Besides, I'm not sure I've figured that out for myself yet." Myra pondered the implications of this woman tagging along for her final book. She fully expected a posthumous release of her final novel, when embarrassment would be impossible. Was she actually ready to unveil her personal secrets to a stranger pre-mortem?

"So, what do you have to offer me as an assistant?"

Without hesitation, Alexia offered a list of tasks she could perform from making tea and coffee, to setting up appointments to research to proofreading. After all, she did have the literary chops to make it into the USC doctoral program. Surely, she had the skills to help.

Also without hesitation, Myra found herself accepting Alexia's proposal. How the word "yes" formed in her mouth, she didn't understand, because in her mind she didn't want to accept her need for an assistant. Moreover, she certainly had no desire to have a babysitter. So, where did that word "yes" come from?

"Thank you," replied the surprised grad student.

"Wonderful," stated Samuel, clapping his hands twice. "I knew you'd find her helpful. I've already booked her flight and into the Mabel Luhan house with you."

"You did what?"

"Well, I had her make the arrangements. She was quite expedient at it. I've arranged a per diem for her, to cover meals and miscellaneous expenses. Her luggage is in the car and I figured she could spend the night here. You know, to make it easier for you both to make the flight together on time tomorrow."

"Don't think so," replied Myra. "I am not prepared for a house guest on such short notice. Besides, I'm flying by private charter, so I'll be leaving from Monterey Peninsula Airport. Get her a motel room here in town or near the airport and I'll arrange for the car service to stop by on our way."

"She's not a guest. She's your new assistant and you have so much room here you could house a college dorm load of assistants."

"No, not this time, Samuel. I don't need help packing. She starts that job effective upon our arrival tomorrow at the airport." She turned toward Alexia. "Sorry, nothing personal. I-I just think I need the rest of the day to be alone. To get some things done that I truly don't need, or want, help with."

She stood up and moved toward the front door to usher them out. Samuel and Alexia followed. As they walked past the living room, Alexia pointed to all the flowers and said, "You know, those are going to be a big mess when you come home."

Myra turned to Samuel. "She's right. Could you arrange to have them sent to some nursing homes or someplace?"

"Sorry, Myra, not in my job description."

"Alexia, could you do that?"

As Samuel opened the door and led Alexia outside, he responded, "Sorry, Myra, you made it quite clear she's not your assistant 'til tomorrow. We're going to find a nice place for lunch, so's I can fill her in on all your eccentricities and pet peeves. Then I'll find her that room for the night you asked me to find." He stopped a few feet from the door and turned back. "However, if she stayed here, she could no doubt handle that for you. Probably take all afternoon. Plus, there's a good chance you'll be getting more. She could arrange to divert any future deliveries to the locations of your choosing, out of your generosity and good name, of course."

Myra stood speechless, exchanging glances between her agent and the floral menagerie overflowing from her living room. She hated to surrender them to the compost pile before their time, but the thought of coming home to a room, or worse, a houseful of rotting flora held no appeal. An even worse thought hit her – her diva's crown must be slipping. Samuel actually got the better of her this time.

Seventeen

Emory Albritton had just finished his speech at a fundraiser when the phone in his jacket pocket vibrated. He suspected who was calling, but had to delay returning the call until he sat in the back of his campaign's SUV. The driver had instructions to take him back to the motel in Charlotte. Being careful with his words, he returned the phone call.

"You saw what?" barked Emory Albritton. Dewey had his full attention.

"Just what I said. Some guy in his fifties picked up the Hamilton gal early this morning. He arrived about dawn. Overweight, bad rosacea, thinning hair. Expensive clothes, though. Hadn't seen this guy before and he seemed out of place with the girl, so I sprinted to my car and made it back to her apartment in time to watch her load some luggage into his trunk and leave. I followed them all the way to Carmel. Pretty sure the car's a rental, and I'm thinkin' the guy might be Mitchell's agent. He's been in town with her in the hospital."

The man paused and Albritton felt the full impact of this disclosure, more than Dewey could have imagined.

"They ended up at a gated community in Carmel, a place called Tehama. Very upscale. I couldn't follow past the front gate, but I learned that's where Mitchell lives. I waited and finally saw the guy leave, alone. I can only assume the girl's now staying with Mitchell."

Albritton drummed his fingers on the car door's armrest. "Okay. Let me think on this and I'll call you back. See if you can find a way to watch the house."

Back in the motel, he found his suite empty. Misty was at a Democratic women's function, but he expected her return soon. He would be freer to talk while she was gone, but he didn't want to rush his answer. Instead, he paced between the front room and the bedroom. After a few minutes, he approached the bar and poured two fingers of fine single-malt, neat, into an Old Fashion glass. He then opened the French doors onto the balcony and looked out over Charlotte's skyline and its night-lights. His schedule required his return to Raleigh in the morning, where he would become too busy to attend to the matter at hand.

He felt two hands run softly up and over both shoulders from behind. He smiled and turned to his wife of thirty years and college sweetheart for the four years before formalizing their relationship. He hadn't heard her enter the suite.

"Deep, weighty matters of state?" she asked in a playful tone.

"What?"

"You've spent the evening glad-handing and drinking with the big boys and now you're out here with scotch in hand. Must be something heavy on your mind."

He shrugged. *Heavy? Only if you consider losing everything heavy*, he thought. "Only the usual conundrum wrapped in enigma … but without the riddle."

"What? No riddle? Where's the fun in that? You should have this solved in no time."

He took her hand and pulled her closer, kissing her on the cheek. "Got a phone call to make. Then, if you're willing, we could go upstairs to the club for a little dancing."

She kissed him back, on the lips. "I was thinking of something a little more private," she whispered in his ear before turning and walking into the bedroom. He remained a prisoner of her charms, but the stress of the previous few weeks had forced him to get a confidential prescription for

Cialis™. He knew his performance problem was all in his head, but how could he share this problem with Misty? No, he would not threaten his marriage by confessing to past sins.

Earlier, on his way to the balcony, before Misty had arrived, he had caught sight of the day's Raleigh News & Observer on the coffee table. He retrieved it as he returned to the bedroom, but had not taken time to peruse the pages. As he tossed it on the bed, he noted a story headline on the bottom half of the front page – "Chief Justice Hoglund Retiring." He now picked up the paper and began to read.

"Ending months of rumor and speculation, State Supreme Court Chief Justice Michael W. Hoglund has announced his retirement with the end of the current court session. Justice Hoglund, who recently turned 82, has served the high court for over twenty years and ..."

Albritton scanned the story as it listed the Justice's contributions to the state. However, as he undid his tie, the final paragraph caught his full attention.

"The Justice will leave for Santa Fe, New Mexico to live with his son and family, a move he makes with great sadness in leaving the state he served well and loves so much."

Albritton felt a lightening of the load on his mind as he realized his problem might no longer be so critical. With the Justice leaving the state, one crucial dot would become more difficult to connect to the remaining ones. Not impossible, just more difficult. The unknowing role played by then Superior Court Judge Hoglund in a certain legal trust case would require a few more steps to ferret out. After all, not everything pertaining to the case could be found in publicly available records. Only a sharp memory would recall some of the behind-the-scenes maneuvering. The Justice had such a memory, but maybe, just maybe, the details of the official court record would not arouse enough suspicion to warrant an investigator's cross-country trip to visit a retired justice.

So, again, he faced his conundrum wrapped in enigma. Just what had Alexia Hamilton discovered? Could she connect the dots leading back to the Umfleet trust? He hoped not. Maybe she knew nothing.

Yet, the senator knew better than to rely on hope and maybes. He quickly returned to the balcony, out of earshot from his wife, and quietly placed his call. Dewey held few scruples and had never shown a drop of remorse in prior dealings.

Eighteen

By suppertime, Myra had come to respect several good qualities in Alexia. She was highly efficient, having found "homes" for all of the floral arrangements, as well as transportation to those homes at no cost to Myra. Alexia had reclaimed the living room without need of a machete. The woman had also arranged for future deliveries to go straight to a deserving charity that promised to note the type of floral array on the card accompanying the piece and to hold all cards for collection at a later date, should Myra chose to individually acknowledge receipt of the gift, as Alexia suggested. The PR potential of sending such "thank yous" hadn't crossed Myra's mind, although in her current circumstance the PR advantage would make little difference.

Myra greatly appreciated Alexia's not being intrusive. The gal acted when called upon, but otherwise stayed to herself and out of Myra's way. Not once had she inquired about Myra's health or about what had happened to lead to her hospitalization. She seemed quite bright and Myra had no doubts that, one, Samuel had given her some account of the situation, or two, she simply added up easy observations – Myra's pastel pumpkin color, her public reputation as a hard partier, and Samuel's instructions to keep Myra clear of any and all alcohol. He had given that instruction clearly in Myra's presence on two occasions before leaving, just so there would be no confusion.

Alexia also knew her way around a kitchen.

"This is absolutely delicious," said Myra. She twirled her fork in the air. "How in the world did you put this together from *my* pantry?"

"I didn't. I only needed five minutes in your kitchen to realize you never actually *cook* anything in there. I stopped at the market while I was out." She scooped up some pasta and chicken, placed it in her mouth, and chewed. A minute later, she added, "And don't worry, this is within the guidelines of your prescribed diet. I took the liberty of surfing the Internet for information on diet restrictions in liver failure, as well as finding a few recipes to get us started."

Myra raised one eyebrow and looked at the girl. So, Samuel was a snitch. "How much did Samuel tell you about me?"

"Not much really. Unfortunately, this isn't my first go around with someone in liver failure."

Myra heard a subtle chime and looked about the room in confusion. Was she hearing things? She thought the DTs were over. She relaxed when Alexia pulled her smart phone from a back pocket.

"What's that?" Myra asked.

"My iPhone."

"No, I meant the chime."

"Oh. I subscribe to a handful of RSS feeds. They get channeled to my phone so I can keep up-to-date on news events and such."

"RSS? Sorry, but I'm a bit old fashioned. I still wrote my books freehand on paper until a few years ago when Samuel bought me a laptop and lessons for a Christmas gift."

"RSS – Really simple syndication. It's just a format for sending out news updates across the Internet. This one's a blog update from an old co-worker back in North Carolina. The state Supreme Court Chief Justice is retiring. I interviewed him once, when I was volunteering for Project Innocence. We were looking at a couple cases where he presided. Interesting man.

He actually started in a law practice near where I grew up." She paused for a moment, caught up in the blog. "Wow, this is interesting. He's moving to Santa Fe to live with his son. Gee, I wonder when he's arriving. Maybe I can connect with him again. How far is that from Taos?"

Myra looked at her new assistant, wondering how her writing career might have been affected by today's technology.

"Hendersonville."

Alexia looked up. "What?"

"Hendersonville, North Carolina. That's where you grew up, right?"

Alexia looked startled … and upset.

"H-how do you know that?"

"Dear, you don't get to my level of writing without a network of resources. Why'd you give up journalism?"

Alexia didn't answer right away and Myra felt her glare from across the room. How much information she'd share with the young woman was yet to be determined. A single phone call to USC not only provided Myra with Alexia's complete resume but with it, a faxed copy of her application to the creative writing program and an invitation to sit on Alexia's doctorate committee. Celebrity certainly had its perks at times and leverage was good to have at all times.

"What? Don't look at me like that. I *am* on the board for your program at USC. Did you think I'd let you stay on as my assistant without checking you out? I was busy while you were out." She paused. "You're still here, by the way. Reflect on that."

Alexia finally answered. "I found it interesting, at first. But, it became as clear as the nose on my face that –"

Myra held up her hand to stop the woman, and slashed her finger across her neck as she gave Alexia a stern look. She mouthed, "No clichés."

Alexia rolled her eyes and continued, "I realized a career in journalism was never my goal, but it was a means toward getting there. Tent making, to use a Biblical concept. The Apostle Paul made –"

"Yes, I'm familiar with the term."

"I want to write fiction, to tell stories."

"And having a doctorate is somehow going to make that easier?" Myra made a habit of keeping her past life a private matter, as attested to by Samuel a week earlier. However, life no longer held promise to be long and healthy. "Alexia, as we get to know each other over the next few weeks, I've decided to share some things with you that less than a handful of people know about me. The first of which is that I have no high degrees. I didn't even finish college, but my life experience taught me, gave me insight into people that I used to craft characters, and sometimes even the stories to tell. Don't expect a fancy Ph.D. to magically transform your career."

Alexia mulled that over for a few minutes as she finished dinner. "I believe that. All stories come from life in some way, shape, or form. The doctorate isn't for that so much, as I'd rather teach than chase newsworthy events ... if I have to fall back to something other than writing."

"Then, I think you've made a good choice." Myra stood and began to clear her dishes.

"I can do that for you," insisted Alexia.

Myra shook her head. "You might not believe it from the looks of my private rooms, but I do clean up after myself and divas still do dishes ... well, on rare occasions, anyway ... if and when I actually attempt cooking." She smiled.

Working together, they cleaned the kitchen in less than

fifteen minutes. As they did so, Myra experienced a never-before feeling – that this must be what having a daughter could have been like. She shook it off. Too late for children. Her mood sank at the thought that it was too late for many things. She couldn't let such thoughts drag her down. She was known for being lively, the life of the party. How could she not live up to that, even at the end?

Myra's fatigue returned, but she refused to be a bad hostess and offered to show Alexia the rest of her home, including her study. The unused parts of the house remained sterile, while areas of private use showed the usual clutter of a single woman, albeit that of a single woman of wealth and refined tastes. Just outside her study, Alexia came to a halt and gazed at the framed prints on the walls.

"Sweetie … and George! I love that comic strip, but I don't think I've ever seen these before." She leaned closer to the glass of a nearby print and scrutinized it. "These are much more risqué than the ones I've seen in print."

The nearest eight-by-ten sketch showed Sweetie in bed with a book, while scrawny George stood at the doorway dressed as a Chippendale stripper at Christmas holding a sprig of mistletoe high in front of him. To George's "Ho! Ho! Ho!" Sweetie replied, "No! No! No!"

"Who's Weston? I thought the authors were Sanders and Ross."

Myra smiled. "These are among my most precious possessions. I have a Picasso and a Monet. You saw those, but I'd give them both up to have more of these. This is secret number two about me. I've idolized Sweetie since her first appearance. Her irreverence. Her wit. Even her sarcasm. She is a diva among divas." She paused to let that sink in. "These, Alexia dear, are signed originals by the creator of 'Sweetie … and George,' Betsy Weston, who, sadly, is no longer with us. Sanders and Ross took over for the publisher when Weston sold them all rights to the series and disappeared."

Myra watched as Alexia scanned each print, chuckling at most of them, laughing loudly at several.

"What happened to her? These are much funnier than the current ones."

"Ahhh, what happened to Betsy Weston is a mystery awaiting revelation. One that I think we're both going to find … what word should I use? Interesting? Too simplistic. Troubling? Perhaps. Intriguing? I hope so. I hope it has the makings of a great book because that's what you'll be working on."

Myra could sense that the young woman was indeed intrigued.

"What do you already know about her?"

"She came from Asheville, North Carolina and moved to Cincinnati, Ohio where she freelanced creating cards for Gibson Greetings. When she came up with this idea, the company thought it too risqué, as you put it, and turned down her idea. So, she struck out on her own, built the series up and then suddenly sold it and disappeared. Do you remember my mentioning to you that I'd been to Asheville about ten years ago? I thought I had a lead on more of these originals. Ended up being only that one."

She pointed to a drawing of Sweetie in a garden with George bent over in the distance, his butt crack prominently showing. The caption read, "The old fart! I asked for hemerocallis and all I see is hemorrhoids."

"I found it in an old motel that locals told me had been a

165

brothel at one time. The current owner told me each room had an original at one time until that building burned down in the early eighties. Only the office and owner's quarters survived and that's why he still had that one. He met Betsy once in the mid-70's when she went back to Asheville for the funeral of Sally Fleming, her inspiration for Sweetie."

"Are there others out there somewhere?"

Myra shrugged her shoulders. "None that I've been able to locate, but I believe there is another small collection in Arkansas. These are one-of-a-kind originals that some think are more priceless than the Picasso, but value is in the eye of the beholder and like all collectibles, the true worth is set only when someone buys it."

Alexia stood and scanned each sketch over and over. Myra wished she could read minds, to get a glimpse of what Alexia was thinking at that moment. She hadn't told Alexia everything she knew about Betsy Weston. No sense scaring her.

Nineteen
(Spring – 1969)
❧✦✦❧

Betsy ran past the police cars with their rotating beacons, past the main drive and office, and approached the brothel from the rear service drive and private garden. The yellow '65 Mustang convertible sat outside the garage doors. The police hadn't thought to secure that area, so she eased past the car, alert to anyone hiding inside or behind it, and entered the garden and patio. She gazed through the large glass sliding doors into the living area to see the girls crying and shaking. Jim moved from girl to girl, trying to console each one. Everyone seemed to be there except Jennie, Billie, and Sally. Betsy's heart ached at that realization. Jim looked up as she entered the room and rushed over to her. He took her softly by the shoulder and ushered her back outside onto the patio.

"What's going on?" she asked.

"Please, sit down." He pointed to a pair of wicker chairs. After sitting next to her, he continued. "I-I don't know how to tell you this. It's tragic. Nothing like this has ever happened here before." A tear fell from his eye and he swallowed. "I, uh …" He took a deep breath. "Billie's dead and Jennie's critically wounded. This john, went by name of Ned, wanted to have two girls tonight. We tried to talk him outta Billie, you know, because… But this guy insisted on Billie and Jennie and offered twice the rate for both. All we can figure is Billie didn't want to oblige him. He went into a rage. Shot her, Billie, in the chest and then Jennie in the back as she tried to run from the room. Then he took off. Police are out huntin' for him now."

Betsy struggled to breathe and to understand the why and how of this grim news. She inhaled deeply and wanted to

167

scream. Why had this happened? Suddenly she felt like an angel of death. Everyone she loved, everyone she touched, was gone or hurt. JT, Jimmy Bob, Jennie, Billie, and Lester. Would Sally or Jim be next? Who was behind this? Dewey? Her pa? Or was she somehow cursed?

She felt drained. She'd cried over Lester, and Roscoe. Where would the tears come from for Jennie and Billie? She steeled her emotions as she responded. "They got him," Betsy answered as tears now flowed down both cheeks. Her speech choked with emotion, she gave Jim a synopsis of the events at the bus yard, including something she'd heard by a policeman on the side, that the man had come to town on the bus and must have wanted it to escape. The comment made sense to her now.

A smile crept onto Jim's craggy face. He stood and walked to the door, which he pulled open to address the women inside.

"Ladies, there's nothing to fear anymore. Betsy nailed the son-of-a-bitch. He won't be comin' back here no more."

Betsy stood, grabbed Jim's shirt from behind, and pulled him back near the chairs. She explained her predicament. Jim's face turned serious again, as he stiffened upright and stuck out his chest like the theatrical hero he might have been once.

"Not here, he won't. Young lady, you've become like family here and you will be protected here."

Betsy appreciated the man's posture and bravado, but the truth sat on the other side of the fence behind her. Jennie and Billie had felt protected, too.

"I need to get to my room," Betsy replied.

Jim hemmed and hawed. "Not tonight. Police have the whole area cordoned off. They wanted to search your room, but Sally was there, told them you had the only key to the padlock. After awhile, they stopped asking. I guess they'd already learned what happened at Lester's. You should be able to get back in first thing in the morning. Meanwhile, we're all camping out here in the living room and Sally's at the hospital with Jennie. She said she'd call with news."

Betsy never slept that night and from her random peeks around the room throughout the night, none of the others had either. About 4 a.m., Jim came into the room and announced that the police were finished with their inspection of the crime scene and had released the property back to the owners, with a stern caution to stop all illegal and immoral activities. The ladies murmured.

"Hey, we been down that road before. We lay low for a couple of weeks and they stop bothering us," said Jim.

"Any word on Jennie?" asked Joan.

Jim shook his head. "No news is good news, so I'm told. I imagine Sally will be back soon, one way or another. She knows she's got things to deal with here."

Betsy raised her hand as if she were back in school, and then, embarrassed, lowered it. Jim chuckled. "Yes, Miss Betsy?"

"Can I get into my room now?"

The man nodded. "Need a bodyguard?" He smiled.

This time the girls giggled. One of the older hookers, asked, "Sure she does. Do you know one?"

Betsy didn't find it funny. Jim's question needed no answer, but the last thing she wanted was for Jim to get hurt. Her pa could break him in half with one hand. Dewey would use his knife or gun, but the result would be the same. She didn't want anyone else hurt on her account.

Jim gave the woman a strange look and then returned his attention to Betsy. "I'll come along anyway. For good measure."

Betsy walked across the patio area, through the gate and to her room, inspecting the door as soon as she got to it. It looked undisturbed, as did the large window ... as far as she could tell. She unlocked the padlock, entered the room, and gazed about. It, too, looked just as she left it.

"Lock up behind me and I'll keep an eye out while you're here." He backed out of the room and Betsy did as he asked. She checked her hiding spot and found her money and papers as she left them. Relieved to find her things undisturbed, she laid back on the bed to think. *What should I do next?* she asked herself. Exhausted, she quickly fell asleep.

A series of knocks on the door awoke her from a deep sleep. Confused and dazed, she sat up to get her bearings and realized the sound that woke her was indeed someone at the door. Betsy slipped off the bed and checked the peephole in the door, to find Sally there, tearful and haggard in the early dawn light.

Betsy unlatched the locks and let the woman into the room. Sally plopped down in the nearest wooden chair, distraught and disheveled.

"Jennie's gone," she whispered. "She made it out of surgery, but had lost too much blood. Oh dear God ..."

Betsy sank onto the bed at the news and wept.

The woman held her head in her hands and spoke to the floor. "Less than a year to go in school. Then she was going to make something of herself, get out of this awful business." Sally's ample chest heaved with a sob. "That's all I've ever wanted for my girls, the chance to do what they wanted, not what some pimp ordered them to do. She would have been my first to complete college."

Sally took a deep breath and looked up to Betsy. "Thank you." She paused, and then with a coldness in her voice that Betsy did not expect, she said, "Thank you for avenging their deaths. I was at the hospital. The killer didn't last as long as Jennie. For whatever that's worth."

Betsy's heart dropped at the realization she had killed him. Intentional or not. Self-defense or not. That he deserved it or not. The man was dead … from her actions.

The look on her face must have given away her despair, because Sally moved to sit next to her and put her arm around Betsy's shoulders. "Don't blame yourself. You couldn't have known what would happen. It would have been you or him on that bus, with Lester wounded and Roscoe dead. He had the gun, not you. What do you think he would have done? Let you go? You had to do it … and he deserved it. I talked with a detective at the hospital. They see this clearly as self-defense. You aren't in any trouble. None at all. In fact, the man told me the DA has agreed. 'Course, if he hadn't he'd be hearing from me and that's not something a man in an election year needs. They won't be holding you for anything."

Betsy knew in her head that Sally was right, and she knew with time, her heart would come to accept that as well. Today, however, she had to face up to what had happened.

Sally continued, "Lester made it through. The doctor said your quick thinking with the pressure dressing might have just made the difference. I think Lester'll do just about anything you ask of him now." She paused and locked onto Betsy, eye to eye. "He told me about the man at the bus stop. Your father?"

Betsy nodded.

"What do you want to do?"

"I think I need to leave. Find someplace else."

Sally returned the nod. "Well, I know this won't come easy, but you're gonna leave in style. In my last brief conversation with Jennie, before her surgery, she made one request. Sally held up a set of car keys. "It's yours. She willed it to you on her deathbed, to help you find your son."

Betsy lost her breath. "I, uh, I can't, I ..." she stammered.

"Look, they co-owned it. It's paid for, and there sure as hell ain't no next-of-kin I care to take time locating. This Mustang is yours now, girl. I can get you a title transfer by tomorrow. It'll take the state a week or two to process it. They can mail it back here and I'll get to it to you, wherever you are."

Betsy nodded.

"That much is settled then." Sally rose from the bed and took a step toward the door. "I've got …. things to tend to." Tears welled up and spilled onto her cheeks, as she left the room. Just outside the door, she turned back to Betsy. "Make something of yourself, Betsy Weston. You're a survivor. You got what it takes, so don't end up like me." She turned and scurried back through the gate to their living quarters.

Betsy pondered the comment for a moment and rose from the bed to close and lock the door. She'd only taken one step toward it when a hulking dark figure blocked the doorway, a silhouette she'd known all her life. He stepped inside and closed the door. She was trapped.

"Mornin' girl."

"H-how'd you get back here? Get away from me, you drunk! Or I'll scream and the owners'll come running."

"Yeah, like I'm scared of them. First off, I ain't drunk.

Might be in an hour, but not now. Second ... didn't come to make trouble. So just hush up, or you'll never know what I come to tell you."

Betsy stepped back, but refused to sit down. He might be sober, but he would never be trustworthy.

"Got wind of someone asking 'bout a baby. Give it up, girl. Never was no baby. No birth certificate on file anywhere. Made sure of that. You'll never find him and I ain't never gonna admit to anything but his being stillborn. Might be the boy's not even in this state, so how you or some lawyer ever gonna find him without me? Just give it up. Just know he's with a good home, a home what can give him the things you'll never be able to give 'im."

Betsy looked at her father with fear and loathing, knowing that without a birth certificate filed somewhere, her only proof lay buried at her old home. Yet, trying to reclaim that evidence was akin to suicide. If Dewey knew she was responsible for Ned's death, her death would be a slow and painful one. Plus, his point about the futility of searching county by county, even if just in adjacent states, rang true.

"Why? Why'd you do this to me?"

He pulled a thick, legal-sized manila envelope from inside his coat and tossed it on the bed. "I promised your mama I'd do one thing for her after she was gone. Hell, promised lots of things, but weren't really able to make good of 'em, 'cept this one." He paused and stared at Betsy for a minute as if trying to see something in her that he'd lost years earlier. "You know, I weren't never cut out for this father stuff, so I make no apologies. But, this is one thing I can give you ... the dowry your mama saved and saved for you. You might not believe it, but I loved your mama more than anythin', and I promised her I'd give it to you on your weddin' day. Since I ain't likely to ever see that, here it is. She also left you her favorite necklace. It's a family heirloom passed down from her great grandma. She hoped you'd like it."

Betsy picked up the envelope and saw that it remained sealed. Had her ma packaged it and sealed it? If so, she found it surprising that her pa had left it undisturbed all these years. Without looking up, she repeated, "Why did you take my son away from me?"

When she looked up for an answer, her pa had already stepped outside. He turned back toward her and said, "I know you hate me and can't say as I blame you. As your pa, I'm doing you one last favor. Best you leave. Dewey knows you're here."

Twenty
❧ ✦ ✦ ❧

Don't you worry none, hear?" Counselor Albritton said, as he ushered the older couple to the front door of his office. "I will make sure your family's land is protected from the developers."

The old woman turned to the lawyer and grabbed his hand. "Thank you, Sir. That land's been in my family since before the War of Independence." Her frail voice sounded reassured. "I don't think I could live, if it fell into the hands of the likes of those nasty men who came to our door and tried to force us to sell."

"Yes, Sir, Mr. Albritton, that land's meant to go to our grandchildren and great grandchildren. We're obliged that you're helpin' us make that possible."

"Mr. Carlson, Mrs. Carlson, consider it done." He smiled, and thought of his childhood days of crossing his fingers behind his back. He watched as they climbed into their decrepit sedan and crept off his lot onto Canoe Place and Valley Road. The old man was the kind of elderly driving hazard who incensed the drivers who came up on him as he crawled along the narrow, twisting, two-lane roads of the area and caused those stuck behind him to pull out their hair in large clumps.

As the car left his sight, a head popped up behind him. "Did that old bag call me nasty? "

"Quiet, Pryor. I'm sure if they'd seen you here they'd have found a better compliment."

"Yeah, and a few for you, too."

Albritton clapped his hand on the man's shoulder and laughed. "Enough to make their Baptist preacher's ears turn red, I'm sure."

The two men returned to the lawyer's office where a third man now sat. "Another client, another option. Do these folks have any idear at all what they's signin?"

"If they did, they wouldn't be giving me their John Hancocks now, would they?" Albritton gathered up the papers on his desk, placed them into a labeled manila folder, and filed them in a special drawer. "And with a little patience, two years, five, maybe ten, we'll have a nice piece of land ripe for developing." He went to his map with a red marker in hand and colored in another plot. He replaced the cap on the marker and used it to tap another spot on the map. "These folks are next."

However, the key to his dream remained elusive. The marked areas surrounded nearly two thousand acres that, when combined with his other "conquests," would make him a wealthy man.

"Middle of next week. Let's give this couple time to talk it up with friends, at their church, whatever. There's nothing like word-of-mouth advertising."

"Just say where and when, and Charlie and me'll go banging on some doors." The two men exchanged glances. "So, what's up with Dewey? We could use his help."

"He's busy with an important project, so don't pay no mind to him right now. He'll be back when he's done."

Gilmore started to say something, but stopped and stood up to join his partner. "Time fer supper."

Albritton prepared to go out to eat in celebration. In the past week, he'd picked up a dozen new clients, five of which were the result of his ploy, and the phone rang regularly throughout the day now. After a few more weeks of growth like that, he'd need a secretary, preferably young, buxom, and blond.

As he locked up his files, the phone rang.

"Emory Albritton."

"Well, little brother, told you I'd keep you informed and that's what I'm doing. A young woman's body washed up on shore near the dam on Thorpe Reservoir this afternoon. Been in the water awhile from what the coroner says, but Sheriff Connelly thought her size and hair matched the missing Cummings girl. So, we called Amos Cummings 'bout her, described the clothing, good teeth, no dental work, and a couple of small birthmarks, and he says it's her. Started cursin' Curt Umfleet up, down, right and left for takin' his little girl from him. Never was much good blood between the two men. Anyway, with the bloody clothes found at the Umfleet place, and now a body, the PA issued a warrant. The Sheriff's on his way as we speak to arrest Umfleet for her murder. Folks from Social Services are with him to take the children."

"What about Umfleet's statement that he took the girl to the bus stop and she left town."

"Yeah, well, I was with the Sheriff myself when we interviewed that driver. He'd been shot in Asheville and was still in the hospital. He told us he picked up a girl by name of Betsy Weston and, in fact, hired the girl to help him with the bus. She'd been in to visit him just the day before. He described her as about a hundred twenty-five pounds with shoulder-length, auburn hair. Wife backed that up outside the room. Seems the same girl was there when he was shot and she killed their attacker, so we talked with the detective. His description of the girl didn't match Alice either. He also mentioned she had a valid driver's license in the name of Betsy Weston and she'd just bought a Mustang convertible. DMV confirmed a pending title change for such a car to a Betsy

Weston. So, that story don't add up. Looks like ol' Curt Umfleet will be in jail a mighty long time, if the jury don't agree to execute him first."

Emory Albritton hung up and returned to his map. He was tempted to color in that two thousand acre plot right then, but he knew better than to act prematurely. First, he needed to convince Umfleet to let him help. There were papers to be signed and a petition to be placed before the court to become trustee on behalf of the children. Each step held its chance to sideline his ambitions, but he remained confident. He'd finish his coloring soon enough. That land wasn't going anywhere.

Twenty-one
(Present Day)
✥✥✥✥

As the Lear 60 XR reached cruising altitude, Myra glanced at Alexia who appeared to be savoring her first flight in a private jet. The fifty-eight foot fuselage could seat six as configured, so the two women had an abundance of room. Myra had flown with this company on more than one occasion so there was also an abundance of oenophilic temptation secured in the bar. Alexia had positioned herself between Myra and the libations, a move Samuel might reward with a bonus.

The young woman sat with a well-worn Bible in her lap. As she opened the book and began to read, Myra thought, "*Oh gawd, I hope she's not a Bible thumper.*" She watched Alexia as she read. After a few minutes, the woman glanced up and noticed Myra looking at her. She closed her Bible and said, "I think I could get accustomed to this." She ran her fingers along the soft leather upholstery.

"Not on a doctorate's salary," quipped Myra.

Alexia smiled. "So, how many books did it take to get to this level?"

"Too many."

"No, seriously, how long did it take to be able to afford this type of luxury?"

"After my third movie option, I chose to travel this way, but it was a stretch for my bank account. The next book and movie option made it much easier. But, remember, I'm single. My expenses, short of the mortgage, are minimal."

"Yeah, right."

Myra watched Alexia roll her eyes again. "Exaggerate the

eyes a little more and we might make a diva out of you, too."

Alexia smiled and repeated her gesture with more passion.

"Better. I guess if there was such a thing as a physical cliché, rolling the eyes would be near the top of the list. So, to answer you, I realize 'minimal' is a relative term."

Alexia put her Bible into her satchel, pulled out a steno pad, and jotted down a few notes. Myra nodded her head toward the notebook.

"About me?" She pointed to the steno pad. "Your notes."

"Sometimes. Sometimes an idea for a plot twist, or a character trait, comes into my head and I note it."

"Good discipline to have. And?" Myra nodded toward the pad again.

"And what? Oh. A character trait, definitely a character trait."

Myra chuckled, wondering what kind of trait that might be, modeled after her. Samuel was right. She might find this girl likeable after all, but she held on to her reservations about that.

"Are you working on a book?"

"Kinda. I have an idea, but I've been so preoccupied with school and moving, I don't have much right now."

"What about short stories? Anything. I need something to read."

Alexia sat upright in her seat. "Seriously? You'd be willing to read some of my stuff and brainstorm with me?" The young woman's countenance brightened.

"We have an hour to go on this flight. Go for it. I'm willing … if you can take the heat."

Alexia dug into her laptop case and pulled out a short sheaf of paper that Myra saw consisted of several works stapled at their top-left corners. Alexia handed her the second from the top, smiling.

"I, um, kinda hoped you would, so I came prepared. Samuel told me you like to read hardcopy, so I took the liberty."

Myra chuckled. "Maybe you should have been a Boy Scout."

Alexia gave her a sheepish grin. "Actually, I kinda was. Honorary. My dad was a Scoutmaster before he passed away."

Myra saw her fight to keep the tears at bay. She had been told about the relatively recent deaths of Alexia's parents. "I'm sorry about your parents."

Alexia wiped the tears from her cheek. "Thanks. It's been a rough year." She sniffed and sat upright. "Okay, so this is a short story I wrote in college and was among the several I submitted with my application for the doctorate program. My college prof really liked this one."

Myra didn't make it past the first page before commenting. "So, where's the hook, that first paragraph that grabs the reader and obligates her to continue? Nothing here says 'read on.'"

Alexia looked flustered. "I, uh … it's more of a literary piece than a thriller or mystery."

"Doesn't matter. All books need that hook to push the reader into the story."

Myra sped through the rest of the story and agreed with Alexia's assessment of the genre, as the piece was primarily character driven. The girl showed good command of structure and characterization, but her pacing was off and her prose needed tightening. What did they teach wannabe writers in college these days?

Within twenty minutes, Myra had Alexia near tears, until she admonished the young woman to grow thicker skin and shared her early life experience with rejection after rejection of her first books. Then, as if some switch turned on, Alexia began to grasp the core of Myra's criticisms. For the next hour, Myra gave Alexia a writing lesson every aspiring author in the country would donate their right arm to have, except they might need it to write.

By the time they landed, the young woman had filled of her steno pad ... and Myra knew Alexia would be up to the task, should Myra not survive to finish the story.

Two hours later, Myra's rental car pulled up the secluded drive at the Mabel Dodge Luhan House, its classic Pueblo Revival architecture in harmony with the surrounding sagebrush desert of the Taos Plateau. Built from an existing four-room, adobe structure by a crew from the Taos Pueblo around 1920, the house became a center for the arts and counterculture of that era. Willa Cather and D.H. Lawrence were among Mable's famous guests, a fact that had drawn Myra to the center early in her literary quest.

Alexia climbed out of the driver's seat and stared at the historic home.

"So, this is it, the place mentioned so much by the Utopian writers of the early 20th century."

"The one and only. Rustic, comfortable, and inspiring. Dennis Hopper edited 'Easy Rider' while staying here. I arrived here for the first time about fifteen years later, but slept in the same room as I looked for a cottage to rent while I wrote 'Rebecca's Bargain.' I've been back several times, once a year actually, always in the same room, the Ansel Adams Room."

Alexia examined the herringbone vigas supporting the roof and the traditional arched doorways of adobe construction on their way to the front desk.

"A reservation for Mitchell," Myra told the girl at the desk.

"Rustic is the word for this place, alright. I've, um, heard there're bugs in adobe homes."

Myra laughed. "True. Adobe bugs, but they don't eat much."

The young clerk inspected the reservation and announced, "Here we are. We have you booked together in Auntie's House."

Myra furrowed her brow. "What? I asked for and confirmed the Ansel Adams Room for myself."

An older woman stepped out from a nearby office.

"Myra, I thought I recognized your voice. It's good to have you back."

"Hello, Diana. I thought I had my usual room."

Alexia stepped up. "Sorry, it's my fault. I changed your reservation so we'd be together. I, uh …"

Alexia withered at Myra's stern look, yet Myra knew Samuel was behind it all. She looked at Diana.

"I'd like my usual room, please."

Diana scanned the computer screen and pressed a few keys, before scrunching up her lip and nose. "I don't think we can switch it now, Myra. I'm sorry. That room is tied up 'til the first of next week, maybe later. I could give you the Gate House Cottage, if you want more room."

"Can I bribe the occupant?"

"Actually, it's not occupied. We're repainting and putting in a new bed. The adobe bugs finally ate the old one." She winked at Myra while watching Alexia squirm.

Myra smiled. "Can I bribe the painters and pest control guy?"

"Sure, if you don't mind sleeping on the floor."

Myra gave a quick nod. "It's settled then. We have Auntie's House." She walked around behind the desk and gave Diana a hug. "Good to see you, too. I'm looking forward to a little peaceful solitude. Life threw a hard ball at me last week."

She heard Alexia whisper, "Cliché." As she turned toward the young woman, Alexia raised her brow and glanced away, as if saying, "Did I say that? Gotcha."

"So I heard." The manager looked Myra up and down and then addressed Alexia. "In Mabel's own words, she envisioned this house as a retreat for the movers and shakers of the earth, as a place to relax and recover their energy. Many come here for solitude and a time of peaceful contemplation. So, one of our main rules here is ... 'No divas allowed.' I hope you'll keep her in line." She smiled. "Again, welcome. If I can do anything for you, please, let me know … and, Myra, I have your lab visit all set up. End of the week, as requested."

"Thank you, dear."

After Alexia left the reception area to move the car and retrieve their luggage, Diana motioned Myra to join her in the back office.

"Are you okay?" she asked.

Myra plopped down into a chair, unsure if she had the energy to stand again. They'd known each other for almost two decades and Diana knew more about Myra's past than all but one other friend.

"We all have to die sometime," said Myra.

"Wow, that's not something I ever thought I'd hear you say."

"Well, it's true. I've come to accept it and if I ever begin to dwell on how much that scares me, I-I don't know what I'd do."

Diana sat down next to her and took her hand. "What can I do?"

"Nothing, unless you can conjure up a close relative as a living donor."

"I'm willing."

Myra gave her friend a wan smile. "I know you are, but I already know we're not a match. Different blood types. Remember?" Myra smiled at a memory. They had both volunteered to donate blood for a mutual friend. Both had been incompatible with the friend and with each other. As it ended up, Myra's incompatibility with that "friend" extended beyond blood types. Marriage number three wasn't meant to be.

A tear trickled down Diana's cheek. She looked Myra straight in the eyes.

"He still asks about you, you know. Just last week, as a matter of fact."

"Before or after I made the gossip rags?"

"Before. I haven't seen him since I heard about your collapse at the hotel."

"Probably drunk somewhere. Tell him you haven't seen or heard from me. I want nothing to do with him."

Diana sighed and nodded. "Ironic. You left him because of his alcoholism and now look at you."

Myra felt as if she'd been slapped hard in the face, but the comment was true. Why did she always end up with the same type of guy? Wine had been only a social tool before meeting Ricardo, not a food group. However, she fell into his hard partying lifestyle until it merged into her own soul and became part of her. He might have become husband number three had she not grown tired of his late night binges, missed appointments, and frequent overnight stays in the Taos drunk tank. She left him sober, missed him terribly, and took up drinking to forget him. *That* hadn't worked out.

By the time Myra entered the front door of Auntie's House, Alexia had carried all of their bags into their respective bedrooms and unpacked one of her suitcases. Myra walked toward the kitchenette to find water near boiling on the stove.

"I thought you might like some tea," said Alexia, poking her head out the doorway of her bedroom.

"That's not exactly what I had in mind," Myra replied as she poked around the cabinets. "But I have no choice, do I?"

A minute later, Myra sat outside on the small patio with a steeping mug of Earl Grey. She felt the warmth of the brew in her hands and stared northeast toward the Taos Mountain, popularized as a sacred site by Mabel Dodge Luhan who credited learning about the power of *Mó-ha-loh* from her husband Tony Luján of the Taos Pueblo. Myra had been privileged to make the trek to Blue Lake, but could make no claim to witnessing the "Faceless Ones," the ancestral dead wrapped in blankets and standing by the trees watching over their mountain and their people.

She sat lost in thought as memories of past trips flitted through her mind. Maybe the Mountain did like her, but she never gave much credence to a mountain having "power" or that the dead could directly influence the living. Yet, as she sat there, she felt peaceful, as if none of the past week's events had happened.

"You're different here."

Myra woke from her reverie and looked up to find Alexia standing next to her.

"As Diana said, no divas allowed."

"Seriously."

Myra thought about Alexia's comment for a moment. "Maybe I am. I was just thinking about the history of this place … Taos, not the house, and the other pueblos for that matter. Each has its own sacred mountain. The Santa Clara Reservation has Chicoma Mountain. Here, they have Taos Mountain, or Pueblo Peak to some … about ten miles that way." Myra pointed toward the mountain. "No matter what you believe in, for me, I've always found peace here … and inspiration."

Alexia looked off toward the mountain and then back to Myra. "Christianity is my key to living. I grew up with two alcoholic parents and my mom died of liver cancer when I was in my early teens. That's what I meant when I said I was no stranger to liver failure. My dad abandoned me and without any other family, I went into the foster system. The parents who just recently passed away were actually my adoptive parents. They saw something in me I never saw in myself and with a life centered on Christ, they offered me a home, gave me my education. Personally, I wasn't sure about all that religion stuff. I withdrew, looking for answers in books. In college, I had a course that required reading the Bible as a literary source. I found more than that there. I saw the source of my new parents' love. Something in Christ's teachings just clicked for me and then I found a vibrant church with a young pastor who showed us that living for God was not the stuffy, "Thou shall not" kind of lifestyle portrayed by so many. After that, the bond between my parents and me just grew and grew. That's why their deaths this past year hit me so hard."

She paused and Myra caught her watching, waiting for Myra's reaction, which was one of subtle resistance outwardly while inside she wondered what she had done to Samuel to make him inflict this girl on her. Never mind. She knew what she had done, repeatedly. Still, something in Alexia's story touched her. Alexia had been given something special. Few people, including Myra, ever experienced such love.

"Sorry, I know a lot of people hate preachy Christians, so I'll stop. I don't want to overstep any bounds here, but I do want you to know I'm praying for you, for you to have peace and for God's gift of healing for you. There, I'm done. What can I do for you?"

Myra, too, had read the Bible as a literary source but certainly had not come away from the experience with anything more than a collection of stories and allegorical phrases that all writers needed to connect with Western culture. Nevertheless, something in Alexia's statement filled her with hope that God, if He existed as described by Judeo-Christian tradition, offered healing as a gift. Myra wanted to know more, but hesitated to ask in fear of being overwhelmed by zealotry.

"I'd like a little time to myself, please."

Alexia nodded and returned inside. A few minutes later, Myra watched her new assistant walk toward the office. She remained outside until sunset and the nocturnal chill of the desert forced her inside to the kiva fireplace. She held a vague recollection of Alexia returning, helping her to bed, tucking her in as a mother would her child, and kneeling silently at her bedside.

The next morning, Myra found Alexia sitting on the patio gazing at the mountains as the sun rose over them. The pastel pinks of the sky backlit the Taos Range of the Sangre de Cristo Mountains.

"Did you see them last night?" Myra asked.

"Them?"

"The mountains."

"I guess not. I was busy trying to locate someone."

"They were gorgeous. You know they got their name from the Spanish because the snowcaps of the higher mountains glow red with the setting sun. Thus, Sangre de Cristo, the 'blood of Christ.' I, uh ..." Myra wanted to ask her question from the previous night but stopped. Not now. "Umm, no never mind."

She turned away to head to the Big House for breakfast, although she had no appetite. She stopped about ten feet away and turned back to Alexia.

"Ready for breakfast? I have a task for you when you're done."

Alexia looked up again, closed the book she held in her lap and replied, "Sure. I'll be ready in a wink."

Myra started to comment about the cliché but noticed a glint of mischief in Alexia's eye. Alexia was baiting her. She let it ride but noted the book was a well-read, make that a worn, copy of the Bible. Alexia walked into the cottage and exited a moment later without it. Myra waited as Alexia caught up to her.

"I guess I should thank you."

"For what?" asked Alexia.

"For your prayers. I've never had anyone tell me that before ... but, to be honest, I'm not sure I believe it will do anything. Still, I thank you for your sincerity and concern."

Alexia shrugged. "Then I guess I should say you're welcome. I can't say I've ever had anyone thank me for that." She smiled. "What's the chore you have for me?"

"Nothing much, really. I want you to return the rental car. We won't be needing it."

189

*　*　*

"What? Dewey, tell me that again!" Albritton nearly screamed into the phone.

"I couldn't actually get into the Tehama community through the front door. The residents even clear deliveries to get 'em past the gate, so I couldn't fake one. I managed to find a way through the wooded hillsides to an overlook where I could watch the Mitchell lady's house. No one. Nada. No sign of life there."

"So, find out where they went."

"I'm working on it. Alright? I managed to learn that floral deliveries is bein' turfed to two nearby nursin' homes. That means the lady didn't want any more, or she was leavin' town and knew to expect more flowers. I also learnt a car service picked up two women at that residence two days ago. I expect all this bribe money to be reimbursed, by the way."

"And the car took them where?"

"Monterey Peninsula Airport, and that's as far as I got."

Albritton rapped his knuckles in four-quarter time on the desk as he thought, but stopped before they might bruise. He had run over his opponents in the senate primary, but his Republican rival was a savvy foe who wouldn't hesitate to use any dirt he could come with to win. He needed to know what the Hamilton girl had. "Find them!"

Twenty-two
(Spring – 1969)
❧✦✦❧

Betsy awoke at first light in the back seat of her car. Her neck and low back ached as her stomach growled. She had left The Rest Stop by noon the day before, but she hadn't gone far. The owner of the diner across from the brothel had allowed her to park in his shed behind the eatery. She heard a knock on the door. The owner opened it just wide enough to squeeze through.

"You up in there?"

Betsy opened her door and eased out of the car.

"There ya are. Want the light on?"

Betsy paused. She hadn't used the light for fear of someone seeing it during the night. But now, it was unlikely anyone would notice. "Sure. What time is it?"

"Almost eight. Figured you might be hungry. Brought your favorite." He handed her a plate covered with a clean dishtowel.

Steam and the most delicious aroma Betsy knew arose from the plate as she uncovered it. A garbage plate. Indeed, one of her favorites. Scrambled eggs, hash browns, red and green peppers, ham, cheese, onions, jalapeño, bacon, and anything the cook decided to throw in, all cooked together. Today, Betsy saw some mushrooms. She smiled.

"Nice to see you smile again."

"Thanks, Cal. How much do I owe you?"

He shook his head and waved his hand back and forth. "Nothin'. It's on me today."

"You sure? I can pay for it."

"Nope. You'll need the money. Besides, that cartoon you

191

gave me last night is payment enough. It'll be worth somethin' someday. I know it and you can count on it."

Betsy smiled again and then took a bite, closing her eyes to savor the taste. "Thanks, Cal." She had a long day ahead of her, provided Sally came through with the papers for the title transfer. The day marked a new day of exhilaration and anxiety for Betsy.

"Hey, um, Betsy, I couldn't help but overhear you talkin' with the others a few days ago. You mentioned somethin' when talkin' about the home where you had your baby, a newspaper."

"The Mountain Press?"

"That's the one. I got a cousin in Sevierville that sent me some things last Christmas and they was wrapped in old copies of that paper. Were you near Sevierville somewhere? That's where that newspaper's printed."

Cal had Betsy's full attention. Sevierville did ring a bell. Her pa's cousin's husband, Erby, had been gone for a day to pick up a new wood stove in that Tennessee town. She nodded. "Maybe so. They didn't take me out much, but some of the men stopped by to get Erby saying they were going to a saloon called the Rebel Railroad."

Cal nodded. "Pigeon Forge. A couple a boys from Blowing Rock had what they called a theme park by name of 'Tweetsie' in Blowing Rock. Involved an old steam engine train up the mountain. They started up another in the Forge and they call it the 'Rebel Railroad.' Been to both of them personally. You want to find your family there, that's the place to start, Pigeon Forge."

Cal provided driving directions along U.S. Highways 19 and 441. Once in Pigeon Forge, Betsy was on her own.

* * *

Shortly after 10 a.m., Cal and Sally emerged from the back door of the diner and walked toward the shed. Betsy watched them through the window where she'd sat most of the morning trying to remember what she could about the area around Erby and Maisy Duncan's home, entering those random thoughts in her journal. She would soon need a second book. She also used her sketchpad to draw a picture of the house itself and was very satisfied with the result.

Cal opened the door and allowed Sally to enter first.

"Morning," said Betsy.

Sally looked ten years older than when Betsy had first arrived. The emotional strain of the previous forty-eight hours had taken its toll on them both, for different reasons. Today, though, Betsy felt a renewed energy surge. Thanks to Cal, she had a new focus, and the hope that she would find Maisy Cummings Duncan, and through her, Jimmy Bob.

Sally handed Betsy some papers. "Here's the paperwork you need to sign. I'll make sure it gets mailed to Raleigh and will hold onto the new title until you let me know where to send it. You keep one copy to show as proof that the transfer is being processed. You'll need to repeat this process in whatever state you end up in, to get it titled in that state."

Betsy signed the form and Sally took the copies she needed to mail. "I'm gonna miss you, Betsy Weston, but I ain't gonna try to talk you into staying. I wouldn't want to lose you, too." Sally looked over to Cal. "Tell her, Cal."

"Man came in for breakfast this morning, 'bout half hour after I brought your food out here. Rough lookin' man. Started askin' questions about The Rest Stop and if any new girls had started there. Told him 'no' 'cause, in truth, you never actually worked there. But he kept eyein' your cartoon. He'd look at it, then at me and back and forth while he drank his coffee." Cal paused and glanced down. "He finally asks 'bout the cartoon, says he knew a girl what could draw like that. I told him a famous artist from out East stopped in for lunch, and enjoyed it so much she drew the cartoon in about ten minutes and gave it to me. Lord forgive me for lying but I sure wasn't about to tell him the truth."

Dread filled Betsy from the top of her scalp to the tip of her toes.

"Uh, w-what did this man look like?"

"About my height, but wiry. Strong. Mean. Dark haired. Mostly though, what really stands out is the scar along the left side of his face, from here to here." Cal demonstrated on his face.

"D-did this man ask any more questions? Did you see where he went when he left?"

Cal shook his head. "Sorry. Had customers to wait on. From the look on your face right now, though, I wish I had. I'm real sorry, Betsy."

Betsy nodded and stepped forward to give the man a hug. He'd done nothing wrong. "Cal, you had no way of knowing, but I have to leave right now. I can't stick around any longer."

Sally nodded and tears formed in her eyes. She moved toward Betsy and took both of Betsy's hands. "You have a gift in these hands, and in that head of yours. Don't waste it. Will we see you again?"

Tears welled up in Betsy's eyes as well. "Can't say as I know. I'd like to say 'yes,' but how can I promise such a thing?" She hugged Sally and then briefly placed a hand on Cal's arm. "Cal, if that man comes back and asks any more questions, tell him you heard the artist was in town to tour the Biltmore and then would be heading back to New York. I think you'll be forgiven that little lie, too."

Betsy moved toward the car, but Cal stopped her. "Here." He held out a wicker basket lined with another dish towel and covered by the same one he'd used at breakfast to cover her plate. "Some sandwiches. Fried chicken. Apples and sweet tea. Should last you a couple of days."

She stepped back toward him, gave him a kiss on the cheek, and took the basket. She placed it on the back seat and climbed behind the wheel. A soon as Cal had fully opened the door, she eased out of the shed and turned down the alley away from the diner and The Rest Stop. She kept glancing into her mirrors and between buildings, looking for any sign of the man with the scar, Dewey Hastings. She moved slowly, with the car at a near idle, hoping to avoid any engine noise that could draw attention to her. Three blocks down, she turned onto a back road heading west and gunned it.

"Are you sure there's no family by name of Duncan?" Betsy's heart sank at the clerk's denial of their Post Office branch delivering to such a family. She pulled her drawing from her purse and showed it to the man. "Does this house look familiar?"

"Sorry, Miss. Lotsa houses 'round here look like that but, again, we don't deliver to any Duncans."

Betsy had arrived in Pigeon Forge around 1 p.m. and found her way to the Post Office. She had figured that they would know of the family, if anyone in town knew of them. Why had she convinced herself that this would be easy?

"Are there any other Post Offices nearby?"

"Well, sure. Sevierville has a few to our north. There's Gatlinburg to the south and Townsend to the southwest. Further west is Walland, near Chilhowee Gap. Further east is

Cocke."

Another memory came to Betsy. "There was a river flowing through the town."

The clerk rubbed his chin in contemplation. "Let's see. Cocke and Gatlinburg don't fit that bill, although the Little Pigeon River runs between 'em. Townsend and Walland both got the Little River. That help any?"

It did. Erby Duncan had mentioned the Little River several times when he wanted to go fishing. "Thanks. That does help. How do I get to Townsend?" Betsy's emotional roller coaster was on its way up again.

After getting directions, Betsy stopped at a nearby filling station for gas and began the thirty-minute drive to Townsend. The other town was but ten minutes further down the road.

At the Post Office in Townsend, she repeated her questions. They had Duncans in their delivery area, but no Erby or Maisy. Betsy felt confident. At least the family name was common there. There had to be Duncans just minutes away. She thanked the clerk and continued down the road. She had plenty of time before the office closed for the day. Just a minute into her drive, she passed an IGA store and recognized it as the one where she and Maisy had shopped for groceries a few times together. Yes! She was on the right track.

In Walland, she approached the postal clerk after waiting behind two other customers.

"Yes, Miss. How can I help you?"

"I'm looking for an Erby and Maisy Duncan. I've been there once but can't recall how to find their house." She held up her drawing. She started to mention they were family, but stopped short.

The clerk looked sad and shook his head. "Such a shame. Did you know them well?"

Her pulse quickened. She wanted to say, "Yes, that she had lived with them for six months," but something inside warned her to remain cautious. "Not real well."

"You knew that Erby had a bit of a drinking problem, right?"

Betsy nodded. The man had been much like her pa, but limited his alcohol to weekends and holidays. The clerk started jotting something down on a piece of notepaper.

"Sad, really," the clerk said as he continued writing. "All they could guess was the man got drunk and accidentally started the fire. Place burned down around them as they slept. Poor souls. I hope they didn't wake up in the middle of that one. Damn near set the mountain on fire."

Betsy's mind went blank as her heart went numb. Her final chance for finding a lead to her baby, gone. Too many deaths. Maisy had been so kind to her. The thought of dying like that made every nerve in her body rattle. She struggled to maintain her composure and to keep tears from her eyes.

"I-I'm so sorry to hear that. I, uh, when did this happen?"

"Saturday, a week ago."

Betsy realized her pa might have played an unwitting role in their deaths. He had provided Erby with an ample supply of white lightning in return for his "help." Maisy did all the work, but Erby was "paid" for putting up with Amos' problem child. If even just one of those Mason jars had broken near open flame, the result would have been like a gasoline bomb exploding.

The man kept writing, glancing up at Betsy intermittently. "Funeral was five days ago. They're buried over at the family plot in Miller's Cove Cemetery. Here's directions on gettin' there, if you want to pay your respects." He slid the note across the counter toward Betsy.

She was about to ask about a midwife named Sue Ellen when one glance at the note made her grab it up and her adrenaline flow. "Thanks, I might do that," she said before spinning around and darting from the building. She climbed into her car and sped east, the way she'd come into town. She kept a close eye on her rear view mirror and didn't slow down until she reached the northern city limits of Sevierville, TN. Convinced that no one had followed her, she pulled over at a little park with picnic tables overlooking the Little Pigeon River, according to the plaque there.

She unraveled the crumpled note and took this opportunity to read it in full for the first time. "Duncans died like I said. Don't want no trouble." His last words were the ones that caught her attention at the time. "Beware. Dewey Hastings in town."

Dewey Hastings sat in his pickup truck in the drive behind the Millers Cove Baptist Church. He had a good view of the adjacent cemetery and was convinced he'd be seeing a yellow Mustang drive up soon. From his one quick look in Asheville, the gal driving it looked nothing like Alice Cummings, but she knew where Alice was. Of that, he was sure. He figured her to be working for the lawyer who'd been asking around about Alice's baby. A yellow Mustang had been seen in Frampton Corner on at least one occasion since Alice left. A car like that stands out in a small town.

But he had no interest in the car, 'cept of course should he "inherit" it by some unfortunate event. He smiled at that thought. Sure 'nuff, that was a nice car. Classy. Suited to a man like him.

His real interest was in finding Alice Cummings. He had

learned from Amos that she'd witnessed him killing those two people. He couldn't leave such a loose end untied. Folks, including the sheriff and DA all believe her to be dead. He needed to make sure they were never proven wrong. She could put the noose around his neck. There was no statute of limitations on murder.

He nibbled on corn chips and sipped a soda as he waited. He had one other dilemma to solve. That cartoon in the diner. It looked like Alice's work, but the name on it said "Betsy" somebody. On his way home, he would detour back to Asheville and claim that cartoon for himself.

Dewey glanced at his watch. No visitors to the cemetery and the Post Office would be closing soon. He started his truck and headed back to town. He barged into the Post Office and ahead of the line of last minute customers.

Dewey slammed his fist onto the counter. "She show up?" His scowl left those in line silent.

The clerk looked nervous as he nodded. "Yes, Sir. Around two-thirty. Yellow mustang, like you said. I did just as you asked. I gave her directions to the cemetery."

"She didn't show up there."

"What can I say? She left in that direction. I couldn't force her to go there. She must have kept driving east."

Dewey wanted to wring a neck. Anybody's neck. But he knew better. This was a small town, backwoods Post Office. The clerk probably had a shotgun behind the counter. He growled and stormed back out the door.

Headin' east, he thought. Back to Asheville. He had no chance of catching up to her, but he had to get that cartoon anyway. He could afford one more day of watching that whorehouse and diner. Maybe he'd even make use of their services.

Twenty-three
❧✦✦❧

Betsy had found a clean residential area that looked safer than the environs of The Rest Stop and parked in front of a house with a bright front porch light. For the second night, after her routine journal entry, she slept in the back seat. Tonight, though, she would have to spring for a motel room. She needed a shower, change of clothes, and a bed, not necessarily in that order.

That morning, she rose early and drove north, out of Sevierville where a newer road led north to the new Interstate Highway System. She'd heard about this highway project started by President Eisenhower, and had seen the cars and trucks speeding through Asheville on the recently completed Interstate 40. No way was she confident enough in her driving to compete with those high-speed idiot drivers.

Now, however, following a detailed consultation with her road map before sleeping, she knew she must brave these new highways if she wanted to cut down on her travel time. Her meager funds mandated an expedited trip, and Cincinnati was her destination. Of the top three greeting card companies, Gibson Greetings in the Queen City was the closest and therefore, first on her list.

She crossed over the Interstate and pulled off at the top of the entrance ramp. Below her, cars and trucks of every size zipped by at speeds she found dizzying. She exited the car and paced beside it, taking deep breaths while periodically glancing at the road below. She glanced over her shoulder at one point and upon seeing a long break in the traffic, decided to go for it. She raced back to the driver's seat, put the car in gear, and started down the ramp at 35 m.p.h. As she moved into the near lane, she managed to take her eyes off the road ahead and glance into her rearview mirror in time to see an eighteen-wheeler bearing down on her. At that moment, the rig's air-horn blasted the driver's displeasure with her with one long blast, followed by her heart racing to Indy 500 track speeds.

Her knuckles blanched on the wheel as she prepared to die in the impact, but the semi whizzed past her in the adjacent lane, the driver throwing her one more irritable blast of the horn for her dastardly driving. She kept her eyes forward, preferring not to see death coming from behind and slowly increased her speed.

After a few miles and dozens of additional sonorous snorts from passing vehicles, she realized the lanes were wide, the pavement smooth, and the curves tamed so that higher speeds were more comfortable than the slow speeds she was accustomed to on the mountainous two-lane widow-makers where she learned to drive.

She crept up to the speed limit in time to slow down for the Knoxville city limits. A new panic set in. She needed to take I-75 north. How did that work? She noticed a sign above the lane announcing the northbound and southbound exits for I-75 and wondered if she would have to exit or come to a stoplight to make the turn.

She found herself distracted by the city's buildings. While Asheville had seemed big, Knoxville appeared enormous. Another blaring car horn brought her attention from the skyline back to the road where she suddenly realized the exit for the next leg of her journey was upon her. She veered into the exit lane, narrowly missing a car coming up behind her in that lane, and a minute later found herself on northbound I-75. She smiled at the seamless transition and admired the efficiency of this new highway system, despite her near miss as a motor vehicle fatality headlining the evening news.

Three hours and one gas stop later, she found herself driving past towns named Erlanger and Fort Mitchell. They had been little more than names on the map of northern Kentucky, but as she passed through she knew they signaled the beginnings of urban development for a city larger than anything she'd experienced before, her final destination, Cincinnati. She entered a sweeping, downhill curve through a cut in the hill and the downtown skyline appeared, dominated by a tall building with a large orange "Central Trust" sign at the top and a taller building behind it.

Awed by the tall buildings, confused by the Interstate signage, and dazed by the traffic, she had made two wrong turns, stopped for directions three times, and found herself heading toward Columbus on I-71. She pulled off to the side of the road at the first spot she thought as being safe to do so. Traffic whizzed past her as she stood by the trunk of the car, trying to make heads and tails of her map.

Flashing lights caught her peripheral vision and she turned to see a State Highway Patrol car pull in behind her. The officer donned his hat as he emerged from the car.

"Are you okay, Miss? It's not really safe on the side of these highways."

"I'm sorry, officer. I've never been to a city this big and I'm totally lost."

The officer smiled as if she'd said something funny. His look confused her. "So, where are you heading?"

She showed him the map and pointed to a spot on it. "This place. I need to go to Gibson Greeting Cards in the morning."

"Easy. You just go ..." He gave her simple directions. "By the way, there's a motel just a half mile or so north, here on Reading Road. It's called the Carousel. You might find it acceptable."

She smiled. "Why, thank you, Officer ..." She scrutinized his nametag. "... Mueller. I will surely look into it."

He gave her that funny smile again and she stepped toward the road, heading toward the driver's door. That second, the patrolman's arms grabbed her and pulled her back, just as a garbage truck careened past, close enough to have trashed her with one more step.

The following morning she left her room at the Carousel Inn and walked down the steps to the motel's front office. Despite clear directions, ones she thought she had understood, it had taken her almost an hour the previous afternoon to find the motel and the little community of Roselawn, which was supposed to be only a twenty-minute drive from where she'd stopped on the highway.

"Good morning, young lady," said the clerk as she entered the office. "How may I help you?"

"I'm looking for a good place to eat, not too expensive, and a bank."

He pulled out a small assortment of local menus and prepared to present them to her. "Couple of banks along Reading Road here – Provident, Fifth Third, and a couple of savings and loans. Just head south. That way." He pointed to his right. "Here visiting?"

"No Sir. Job hunting. I'm applying for a job as a writer at the greeting card company."

He looked her up and down and gave her the same funny smile as the highway patrolman. "Have you applied already?"

"No, Sir. I just arrived in town yesterday."

"Know anybody who works there?"

"No, Sir."

"I see." His manner became abrupt. "Well, uh, here's what I have in way of local menus." He handed them to her and gave her time to peruse them.

As she handed them back, she asked, "If I might ask, why did you ask if I knew anyone there, at Gibson?"

"Just wondered. It's a solid company and folks seem happy there. I don't see many ads for jobs there and I know 'cause I'm always lookin' for something better than this. I figure folks who know someone there might just have a better chance."

Betsy scrutinized the man. She read between the lines that he hoped to find an "in" for himself as well.

He smiled and said, "Anything else?"

"No, Sir. Thank you for your trouble."

He chuckled and repeated that same odd smile. "Love the accent."

She smiled and headed out the door. Her accent? She climbed into the Mustang and drove south until she found a small bagel bakery. She'd never had a bagel before, but soon found herself imitating others around her in slathering cream cheese onto a warm cinnamon, raisin bagel and devouring it. Her belly satisfied, she drove further south until coming upon a Fifth Third Bank. She opened a passbook savings account with all but a hundred dollars of her cash and took a small safety deposit box for her important papers and her great, great grandmother's necklace.

As she left the vault, the young woman assisting her commented, "Love that accent. I bet it drives the guys crazy."

Betsy laughed. "I wouldn't know. Back home we don't have any accent."

She tucked her box key into her wallet, but then thought better of it and moved it to a zippered compartment in her purse. Moments later, she sat in her car, contemplating her next move. She had dressed for a job interview, unsure but hopeful that she would get one on the spot, and now realized she had another potential asset besides the samples of her writing tucked into her purse. "My sweet southern drawl," she said aloud, laying it on thick as sorghum, as she had when she had called the Umfleet house and talked with the deputy. She wondered how Curt and his kids were doing without Mary. She made a mental note to call him, once she had a job and some money rolling in. She also needed to send Sally a forwarding address, once she had one.

She noted the time on a clock in the bank window and took a deep breath. It was time.

She drove north and turned east onto the road where the bakery sat. Less than a mile later, she turned into the long drive down a grassy slope to the Gibson Greetings, Inc. headquarters. Gibson was number three behind Hallmark and American Greetings, but she found her confidence flagging at the thought of trying the top two companies. Besides, Hallmark was another long day's drive west to Kansas City, and American was in Cleveland. Who'd want to live in a place where the river catches fire?

She found her way to the employment office where a middle-aged woman in a perfectly fitted, skirted suit greeted her from behind a cluttered desk.

"Good morning, Ma'am. My name's Betsy Weston and I'd like to apply for a job as a writer."

The woman paused for a moment, gave Betsy an amused glance, and looked about before answering.

"Mr. Gordon isn't available today, and I don't believe

205

we're looking for any new writers right now."

Betsy shuffled her feet a bit. She felt like a small town country bumpkin at that moment, but she had done her research. The thought came to her that she'd stopped a cold-blooded killer, why was she feeling so timid? Where the surge came from she had no idea, but her confidence soared. "I see. Might I ask you a question?"

The secretary nodded. "Sure, sweetie."

"Well, I, uh, I've read maybe a hundred of y'all's greeting cards in the past week, so I think I've got a pretty good feel for your writers' work. They're all men, aren't they?"

Betsy noted a slight gleam in the woman's eyes as a brief smile crossed her face.

"As a matter of fact, I think you're right."

"And they're all middle-aged or older, right?"

The woman's smile returned and stayed. "Right again, sweetie. You picked this all up just reading our cards?"

"Yes, Ma'am, and I bet other folks can tell, too, subconsciously anyway. I think y'all need some young blood and a female perspective on that writing staff of yours."

The older blond woman took a deep breath and eyed Betsy from head to toe and back. Betsy knew the woman had underestimated her and sat there now, re-evaluating the young girl with the southern drawl.

"And you're just the woman to fill the bill, right, Sweetie?"

"Yes, Ma'am, I am. Can I make an appointment to meet with Mr. Gordon?"

"Hmmm. Sweetie, I want you to know that I agree with you one hundred percent, but good luck selling yourself to Mr. Gordon. He plays golf with those middle-aged writers. He and his wife socialize with those writers and their wives, and he's as old-fashioned as they come when it comes to hiring." She leaned closer to Betsy and whispered, "That means he's as chauvinistic as they come about hiring women."

She sat back in her chair. "But I'll be happy to make that appointment for you. Do you have any samples of your writing?"

"Sure do, Ma'am." Betsy opened her purse and retrieved the samples she had created. They were dog-eared and crumpled, so she placed them on the edge of the desk and tried to flatten them out with the palm of her hand. "Sorry. I didn't think they'd get so wrinkled in my purse."

"Don't worry, sweetie. I'll take care of them before he gets to see them. May I?" She held up the top two sample cards. "Did you draw these as well?"

Betsy nodded.

"Wow, you draw very well. Maybe you're applying for the wrong job." She opened the first card and smiled. She repeated the process through all dozen samples, giggling at a couple of them. "I must say, I'm impressed. Sweetie, tell you what. Mr. Gordon will be back day after tomorrow. Why don't you come in after lunch, say one-fifteen and I'll make sure he meets with you. That'll give me time to work on him."

Betsy's smile illuminated the room. "Thank you, Ma'am. Thank you."

At that moment, another woman, younger and brunette, entered the room and the lady behind the desk stood to give up her seat to the new arrival. The younger woman handed some papers to the older blond lady.

"Thank you," said the blond lady. "Carol, this is Betsy Weston. I promised her an appointment with Mr. Gordon for one-fifteen the day he's back."

Carol looked at the older woman and narrowed her eyes,

questioning her.

"I take full responsibility. I'm taking these samples with me. I'll make sure he sees them. Well, I have to get to the Woman's Club."

Betsy looked back and forth between the women, confused.

The woman she had assumed to be the secretary approached Betsy and held out her hand. "Nice to meet you, Betsy Weston. I'm Georgia Gordon, and I promise to work on my husband as soon as he gets back from Memphis. I look forward to seeing you again."

Betsy was not accustomed to sweating. No matter how hard she worked, played, or worried she rarely broke a sweat. It wasn't in her nature. Yet, she sat in the employment office at one-ten, five minutes until the biggest appointment in her life, feeling as if someone had drenched her with a bucket of water. She worried that it showed and longed for a mirror to check her armpits, neck, and any other place that might display her nervousness.

She had spent the previous day and a half working on new cards. When she blocked on ideas, she got into the Mustang and drove, both to familiarize herself with the city and to gain confidence driving in city traffic. She also looked for a place to rent, preferably furnished, and found several possibilities in Roselawn and nearby Gulf Manor. Mostly, though, she worked on her goal of a dozen new cards.

At one-fifteen precisely, by the clock on the wall, the phone rang and Angie nodded to whatever she heard after picking up. She stood and took three steps to her boss' door.

"He's ready for you."

Betsy took a deep breath and stood.

"Hey, you look fine. Don't be nervous. He's really a pretty good guy, just old fashioned. Besides, you have Georgia on your side. If anyone can soften him up, she can. Good luck."

Betsy thanked her, held her head up, and walked through the door. Greg Gordon stood at his desk and beckoned Betsy to have a seat. To Betsy's eye, he stood just shy of six feet tall, erect with the bearing and short-cropped salt-and-pepper hair of a military officer.

"Good afternoon, Miss Weston. I'm Greg Gordon. Please, have a seat." He sat on the corner of his desk and looked her over. "Can we get you something to drink? Water? Tea? A soft drink?"

Betsy sat in the straight-backed chair, knees together and hands folded on her lap. "No, thank you, Sir. I'm fine."

"Well, I must say, you have won a strong advocate in my wife. I don't know what you did to bewitch her, but she chewed my ear off about needing some fresh perspective on our writing staff."

Betsy looked him squarely in the eyes. "I can't say as I know why either, Sir, except that she liked my work. Isn't that really what it's about? The quality of the work."

Mr. Gordon laughed. "Well, Miss Weston, when my wife said you were a straight hitter, she meant it. Right to the point I see."

"Yes, Sir. Your time is valuable and I don't see a need to waste it."

Mr. Gordon smiled and focused on her.

"How old are you?"

"Almost nineteen, but I'm legally emancipated. I have the papers to prove it."

"Any family?"

"No, Sir."

"Well, if we get to the point of hiring, we'll worry about confirming your status." He walked behind his desk and sat down. "Okay, so you're nineteen, almost. Creating cards for the wide variety of life events requires some life experience. What makes you think you have what it takes to work here?"

Betsy sighed inside. This was one question she had already anticipated. "Sir, do you like country music?" She didn't wait for an answer. "It's all about those life experiences you mention, and Johnny Cash and Loretta Lynn could write gold records about my life. My momma died of cancer when I was ten. My pa was an alcoholic. My boyfriend went off to Viet Nam and died a month later."

She started to bring up having a son and losing him, but could feel the emotion welling up and knew she had to remain professional.

"I left the only home I know, on my own. Left all my friends behind to find a better life. The first week after I left, I made two new friends who were murdered two weeks later. I've seen tragedy, yet discovered sympathy in unexpected places. And like most folks, I've experienced my share of happiness and joy, too." She felt a tear warm a path down her cheek, and made no effort to hide it. "Tell me, Sir. Do you think I have the experience you talk about?"

Mr. Gordon stared at her without answering. After a moment, he picked up the phone and dialed a number. There weren't enough numbers for an outside call, so Betsy figured he had dialed an internal line.

"Jacob. Hi. That young woman I talked to you about is in my office. Do you have time to stop in? … Great."

He made small talk with Betsy for the next few minute

until interrupted by a knock on the door. A short wiry man, early-forties, longish black hair swept back over his ears, wearing tailored slacks and open collar shirt, entered the office.

"Miss Weston, this is Jacob Meyer, our creative director. I gave him the samples you gave my wife the other day."

Betsy looked up in anticipation and then reached down toward her purse. She'd learned a lesson two days earlier and this time her samples sat neatly organized in a manila folder that sat under her purse. She lifted the folder to her lap.

"I have some more. I used the time waiting for this interview to make some new ones."

Meyer looked at her. "How many do you have?"

"Another dozen, but to be honest there's only a few I really like. The others need some work."

Meyer smiled as he took the folder from her. "Still, you came up with a dozen ideas in just over a day. Some of our most experienced guys can't do that."

He thumbed through the papers, placing two at the top of the pile as he went. When he finished he removed those two and took three from a folder he'd carried into the office with him. He then showed his selection to her. He had picked the same ones she thought the best of the bunch. Of the five, he lifted two and held them up.

"These two I'd approve right now. The other three need better artwork, but I have to say, your artistic skills are excellent, especially for someone actually applying for a writing job. You have a fantastic way of displaying the sentiment of your words. The humor in this one is very whimsical. We don't often find someone who can draw *and* write." He grinned. "Maybe I should reverse that order since you're applying for a writing slot."

Betsy felt her anxiety lift and hope buoyed her spirit. "I

can apply for something else if that'll help."

The two men smiled, but briefly. Mr. Gordon spoke first.

"We've seen your talent, and you are correct, Miss Weston, quality does count, but other factors play in as well. Tell me, what do see as your biggest weakness?"

Betsy didn't hesitate. "Chocolate, Sir."

Mr. Gordon guffawed. "Th-that's not quite what I meant, but, never mind." He calmed down and an all-business seriousness came over him. "Miss Weston, would you excuse us for a minute?"

He led Mr. Meyer to the outer office and the ebullience Betsy had felt a moment earlier faded. The men's absence from the room lasted only minutes and Mr. Gordon alone returned to the office. He sat down at his desk and made a notation on Betsy's application form, followed by a sigh that Betsy found disheartening. He looked right at her.

"As I said earlier, you have talent and that counts for a whole lot. Unfortunately, it doesn't overcome everything, such as budgets. The reality of the situation is that we don't have a job opening, and to create a new job position would require approval by the executive committee. I can't offer you a job at this time and I can't honestly say when I might be able to make an offer." He took a deep breath and continued, "That said, Mr. Meyer likes what he sees and is willing to look at your work on a freelance basis. He's also offering you the usual freelance fee for the five cards he selected."

Betsy wasn't quite sure what this offer meant and her confusion must have been apparent.

"Do you understand what freelancing is?"

"Um, not quite, Sir."

He nodded. "In a nutshell, you work for free. You come up with ideas on your own, like you did with these samples, and when you have something you really like, you make an appointment to see Jacob and show him what you have. If he likes it, he buys it from you for a flat fee of one hundred dollars per card with both artwork and verse. Verse or ideas only get $15 to $20 each."

Betsy's demeanor fell. "So, there's no job."

Mr. Gordon stood up and returned to the corner of his desk. "Sorry, no job, but I don't think you quite get this. He's just offered to buy five of your samples. You sign a few papers releasing your rights to these pieces and you'll walk out of here with a check for five hundred dollars. That's never happened here before with someone like you, as young as you are, walking in off the street as you did."

He smiled and paused to watch her reaction. In a flash, she realized the potential in what he didn't say. As a freelancer, she could submit ideas to more than one company, and have total freedom to create what she wanted.

"Just realize that it's hard work, but it can be fun, too," he added. "And you have to be smart with your money because there can be times when you don't sell a single idea."

The headline in The Sylva Herald said it all, "Frampton Corner Man Charged with Murder." Emory Albritton read the article, filling in the blanks with the inside information from his brother. He knew the defense attorney, a competent young man, but lacking the experience to go against the District Attorney, who had announced he was handling this case personally. With an election coming up, that came as no surprise.

Albritton set down the newspaper and picked up the petition he'd prepared to gain the court's approval as trustee of the Umfleet family trust and legal guardian of the children. He had already found a solid foster family to care for the children and a phone conversation with Judge Hoglund had been positive. He planned to file the petition in the morning, although there would be no action on it until Curt Umfleet stood convicted. The only potential roach in the soup would be his exoneration, which Albritton saw as unlikely based on the behind-the-scenes evidence presented to him.

The woman's body fished from the lake appeared to be that of the missing girl, based on size and hair. The girl's father said she'd never been to a doctor or dentist so they had no dental records or blood type to match. Amos Cummings had identified his daughter by the clothes she wore and a ring on her finger. The strongest point in the case was the blood stained clothing in Curt Umfleet's burn pit, which he had readily admitted belonged to the girl. But that story died with the bus driver's testimony that a different girl had gotten onto his bus that night, plus the legal documents proving the existence of that young woman. Alice Cummings had fallen off the face of the earth.

Within weeks, he would have control of the largest parcel of land in his end of the county. Land that held almost five miles of shoreline on the highest lake east of the Mississippi. Land that would become "home" to million dollar estates. Land that would make him a wealthy man.

Twenty-four
(Present Day)
❧ ◆ ◆ ❧

The first few days in the Luhan House proved to be a struggle for Myra. Her stamina continued to deteriorate. Her concentration flagged. The temptation for a bottle of merlot increased with each nonproductive hour. By the end of the week, Myra had produced little more than a rough outline for that story she'd held inside for years. She wondered if maybe she'd been wrong. Maybe this wasn't the story she had thought it to be off and on over the years. Maybe this wasn't her "alpha story." A story like that shouldn't be so difficult to start.

Despite being dragged, pouting and silent, into using a laptop, she still preferred editing on hardcopy and modern technology would never change that. She had hoped to test Alexia's skills with the first few chapters of the book, but that wasn't going to happen in as timely a manner as she had imagined. She made a series of notes in the margins of an old short story, incorporated them into the story on her laptop, and reprinted it. Now, she stood next to Alexia and handed the sheets to her.

"Here you go. You say you can proofread, so now prove it. I'll warn you upfront, I've actually left a few typos in on purpose just to test you."

Alexia chuckled. "On purpose, uh? They won't get past me."

Myra laid her hand on the young woman's shoulder and smiled. Alexia had spent the last few days winning her over. She did whatever Myra asked, without complaint, with a smile on her face, and at any time of day, a task made more miserable by what was becoming Myra's irregular habit of writing. Once upon a time, she would write through the night, but her strength and stamina, or lack thereof, now had her writing, then napping. Sometimes the nap consumed more time than her writing.

When Myra commented on Alexia's work ethic, the girl's response was simple. "The Bible instructs us to work as if unto the Lord, so I'm working for Him as much as for you."

Myra retrieved two bottles of spring water from the kitchenette and returned to the sitting area where they had been working.

Alexia silently handed back the first three pages, each littered with red correction marks.

"What? You couldn't have found that many errors."

Alexia grinned. "I didn't, except the ones I assume you left for me to find. I just wanted to see if you're paying attention."

Myra laughed. "Okay, you got me."

There was a quick rap at the door, and Diana popped her head through. "It's good to hear you laugh. Been a while."

Myra nodded. It *had* been a while.

"Ready for a break? I can take you over to the warehouse now. There's no time like the present."

"Cliché," both women muttered in unison. Diana laughed as Myra gave Alexia a funny look.

"Perfect time for me," replied Myra. "What about you, Alexia?"

"A warehouse? Umm, I guess so. If that's what you want." Her tone revealed her bewilderment.

Myra gave Diana an amused look at the girl's reluctance. Going to a warehouse wouldn't excite her either, except that this warehouse was hers.

"C'mon. It's time to take a break. You'll like this, I think. All girls like ponies."

The look of bewilderment on Alexia's face deepened.

Ten minutes later, Diana pulled the MDLH van up to the gate of a tall chain-link fence. Myra pressed the button on a remote switch and the gate rolled open, allowing Diana to pull into a dusty lot fronting a prefabricated metal structure on DEA Lane in the southern end of town. The adobe-colored building was fifty by one hundred feet with no discerning features except a doublewide vehicle door and a single man-door. No signage indicated its use or owner, but security appeared prominent.

"What is this place?" asked Alexia.

"Follow me," answered Myra as she climbed out of the van and walked to the man door. Alexia, followed by Diana, entered behind Myra, who had moved to a circuit box and began flipping a number of circuit breakers. Bright lights now bathed the inside.

"Wow! Ponies, huh?"

"These are my diamonds, a girl's best friend."

Two rows of vintage Ford Mustangs lined both long walls of the warehouse with a mechanics bay holding two spaces at one end. A small office area filled the equivalent of one space and held a desk and several filing cabinets.

With a loving pat, Myra showed off the nearest car. "Steve McQueen's Mustang from the movie 'Bullitt.' This is the remaining original 1968 GT390 Fastback, not one of the limited-edition production models. I bought it in a hush-hush deal from a man in Ohio who had it stored in a hay barn. She's all fixed up now." She pointed to a car across the aisle. "And that one is the Shelby that Morgan Freeman drove in 'The Bucket List.' My only other movie Mustang is that one over there, from a bit part in 'Back to the Future II.' However, the ones I wanted to show you specifically are those two at the end."

Myra walked to the last two cars on the far wall, a 1965 yellow Mustang convertible and a red 1975 Mustang Mach I. Both were in pristine condition, save one small dent in the convertible's bumper, and both showed signs of a recent bath. Alexia remained standing where she had stopped upon entering the building and continued to gaze from car to car.

"C'mon. Over here," Myra insisted.

Alexia dawdled toward Myra but stopped at a noise behind her. She turned to see Diana pulling a chain to open the large vehicle door, and then resumed her stroll to the end of the building.

"I'm thinking of making these two cars prominent in my story. Well, this one, the yellow convertible, was Betsy Weston's first car. She sold it to the motel owner, a Jim Fleming, where I found the original 'Sweetie' print. On a lark, I bought it from him. I was collecting "Sweetie" memorabilia and prints, why not the artist's car? Then he told me she had purchased a 1975 red Mustang Mach I from the local Ford dealer while she was in town. I found the dealer's son, who described his father as a pack rat. Lucky for me, the pack rat kept records for every sale and the son hadn't taken the time to clean out the file cabinets. We found the original sales papers for such a car but the dealer sold it to an Elise Kenwood, not Betsy Weston, and she paid cash. I was able to track down the car in Arkansas by its VIN, and I went there and bought that one, too. After that, I was hooked on old Mustangs, and you see the result here. But who was this Elise Kenwood and where did she end up? That's a mystery you get to solve."

The idea of an investigative task seemed to perk up

Alexia.

"How am I going to do that here, in New Mexico? I'll probably need to work back in Asheville or Arkansas, using the car as a starting point."

Myra expected that response and nodded. "Yes, you will. That's one of the reasons why we're going on a little road trip after my lab tests. In the meantime, I'm going to keep writing, or trying to, anyway, and you're going to start the research on this."

Myra walked back to the office area and sat on the gray metal folding chair next to the matching metal office desk. She felt like she could lay her head on the desk and fall asleep right there. She pointed to the file cabinets. "Over there. Open that bottom drawer and pull out the dozen or so file folders in there."

Alexia obeyed and placed them next to Myra, enough to create a foot-tall stack on the old wooden desk. Alexia opened the top folder and browsed a bit.

"There's a box over there to put that in."

While Alexia claimed the empty paper carton, Myra retrieved a set of keys from a lock box in the desk and tossed them to Alexia. "Here you go. Get the yellow Mustang. You can drive a stick, can't you?"

"Um, no. I never needed to learn."

"Damn, this is ..."

Diana interrupted, "I'll get it." She took the keys from Alexia.

"... gonna be a long drive. Guess you're going to learn today."

Alexia piled the folders into the container as Diana drove up in the old convertible. Diana popped open the trunk so Alexia could deposit the box inside and then said, "You go on ahead. I'll lock up for you. See you at dinner."

Myra thanked her old friend and with Alexia in the driver's seat, she began to give instructions. "Okay, left foot pushes in the clutch. First gear is here, second here ..." Alexia let out the clutch too quickly and the car stalled. A minute later, they lurched out through the door, only to stall outside the building. On her third attempt, Alexia managed to keep the car running, and in random jerks, drove off, back to the Luhan House.

"So, what do you have for me?" Albritton walked away from the three others in his foursome, toward a wooded area off the fairway, as he spoke into his cell phone. He chose his words carefully until out of earshot of the men, developers eager for more land in western Carolina.

A man in the foursome behind them yelled, "Hey there, Senator. You want my vote, then hurry up. We have a game to finish!"

Albritton smiled and waved, but his attention was on the phone call.

"Before I tell you, I want you to understand what it took to get the information."

"I don't want those details."

"But you're gonna get 'em," said Dewey. "If anything turns sour, I ain't taking the heat alone while you talk up some, whadayou call it, plausible deniability bullshit or whatever. See, I tracked the car service to a private airline company. Seems this author lady is a regular, and pays well, so bribe money wasn't working. The owner and crew was ferrying some celebrity to Hawaii or someplace and were gone for a week. Broke into the office but couldn't find anything helpful. After the plane came back, I couldn't find the pilot or owner. I was finally able to track down the co-pilot. He eagerly complied after I broke a few fingers and threatened to shoot a kneecap. Ready for your answer?"

Albritton sighed. He preferred anything short of physical intimidation, which he'd found necessary only on one previous occasion. He turned a figurative blind eye to this information though, as he had more at stake now than ever before and the timetable for finding a resolution seemed to be shrinking.

"They flew to Taos."

Albritton blanched at the news, but felt confused. Taos? His first reaction was that the judge would be retiring to Santa Fe and the women could be meeting up with him. Taos was but ninety minutes away, but why fly there? If the young woman had something, knew something, and had convinced Mitchell to meet Judge Hoglund, why not just fly to Santa Fe itself? Even Albuquerque was a little closer. Taos made no sense, unless she meant to throw Dewey off the track. Had she made Dewey? Did she know she was being followed?

"Get there! Now! Whatever it takes, do not let these women meet with Judge Hoglund. He shouldn't be too hard to find. He's moved in with his son."

"Whoa there, Senator. We need to talk about money. This is gonna cost you more than we talked about. Also, I might not get there before tomorrow afternoon. Doubt I'm gonna be a favored customer of the only private charter to fly to Taos from here regular-like. Might convince another charter to take me, if the money's right, but the first two I called were booked and unwilling to abandon regular customers. I can get there by tomorrow on a commercial flight if it comes to that."

Albritton cursed under his breath.

"Do whatever. I'll cover it. I've never cheated you before.

If those women even look like they're heading to Santa Fe, stop them!"

Myra awoke to incessant pounding on the cottage's front door. Her watch revealed the time at nearly noon. How in the world had she slept so long? Despite thirteen hours of sleep, she dragged herself out of bed. She looked into the second bedroom to find it empty. Alexia had found it easier to use the Convention Center classroom to spread out and organize the notes Myra had left in her charge. Myra had no doubt she would find the girl there, but who was at the door?

She engaged the peephole of the door and her heart began to race. Ricardo! How had he learned she was staying there, or that she was even in town, for that matter?

No, this was not a confrontation she needed right now. Or ever, if she was honest with herself.

She stole back into the bedroom and quietly closed its door. Ricardo would go away, she hoped.

She heard him yelling her name at one point and the assault on the door became so violent she feared its collapse. Then, quiet. She eased the bedroom door open, half expecting to find the man standing there. The front door remained intact and she heard voices outside. She peered around the edge of the curtain to see a patrol car and an officer leading Ricardo away. Myra sighed in relief. The staff had called the cavalry. Maybe the man would eventually forget the ten thousand dollars she had taken from his bank account before leaving him. Repaying him had never been an issue. Not wanting to see him transform those dollar bills into liquid entertainment had been her excuse.

She still cared, but maybe it was time to accept him as an

adult, give him back his money, and let the bottles fall where they might. Yes, she decided. She needed to make amends before it was too late. Just not in person.

A few minutes later, a softer knock rattled the door. This time Myra's peep revealed Diana and she opened the door to her friend.

"Sorry about that. From what I picked up in his slurred words, he saw you riding in the convertible. I'm surprised he had the mental acumen to figure out you were here. You okay?"

Myra nodded. "Is Alexia in the classroom?"

"I think so. I can call over there to check."

"Would you, please? Tell her to pack everything up for traveling. We're leaving now."

"Now? Your lab tests —"

"Now. I'd love to stay, but ... you know. I'll stop at the lab on the way out."

Diana raised both eyebrows and rolled her eyes.

"You need to practice. Alexia does a much better job with that gesture."

Myra walked up to her friend and hugged her. "Diana, if anything happens before I see you again, I want you to know that I love you like a sister. I'll be in your debt forever for all of the kindnesses you've shown me over the years." She wiped the tears from her eye, while a whitewater torrent flowed down Diana's cheeks.

"I-I don't want to think about that. You're going to get better. That's all there is to it." She wiped her cheeks. "I *will* see you again."

Myra hugged her again, released her, and walked into the bedroom where she retrieved her checkbook from her purse. Back in the sitting area, she wrote out a check and handed it to

Diana.

"Make sure Ricardo gets this, please. There's even a little extra for interest. Oh, and tell him if he comes near me again, I'll do more than get a restraining order against him. I'll make his life miserable."

Diana, her composure regained, shook her head. "That last part he'll understand. What's this for?" Diana held up the check. "Aren't you just enabling him?"

"He's a big boy. I've given up trying to help ... and I didn't make his life miserable, thank you very much."

Diana shrugged. "Semantics. I'll go track down Alexia now."

Myra watched her friend cross the dusty yard and parking lot. She returned to the bedroom and began to pack. A stop at the lab, then Taos to Eureka Springs, Arkansas. Due east. One long day's drive along U.S. Routes 64 and 412 until they hit the Razorback's state line, and then a few zigzags to finish the trip. Myra had done the trip non-stop before. This time, though, fatigue sapped her. Maybe they'd take it in two, or even three, days, and she was probably going to need a cervical collar with Alexia driving.

Albritton watched the sunset from his deck, three fingers of Scotch in hand. He resisted pacing the wooden planks, afraid of stirring Misty's suspicions that something was dramatically wrong. However, leaning on the deck rail, elbows resting on top, was as natural for him as kissing babies while on the stump or grabbing photo ops with soldiers returning from the Middle East. She might comment on the amount of Laphroaig single malt in his glass, but he'd consumed more at other times.

He ran his fingers across the smooth wood. He'd had this home built for Misty as her wedding present. Their kids had been raised here. One grandchild's birth took place unexpectedly in the guest room. They'd hosted parties of all flavors here. Their church held an annual potluck luncheon there. And he could lose it all.

He noticed his heart beating fast and could feel the pulse in his neck without putting a finger to it. Where was his man at this moment? The guy should have called before now. Had he arrived in Taos? Or had another obstacle dropped into their way? Where were the Judge and the Mitchell woman? Was his world on the edge of that ever-deepening abyss or was he simply paranoid?

He heard the sliding door behind him grate as it opened. His wife walked toward him, holding out his cell phone to him. He quickly patted his back pocket and felt a void where his phone should have been.

"Thought you might want this. I heard it ring a few times while I had my hands messy in the kitchen."

He took the phone and kissed her on the cheek. "Thanks, Hon." He'd been so pre-occupied he'd forgotten his phone in the den.

"Mike and Emily should be here in half an hour and then we need to leave for the club."

Emory had been like a father to Mike after Mike Sr.'s death. Despite Emory's concerns, Mike had gone into law enforcement, like his father. With Emory's influence, however, he had been accepted by the State Highway Patrol and fast-tracked to the State Bureau of Investigation. In an ironic twist, Mike had accepted an assignment to the Professional Standards Division, the unit responsible for investigating financial crimes and political corruption.

"I'm ready."

She raised her eyebrows and nodded toward his glass.

"Will I need to drive? Wouldn't want Mike arresting you."

He had tried so hard not to arouse Misty's suspicion only to raise her concern over his sobriety.

"Is there something we need to talk about?"

"No, no. I'm fine. Just thinking through some numbers for a proposed road project ... and no more Scotch after this one. I'll be okay to drive. Honest."

"I'll be the judge of that." She turned to enter the house, pausing at the door. "Please. No more after that glass. You've been drinking a lot lately and it worries me. If I didn't know better, I'd think you were having an affair."

She gave him an icy stare that unsettled him further, but she said no more and turned back toward the house. He watched her disappear into the interior shadows and leaned back against the deck rail. He checked the last missed call, and pressed a key to recall the number.

"'bout time. I've been trying to reach you for half an hour."

"Sorry. Tied up. Where are you?"

"Santa Fe, headin' for Taos. Like I said I'd be. Good news. That judge ain't in town yet. You were right that his son would be easy to find. I managed to find a gabby neighbor who was more than willing to tell me the whole story. Seems the whole family's happy as a bear in a berry patch that dad's coming to town, but he's not due in for another week."

Albritton sighed in relief. Life as he knew it had been granted another respite.

"What about Mitchell and the girl?"

"I don't got any exact whereabouts for them yet, but I done some readin' on my flight over here. Learned that

Mitchell wrote at least two of her books here and the blurbs in those books mention a place, a Mabel somebody house. I got it written down in my notepad. I'll be asking around about that after I get off the phone. If I find 'em, whadayou want me to do?"

Albritton tired of the stress. Despite his best efforts to look normal, Misty had noticed his obsession with this problem and the result – his increased drinking. He didn't like her misinterpretation of the events. He'd never cheat on her, but what if she discovered what was really going on.

He had no way of knowing what the girl knew, or if she had connected the pieces of a puzzle she might not even know she had. Nevertheless, he couldn't risk that she might stumble upon the key piece that could start a cascade of discovery and recognition that could destroy him. And what about the author? The tabloids placed her on death's doorstep, yet here she was traveling. Was she really that ill? What might she now know?

Didn't Dr. Phil teach that you had to accept what you couldn't change and deal head-on with the things you could? Desperation weighed on him. He took a step he might forever regret.

"Make the girl vanish, but not before learning what she might have told the Mitchell woman. On second thought, just make them both vanish. Do your usual good work. Nothing left behind. No evidence to find."

Twenty-five
(Summer – 1969)
ง⊕◆◆⊕ย

The truth of those final words from Mr. Gordon rang so true two months later, with no additional cards sold in the interval. Betsy's first, and only, check from Gibson had covered her deposit and first month's rent on a furnished apartment just a half mile from the company. She cut back on her driving as the cost of gasoline rose from twenty-five to over thirty cents a gallon. Instead of the long drives, she found walking through the wooded trails of nearby French Park a relaxing respite to her occasional writer's block.

Much of her time that first two weeks after meeting Jacob Meyer had been spent finding the apartment and settling in. Since then, she'd had three more meetings where she'd shown him a dozen new cards each time, but nothing clicked. She spent hours at local grocery and drug stores poring over the racks of cards, looking at new styles, watching other people at the racks to see what they laughed at, what they held onto and contemplated, and ultimately what they purchased. She even got up the nerve to ask a number of women what they liked about the cards they chose. From her "research," she developed an idea of what local women wanted, but she also realized that such tastes didn't necessarily translate to national sales.

Betsy figured she had the funds to last another month, maybe two if she ate only twice a day and used her car sparingly. Many might have called her first sale "beginner's luck" but she felt a growing confidence in her ability to draw and write. She could do this. She could, and would, make a living doing this. Not just because she had the talent, but because she had discovered she loved being creative and seeing people appreciate her skills. She had found a new passion for her work as she defended it to Jacob.

Still, she had never been purely a dreamer. She had experienced too much "reality" in her short life. One more month. If she hadn't sold more cards by then, she would force herself to find another source of income. Waitressing, baby-sitting, anything – anything legal anyway – that could add to her savings account. And when she had saved enough to have a surplus over her living expenses, she would consult a private eye about the realities of finding Jimmy Bob. She would never give up hope of reuniting with her son.

Betsy sat at her makeshift drawing board and drew a final addition on her latest creation before signing it. While the ink dried, she walked to a nearby gas station where she used the payphone to call Jacob. Having her own phone was a luxury she could not yet justify.

"Jacob Meyer."

"Hi, it's Betsy. Can I stop by this afternoon? I have some more ideas to show you."

There was a pause on the other end of the line.

"Umm, you know, Betsy. We might want to, well, just set up a once-a-month regular meeting where you can show me what you've done. It's hard for me to break free every time you call."

Betsy felt the tug of disappointment. She knew deep down that she had some good cards this time, and she needed the paycheck. Another month's rent would be due soon and everyday expenses slowly eroded her savings. She began to see that her first sale had been too easy. Reality now became the dragging foot that slowed her eager optimism.

"Okay, I understand. I, uh ... When would be convenient

for you?"

"Tell you what, we have weekly meetings with the writers, but our big monthly brainstorming session is on the tenth of the month, or the closest day to it if that's a weekend. It would work best for me to see your stuff the following day, to see how it fits with what we're thinking and doing."

"The tenth is tomorrow."

"Lucky for you, it is. So, come on over at 9 a.m. the following day. Take tomorrow to really critique your work and fine tune it for me, and we'll see what works."

"Yes, Sir. Thank you. See you then."

Her optimism took off at a full sprint to match her run home. She wanted to celebrate by opening her last Godiva bar, but restrained herself. *I'll save it for after I've sold some cards.* She found a Hershey bar in the kitchen and sat down at the drawing board to review her proposed cards.

Betsy felt another surge of confidence as she packed up her portfolio. She knew she had some winners. She'd taken what was to her a bold step and, armed with half a dozen of her favorite cards, had driven to the local Kroger's store and asked for opinions from the women shopping for cards. Emboldened further by their positive feedback, she'd even gone so far as to ask a few men -- the older, grandfatherly ones -- for their opinions. With their comments in mind, she returned to her apartment, made a handful of changes and "fine tuned" her cards for Jacob. Just as he'd asked her to.

At 9:05, she sat in the leather chair opposite Jacob's drawing board and refrained from biting her nails as he surveyed her collection. At nine-fifteen, she remained sitting in that chair, without so much as a word, smile, frown, or nod from Jacob. Five more minutes and her nails would become fair game. This was awful.

With a minute to spare her cuticles, Jacob pulled out a card, and another. Then five more. He leafed through the folder one more time and pulled out three more. All of these he laid out on his drawing board before standing back and looking at them collectively. He raised his left hand to his chin while placing his right hand under his left elbow.

C'mon, say something, anything! Betsy wanted to scream.

He turned his gaze from the cards to her and said, "Can you do two more like these? Maybe something for a 'get well' card or a 'thinking of you' card?"

Betsy's jaw dropped. Did he want to buy twelve of her cards? A full dozen? She stood and joined him. "Sure. I guess. Why?" Only a couple of the cards in his selection were from her group of personal favorites. What did he see that she didn't?

"Look at these together, as a group."

Betsy complied but still didn't see anything special.

Jacob smiled. "Okay, I can tell you still don't see it." He reached for her folder and pulled out two other cards, two of her favorites, and placed them on the board with the set. "Look again."

Betsy could see that these last two seemed out of place in the group, but why? She couldn't quite grasp it at first, but then she saw it. The lines, the somewhat abstract coloring, and the caricatures she had used all blended into a uniform style. As much as she liked them, the other two cards didn't follow that style.

"Are you sure you want to be a writer? Don't get me wrong, your prose is solid. You have a nice way of expressing the sentiment. But your artwork, this work, is unique. It's

231

catchy. Modern, to use a word that's greatly overused. I can see a whole line of cards with this style. In fact, I even like the stylistic signature. It gives each piece the sense of being true art, like signed paintings. We could extend this to a whole line of products -- party supplies, balloons, ball caps and T-shirts."

Now Betsy stood there, wordless.

Jacob stood there gazing at her. "How did we get so lucky that you popped into *our* door?"

Betsy gave a simple shrug. "Y'all were closest to my home."

Jacob laughed. "Then we certainly did get lucky." He pulled off the two last cards, leaving only the original ten he had chosen. "Look, I want to present these to my executive board, along with the two I asked you to do. I'll buy the dozen. Also, I want to ask them to create a new job position for you. I'll call you after I get their decision."

"Um, I don't have a phone." Yet, she wanted to run right out and order one. And jump, shimmy, and sing in joy.

"Then call me the first of next week. I'll have a check for you as well. Does that work for you?"

Betsy floated well above cloud nine. She settled at cloud twelve ... for twelve hundred dollars! That was a whole lot more than her pa had ever made in one month. Twelve hundred. She could breathe a whole lot easier about paying her rent and covering her expenses. She could loosen up and buy real groceries for a change, although her frugality had enabled her to drop fifteen pounds and she liked the slimmer image in the mirror.

Jacob escorted her to the reception area where Betsy saw a young man signing into the guest registry just as she had earlier. The man looked to Betsy to be about six foot tall, slim, and athletic, with longish, sandy brown hair swept back behind the ears. His profile appeared strong and when he looked up and toward them, the strength of that profile carried to his face with a rugged handsomeness that she found appealing.

"Hey, Pop. I was just coming in to see you."

Betsy noticed Jacob's face take on a stern demeanor.

"Rod, aren't you supposed to be in class? I'm not paying all that tuition money for you to skip out."

"We're cool. No classes until after lunch." Rod's gaze settled on Betsy, which made her unsettled.

"Sorry," Jacob said. "My bad manners. Betsy, this is my son, Rod. This is Betsy Weston."

Betsy extended her hand, which Rod took gently to shake. His touch transmitted a tingle that extended up to her elbow.

"Betsy is an artist and writer, and may be just the person to shake up this company and bring some new life to it."

Rod's smile seemed to glow. "Wow, he doesn't give compliments easily, Betsy. You must be good."

Betsy felt her face flush. "Beginner's luck. Nice to meet you." She turned to Jacob. "I'll call you next week."

She left the building, listening as Rod began to talk with his father about some expense or another at school. She had walked halfway up the long drive toward the sidewalk, when she heard her name."

"Betsy! Betsy Weston! Hey, wait up!"

She turned to see Rod running across the pavement and up the hill toward her. Despite the sprint, he showed no shortness of breath and his smile lit up again.

"Hey, my dad says you're new in town. Look, I don't have class until one o'clock and it's the last week of this old boring accounting class. Can I treat you to lunch? Ever had Skyline Chili? It's a Cincinnati original."

As intriguing as Rod seemed, Betsy needed only a

233

moment to decide she wasn't ready for a relationship. Plus, she had work to do, a job to earn.

"That's mighty sweet of you, Rod, but I can't right now. I've got other things I need to do."

"What about dinner then? You have to eat sometime, right?

"Not today. Thanks." She turned to resume her walk home, but he stepped in front of her and blocked the way.

"Not today what? You don't have to eat today? Or, you don't want –"

"I don't have time to go with you today." She eluded him and started to walk, but Rod raced in front of her and blocked her way again. Despite his physical appeal, his actions were inching toward an aggression that made her nervous. She didn't want to be rude, but he wasn't taking her 'no' for an answer.

"Move, please. I'd like to go home."

"Walking? So, you live nearby."

Betsy realized she'd revealed too much. She didn't want him following her to her apartment. Or did she? She found Rod attractive. Confident. Certainly bold. Not like the guys her age she knew back in North Carolina. She felt flattered by his invitation, yet also apprehensive at his insistence. She looked into his hazel-green eyes and saw … what? Desire? Well, that came across through more than his eyes. Laughter? Life? No, distraction. She could melt into those deep, dazzling wells. He could indeed become a disruption to her plans. The last thing she needed was for him to know where she lived.

"My car's down the street, for an oil change."

"C'mon, I'll give you a lift."

"Thank you for the offer, but, no. I want to walk and think."

"About what? About where I can take you to dinner?"

Betsy took in a deep breath and let out an exasperated sigh.

"Rod, you seem like a nice guy, but we just met ... and, I'm trying to get a job with your father. That means I have to show him I can meet a deadline. That means no distractions."

Rod's smile broadened as well as brightened. "That's a good sign. At least you're interested enough to find me distracting. How about dinner Monday night? We can celebrate your new job."

Or commiserate not getting one, she thought. She weakened. "Okay. Monday night. I'll meet you somewhere."

"I can pick you up, say, seven."

"No, I'd prefer meeting you someplace."

"Hmmm, okay. Right here, at seven."

"No. At the restaurant ... or call it off." She looked him straight in the eye. "And let's keep it simple, like that chili place you mentioned."

Betsy watched as Rod's eyes scrutinized her, but the smile never left his mouth.

"I get it. You want to be able to dump me if the date doesn't go well."

"Exactly."

Rod laughed. "You're certainly to the point. Trust me; I don't bite. I might drool, but that's only because you're the prettiest woman I've met in a long time ... and worldly, too, it looks like."

Betsy wasn't sure what he meant by 'worldly.' She could never call herself experienced, but she was a quick study and the stories she'd heard from the ladies at The Rest Stop had been cautionary tales.

"Why, thank you. I think," she replied to his compliment.

He was by far the most handsome man she'd ever met, and no doubt much more sophisticated than she could ever be. A dangerous combination, according to her mentors.

Suddenly, her mind filled with thoughts of Jimmy Bob's father and her lost son, and guilt sluiced through her. How could she even think of resuming life and finding love when she'd failed to find him? She fought the tears.

"I-I have to go. I-I …" She choked on the words, and then pivoted and raced up the remaining drive, leaving Rod standing on the blacktop alone.

"Hey! What'd I say? I didn't mean …"

Betsy kept running, tears streaming down her face.

"What about Monday? Which Skyline? Do you know …?"

She ran, leaving his question unanswered.

Twenty-six
❧ ◆ ◆ ❧

Betsy looked up from the small creek in the park, out across the grassy slope. Two young children laughed and screamed as they held their arms stiff at their sides and log rolled down the hill. Their mother laughed as they stood up and wobbled with dizziness, and encouraged them to run back up and do it again. A happy family. A mother in love with her children.

She thought she had resolved the conflict in her heart by accepting the harsh fact that her father had succeeded in his threat. She might never see Jimmy Bob again, plain and simple, although she would always hope. Life marched on. She had to move on with it, or fall into such despair that life could no longer hold any meaning.

The high tide of emotion that swept across her like a tsunami after accepting her first date since JT joined the Army and then finding herself pregnant, had destabilized her. After an hour of staring at an empty drawing board, she had retreated to higher ground and spent all afternoon walking the trails in the park. Now, as dusk approached, a park ranger found her seated on a log above the dry creek and escorted her to her car in preparation of closing the park.

"Miss, I don't know what's bothering you, but I can tell something's wrong. Can I help? Do you have anyone to talk to?"

Betsy shook her head.

The man took a pocket-sized spiral notebook, along with a pen, from his shirt pocket and wrote something. He tore the sheet off the spiral wire and handed it to her. "Here. I won't presume that I can help, but my pastor's a great guy. I know he'd be willing to listen and help in any way he can."

Betsy took the paper and stared at it.

"Time to close the park, Miss. I'll follow you out, if that's okay."

Twenty minutes later, Betsy realized she now sat parked in her slot behind the apartment building. She did not recall driving back from the park to her apartment. She wondered how long she'd been sitting there, dazed, with the car running. She vaguely recalled the ranger handing her something and escorting her out of the park. She looked around and found the paper. On it was written the name of a man, a church, and its address and phone number.

She couldn't recall the last time she'd been to church. It must have been with Maisy Duncan. What had Maisy's religion earned her? She thought about that and crumpled the paper in her hand. She emerged from the car and as she entered the building, she tossed it into a nearby trashcan. *God?* she thought. *How could a loving God allow her mother to die from cancer, her baby to be stolen, her friends to be murdered, and Maisy's death in an inferno?* No church or pastor would be able to help her. Sally had said it, "You're a survivor. Make something of yourself, Betsy Weston."

With hardened tenacity, Betsy pushed ahead with her work and by Monday morning had completed not only the two requested cards, but six additional cards as well – all following the design style she had subconsciously developed over the past few weeks. After a call to Jacob, she walked to the plant and signed in at the registration desk as the receptionist worked the phone switchboard. She turned to wait for Jacob.

"Betsy." The receptionist rose from her seat and tapped her on the shoulder. "These came for you earlier."

As Betsy turned back to the woman, a large floral bouquet on the desktop surprised her. "Th-they're beautiful." No one had ever sent her flowers. Had Jacob arranged this?

"There's a card." The receptionist pointed to a small envelope nestled in among the flowers.

Betsy opened it and read, "Skyline, 7pm, looking forward to a celebration." An address for the restaurant followed. Betsy smiled. *Handsome and thoughtful.*

Jacob's voice interrupted her thoughts. "Good morning. Let's go back to my office."

Betsy looked at the receptionist. "Can I leave these here and pick them up on my way out?" The woman nodded.

Upon walking into Jacob's office, Betsy noticed her cards laid out on his drawing board. She opened her portfolio and placed the eight new cards next to them. The creative director looked at the additions and smiled.

"You amaze me once again." He picked up each card and examined it. "Very nice. Don't take this the wrong way, but we will rework the prose a bit. Maybe even the artwork. As you'll learn, every card we do goes through a process to tweak and perfect it. You're talented, but you're new at this. Take the opportunity to learn from the experienced guys, but don't take their comments as gospel. I want your work to be fresh, to be your own."

Betsy understood. After all, she hadn't seen what Jacob saw in the style she had developed. She could take criticism. She'd lived with it for years under the most negative of terms. Positive feedback would be a welcomed change. But, what about the job?

"Okay. I'll buy them all."

"Wow! Thank you." *And the job?* Was this going to be as tense as the waiting during her last meeting?

"I presented your work to the board and they want to start a new signature line of cards, gifts and the like, using your work. That's the good news."

Uh oh, she thought. *That means there's bad news.*

"The better news is that they've authorized me to pay you a premium for these. I think you'll like the check you're going to get."

And the job?

"I'm afraid, though, that the board won't authorize a new job position until the new fiscal year, which is October 1st. I tried. Honestly, I tried. Can you work with me this way until then? You can attend our weekly sessions with the writers and artists, if you want. Plus, I still want to meet with you monthly to see what you've developed. I just can't give you a regular paycheck or a workspace."

No job. She sighed inwardly. *No celebrating tonight.* At least he held out the chance for a job in four months. If she continued selling as she had, she could hold out even longer than that.

"Well, I was really hoping for that job, but I can live with this. I guess." She hoped her disappointment didn't show. "I really, really appreciate your interest and support ... and buying my work."

Jacob walked over to his desk and picked up a short stack of stapled papers. "This is like the papers you signed to give us rights to your first cards. It's a little different. It gives us the rights to these works, as well as the right to first refusal to anything new you produce. You can take that home to read, or have your lawyer check it. Once you've signed, I can ask accounting to cut you your check."

Betsy paused a moment. Did she really need a lawyer? She liked Jacob. "Is there anything in there I need to worry about? I'm not much into contracts and the like."

"It's mostly standard stuff for freelancers in this industry."

"Yes, Sir. I trust you." She took a pen from the drawing board and signed her distinctive signature to two copies of the contract. Eighteen hundred dollars! And then she remembered he said they had approved a premium. What did that mean?

Jacob smiled, took the contracts, and placed one into a manila envelope for Betsy. He then picked up his phone. "Harold, it's Jacob. Betsy Weston is with me ... Yes, that one ... She's signed the contract and I'm buying eighteen cards ... Right. At the new rate ... Thanks." He looked up to Betsy. "They'll have your check here in a few minutes. So, tell me, where'd you learn to do this?"

They talked for about ten minutes, with Betsy saying nothing about her past but that she grew up in North Carolina and learned to write and draw in high school. She'd said more than she should have to Mr. Gordon. In reflection of that meeting, she'd decided to be more discreet about her past. She learned a bit about Jacob and his family, particularly Rod, whom Jacob seemed to be "selling" to her. She wondered what the son had said to his father.

A knock on the door interrupted their conversation. A balding, middle-aged man opened the door a bit and peeked in. Jacob rose to meet him and took an envelope from him, which he then turned over to Betsy. "I think you'll be happy with this."

Betsy took the envelope and fingered it.

"Go ahead, open it."

Betsy complied and her jaw dropped when she saw a

check for $5400. That was three times the rate per card that she'd been paid for her first cards. She would surely be able to hold out for several months on the money she'd already made. Maybe tonight would be a time to celebrate after all. She jumped up and gave Jacob a huge hug, but shrunk back quickly. That wasn't a very business-like response.

"Sorry." Betsy blushed.

Jacob laughed. "That's okay. Now, if one of my male staff writers did that ..."

They both laughed.

Betsy floated to the reception area and picked up her flowers. As she turned toward the front door, Mrs. Gordon walked through and smiled as she spied Betsy at the front desk.

"Why, good morning, Betsy Weston. I hear you're shaking this place up."

"Hi, Mrs. Gordon. I just –"

"Please, call me Georgia. You certainly look excited and happy."

"I am, Ma'am. I just sold more cards to Mr. Meyer and they're using my cards to start a new signature line."

"Congratulations. That's wonderful." She chuckled. "I just hope they didn't make you sign some contract that gives away your first-born child."

Betsy froze and dropped her flowers, the glass vase breaking on the tile floor.

Albritton and his brother Mike, the deputy, sat in the back row of the courtroom talking while the jury filed back into the box. The worn oak bench glistened with the patina of age, polished by thousands of derrieres sliding in and out during almost a hundred years of use. The wood of the straight-backed chairs of the jury box matched that of the benches in age and color. Light filtered into the room through tall windows on the east side of the high ceilinged arena of justice.

"That didn't take long," said Mike.

"Sure didn't." Albritton scrutinized the jurors, hoping to gleam their decision from their countenances. "Don't know if that's a good sign or bad."

"Guess that depends which side of the room you're seated on."

Curt Umfleet sat on the left side as one faced the judge, according to western legal tradition. He appeared calm and seemed to be praying quietly to himself. His seat put him on the judge's right side, but furthest away from the jury. Albritton had never discovered the origin of this seating tradition, but had been told that the prosecution took the chairs closest to the jury in order to curry favor subconsciously with them.

"Sure don't seem right him calling himself a Christian, and then killing that poor Cummings girl," said Mike.

The counselor nodded in agreement. Before he could comment, the bailiff stood and said, "All rise."

Judge Hoglund entered the chamber from behind the dais and spoke as he sat down. "Be seated." There was a moment of rustling as dozens of people sat in unison and the judge rearranged his robes and adjusted his position to become more comfortable. He then turned toward the jury box and asked, "Mr. Foreman, I understand you have already reached a verdict."

"We have, Your Honor." The man seated closest to the judge arose and held out a folded slip of paper, which the bailiff took and gave to the judge. Albritton noted Umfleet's eyes remained closed and the silent working of his mouth became more active.

The judge read the paper and looked at the defendant. "Will the defendant rise?"

Umfleet stopped his silent intercession, opened his eyes, and stood, facing the judge.

"Curtis Umfleet, a jury of your peers has reviewed the evidence and do now find you guilty of second-degree murder and obstruction of justice. You are remanded to the custody of the state prison system, pending formal sentencing two weeks from today.

Judge Hoglund struck his gavel and waited for the flurry of commotion to settle before asking the prosecutor to approach the bench. Albritton couldn't make out the conversation, but the lawyer remained serious and business-like. His brother's stirring beside him took his focus off the bench. He looked to his left and saw a deputy whispering into his brother's ear. Mike turned to him.

"Gotta run, little brother. The bad guys are busy. Robbery in progress. Time to give chase."

"Careful, Mike."

"Always."

Albritton watched his older sibling leave the courtroom and turned his attention back to the bench. Judge Hoglund peered right at him and wiggled his finger for the counselor to approach the bench.

Albritton pointed to himself and mouthed, "Me?"

The judge nodded. As Albritton approached the bench, the judge rose and said, "Come back to my chambers, Emory."

The lawyer followed the judge into his private office and sat down in the chair offered by the magistrate.

"I've reviewed your petition to become trustee of the Umfleet trust, as well as legal custodian of the children. The father has conveyed to me, through his lawyer, that while he wished he had more time to assess his options and to evaluate your abilities, he acknowledges his situation and will leave the decision to my discretion. Be honest with me, Emory. Do I have any reason to be concerned? Will you have the children's best interests at heart?"

A warning claxon blared in Albritton's head. Had he done something to draw attention to his activities? He had amassed options to thousands of acres of real estate, but had yet to act upon a single one. The wave of land development remained east of Cashiers, but five years, maybe ten, would see it crash along his shoreline. He could be patient.

"Yes, Sir. As you saw in my petition, I've already found a stable Christian home for the children. I believe you even know the family. Also, the family's land will remain in trust for their benefit. My petition shows the estimated income from farming that land. Plus, limited timber rights can generate more capital, all of which will go to the benefit of the children. The family's home in Frampton Corner will be maintained for the children until they reach the age of majority, as requested by Curt Umfleet. I think everything is in order, Judge."

Judge Hoglund eased back in his chair and scrutinized Albritton. The lawyer tolerated the first thirty seconds of silence, but by the sixty-second mark, he began to feel a bit nervous. He struggled to hide the emotion.

The judge finally sat forward and pulled some papers from the corner of his desk. He took his pen and leafed to the back page, where he started to sign his name. Albritton recognized the paperwork as being his petition and quietly sighed relief, holding in the jubilation that wanted him to pump his fist in the air with a resounding "Yes!"

"Thank you, Judge. I won't disappoint you." He shook

the jurist's hand and turned to leave.

He let the grin overcome his mouth as soon as the door to the judge's chambers closed behind him. He sauntered down the hall into the courthouse lobby and out the front doors toward his car. He subconsciously patted his briefcase and the signed papers within it, as he thought about celebrating with Mike. Beyond that, he felt secure in his future and could now focus on a certain young woman, his college sweetheart. While they continued to see each other regularly, Misty Caldwell's father had made it clear that any suitor for his daughter's hand had best be financially grounded. Albritton could make that claim now.

As Albritton approached his car, a deputy sheriff's car pulled up next to him, but it wasn't his brother. Jeremy Herndon climbed out of the car.

He seemed out of breath as he caught up with Emory.

"Glad I caught you, Emory."

"Hey, Jeremy. Catch the robbers?"

The deputy shook his head, looking grim. He pointed to a nearby park bench. "Might want to sit down. Got bad news, Emory, bad news."

Albritton's gut churned. Jeremy led him to the bench and Albritton complied by sitting down, even though he didn't want to.

"The robbers were armed and waitin' for us. Mike got shot before we even knew what was happening. Sorry, Emory, he didn't make it."

Emory had given a tearful eulogy at his brother's funeral, while Misty stood with him and his parents through every step of the sad event. He had wanted to postpone their engagement. It didn't seem proper, but his mother chided him, saying, "Don't you dare delay the important things in life. If your brother's death tells you anything, it should be how fleeting and precious life is, and how quickly and suddenly you can lose it."

So now, Emory and Misty regaled their friends – old family, college, and recent – at the Greensboro Country Club engagement party hosted by both families. The warm summer evening was ripe for a dip in the pool and the smell of backyard barbeques permeated the Irving Park neighborhood where Misty grew up.

The couple whispered to each other at the head table, laughing at her father. 'Guff' Caldwell had tried his best to act the stern, doting dad when Emory asked him for his daughter's hand, but his wife had already prepped Emory. The 'old goat' had been eager to take Emory into the family since he'd started law school and had been worried that maybe the young man's intentions had changed since moving to the western end of the state.

"Just how many drinks do you think he's had?" asked Emory.

"I have no idea. But he's sure enjoying himself." Misty patted his hand and pointed. "Look, my cousin Henry is taking a movie of Dad. He'll never live this down now."

Emory's face turned somber and he pointed to the entrance.

"Misty, she decided to come after all, and she has Mike Jr. with her. Excuse me for a moment."

Emory stood up and navigated his way to the main door. Misty followed. As Emory approached his sister-in-law, Hannah, and his nephew, the woman smiled and the young boy ran and jumped into his uncle's arms.

"Uncle Em'y, this place is neat."

"It is, isn't it?" replied Emory as he tussled the boy's hair and set him back down to embrace Hannah. "Hi. Thanks for coming. It means a lot to me."

"To both of us," added Misty as she joined them.

"C'mon, I have a seat for you with us."

"No, really, Emory, I, uh … not at the head table. We –"

"Please? It's where Mike would have been."

Hannah hesitated, but nodded and followed the couple to the head table. Emory noticed his parents threading their way through the crowd toward them.

"Ganpa, Ganma!" Mike Jr. broke free of his mom's hand and ran to his grandparents.

After greetings, Hannah parked her things at the head table and at the prodding of her father-in-law accepted his offer to dance. Mike Jr. watched her head to the dance floor.

"I wanna dance, too."

Misty smiled at Emory and curtseyed to the boy. "I accept your offer, young sir."

She led him to the dance floor as Emory's eyes misted over. Mike's funeral still seemed like a nightmare, and his death had left a larger hole in Emory's life than he'd ever imagined. Misty could sense it; he was sure of that. She went out of her way to include Hannah and Mike Jr. in their outings and never complained when Emory stepped in as a surrogate father to his nephew, a commitment Emory had made to himself as Mike's body was lowered into the grave.

Watching Mike Jr.'s comical dance made Emory smile, but watching Misty interact with the child really touched him. They looked forward to having their own children and he knew she would be a fantastic mom. The scene before him confirmed that.

Movement in his peripheral vision made him glance away. At the doorway, Dewey Hastings, dressed in an ill-fitted brown plaid suit, waved to catch his attention. Emory rushed to the lobby to meet the man, wondering how he got into the building unquestioned. Hastings held up a large manila envelope as Emory approached.

"Sorry to interrupt. The photo lab messed things all up, but I got it all straightened out. Here's them papers and pictures you wanted."

Emory grabbed the envelope. "Thanks, but do me a favor and get out of here before folks see you. It's not good for us to be seen together."

"Crap. And here I got all dressed up for this. What's wrong, Counselor? Not good enough for you?"

"You know what I mean, and why. Now, beat it."

The man shrugged, turned, and left. Emory sighed in relief as the main doors closed behind the man. He hoped no one significant connected the two of them. He opened the envelope and leafed through the papers, smiling. Easy pickings from one of his first elderly clients. Now, his engagement present to Misty.

He returned to the room and found his fiancée at the head table, helping Mike Jr. with a Royal Crown cola while Hannah retrieved some food for them. He tapped her on the shoulder to get her attention.

"Happy engagement." He handed her the envelope as she gave him an inquisitive look.

"What's this?"

He gave her a few moments to look at the contents before answering.

"An engagement present. Our first piece of property … where our home will be built. Like the view?" The Kodak color photos revealed a mountaintop view overlooking Thorpe Reservoir to the west. A map showed the plot layout. The deed showed it owned in full by Emory Albritton. "Twenty acres, mostly wooded. There's an old logging road we'll upgrade to get to the building site. I see a grand house, with lots of windows and a long deck offering this view. What do you think?"

"How did you …?" She smiled and hugged Emory, ending the embrace with a long kiss. "It looks beautiful. May I?" She nodded toward her parents, who had finally taken a break from dancing to sit at an adjacent table.

Emory pushed aside a sudden feeling of guilt. He had not missed the irony of his brother's death. Mike had been 100%-by-the-book, law abiding and in love with law enforcement. He, well, wasn't. He skirted the law, manipulated the law, and yet Mike was the one to die. Mike had the loving family, the most to lose. Yet, Emory was the one still there. There was something universally unfair about that, but Emory didn't want to dwell on that. He had his life to live.

Emory nodded and watched as Misty showed his "gift" to her parents. Guff smiled broadly and gave him a quick thumbs up. Emory basked in the moment. He loved making Misty happy and looked forward to a lifetime of such surprises for her.

Twenty-seven
(Present day)
ఇ◆◆ఞ

Dewey Hastings and Senator Albritton went way back, to the first time Dewey extorted Albritton's lunch money on the middle school playground. Dewey didn't have the book smarts of the younger boy, but he had the street smarts and the bluster to pull off just about anything. After that first hungry week, however, the younger boy's brain had outwitted Dewey's brawn and Dewey realized he had limitations. Still, he wasn't finished with the lad. He cautiously "coached" Albritton on the ways of the street and saw that the boy had a talent for working along the fringes of the law to the advantage of both of them. Now, thirty-some years later, Dewey bristled at the mention of working "for" the senator. True, Albritton held the purse strings, but Dewey liked to think he'd been the politician's mentor through all those years.

Those street smarts hadn't been needed to locate the 'Mabel somebody' house. A brief stop at the local tourist information center led him to a display of local attractions in which the brochure for the Mabel Dodge Luhan House and Conference Center sat prominently near the top of the rack. Every bit of his experience, however, would be needed to pull off the task before him. In western Carolina, he knew every crag and dale, every twist of the commonly used roads and, more importantly, every rarely used back road. He could make a body disappear forever in his own stompin' grounds. Here, he didn't know how to get from one end of this dustbowl town to the other.

He drove his rented Corolla down Paseo del Pueblo Norte and marveled at the names. Too many 'caminos' and 'paseos' and 'de la' this or 'del' that. Where were the American street names? At least Kit Carson was a real name, a name he recognized. Besides, who the hell would plant a bunch of prickly cactus and call it a garden? He missed the familiar flora of western Carolina. The mountains in the distance held some promise as a body dump, but what kind of vehicle would he need to accomplish that? The Corolla wasn't likely to cut it. How easy would it be to move about the Taos Indian Reservation?

Those details could come later. At this point, he needed to confirm the women's presence at that Mabel's house. He pulled into the Kit Carson State Park and parked by the ball fields. According to his map, Mabel's sat in the tree line at the base of the scrubby foothill. He hoped to find a vantage point in the park where he could casually sit and stake out the place. The area around the tennis courts gave him his only clear view of the historic inn's property but trees, fences, and buildings obstructed any valuable observations. He would need a different tack.

He meandered around the park a bit, acting like a tourist, before getting back into his rental. His only option was a direct attack. He checked his appearance in the rear-view mirror, started the engine, and drove right into the lot of the Mabel Dodge Luhan House. Only a few cars sat there. He wondered if they belonged to guests or the staff. He parked, and climbed out into the dry, warm air. He calmly strolled around the grounds, pretending to admire the architecture. A short man of American Indian descent, who appeared to be a groundskeeper or maintenance man, watched him closely. Dewey walked up to him.

"I've heard so much about this place. I just had to stop by and see it for myself." He glanced around but could not discern which rooms had occupants. A thought came to him, prompted by his reading the travel brochure earlier. "So, could you show me where Dennis Hopper wrote 'Easy Rider'? The Ansel Adams room, wasn't it? I can't wait to tell my buddies I actually saw it."

The man pointed toward one spot on the property. A small patio shared by two rooms, but he didn't say which one was the Adams room. Dewey saw no indication that either room held occupants.

"The front office had more on the history of the place." The man moved to return to his duties.

"So, which room does Myra Mitchell use when she's here?"

The man continued to walk away, but shrugged his shoulders.

So much for that approach, thought Dewey. He would have to take a different one. He put on his best smile, and walked into the reception area.

"May I help you, Sir," asked the college-aged girl at the reception desk.

"Good afternoon. My name's Carl Hamilton and I'm here to surprise my niece, Alexia. My sister-in-law told me she was here with a Ms. Mitchell. Could you tell me where they are so I can surprise her?"

The young woman knitted her brow and gave him a curious look. "I'm sorry, Sir. I can pass on a message for a guest, but we respect their privacy and don't give out information on them."

Dewey half expected such an answer. At least her body language admitted that she knew the girl and the Mitchell lady. In his mind that confirmed they were there.

"Perhaps I could call her on the house phone. You could

connect me without divulging anything." He hoped to watch her make the connection and determine the room. He looked about for a phone.

"I'm sorry. We don't have a house phone."

Dewey's frustration mounted but he knew that sugar was needed, not spicy contention.

"Surely there must be some way. I drove all the way up here from Santa Fe to treat her to dinner and catch up on the family. I'd be much obliged for some help here."

"Just a minute."

The young woman exited to a back office and Dewey could hear her talking with what sounded like an older woman. He stepped closer to the doorway, watching the shadows on the floor to alert him to any movement toward him. He turned back toward the front desk and thought luck was finally with him. The computer screen listed all of the rooms and occupants' last names. But his only luck recently had been bad luck. Neither woman's name appeared on the screen. Were they there under an alias, or had they again moved one step ahead of him?

"No." The next words were muffled. "You know the policy ..." Again, he couldn't make out the words. "... don't want paparazzi around ..."

He realized he wasn't getting anywhere and wouldn't get any info the easy way. Plus, he was tired of playing catch-up. How did they keep managing to elude him? Anger management was only the name of a movie in his book. His Plan B had consisted of taking Mitchell and the girl by force and just driving until he found a suitable dumping ground. Plan B had now become Plan A. He snatched up the desk phone and unplugged the cord before pulling the rest of it out from the wall. He retrieved his knife from his back pocket and cradled it in his left hand. Next, he stepped into the office and closed the door. He saw an older woman move to pick up the phone on her desk. A glimpse of her nametag told him that she, Diana, was the manager.

"Not a good idea!" He brandished the knife openly and the woman, Diana, slowly removed her hand from the handset. "Sit down, both of you! Hands where I can sees 'em." He grabbed that phone and pulled the cord from the wall.

Dewey walked up behind the chair holding the young woman. "Put your hands behind the chair." He held the tip of the knife to her throat as she began to weep. He quickly tied her hands together and took the excess cord to hogtie her ankles under the chair, all the while keeping an eye on the manager. "Your turn," he said to the woman. Her rolling desk chair had arms, so he secured each wrist to an arm and tied her legs to the central post of the chair.

Satisfied that both women were secure, he sat on the edge of the desk.

"Now, I need to know where Alexia Hamilton and Myra Mitchell are."

Diana looked at him defiantly while the clerk broke down sobbing. He focused on the girl, placing the tip of his knife on her throat again and applying just enough pressure to draw a bead of blood. He watched the sweat ooze on her brow. The girl looked at her boss. Dewey followed her gaze in time to see Diana give a subtle nod.

"Th-they're not h-here."

Dewey's face flushed as the anger flamed inside. Was she lying? Or was he once again a step behind? He controlled his emotions. He would take the lead soon enough and finish his assigned task. At the moment, he needed the information required to make that happen.

"Where are they?"

"I-I don't know. H-honest."

He applied a bit more pressure to the knife. She started to quiver and he noted a pool of urine settling in the wooden seat of her chair.

"H-honest. They left yesterday and I wasn't working. I-I don't know where th-they went."

Dewey saw a roll of duct tape on top of a nearby file cabinet. He removed a short strip of tape and applied it over the girl's mouth. "Behave, or I'll cover your nose, too." He turned his attention to the girl's boss.

"So, where'd they go?"

"Who are you?"

Despite her attempts to remain calm, Dewey could sense the tension in her voice and see the perspiration starting to soak the armpits of her blouse.

"Where did they go?"

"You're not Alexia's uncle. She has no living family. Who are you and why do you want Myra?"

Dewey smiled at the assumption made by the woman. After all, who'd be after the girl when the famous A-list author had all the money? He'd let that assumption ride.

"Where?"

He slowly tore off another piece of tape and applied it to the clerk's nose. Panic flared into the girl's eyes as she realized she could get no air.

"St-stop it! Please! Don't hurt her. Please."

The girl's chest began to heave with her mounting panic. He looked at Diana and raised his brow in a silent "*So, answer me.*"

"Th-they left yesterday. Right after noon. They're driving east. That's all I know! Please! Take that tape off! She's suffocating."

Dewey reached for the tape just as the girl's head slumped over, limp. He pulled off the tape and watched as she took in a huge reflex breath. She would come to, eventually.

"I don't believe you're telling me everything. Where are they going?"

Diana stood her ground and remained silent. He didn't really want to kill the girl, so he let her be. He looked about the room and discovered a large toolbox in one corner, on top of a box of paper. He rummaged through it and found a hammer. He returned to the desk and picked up the tape, tearing off a piece and placing it over the manager's mouth. He then stepped behind her, where she couldn't see him and anticipate his movements. He took a heavy swing of the hammer onto her left long finger as it rested on the arm of the chair. The woman's scream stopped at the tape across her mouth, but the tears gushed easily.

He stepped in front of her. "Ready to tell me?"

Her face settled into a flint-like iciness, remaining unchanged even after the third finger hung from her hand, crushed. Her breathing had increased, but the tears had stopped. Dewey could see that she would give up her entire hand before betraying the Mitchell woman. Maybe.

He poked through the toolbox and smiled as he picked up a pair of tin snips. The fingers would yield easily where the bone sat already fractured. He sat in front of her, opening and closing the snips. Her face showed no fear. What was this woman made of?

Once again, he stepped behind her.

"A broken finger is one thang. You can use it again once healed. Losin' the finger altogether is another matter."

She tried to say something, but the tape transmuted it into

mumbling. She tried to move her hand but he had tied it well. She started to shake the chair. Her muffled cries barely rose from her.

With his left hand he held her injured hand down, while with his right hand he directed the snips to her ring finger and began to apply force, her hand flinching. He heard her sobs as the skin began to tear, but he stopped at the sound of movement in the outer reception area.

A deep bass voice asked, "Diana?" followed by a knock at the door.

"Damn it!" he muttered under his breath. He scanned the room for another way out. The window was convenient, but he had no idea where he would be in relation to his car. He hesitated, hoping that no response would send the inquirer away thinking Diana was elsewhere.

Suddenly, Diana kicked out with her restrained feet, sending her and the chair toppling.

"Diana!" The male voice reflected urgent concern. The knock became a pounding at the door. Dewey slammed the snips in anger at Diana's head and rushed to the window. The latch opened easily. The lower sash barely budged. The door cracked at the sound of a shoulder's impact. "Diana!"

Dewey ran to the toolbox, picked it up, and threw it at the unyielding window. The wooden sash and glass shattered on impact. Dewey pushed aside the remnants and escaped to a nearby courtyard as the office door splintered open and a man wearing an inn staff shirt charged into the room. Dewey ran around the building to his car, and floored the accelerator, spewing up rock and dust, as he fled the parking lot.

He knew the women inside had no idea what kind or color of car he had, but the man who'd interrupted his fun might have the details on his rental. He would need another vehicle ASAP. He thought through his situation. If the woman, Diana, talked, which she would, she'd let authorities know that she'd told him that Myra Mitchell was heading east. They would assume he'd be following that route. Would he be better off getting out of Taos now or under the cover of dark? Should he deflect any search for him by driving north? He could drive south, back to Santa Fe, and fly east to … to do what? Intercept them? What were the chances of that? And where? "Heading east" meant what? Was the Hamilton girl taking Mitchell to North Carolina? The east coast? How far could Mitchell go in her condition? Somewhere in between?

He picked up Highway 64 and moved north to the first gas station, where he observed the traffic in and out of the pumps while inspecting his road atlas. He selected the car he wanted and followed it as the driver pulled away from the pump, smiling as the driver entered the lot of a nearby grocery store and parked. Dewey surveyed the lot for video cameras and saw only one covering the store entrance. He parked next to his target and started to exit his rental when he spotted the driver and a young teen emerging from the store and walking back toward the car.

He cursed at the realization that the woman had simply stopped to pick up her child. He took the time to consult his map again and realized he had lost his quarry. She had a day's travel on him and could be on any one of a number of routes east by now, but only a few were quality roads with enough towns that if Mitchell got into trouble with her health she could get help rapidly enough. Heading north made no sense that way. They could head to U.S. Highway 50 but that led through desolate areas of western Kansas. After that, they'd have to go to Denver to pick up I-70. U.S. Highway 64 was the most direct route east and would lead her to Tulsa, but it, too, led through some sparse country. No, the U.S. highways would lack cell phone coverage and quick access to medical care, but I-40, just to their south, qualified and would take her to Oklahoma City, Memphis, Nashville, and ultimately, western North Carolina. Trying to chase her down by car would be fruitless.

He pulled out his smart phone and checked airlines. He could be in Oklahoma City that night, hopefully ahead of her by at least a day and right in her path unless she had driven north to pick up I-70 or further south to I-20 in Texas. He could cover only one route and his gut told him he was making the right decision. But he still needed a plan. How could he possibly find them? They could be going just about anywhere "east."

Twenty-eight
(Summer –1969)
❧✦✦☙

Betsy had blamed dropping the flowers on slippery hands, but Georgia's innocent comment stung like a literal slap in the face and delivered Betsy into such a funk she abandoned that first date with Rod. But he persisted, and a week later, they met at the nearest Skyline Chili. Then she put him off with a variety of excuses, until two weeks later, at Frisch's Big Boy, he introduced Betsy to fresh strawberry pie from heaven. After another week of excuses, she accepted another date. She wasn't playing hard-to-get. Her emotions went from high tide at full moon to low tide at new moon. Was she ready for a new commitment?

During that time, several things happened that seemed to push her past aside. After multiple failed attempts to call Curt Umfleet, her last call had been met with a recording that the number had been disconnected. Undaunted, she mailed him a registered letter including a check to pay him back, with interest. She had received no reply. Nor did the letter return to her, but the check had cleared the bank so she assumed life went on for the Umfleets. Harder perhaps, without Mary, but life went on. She would forever feel indebted to him for his role in helping her, but in her mind, she had settled her financial obligation.

In addition, she quietly asked around and finally splurged by consulting a private eye, or private investigator as they preferred being called.

"Good morning, Miss. Just how can I help you?"

"I'd like you to retrieve something for me, quietly and secretly, from a house where I grew up in western North

Carolina. Can you do that?"

"Maybe. I need some more details."

He sat behind his desk taking notes as Betsy told him about the chest she wanted him to collect. She gave no details as to its contents, other than it held important papers for her. She said nothing about Jimmy Bob. As for the reason she needed help, she explained that she had witnessed a crime there and for her to return would likely result in harm. She told him the local sheriff was in cahoots with the home's owner, and wouldn't help her. Maybe that was slandering Sheriff Connelly but the more she had thought about her pa's activities, the more likely that seemed. He agreed to take the case, despite arguing that she should be a responsible citizen and report the crime she witnessed.

Five days later, she received a phone call to meet the man at his office. Had he found it? She was surprised to realize that her hope no longer soared in anticipation.

"Sorry, Miss Weston, but I couldn't complete the job. The lumber stack you mentioned was used to build a pole barn addition to that shed. The place is filled with more junk than I've ever seen in one location. Heaven knows what he plans to do with some of the stuff I saw in there. I couldn't begin to get near the spot you mentioned to start digging. I'm sorry."

Knowing her pa, that junk would be there until he died. Betsy felt what hope she still had fade to black. Yet, she no longer felt the ache in her heart as with past disappointments. She reflected on her thoughts about the Umfleets. Jimmy Bob would not be found. Just as with Curt Umfleet's losing Mary, she had lost her son. Life had to move on.

The following Friday night, Rod helped her discover Graeter's Ice Cream where the bittersweet chocolate chunks, in the creamiest vanilla ice cream she'd ever tasted, could compete with Godiva's best. The following day, she returned on her own for three scoops of the chocolate chocolate-chip ice cream, and a new stash of their homemade chocolate bars. She waddled from the store feeling like her stomach was a bloated watermelon.

Rod told her he wanted to wine and dine her, but she refused the wine aspect of his offer, so he fed her, laughed with her, shared his dreams, talked about school, complimented her on her work, and told her how impressed his father had become with her. He introduced her to treats unlike anything she'd ever tasted. Over the next month, he took her across the river to The Conservatory for dancing, to Mt. Adams' Blind Lemon for quiet conversation, and to a Reds' game where she actually got to meet Pete Rose *and* Johnny Bench. Rod swept her off her feet.

Jacob Meyer aided and abetted his son. He'd made it clear that never in his career had he met such a natural talent. He coached and groomed her. He became a mentor and in turn, she saw in him the father she'd always wanted. She played on these new emotions to add to her new card line and Jacob snatched up 90% of what she presented to him. To Betsy, he was the most artistic man she could imagine and the thought of his becoming her father-in-law made her heart leap with Rod's first hint at marriage.

With that, her past slammed her into an emotional wall. She wanted to be honest with Rod, to tell him about Jimmy Bob, her escape from her pa, and Dewey Hastings. She didn't think Dewey would ever be able to trace her to Ohio, but only time would give her full assurance that he no longer posed a threat. More importantly, Rod deserved to know she'd had a child before, out of wedlock. Yet, it scared her more to think of losing him now. Another loss would be too much. The timing had to be just right for such a revelation. And what would Jacob think? Or Georgia? Or her new friends? She had succeeded in forging the new life she'd always dreamed of. Could she risk losing it now?

After a tumultuous and joyous three months, Rod told her to get all dolled up for their next date to celebrate his graduation. She did, and he surprised her with dinner at the 5-star Maisonnette, at the end of which he got down on one knee and asked, "Betsy Weston, will you marry me?"

A year later, on the third of October, at two p.m., she became Mrs. Betsy Meyer and turned down her new father-in-law's job offer to remain a freelancer. At the end of October, Rod's third employer since graduating fired him and Rod remained a freeloader.

In reality, the honeymoon had ended with the wedding, and she realized she had been as enamored by the father as by the son. If only she had recognized that fact earlier.

Early in the new year, with snow on the ground and frost on the inside of the windows, Betsy glanced out the apartment window to see Rod sliding toward the main door. It was too early in the day. Had they lost heat at work? Or had something else happened? She stood next to her drawing table as the door to their apartment opened. The look on Rod's face revealed a replay of the previous firings.

"What happened? I thought this job was going great," Betsy said as Rod slinked into the apartment, her apartment, under her name, the only name on the lease and responsible for the rent.

"It was great. I don't know what happened. Honest. Maybe I'm just not cut out to be an accountant."

"Rod, you've got to find a job you can hold onto. If we're going to have a family, you need to be able to support us. I want to focus on our kids, not being the breadwinner."

"I know, I know. We've had this argument before. I'm not deaf and my memory is fine."

He was right. They'd had this argument after the second dismissal.

"You must have some idea why they let you go. What'd they tell you?"

He glared at her but said nothing. His silence irritated her. She frowned and released a long sigh.

"Fine. Don't tell me." She grabbed her purse. "I need to get out of here for a little while. Don't worry. I'll be back to cook your dinner."

With that, she dressed for the weather and stomped out the door. The road into French Park had been freshly plowed and by the time she reached the parking lot, she regretted the brusque, sarcastic tone of her last comment. She saw people standing around a fire built inside a 55-gallon drum and joined them briefly. Then she parked herself on a nearby picnic table and watched kids and adults alike sledding down the same hill where she'd watched the children roll just months earlier. The snow made it peaceful. The laughter around her should have lifted her up, but the inner turmoil would not yield. What had happened? She felt convinced that Rod knew that answer and resented his unwillingness to open up with her. He'd been so open and sharing while they dated. Now he acted like he had tetanus – was there such a word as 'tetanic?' – completely lock-jawed.

Even more than that, his presence in the apartment, with his constant demands of her, made it difficult at best to find her creative muse, to create the works that their livelihood depended upon, still. She recalled the creative famine she'd suffered after his last firing. Then, she had refused to tell Jacob why. This time would be different.

Still, the question "why?" stalked her. She returned to the main parking lot where a payphone occupied one corner of the nearby picnic pavilion. Doffing one glove, she searched through her purse and came up with some loose change, as well as the note with Rod's work number. She popped in a quarter and called the company.

"Mr. DeVois, please."

It took a minute to convince the man's secretary to let her talk with him, but he came on the line. "I don't have much time, Mrs. Meyer. What can I do for you?" He seemed irritated and she guessed he didn't want to talk with her but was too polite to refuse.

"I'm so sorry to bother you and I won't keep you long, but Rod came home and told me he was dismissed." She watched the mist of her breath dissipate into the cold air. Was it an omen of something to come?

"That's correct."

"He won't talk to me about it. I don't understand what happened and I don't know how I can help him if I don't understand what the problem is."

There was a pause, but when he spoke, his tone seemed to have softened. She got an earful of shortcomings: coming in late, leaving early, criticizing everyone else's work while not finishing his own, mathematic errors and disputes with customers.

Betsy thanked Mr. DeVois and hung up, stunned. How could *she* help? If she mentioned these issues, he'd get defensive and complain about her nagging. He'd get angry if she revealed that she'd called his ex-boss. How could she affect his apparent lack of work ethic? But even more alarming was the fact that since she worked from home, she knew what time he left for work and that he always returned home at the expected time. What was he doing? Did he regret getting married? Did he have someone else?

She reflected on their finances. She could afford to give him a week at home with all of his interruptions. Maybe she'd get some, a little, a tiny bit of work done. If he remained jobless after a week, she'd go to Jacob and ask for a temporary workspace.

She arrived home to prepare dinner at their usual time. The apartment was empty.

Betsy lay in bed, wide-awake. She had no tears left and a trashcan next to the bed sat full of used tissues. Married a full three months and two weeks and she lay there alone, her husband's whereabouts unknown. What cosmic wrong had she committed? Why were all of her relationships lemmings, doomed to jump off a cliff to die a quick death?

The door to the apartment opened in the middle of the night and Betsy jumped out of bed and rushed to the bedroom door. Rod staggered to the bathroom, neglecting to close the door. She waited. He emerged and turned toward the bedroom, stopping as he saw her silhouette framed by the doorway.

"I-I'm sawree," he said, his speech slurred. "I ..."

She stepped forward and caught him as he started to slump over. Placing an arm under his, she helped him to bed. She didn't like that he'd turned to alcohol for solace, but recognized that she'd left the apartment first. She hadn't been there for him, hadn't given him the support he needed. Lying next to him, she stroked his forehead and watched his face in low ambient light. She saw no peace there, despite the alcohol-induced slumber.

She awoke the next morning to the blended aromas of bacon and coffee. The bedside clock told her she'd managed to claim almost five hours of sleep. Not enough to find any creative traction. She donned her robe and walked to the kitchen where Rod tended to a frying pan full of thick-sliced Kahn's bacon, her favorite. Several eggs sat next to the range, waiting their turn in the skillet. Beside them sat a large mug of black coffee, which Rod grabbed and sipped before realizing she was there. He turned toward her.

"I –"

"I'm –"

They both stopped, but Betsy took the opportunity to speak up first. "I shouldn't have left. I'm sorry." She eased up to him, afraid to yield to her desire to wrap her arms around him.

"I'm sorry, too." He stepped forward and took her in his arms. "I-I needed …"

She placed her lips on his to quiet him. An hour later, they emerged from the bedroom and she took over in the kitchen, rescuing the grease-encased bacon, frying eggs, and toasting slices of Wonder Bread. As they sat opposite each other at their small table and ate, she toyed with his legs using her foot. They ate slowly, silently. His plate nearly empty, he stopped chewing and reached across to play with her hair.

"I do love you," he said. "I want you to be proud of me."

Betsy smiled and took his hand and kissed it. "I love you, too … and I …" She started to say, "… and I am," but couldn't force the word out. She wanted to be proud of him. She wanted to encourage him. Why was it so hard to do that? She completed her comment. "... know I will be."

Late the next morning Betsy watched Rod leave to get the day's paper with its want ads and to renew his effort at finding a job. She felt invigorated and optimistic, the honeymoon far from over. After a quick 'run' through the apartment, picking up errant clothes and tidying up the kitchen, she sat at her drawing table and began to sketch a character who'd been incubating in her mind for the past few weeks. The first figure didn't match her vision, so she balled up the paper and tried again. On her tenth effort, her mental image clicked with what she saw on the paper, but she looked too much like Sally Fleming. Betsy would never deny that Sally and Jim Fleming were the muses behind her idea, but she didn't want her character to be recognizable as the real person. Still, the character had to display the woman's verve, quick wit, irreverence, and timely sarcasm – her chutzpah. It was a word she'd just learned and she loved saying it. Yes, chutzpah. She altered the sketch and sat back smiling. There 'she' was.

'She' needed a name. As Betsy worked through a mental list of female names, she slipped past Georgia and Georgia Gordon's habit of calling everyone "Sweetie" came to mind. That was 'her.' The perfect antithesis. Sweetie could be sweet, but rarely would be. Now, Sweetie and ...

She returned to a new sheet of paper and began her sketch of Sweetie's mate. An hour later, with several redraws of the man and a few tweaks to Sweetie, she had the pair, satisfied with each individual alone and as a pair of foils for each other. "Sweetie and ..." The first male name that popped into her head was 'George.' She thought about it for a moment and nodded. "*Why not?*" she thought. 'Sweetie and George' it would be.

By mid-afternoon, Betsy had several cartoons completed and captioned. Sweetie and George in a church pew, Sweetie's nose wrinkled as she leans away and comments, "No, you old fart. We don't need a percussion section." George bent over the garden as Sweetie comments on hemorrhoids when she asked for hemerocallis. George sniping as Sweetie applies a new skin lotion, "Trying to put your old whine in a new skin?"

Betsy started a new cartoon but stopped at the sound of keys in the front door. She jumped up to greet Rod and as the door swung open, she stepped forward only to have him brusquely push past her and plop down on the couch. His face reflected his bad day. She took a deep breath, sat down beside him, and reached up to stroke his face.

"No luck, huh?"

He grabbed her arm and pushed her away, the alcohol evident on his breath.

Betsy jumped up and fled to the bedroom, crying. That was it. She'd escaped one drunk. She would not replace him with another. It was her apartment, in her name alone, and in the morning, she planned to kick him out.

Twenty-nine
(Summer 1971)
๑~◆◆๑

"Why, Jacob?" Betsy stood in front of the creative director's desk, dumbfounded by the rejection of her "Sweetie and George" creation. "Look at the popular comedians: Jackie Gleason, Sid Caesar, Mel Brooks, Steve Martin, George Carlin. Some of their funniest stuff is irreverent, cutting edge. We need to tap that."

Jacob Meyer shook his head and sighed. "Bets, you know I love you. You know I've loved this series since you first showed it to me at dinner months ago. But the executive board is staunchly conservative and won't yield."

Betsy looked at her soon-to-be-ex-father-in-law and took a deep breath. "This ... this doesn't have anything to do with my leaving Rod, does it?" The question had to be asked. She admired Jacob greatly, but she needed to make sure.

Jacob shook his head again. "No." He paused. "You know I'm too fond of you to ever ..." He gazed directly at her, unflinching. "... to ever hurt you ... and I can't abandon Rod; he's my son. You were the best thing ever to come his way and he missed the boat, screwed it up royally. I blame him, not you. Our relationship, both working and personal, will not change because of his failure."

She looked at the man and saw sincerity. Still, the relationship would change. It wouldn't stay the same after her divorce was final. There would always be the awkwardness of Rod's presence between them, the wistful thoughts of what might have been, and the grandchildren who would never be.

"Thank you, Jacob. I love you, too." She reached into her briefcase and retrieved a set of papers. "However, business is still business. You once taught me that." She handed him the papers. "I'd appreciate a signature on these as soon as possible. It's the release of your right of first refusal on the series, so I can market it elsewhere."

He read the papers and looked up at her. "I should get the lawyers to do this, but I see you're already using our own form." He smiled. "You've learned fast." He signed both sets of papers and returned one set to Betsy. "My board's going to regret this."

Betsy tucked her set of papers into her briefcase. "Thanks, Jacob. You've been a great teacher, but maybe you should have read it closer. I wasn't trying to pass one over on y'all, but that form releases me from all future rights of first refusal as well."

Jacob stood up, walked around his desk, and gave Betsy a big hug. "You didn't pass one over on me. I saw that and signed it anyway. My gift to my daughter, and I'll always think of you as my daughter. Now, please don't make me regret it by taking all your talent elsewhere."

She hugged him again and stepped back.

"Actually, I kinda saw this coming and I'm going to syndication. King Features has already given me an offer. You should see 'Sweetie and George' in the Sunday comics within a month."

Jacob laughed. "You really have learned a lot this last year. You know I wish you all the best. I guess I'll have to start subscribing to the Sunday Enquirer."

"Jacob, I know you said our relationship wouldn't change and I appreciate that. I should let you know I'm thinking about leaving town after the divorce."

His mouth dropped and a look of disappointment crossed his face.

"I'll let you know what I decide. In the meantime, I'll continue my work on the current card series until you can get your own team up-to-speed on it. I suspect my 'Sweetie' is going to become very time consuming and I'll be needing to back off the card series."

He nodded. "I hate to say it, but I think you're right … and that's okay with me. I only want the best for you." He chuckled. "I keep saying that. I really mean it."

Betsy gave him one more hug, picked up her briefcase and portfolio, and left. A tear crossed her cheek as she left his office.

Betsy had tried to keep her marriage but Rod stayed in a state of denial. Hours and hours of counseling, but everything was her fault or that of his multiple employers. Reconciliation after reconciliation, but none lasting long enough to earn Rod a return to her bed. Now, after six months of rancorous discord, Betsy's divorce finalized. Being young and female had worked in her favor. The judge took the position that Rod should be the breadwinner and granted him nothing of her increasingly substantial earnings. She kept her scant possessions, including the car and everything she had brought into the marriage. There wasn't much else to split up.

During that six months, her prediction that "Sweetie" would take up more and more of her time came true. She hadn't been prepared for the pace of weekly deadlines, but she never failed to meet them, despite the all-too-frequent heated meetings with Rod and the lawyers. By the time the judge signed off on the papers, she had divested herself of every possession that wouldn't fit into her Mustang and had gotten ahead of the deadlines by a month. More than enough time to make the move to California, the base of the Hearst-owned King Features. She didn't have to move to the West Coast, but why not? She had no desire to live elsewhere.

Part of her felt that the further she moved away from her past, the better. The other part wanted to remain closer to North Carolina. Over the previous year, she had hired two different private investigators to find Jimmy Bob. Admittedly, she had had little money to fund the first attempt, but money hadn't been an issue on the second try. Neither had been successful. It was time to move west, but not to forget.

So, on the 30th of June, her apartment empty and her car full, she first drove to Gibson Greetings to give her tearful goodbyes to the creative staff and others she had gotten to know so well.

"Surprise!"

Georgia Gordon and Carol presented her with a farewell cake, and the creative staff presented her with a personalized, signed collage of her work.

"Is, uh, Jacob here?" Betsy asked around.

No one had seen him and he hadn't called in.

An hour went by, but no Jacob. So, with a heavy heart and saddened by Jacob's failure to show, Betsy left Cincinnati, heading west. From St. Louis, she picked up the "Mother Road," Route 66, now partly replaced by the new interstate, and made the scenic drive through the Ozarks to Springfield, MO. At the northeast end of town, she came across a rough-hewn rail fence separating the road from a dozen or more stone cottages. The sign said "Rail Haven Motor Court." She pulled into the lot, checked into the office, and rented a cottage for the night. Although the place had a kitchenette, she was not prepared to cook dinner, so she took to the road and a few miles further along she stopped at Red's Giant Hamburgs for dinner. Perhaps, "stopped" wasn't the right word for a place that billed itself as the world's first "drive-thru" restaurant.

Intrigued by the promotional flyers for local attractions, Betsy decided to explore the Ozarks a bit the next day instead of heading straight out on Route 66. By lunchtime, she found herself in Eureka Springs, AR ... and immediately fell in love with the place. The winding tree-lined streets, the quaint Victorian homes terraced into the hillsides, its eclectic shops all combined to give the town a unique appeal. She parked her car and began to walk ... and walk ... and walk. By dinnertime, she had covered most of the town and California no longer held any appeal.

She returned to Basin Springs Park at the center of town and checked into the massive, stone Basin Park Hotel. Built against the hillside, all eight floors had "ground floor" entrances.

"How many nights, Miss?"

"Three, please."

The clerk filled out the paperwork and asked for cash. Betsy completed the transaction and asked, "Do you have any brochures on places to rent?"

The clerk looked at her with a bit of surprise on his face.

"O'er there on that table is the real estate information, but most young folk migratin' to town seem to end up in one o' them communes around town. Cheaper."

"Thanks, but I need a quiet place to work. Something nice."

"Got a job?"

"Yes, Sir."

"How old're you?"

"Old enough." This man was becoming irritating.

"Run-away?"

"Look, it's no business of yours. May I have my key, please?"

The man handed her the room key, and continued his twenty questions.

"What kinda job?"

Betsy's patience wore thin. "I have to park my car." She turned to exit the lobby.

He spoke up behind her. "I'ma askin' 'cause my sister has a cottage on top the hill here, on Eureka Street. It's not advertised, but she's lookin' for a renter. She don't want no bunch of flower children, or marijuana smokin' hippies, or rent skipping drifters, so I'm doing due diligence, I think they call it."

Betsy hesitated at the door, her hand on the brass push plate ready to open the door.

"Beautiful place. Best deal in town ... for the right person."

Betsy turned around and returned to the desk. The way he'd said those words caught her attention. The owner's apparent willingness to let the place sit empty while waiting for the right person or persons as renters spoke volumes about the owner and her pride in her property.

"How nice?"

"Two bedroom, kitchen, large main room, bath and a half, smaller workroom, detached garage, full width front porch lookin' southeast over the valley. Well maintained, everything works like it should. Even got a flower garden."

"How much?"

"Hundred fifty a week or four hundred for a month, includes utilities. Might be willing to negotiate for something long term."

The price didn't scare Betsy this time. She had the money.

The man had her interest and she could tell he knew it.

"You the right person?"

"Maybe. But I don't know what the competition is, and I'd sure want to see it first."

"Gotta prove to me you're the right person. Age?"

"Twenty-one." *Well, almost*, she thought.

"Job?"

"Do you have a copy of Sunday's Arkansas Democrat-Gazette?"

"Should be extras in back waitin' for the distributor to pick up." He walked into the back office and Betsy took that moment to rush to the table holding the real estate flyers. She quickly scanned the rental section of one to see that the man was correct in calling it a good deal. However, she didn't have time to scrutinize *all* the papers to prove his claim of being the 'best deal in town.' He returned to the desk with a copy of the newspaper.

She extracted the color comic section and found the "Sweetie and George" block. "Here." She handed the section back to him and pointed to the comic.

"What about it?"

She pointed to the by-line and then to her registration. "That's me."

He looked at the cartoon and compared the signature with the one on the room registration. "No way." He scrutinized her, his brow furrowed. "You're only twenty-one and you do this?" She nodded. "Damn," was his only reply.

She turned toward the front door again, ready to move her car.

"Alright then. Tomorrow morning, 9 a.m. Meet me here!" he yelled after her.

* * *

Four days later, after scrutinizing more than a dozen rentals, Betsy left the Basin Park Hotel for her new residence, a three bedroom, two-bath home with a loft workspace and great light … right next door to the hotel clerk's sister's rental. But he wasn't upset. Neither was his sister, Tammie.

"I know you're going to love it here," said Tammie as she passed the keys to her home to Betsy. Angela, her teenage daughter, pouted as she looked on.

"Mom, why do we have –?"

"Shush, girl. We've talked about this already."

Tammie and Angela had spent the previous two days moving their belongings from their home to the rental next door. Betsy was certain the extra two hundred dollars a month above the price of the rental and a yearlong lease had convinced mom into switching.

"Angela, I'm going to need furniture, household goods … all that stuff. Do you like to shop?" Betsy guessed the girl didn't have much opportunity to shop for more than necessities. "I'll need some help … and I need someone to show me around. Are you up for that?"

Angela smiled and nodded.

The following day, the mayor personally invited her to the next city council meeting, where he welcomed her to the community and gave her a ceremonial "Key to the City." After the meeting, a young woman approached her.

"I love your comic. How did you ever come up with the idea?"

"Thank you. I –"

"By the way, I'm Oni Prairieberry." She must have seen the quizzical look on Betsy's face. "Not my given name. I guess that's obvious. When we got married, we decided to change our names to, well, to have meaning. Oni is African for 'born on sacred ground.' I loved it. Oni. The last name was just something to be whimsical. A decade later, I learned that 'oni' was Japanese for 'demon,' but it was too late to change again. I mean, changing your name once is one thing, but doing it again? I'd be as confused as everyone else."

Betsy couldn't help but smile at the soft-spoken brunette with thick-lensed, dark rimmed glasses, tornado whipped hair, and flower-child name. "Nice to meet you." She hoped the smile reflected friendliness, not her abashed feeling over Oni's comment about changing names.

"I'm a writer, too. Well, not like in comics or anything. Couldn't draw a crooked barn if my life depended on it. I write children's books. That's my husband, Chance, over there." She pointed toward the chamber's main door. "Would you like to come over to our place for some tea?"

"Umm, right now?" Betsy was intrigued by the woman's strange name and apparent free spirit. After the stuffy, conservative crew at Gibson, Oni was a breath of Ozark air.

"Well, sure. Or later, if you can't come now."

"How about tomorrow?"

Afternoon or evening?"

"Makes no difference."

"Good. Then come tomorrow about four and join us for dinner. Do you like vegetarian?"

Betsy started to reply, but Oni continued.

"I still eat meat on occasion, but I intend to give it up entirely. It's the socially responsible thing to do."

Betsy suddenly felt socially irresponsible. She was a carnivore through and through. Barbecue with Carolina thin tomato sauce, hamburgers, steak, barbecue with Carolina mustard sauce, grilled chicken, prime rib, barbecue with Carolina vinegar and pepper sauce ... and in a pinch, Texas barbecued beef. That was real good, too. Thinking about it made her crave a Red's Giant Hamburg, even with that imitation barbecue sauce from Kansas City.

"I guess. Can't say as I've ever really tried it, but sure, I'm game."

Betsy spent the next week furnishing her new home while Eureka Springs spent the week ogling their new resident, "that cartoon girl." Betsy loved the thriving arts community and the hills reminded her of home. Even if her art wasn't of the 'fine' persuasion, the community loved an artist who could pay her bills. Betsy loved the town's eclectic population and the town accepted her into it.

By the end of the week, Betsy was fast friends with Angela, her mom, and Oni. She paid the girl for her time, bought her several new items of clothes, and gave the girl a personalized and autographed "Sweetie and George" cartoon. The cartoon, she noticed, quickly found a frame and a prominent position over the head of Angela's bed. Her mom got a new refrigerator for the "rental" home. Oni's gift? Unlimited conversation.

Her life at Gibson Cards had garnered some recognition, mainly from the closed group of artists and writers in the creative group, which had boosted her self-image. Her new life in Eureka Springs, however, brought with it a level of acclaim she was totally unprepared for.

At the hardware store, "Hi, Miss Weston. Love your comic." At the grocery, "Oh, Miss Betsy, Sweetie is my favorite." At various eateries, compliments and autograph seekers interrupted her meals. On the street, kids came up to her and asked to be in her comic. She thought this would blow over within a week or so, but after a month, the disruptions continued. Now, the tourists would come up to her after some local pointed her out.

"Oni, I'm beside myself. I can't go out without someone pestering me. It's distracting me and I don't know what to do."

"Sounds like new material to me."

"Huh?"

"There have to be some comments that you could use as source material. I've always been told that nothing is wasted on the writer. Everything in life becomes fodder. Figure out how to use it in your strip."

After mulling this over for day or two, Betsy had an idea: Sweetie and George would take to the old Route 66, before it completely disappeared from the maps. Chicago. Springfield, Illinois. Saint Louis. Springfield, Missouri. Oklahoma City. Shamrock and Amarillo, Texas. Albuquerque. Kingman, Arizona and the treacherous hairpin curves through the Black Mountains. Finally, Los Angeles. Betsy took a working vacation to make the road trip by herself over a two-month span, without curious neighbors and tourists, and the material became her first "Sweetie and George" book. Her series took off faster than Sweetie gunning it down Sunset Strip and her bank account quickly required professional management.

The following year saw Sweetie and George across the U.S. On Broadway in New York. On the beach in Miami. At the U.S. Capital and Washington Monument in Washington, D.C. The Alamo in San Antonio. Fisherman's Wharf in San Francisco. Pike Street Market in Seattle. Plus, more Chicago and L.A. A year later, her syndication managers had her touring the National Parks.

Yet, the traveling, exhilarating at first, became drudgery. The pace of maintaining a weekly cartoon, along with the expected yearly book, drained her. More importantly, Betsy tired of being alone. Co-workers and tour leaders didn't count. She missed having someone "at home" to share life with. After the divorce, she knew better than to rush into any relationship, but her self-imposed reclusion had ended long ago, only to find a work-imposed seclusion replacing it. She traveled the country, spent hours in exciting cities and beautiful national parks surrounded by a sea of people, and felt more isolated and alone than ever.

Her latest tour had ended and now, on a rainy mid-September day, she flew into Little Rock, and drove home, alone.

"Welcome home, stranger," said Tammie, standing at her front door with a plate of fried chicken, mashed potatoes, and fresh green beans. "I saw the lights come on and figured you to be home again."

"Hi. Nice to be back. I just finished unloading my car and unpacking some groceries." Betsy welcomed Tammie into the house and took the plate. "Ever been to Mount Rushmore?" Tammie shook her head. "Absolutely beautiful, but I feel as cold and alone as those stone faces. It's nice to be back among friends."

Betsy pointed to the dining table, where she sat the plate of food. "Can I get you something to drink?"

Tammie shook her head. "No, thanks. Really. I need to get back to Angela. I'm helping her with a school project."

"Oh." Betsy deflated at the thought of another meal by herself. "Okay. Um, thanks again for the food. You know I love your fried chicken." She walked Tammie to the door. "Say, if you and Angela had a favorite National Park you'd like to see, which one would it be?"

Tammie smiled. "That's easy. Angie loved your postcard

from Yellowstone. Me? I've always wanted to see the ocean, any ocean. I loved the pictures from that place in Maine, on the coast."

"Acadia."

She smiled again. "That's the one."

Betsy smiled. "Both were beautiful. I'm sorry you both couldn't join me on the trip. Hey, why don't you go help Angie and when you need a break, come on over for ice cream. I crave some company."

"It's a deal. See you in awhile."

Betsy rushed through dinner and hastily set up her easel. Within an hour she had cartoons drawn of Angela by Old Faithful and Tammie on the rocky Maine shore. Both sketches had Sweetie and George in background cameos. With that surprise completed, she continued unpacking until a knock on the door interrupted her.

She opened the door to find not only Tammie and Angela, but Oni and Chance as well. She relished the hugs of her friends. "Yay, it's a party. Come in, come in." Suddenly her house was full of chatter and good friends. She soaked it all in.

She and Tammie set up an ice cream buffet with all the fixings for just about any sundae the imagination could conjure. Cold soda sated their thirsts.

Oni spoke up. "Okay, tell us all about the trip."

Betsy complied.

Oni fidgeted on the couch as Betsy described each park in one or two sentences. They all laughed as Betsy displayed some of the rough sketches of cartoons from the trip.

"Okay, okay. Enough," said Oni. "Get to the good part. Did you meet anyone special?"

Betsy sighed and shook her head. "You're insane, you know that."

"What? Me? Insane?"

"Sure. Einstein defined insanity as doing the same thing over and over and expecting different results. You ask me that every time I return from a trip, and the answer is the same." She shook her head.

Oni smiled. "Well, who can argue with a genius? Insane or not, I have someone I want you to meet. There's a new artist displaying at the gallery. A sculptor. Meet me there tomorrow after we open."

Betsy frowned. "Oni ... I don't –"

"No excuses. I'll expect you around nine."

Chance pointed to his wristwatch.

"Okay, okay." She turned back to Betsy. "We gotta go, but I mean it. Tomorrow morning. I expect to see you."

Betsy made no promise as she showed the couple to the door and exchanged goodbye hugs. She turned back toward the room to find Tammie and Angela standing behind her.

"We should probably go, too. School tomorrow."

Angie rolled her eyes.

"Don't go yet. Wait right here."

She scurried to the loft and retrieved her gifts.

"Here. These are for you."

Mother and daughter broke into wide grins and giggled. Angie gave Betsy a tight squeeze.

"How? When?" Tammie paused. "You did these after I left earlier? You had to have. How?"

"I just wanted you to have something to show how much I missed you two. I'm glad to be home."

Yet, as she waved goodbye to Tammie and Angela and watched them walk across the yard to the adjacent home, that sense of isolation returned. She loved Eureka Springs, but she never seemed to be there with all the traveling. Perhaps she needed a year off from the large book projects. But staying home posed a separate problem. She knew all the locals and found none of the single men appealing. And with her increasing wealth, she found herself suspect of every man's motives when asked out socially. She was a big fish in a small pond and traveling was her only way of moving into the ocean. She had certainly found a new life, one she loved, but her dream for a happy family seemed to be fading.

Thirty
(Present Day)
ஒ◆◆ஒ

Myra sat in the passenger's seat while Alexia drove, enjoying the wind in her hair and the sense of freedom only a convertible on the open road could provide. She'd never liked being the passenger, subject to the whims of another driver who commanded pit stops, speed, or whatever else Myra preferred to control. Yet, Alexia had proven herself a competent driver and willing to stop whenever or wherever Myra wanted. Plus, her endurance, or lack thereof, had affected her time at the wheel more than she would have ever expected. Actually, it had affected her time in the car, period. There would be no all-night drives.

Following U.S. Highway 64, they'd made it only as far as Clayton, NM the previous afternoon where she opted to stay at the newly reopened Ecklund Hotel. Rooms were scarce in the town's chain motels due to wildfires forcing home evacuations in the area and she'd hoped the historic stone hotel would reek of history and keep Alexia occupied. Unfortunately, the town's only real historical "claim to fame" was being the home of Thomas "Black Jack" Ketchum – "one of Clayton's most famous outlaws" as described by the only highlight on the city's "History" webpage. She'd thought the city fathers had neglected to add more history to the page until she got the bill for lodgings and food and realized the train robber heritage continued through the city's less famous outlaws' heirs.

Myra watched Alexia as she drove. Her face reflected conflict, which Myra couldn't quite fathom. They were riding the open plains, top down, the sun beating down on them. What could be better?

Actually, the sun held them in a sizzling sauté. Mid-August on the Great Plains. Alexia was sweating, she noticed now, despite the air rushing past them like a gale force wind.

"Sorry."

"What?" replied Alexia.

"I'm sorry. The heat. Putting the top down is usually the best I can do since this car was made before air conditioning became standard on cars."

"Actually, I think putting the top up and leaving the windows down would be better."

Myra liked the top down. She liked the heat, sort of, and never sweated. Besides, it was her car, she was the boss, and Alexia had been so compliant yesterday. Moreover, she was the boss. Oh, she'd enumerated that already.

"Okay, pull over and put the top up."

Surprise pushed aside conflict on Alexia's countenance.

"What? Yesterday, you were barking out commands, dictating speed and when I should start braking if we came up on a slower car, and telling me how many flashes of the turn signal I should give before turning. Giving me grief if I hit the rumble strip. Today, you're giving in to my simple comment?"

Myra felt the flush and knew she'd be blushing, if you could tell through the persistent jaundice. "I wasn't that bad." She paused. "Well, I could be, but I wasn't. Was I?"

Alexia raised both eyebrows and rolled her eyes. "Oh no, not at all." The sarcasm seeped from her voice. "This morning all you've done is complain about the lodgings ... which *you* picked. The rooms were nice, clean, and very reasonable in cost, but nooooo, her diva-ness has to pick apart every flaw." She glanced from the road to Myra. "And did you not tell me, several times, to only let the turn signal flash four times before turning? That four flashes gave other traffic plenty of warning."

Myra did recall saying just that, but giving in for the second time in as many minutes was not in her nature.

"Eww, touchy we are this morning."

"Eww, bitchy we are this morning," retorted Alexia in perfect Yoda mimicry.

Myra crossed her arms over her chest and huffed. "Okay, fine. When we get to Tulsa, we'll get you a ticket to fly back to L.A. I can finish this trip on my own."

Alexia screeched to a halt on the shoulder and turned to Myra. "Whatever." Then her shoulders sagged and she let out a long breath. "Look … I-I'm sorry. I want to stay. It's just, well, back in Taos you were so laid back and I thought we were connecting, actually developing a nice relationship. Since we left … wow, what a difference a day makes."

"Cliché," whispered Myra. She studied her assistant, but realized the car had become like a frying pan without the wind factor. She felt a trickle of sweat form on her brow. But, was it just the heat? Something was bothering her. She just needed to put her finger on that 'something.'

"And there's, uh, one other thing I'm not sure how to bring up. So, I'll just say it. I know you don't put much stock in God and all my Christian hokum, but as I was praying last night, I felt that God told me to tell you that before this trip was over, He would fill your oldest, deepest, most secret desire to prove to you He is real."

Myra sat there, sweating and feeling as if her stomach had bottomed out. She didn't know how to process Alexia's comment. She chose to ignore it.

"Help me put the top up. We're going to dehydrate sitting here like this."

Myra stepped out of the car and began to unbutton the

boot covering the convertible top. After a moment, Alexia joined her, removing the boot on her side of the car and placing it in the back seat. Together they lifted the top into position and returned inside to latch it shut. Myra knocked over her purse in the process and her cell phone spilled onto the floor. She picked it up and glanced at the screen to discover she had no cell service.

"Damn."

In response, Alexia grabbed her phone to discover the same. Like Black Jack's "Hole in the Wall Gang," they had disappeared into a cellular blind canyon. Without saying a word, she sped off.

"We need to get you back into cell coverage. What if they found a donor? Would you hand me the road map, please?"

"Not while you're driving. I'll look," replied Myra.

She rifled through the glove box, and then felt around under the seat. Nothing. She was sure she had a map somewhere, but then, she'd traveled this route before and didn't need a map for the trip. She knew the way by heart.

"Check under your seat."

Alexia cautiously lowered one hand and checked under the seat. She pulled up a loose quarter. "So, you don't have a map."

Myra sighed. "Guess not. It's not like I use this car every day."

Alexia slowed to a stop, pulled a three-point turn, and started back the other way.

"What're you doing? We'll reach service if we keep going straight."

"Maybe, but when? We need to move down into the I-40 corridor if we want to keep 24/7 service. That's an hour or so south and we just passed a route to get there."

Ten minutes later, Alexia turned south onto U.S. Route 83. Fifteen minutes after that, they neared the town of Perryton, TX and both phones pinged with service.

Myra looked at Alexia and said, "I apologize. I recognize now that I'm uptight about getting all these labs done and the risks of a transplant. In Taos, I could forget that and relax. Now, I'm waiting for a call that might never come. I-I shouldn't take that out on you." She paused. "And you're right, we were developing a relationship in Taos and that scares me. My track record on relationships is not on the level of an Olympic meet. Maybe not even Junior High track."

Then Myra's phone signaled awaiting messages. More than one. Her heart rate galloped to match the speed of her Mustang. Had she missed *the* call?

She scrolled through the list of calls. *Curious*, she thought. *The 575 area code is Taos.* She didn't recognize the number. Alexia pulled into Imo's Country Store to fill up at their pumps, and Myra took the opportunity of Alexia being in the store to return the calls.

"Detective Ramirez."

Taos PD? Detective? Myra replied, "This is Myra Mitchell, Detective. I've been out of cell service and just now got your messages."

Myra sat there stonily as he described events at the Luhan House that had taken place just two hours earlier. Diana was in surgery and the monster that hurt Diana was after her, Myra. Who? Why? Nothing computed. This made no sense. She had no enemies. Well, none at that violent level anyway. Myra couldn't wrap her mind around any feasible plot line that could come close to explaining this. Maybe she was hallucinating in the heat. She thanked the detective and hung up as Alexia returned to the car.

"You okay?"

Alexia's voice sounded distant, like Samuel's had at the restaurant before she collapsed.

"Cliché or not, you actually look 'white as a ghost.' Can I get you anything?"

Myra felt paralyzed. She couldn't nod 'yes' or shake her head 'no,' but tears found their path of least resistance. She couldn't think, but one concern emerged in her thoughts. *Why* had this man tracked her to the Luhan House? She looked at the cell phone in her hand.

"Give me your cell phone. Go inside and buy us a throwaway phone."

Alexia gave up her cell phone and Myra made sure both phones were turned off. She would have preferred removing the batteries altogether but that required an engineering degree these days. *That eliminates one method for tracking us,* she thought. Her next thought ... should she continue on to Eureka Springs?

Thirty-one
(Autumn, 1975)
ல•••ல

Betsy hadn't awakened until a pounding on her door aroused her shortly after ten o'clock the next morning. Oni stood at her door, tapping a foot, her arms crossed, threatening to drag her down the hill to the gallery in her PJs. Knowing her friend might do just that, she promised to be there within the hour.

Now, at eleven-thirty, she stood in the middle of the Eureka Art Gallery staring at her personal vision of Adonis. His oil black hair laid swept back in waves across his head, while his bronzed skin stood in contrast to a brightly bleached white T-shirt that clung to tight abdominals he could have chiseled from granite himself. Glistening grey eyes seemed to penetrate her soul and his flawless smile illuminated the room. She felt breathless and speechless.

And immediately on guard. One bad marriage was enough. Still, lust tugged her along and she felt a dangerously passionate physical attraction to Nico Brunori. She had no intention of rushing into a new relationship. Yet, as Oni put it, over four years of abstinence no longer qualified as "rushing."

"So, you're 'that cartoon lady' I keep hearing about."

"Yes, I'm Betsy."

He took her extended hand and kissed it. She felt a warm flush rise to her face … and fill other body parts she had neglected for too long.

She tried to ignore Oni's gestures behind him, but her antics broadened Betsy's smile more than the kiss. In turn, Nico apparently read the smile as a positive sign and poured on the charm. He placed his arm around her shoulders and with a sweep of his other arm, led her toward his closest sculpture, a young boy in straw hat and overalls, sitting on a log with his cane pole dangling over a pool of rippled water.

She glanced around her. His work held amazing detail, but was not at all what she expected. According to Oni, he was second generation Italian, spoke four languages fluently, and trained at distinguished art academies on the East Coast, in France, and in Italy. She expected classically inspired nudes, couples in passionate embrace, virile hunters, and beautiful dancers. She did spot one dancer -- a freckled, young girl in pigtails, tutu sagging on her too-small frame, attempting a pirouette.

"Nico, your work is delightful." She touched the bronze in front of her and traced the details with her fingers. "I, uh, I expected something more, well, classical. This is like Norman Rockwell in bronze. It's wonderful the way it catches the core of Americana."

"Thank you." He guided her to a nearby table and poured her a glass of red wine.

She shook her head and put her hand out to stop him. "Thank you, but I don't drink."

"Aww, I personally brought these bottles from Italy, from my family's vineyards there. I thought you would like it."

His pout melted her resolve and she took the glass. With a nod of his head encouraging her, she took a sip. She'd had sweet wines during holiday dinners with Rod's family and hadn't cared much for them, but this wine had a dry cherry, lightly nutty taste. She looked at the squat bottle in its straw basket.

"Chianti Classico. My family is from the Florence region of Italy. Do you like it?"

"Actually, I do, but one glass will be enough. Thank you."

Oni tapped Nico on the shoulder. A customer wished to meet the sculptor.

Betsy sipped her wine as she watched him interact with several customers. As more people entered the gallery, she became aware that he would be tied up for some time. She placed her empty glass on the table, walked up to Oni, and whispered, "He's beautiful. What are you trying to do to me?"

Oni raised one eyebrow and looked her squarely in the eye. With a saucy tone of voice, she replied, "Simple, honey. Get you laid. What else?"

Betsy blushed. She'd been too busy to absorb the free love manner of the hippy movement. She wasn't sure what she thought of casual sex. What would her mother have thought about it? That was a question she would never have answered. She didn't want to think about what her pa would say. She didn't want to think about him at all, nor Dewey Hastings. Gratefully, she rarely thought of either one and finally felt rid of their haunting presences.

"Tell Nico I enjoyed meeting him. I have to get home to work."

Shortly after 6 p.m., Betsy descended from her loft with her stomach growling. She had started rummaging through her refrigerator when she heard a knocking, no, more of a pounding, like with someone's foot, at her door.

"Nico!"

The man stood there with a grocery bag in one hand and two bottles of family Chianti in the other. Her response was equal portions of surprise and apprehension. Then thoughts of irritation at Oni flit through her mind. Oni knew better than to give out Betsy's address.

"*Buona sera. Io sono qui per cucinare si cena.*"

"Huh?"

"I'm here to cook you dinner."

She looked at him suspiciously. "Oni put you up to this, didn't she?"

"Not at all. She only told me where you lived."

She stood there, pondering what to do. Oni was correct in saying that four years was no longer rushing, but she had just met this man. That conversation lasted all of ten minutes. Why should she feel comfortable having him in her home, much less making dinner for her? Was she that lonely, that "hard up?" What was Oni thinking? And then she remembered Oni's comment and realized no woman with Nico could ever be considered "hard up."

"Can I come in? This is heavy and getting heavier with each minute. I walked all the way from the grocery, and climbing up the hill was no treat."

She stepped back. She'd never had a man cook anything fancier than breakfast for her in her own kitchen. If nothing else, this would be novel. "Um, sure. Why not? Come on in."

He stepped across the threshold, stopped, and raised his eyebrows. "Kitchen?"

"Oh. Right. That way." She pointed in the direction he should go. "Through that door."

Two hours later, following a delicious meal of Chicken Florentine, Betsy uncorked the second bottle of Chianti and poured two more glasses of the dry, red wine. Nico eased up behind her and wrapped his arms around her, kissing her neck. She took a gulp of wine and set down her glass before turning into his embrace. Her inhibition gone, she realized Oni's goal was about to be fulfilled.

* * *

Betsy spent the next year questioning every move, every minute spent with Nico. He had proven himself an amazing lover, once Betsy moved past her inhibitions. His immediate family had visited several times and an Italian aunt and uncle had come to town on one occasion. She'd never witnessed such familial love, such passion. Every meal was like a party. Even their arguments, while fervent, brought ebullient resolutions. She loved the image of the joyful Italian family played out before her.

Yet, the adage, "Fool me once, shame on you; fool me twice, shame on me," played over and over in her mind. She paid close attention to Nico and saw no beacons warning her of abusive shores or alcoholic gales. And his art was successful. He had no need for her money. He was tender and understanding. More so than she ever thought a man could be. She saw that as the artist within – sensitive, accepting, wistful.

He wore her down. Or had she fallen to a ticking biological clock? She was now twenty-six and her dreams for a family beckoned with increasing urgency.

Pre-dawn over the Ozarks sparkled with the promise of a wonderful spring day. Oni finished fixing Betsy's hair with flowers and helped her adjust the Grecian inspired, off-white gown that flowed as Betsy walked. A warm southwesterly breeze rushed through the window and made the petals flutter.

"You're beautiful."

Betsy's gut fluttered, too. Was she doing the right thing?

"C'mon. The limo's outside."

Fifteen minutes later, with Tammie and Angela, they turned off Highway 23 onto the drive to Pond Mountain. Nico and Chance would be there by now, along with a coterie of local and distant guests.

The limo pulled up to the end of the drive and stopped,

but only Tammie, Angela, and, finally, Oni emerged from the vehicle. Oni took command and soon the guests clustered along two sides of a pine needle path heading toward the pond and its dock with a gazebo at the end. Betsy watched all this from the limousine and blinked twice, mouth open, when she saw Jacob Meyer emerge from the crowd, approach her door, and open it. More than her mentor, he'd been the father she'd never had, supportive and loving despite her failed relationship with his son. If he had RSVP'd to her invitation, Oni had kept it a secret, a surprise to her.

"Wow! You're more beautiful than ever." He extended his hand. "If you'll let me, I'd like to give you away."

Tears flowed from Betsy's eyes and she grabbed a tissue to dab them. She nodded. "That would make me very happy," she managed to say. His blessing on this day meant more to her than she could begin to describe.

As the sun rose above the horizon, she stepped out of the limousine and straightened her gown ... and her resolve. A classical string quartet of cello, viola and two violins began to play. She looked down the path to see Nico under the gazebo with his younger brother and Chance as witnesses. The birds began to chirp their welcome to the new day. She noticed her first butterfly of the spring, a cabbage white, as it fluttered along the path ahead of her. Tammie, Angela, and Oni preceded her. Twenty minutes later, she had taken the plunge.

(Spring, 1981)

The tenth anniversary of "Sweetie and George" put Betsy in a reflective mood. Never in her most imaginative dreams had she ever foreseen the success she now enjoyed. Her childhood in poverty with an alcoholic father. The loss of her son. Her escape from the hills of western North Carolina that landed her in a brothel where two young women were brutally murdered. Those first few months trying to eke out a living as a freelance greeting card writer. A failed marriage. Building her dream with "Sweetie and George." Traveling the world, first in the U.S., followed by international travel with her polyglot second husband. All had been fodder for her work, just as Oni had said.

As had her barrenness. After five years of marriage, she'd been unable to conceive. Nico never said it outright, but she knew he blamed her somehow. A growing friction had developed between them. Yet, her fertility specialist had found her fertile. He had discovered no physical obstacles and had laid it all on stress. Too many deadlines. Too much travel. She needed to take a year off to relax and fully enjoy the life she and Nico could easily afford. That year would start right after this celebration.

She looked out over a hall of people assembled in Monterey, California for the decennial of her creation. Banners of Sweetie and George along with their new dog, Roscoe, the Elvis fan, decorated the entrance and area behind the head table. Friends from Arkansas sat at nearby tables. Nico and Betsy sat at the head table along with her agent and the heads of King Features. Waiters removed empty dessert plates and silverware. Coffee carafes appeared on every table.

Betsy had already reaped her accolades and made her speech, mostly a succinct compilation of 'thank yous.' Now, the CEO of King Features spoke at the podium.

"And in closing, I'd like to present to you the latest 'Sweetie and George' book: a special, tenth anniversary edition of 'The Best of Sweetie and George.'" He unveiled an enlarged copy of the cover sitting on the easel behind them. "And for everyone here tonight, we have advanced copies which Betsy has agreed to autograph." He turned toward her. "That's right, isn't it?"

Betsy gulped in some air and nodded. She didn't look forward to the task, which might take another hour or more, but it came with the territory. As the books were distributed, she arose and walked to a table set up for her signing. Nico caught up to her.

"I'm going back to the room to pack. Will I see you before I leave?"

He had to catch a red-eye flight back east for a gallery opening, while she still had business to attend to with King Features.

"I hope so. I'll do my best to be quick." She said that, but her hopes seemed dashed by the growing line of people in front of the table. They kissed and she sat down, watching Nico leave the banquet hall as the first person in line started gushing about how much she loved Sweetie.

Two hours later, knowing she'd missed Nico, she hunted down her agent.

"Chas, do I really have to attend these meetings? Can't you handle this for me? You know I hate business meetings."

He shook his head. "No can do. You need to be there tomorrow. After that, yeah, I can probably handle everything solo."

She frowned and sighed.

"What's up? You don't usually shy away from these things."

She glanced at the man who had helped turn her into a millionairess several times over. She didn't really want to burden him with her personal concerns.

"I, uh ... Our fifth anniversary was last week and between

Nico's late hours preparing for his gallery opening and this shindig, we never celebrated. I want to fly east and surprise him." She'd begun to have other worries about Nico's late hours, but she would not share those with anyone and certainly not Chas.

Two days later, she flew through Dallas to Little Rock and drove home. She had come home to repack for Nico's showing in Florida. Driving down Eureka Street shortly after dusk, her heart accelerated when she saw lights on in their house, lights they had not left on timers when they departed for California.

She pulled up next to Tammie's home and turned off the car, sitting and watching her home. Shadows flit across the curtains of their bedroom, and anxiety cemented itself in her heart. Maybe Nico had come home to repack as well. But, she had their car. How would he have gotten home from Little Rock? Maybe a burglar was ransacking her home. Maybe ... She didn't want to think of the other options.

She knocked on Tammie's door, but no one answered and she remembered that Tammie had promised Angela a trip to Disneyland while in California. Betsy had preceded them home. Nervously, she found a piece of 2x4 for self-defense and crept toward her house. She quietly unlocked the back door and sneaked inside. Wine bottles, empty glasses, and dirty dishes lay scattered across the kitchen counters. She crept into the front room. It looked untouched. Her heart racing and her breathing bordering on hyperventilation, she moved toward their bedroom and threw open the door, 2x4 raised and ready.

Nico was there, in bed. He was not alone.

Screaming in anger, she raced toward the bed already swinging the 2x4. She caught the other man in the butt with a major league connection.

"Get out! Get out of my house!" She prepared another swing as the man hastily gathered up his clothes, while trying to fend off her rage. As he ran from the room, she turned on Nico who'd already jumped out of bed. She caught him on the thigh with an off-balance swing. "You, too, you pervert! Get out! Get out! Get out! How dare you defile our bedroom like this! Don't come back! Don't you dare show your face to me ever again. Get out!"

She chased him down the steps and out the front door. On the way through the front room, she dropped the lumber and picked up a bust Nico had created of her. She threw it and narrowly missed him as he cleared the front porch.

In a frenzy, she ran back upstairs and gathered his clothes from the closet and his chest. She then collected his toiletries, shoes, framed photos and anything else of his she could find, and dumped them all in the middle of the room. She ran to the window and opened it. His belongings began to rain down upon the side yard, until the bedroom stood clear of any and all reminders of him.

Crying, Betsy sat on the edge of the bed and then quickly jumped back up. She stripped the bed of its linens and threw these out the window to join the pile on the ground. The thought of sleeping in that bed, even just touching it, now made her gag.

She walked downstairs and saw the empty glasses and dishes. They soon lay in a pile of shattered shards at the base of the closest wall. Emotionally spent, she plopped onto the couch and sobbed. Her dream of a family lay crushed with the fine china. How could she even consider showing her face in town after outing her cheating, queer husband like that? Her life in Eureka Springs was over.

Thirty-two
(Present Day)
ତ୍ୟ••୧ଡ

Dewey spent the afternoon on the airport's Wi-Fi portal accessing the Internet for every bit of information he could find on Myra Mitchell. He didn't think the girl had discovered the secret that Albritton so feared. Had that been the case, Mitchell and the girl would have flown to Raleigh to expedite the trip. Therefore, she had another reason for the trip and some clue to where she was heading had to exist in the writer's history. Dewey kept running face-first into one solid obstacle: Myra Mitchell seemed to have suddenly appeared on earth in Taos with the release of her first book. To Dewey's mind that meant only one thing. Since Myra Mitchell was not a pen name, then prior to Taos, she had to have been somebody else, from somewhere else.

He glanced at his watch and saw that he needed to check in with the Senator. Albritton answered on the second ring.

"So, are you ready to come home? I have work for you here."

Dewey explained his predicament. Albritton didn't have to voice his displeasure. Dewey could feel the chill through his phone.

After two minutes of deathly still air, Albritton said, "You have twenty-four hours to get back on track."

"What? You're kiddin', right? How am I going to find them across millions of acres? I'm playing a hunch by being here, but you're crazy if you think I'm just gonna stumble across them on the highway. I'm one man. Hell, use your nephew to check cell phone GPS or somethin'. I don't got that kind of access."

"Twenty-four hours, Dewey. You'd better have something more to go on, or our working relationship will come to an unpleasant end. Call me when you've found something, preferably them."

Dewey had never had reason to fear the Senator. He was the man's mentor. He held enough of the cards that Albritton could never act unilaterally without facing ruin. Yet, something in the man's voice disturbed Dewey. *Did* he hold enough cards? He'd been outwitted by Albritton before, even as a schoolboy. For the first time, he actually felt fear of the man, his position, his wealth, and his power.

The senator hung up in a huff. He didn't like this sense of being out of control, waiting to see if the ax would fall … and where.

Albritton began to dial his nephew's cell number but thought better of it. Mike Jr. would balk at such an intrusion, even though the U.S. Justice Department recently ruled that there was no constitutional ban on the government's acquiring cell GPS data from a wireless carrier. No warrant was needed on the Federal level, but state law was not so well defined. Several state high courts had recently ruled against suspicionless GPS tracking and now required state agencies to obtain warrants for such tracking of a car or handheld mobile phone. His nephew was like his brother, too straight an arrow to skirt the law.

He dialed a second number.

An answering machine picked up his call at the other end and Albritton left a message, as he had done numerous times before. "I need a GPS track on the following cell phone ASAP." He repeated the number twice and hung up.

Ten minutes later, the phone rang. "Usual fee and method?"

"Yes."

"Good. It would appear the target's at the Santa Fe airport."

"That's right. Please let me know where he goes over the next twenty-four hours. Next item, a GPS track on this number." He didn't have Myra Mitchell's cell number, so he gave the man Alexia Hamilton's cell phone number and waited for a response.

"Hmm, let me try something else. Just a minute…" After a pause, the man returned. "No go. That number is off-line at this point. I can't find a location. Do you want me to keep trying?"

"Yes. Let me know if it comes on-line and where to find it."

Dewey Hastings had fast become a problem. He'd left behind a trail of broken bones and assaults. These people could and would identify him, eventually. Dewey had always considered himself indispensible, yet to Albritton they'd never been "friends." From that first meeting on the schoolyard, Albritton had disliked the bully, and that persisted for the man. He was a tool, just a tool. And sometimes a tool broke and had to be thrown away.

He dialed another number after disconnecting. "Got a job for you. Our friend Mr. Hastings might be a liability we can no longer afford."

Dewey tried to nap on the flight to Oklahoma City, but sat there in a fitful half sleep. His mind dwelled on his search, while holding onto a nagging worry about Albritton's next action. Unable to doze off, he stared out the window and watched the light of the day fading to the west. Then a thought hit him.

Upon landing, he emerged to the boarding gate area and quickly brought his laptop on-line with the airport's Wi-Fi network. Why had the Mitchell woman been in Taos? The Luhan House was known as a writer's retreat. So, she must be working on a book. Were there any other well-known writer's retreats she could be heading to?

He Googled the phrase "writer's retreats" and came up with thousands of hits. She was heading due east, so he narrowed the search first to Oklahoma and surfed through a number of sites. He did likewise for Missouri, Arkansas, and Tennessee. There were still hundreds of places, most of which were rooms or cabins to rent. *She could afford to do that anywhere in the world*, he thought. *Why here?* That didn't help much. *Maybe she's headin' for Carolina after all.*

He took the time to call half a dozen or so of these places, those that seemed better suited to a writer of Mitchell's caliber. Nothing. All said the same thing, "They'd *love* to have Myra Mitchell stay with them." But she wasn't and hadn't made any plans with them.

At one website, he stumbled across the term "writers' colony" and decided to explore that possibility. From surfing a few sites, he learned that such places focused on educating and training writers, as well as providing rooms to work in. He reasoned that if she wrote her first book in Taos, but was someone else, somewhere else before that, maybe that someplace was a writer's colony where she learned to write. To his way of thinking, where else would someone learn to write like that? Sure, that made sense. If he wanted to learn to write books, maybe he'd go to something like a writer's colony. He scanned the search results page and saw a site, www.writerscolony.org. Maybe they had a list of these places he could use to narrow his search.

But the website wasn't a list. What he found instead was an organization, The Writers' Retreat at Grotto Spring, in the Ozarks. Eureka Springs, Arkansas more precisely. The website announced a special guest speaker in two days, but made no mention as to whom that might be. With a quick consultation of a U.S. map, he realized the place was due east of Taos, a straight shot traveling U.S. Highway 412 almost all the way. The only fly in his sorghum was the place wasn't around when she wrote her first books, much less before that. The colony was founded in 2000. He'd found no references to the colony in any of her books' acknowledgement pages or press interviews. What tie could she have there? Maybe she'd been to the Grotto Spring House country inn that preceded the colony. Maybe she just wanted to go there as somewhere new for her. Maybe she was the special guest speaker. Yeah, that could be it. They would announce who it was unless they didn't want paparazzi descending on the place like locusts on a cornfield.

He vacillated. He had nothing else to go on, but might she be heading that way? Did he take a chance and drive there? He decided to let his fingers do the walking again, despite the chance they had caller ID and might get suspicious of an out-of-area call asking for the Mitchell woman. He needed a better story for this call. He'd met some resistance on a couple of the previous calls. He checked a few more websites to prepare his story.

"Writers' Retreat. May I help you?"

"Hi, this is Tim at Enterprise Rent-A-Car. I have a car for Myra Mitchell and wanted to confirm her arrival there."

There was a pause. "Where'd you say you were calling

from?"

"Enterprise Rent-A-Car. I'm with the VIP services at the regional office in Oklahoma City, but our agent in Fayetteville will deliver the car. I believe she asked for a Ford Mustang." He'd read something about her collection of Mustangs in an interview. He hoped he sounded convincing.

After a moment, the woman returned to the phone. "I'm sorry, but she hasn't arrived yet. We will leave her a note to contact you. Can I have your number?"

"Actually, she can contact our 800 number or the local agent in Fayetteville when she arrives and the car will be delivered within an hour. Guaranteed. Thank you for your help." He didn't wait for a reply and hung up the pay phone. He pumped his fist in the air, grabbed his carry-on case, and walked directly to the Hertz rental desk to use his Gold Plus membership to find something nicer than that Corolla he'd suffered with in New Mexico.

Thirty-three

Just north of Huntsville, AR, Alexia exited U.S. Highway 412 onto northbound Arkansas 23 towards Eureka Springs. Myra refused to voice her concerns about continuing on to the Writer's Retreat at Grotto Spring, but she had agreed to speak to the authors in residence and, in return, the retreat's director, Oni Prairieberry, would turn over to them several file boxes that had belonged to Betsy Weston. Myra felt confident that Alexia would need those files for her research.

"Are you sure we should be heading to Eureka Springs? Maybe I could go alone and get what you want?"

Myra looked at her assistant. No, she wasn't sure.

"We need to keep going. I told you last night I talked with Diana personally and she assured me she did *not* tell the man where we were headed. Short of tracking our cell phones, which I disabled, how could he possibly know where we are? It's a big country. Besides, I promised to speak at the Writer's Retreat and Ms. Prairieberry told me she absolutely would not relinquish the Weston files to anyone but me."

Alexia shook her head but did not reply.

"But, as a precaution, we're going to stay at a place outside of town. It's only about half an hour away, just south of the city. I can call Ms. Prairieberry from there."

True to her estimate, the turnoff to the Pond Mountain Lodge & Resort came along thirty minutes later."

"Turn left, here," said Myra.

Alexia parked in front of the office and got out to stretch her legs while Myra went into the office. Moments later, Myra returned.

"We have the Roadrunner Cabin. It's that way." Myra

pointed toward a forested ridge. "We should have our privacy there."

Myra watched as Alexia scanned the surroundings, frowning. Although built up quite a bit since her one brief visit here years before, Myra still found it beautiful ... and secluded enough to protect them. She couldn't understand Alexia's reaction.

"Isn't it beautiful?" she asked.

Alexia turned back to her. "Sure, but it seems, I don't know, so isolated. If someone is out to get you, he could do it and you, we, might not be found for days."

Myra looked about and her smile disappeared. Smarty-pants was right, again.

"He doesn't know we're here. All he knows is that we took off by car. We could be anywhere in the country now." Was she repeating that to reassure Alexia or herself?

Alexia didn't look assuaged.

Myra continued, "This is where Betsy Weston got married the second time. The property was privately owned back then, not a resort. Five years later, something happened and she disappeared. Sold her rights to 'Sweetie and George' and preceded Elvis for some alien world, or the witness protection program, or something. Never heard from or seen since."

Alexis resumed her survey of the property. Myra could see that she was unsettled.

"Tell you what," said Myra. "Why don't you walk around and get a feel for the place. I'll drive the car to the cabin's parking."

Alexia walked a bit and looked at the disposable cell phone. She walked another direction and repeated the action. Her face showed dislike.

"We don't have any cell service here." She pulled her

regular cell phone from her purse.

Myra shook her head. "Please don't use that. We can use the motel phones."

Alexia disagreed. "Not if we're not here. I'll just turn it on long enough to check for a signal and then turn it off again."

Myra began to protest again, but thought better of it. How could someone track them with just a quick use like that? Alexia seemed satisfied with the result and placed the phone back in her purse.

"We're good with those, if we need them."

As Myra began to climb into the car, a woman rushed from the office, holding two hardcover novels.

"Ms. Mitchell, could you please …"

The woman, who appeared to be around forty, stopped short of the Mustang. Her mouth gaped open and she reached out and grazed her fingers across the back bumper. She stood up and approached Myra, who was now standing next to the driver's door. Her brow furrowed and she scrutinized Myra from head to toe.

"My name's Angela Thoms. I'm the manager here now. Have we met before?"

"I-I don't think so. Would you like me to autograph those?" She pointed to the novels in Ms. Thoms' hands.

"I don't want to seem rude or forward, but where did you get this car?"

Alexia moved next to and a bit in front of Myra, as if ready to protect her.

"I know this car. This is Betsy's car. I learned to drive in this car. That dent in the back bumper is where I backed into a streetlight in my first attempt at parallel parking. Where did you get this?"

She didn't seem angry. Anguish best described the

emotion coming from the woman, and for Myra, it cut through her like a contagious twitch.

"She bought it from a man in North Carolina," said Alexia. "You knew Betsy Weston?"

The woman resumed her caress of the car, as if it connected to some lost part of her. Myra noted the tears flowing down Ms. Thoms' cheeks, and felt a sudden link to the woman, with Betsy Weston as the common denominator.

The woman turned back to them. "Betsy rented our house. My mom and I lived next door in a place we usually rented. I thought my mom was crazy for giving up our home to this stranger, but it ended up being the most wonderful years of our lives. I still have cartoons she drew for me and my mom. They're my most cherished possessions."

"Is, uh … does your mom still live around here?" Myra asked.

The tears flowed more heavily now. "No." Angela choked on her emotions. "Sh-she passed three years ago. Heart disease."

Myra choked, too. She could feel Angela's pain as if it were her own.

Angela pointed to the driver's seat. "May I?"

Myra nodded. "Sure."

The woman sat behind the wheel and closed her eyes, no doubt, reliving a past event.

"I remember sitting behind this wheel for the first time. My mom was as nervous as a chicken with a fox in the henhouse and Betsy was laughing in the back seat, recounting her first attempts at driving, her first time on an Interstate. We had such good times in this car."

Myra didn't know what to say, but Alexia stepped into the void. "We're researching Betsy's life for a book. We know she got married right here, at the pond. What happened?"

The woman had calmed and the tears had stopped.

"It happened right after the tenth anniversary celebration for 'Sweetie and George.' A bunch of us from town here, went to California with Betsy. My mom and me went to Disneyland, Hollywood, and Knott's Berry Farm afterward. By the time we got home, she was gone. The keys to our house were in our mailbox with a short note saying she had to leave but she loved us and would miss us. She left everything behind except her clothes, personal items, and studio, anything to do with Sweetie. A month later, 'Sweetie and George' had a new byline. I couldn't believe she'd given up Sweetie."

"Nico, her husband, was here for a few days afterward, but he wouldn't talk to us. Rumor was she came home and found him cheating on her, in her own bed. Some said it was with another man. Right before mom died, we found out a little bit more. Betsy used her friendship and influence with a local judge to issue a divorce the very next day. Rumor said he also granted her a name change, but Judge Atkinson wouldn't confirm that and he had sealed the records. Only Betsy, if she ever comes back, can apply to unseal them." She gazed wistfully toward the lake. "Every day for years, I prayed she'd come back ... but we never heard from her. My mom took that note and tucked it into the frame with one of her cartoons. She'd look at it every time she felt anger at Betsy for leaving like that. Still have that note, too."

She turned back toward Alexia. "Gawd, I'd love to see her again. I forgave her years ago. Mom, too. I'd just like to hug her and thank her for giving us a life we wouldn't have had if it weren't for her generosity."

Alexia looked at Myra with a look that Myra couldn't quite read, and said, "Now I think we know who Elise

Kenwood is. Do –"

Angela interrupted. "Elise Kenwood? Elise Kenwood was Betsy?"

"We're not sure. Myra owns another car that was supposed to belong to Betsy, but her research found the name Elise Kenwood on the title. How do you know her?" asked Alexia.

Myra suddenly felt very tired and watched the exchange between the other two women, content to let Alexia take the lead.

"Uh, we never met in person, but my mom received a check from an Elise Kenwood that let us pay off both houses, plus some for my college. She told us the money was from an anonymous donor. Everything was done by mail. Mom never talked to or met her. We figured Betsy was the donor, but you think Elise was actually Betsy?"

"It's beginning to look that way," replied Alexia. She looked at Myra. "Do you think we'll be able to track her down?"

"Might be a long shot. Sealed court records usually form a serious roadblock. But as I said in Taos, she must be the key to the mystery." Myra turned back to Angela. "Do you know Oni Prairieberry?"

"Sure do. She was probably, no, she was Betsy's best friend here. She runs the Writer's Retreat."

"I'm supposed to give a talk there tomorrow over lunch and she has some things from Betsy she promised to give me for our research."

"Well, I've been in those boxes. Mom, Oni, and me looked through them for clues to what might have happened. You'll find her old diaries interesting. She had a rough life until coming here. But there's no clue about what happened to her, if that's what you're hoping for."

Dewey sat on the balcony of the Basin Park Hotel, sipping a light beer while watching the main street. He'd been there for two days, waiting and watching. He'd received a text message from the Senator that the Hamilton girl's cell phone had pinged the towers in Eureka Springs. He acknowledged to Albritton that he was already in town, but received no reply. That seemed off.

The Writer's Retreat was at the far end of Spring Street and there were back ways to get there, but everyone who came to town seemed to gravitate to Main Street around Basin Spring Park. Spring Street intersected with Main Street here, and between the covered balcony bar and the park next door, he had an unfettered view of the street. If the Mitchell lady and girl came through, he'd see them. And when he'd confirmed their presence in town, he would call the Senator with the good news. No, even better, he would dispatch the women and then call the senator with better news.

"Here you are, Sir. Enjoy."

The waitress laid a club sandwich platter on the table before him. The place had great burgers, but he'd decided to try as much on the menu as he could. This was an early lunch. He'd maintained a somewhat erratic schedule, befitting a tourist, so as to avoid questions.

Today after eating, he planned a leisurely walk taking photos of the homes along Spring Street to the retreat. He would blend in easily that way. The retreat had confirmed their coming to Eureka Springs, but he had no doubt the women had learned of his "interrogation" of the manager of Mabel's place in Taos by now. Still, they couldn't be expecting him here. He had the element of surprise.

However, Hastings wasn't alone. A second set of eyes followed the activity on the street, as well as Hastings on the balcony. The Senator had been surprised to find that Dewey had preceded the women to Eureka Springs. How had the man gotten so lucky? However it had happened, the Senator was pleased that two problems could now be "handled" much more expediently and had arranged a quick flight for this man to Little Rock. The man had his instructions: complete what Dewey hadn't and then take care of Dewey himself.

Thirty-four

Myra and Alexia drove slowly through historic downtown Eureka Springs, past the auditorium, turning toward Basin Spring Park.

"This town is beautiful," exclaimed Alexia. "So quaint. I love it! I can see why Betsy stayed, so it must have been something awful to make her leave like that."

Myra nodded. "I'm sure it was. I'd say "been there, done that,' but you know how I hate clichés." She turned left at the old Eureka Gallery onto Spring Street. "Up here we'll pass the Post Office and further up Spring Street we'll pass the public library. It's built of solid granite and was donated to the city by Andrew Carnegie himself. Lots of famous people have passed over these same streets."

They passed couples strolling along the tree-lined street, families with young children in tow, and a man taking photos of the beautifully restored Victorian-era homes, many of them operating as bed and breakfast inns. "I read somewhere that Oni Prairieberry and her husband started the first B&B inn here. She's hosted a number of luminaries herself, including the Clintons when he was Governor. She's listed as an official F.O.B., friend of Bill," Alexia commented.

"That's right. They turned the inn into the Writer's Retreat just before her husband died too young of cancer."

Myra continued, "Did you also read that these streets were built up to prevent mud slides that had become a problem? That's why most of the homes on the downhill side are altered to have main entries on what would have been the second floor originally." Alexia nodded, acknowledging that bit of trivia as they passed a dozen more homes and inns. A minute later, they arrived at Grotto Spring. As Myra turned into the gravel drive of the retreat, a young woman emerged from the nearest building.

"Ms. Mitchell, it is such an honor to meet you. I'm Maria, chief go-fer here. Oni's on the phone, but she'll be right out."

Myra introduced Alexia and took a deep breath of the clean Ozark air. A front had passed through overnight and the atmosphere seemed recharged. The air refreshed her, but she missed the smell of the ocean at home in Carmel.

"I see you picked up your rental okay. Wow, I never knew Enterprise rented vintage cars. This is great. Did you know we have one of the country's biggest Mustang car shows here in town?"

Myra knitted her brow. "Rental? This is my own car. I know nothing of a rental."

Maria continued examining the car. "Funny, a guy named Tim called a few nights ago, asking if you'd gotten here yet and that your rental was in the lot in Fayetteville." She stopped at the back bumper. "Too bad about that dent. This car is perfect otherwise. I know a guy who –"

The squeaky screen door interrupted her, while alarm raced up Myra's spine.

"Ms. Mitchell!" Oni Prairieberry walked toward them, arms extended.

"Ms. Prairieberry." Myra braced for a hug. "Please, call me Myra. Both of you. Please."

"Absolutely, and please reciprocate. Everyone calls me by my first name, unless they're mad at me." She laughed. "I even get mail just addressed to Oni in Eureka Springs. No street necessary, everyone here knows me."

Myra introduced Alexia.

"Oni," echoed Alexia. "What a unique name."

"Yes, well, would you believe it's not my given name? Of course you would. It's a short story really. I got married at age sixteen in the middle of the hippy era. My husband, my first husband that is … he and I decided we needed names that had meaning. I selected Oni because it means 'born on sacred, or spiritual, ground.' Well, in Africa, anyway, not Japan. The last name was simply something whimsical and impulsive." She laughed. "Now, thirty-plus years later, I'm forever Oni Prairieberry. Well, come on in. The gang is anxiously waiting."

Myra scrutinized the area around the old home before moving and approached Alexia. She whispered in the young woman's ear, "You heard that, right? Someone called asking about my rental. Keep your eyes and ears open. I think whoever this is, is after me. He won't strike while we're with others, but we might have to leave quickly." Alexia nodded. Myra hoped she was correct.

Myra's luncheon session extended well beyond her scheduled time. As she had done with Alexia on the charter plane, she read excerpts of everyone's writing and gave honest critique, no holds barred. More than a few tears erupted, but all were grateful.

Oni approached her. "Thank you so much. You went far beyond what you'd agreed to do. I don't know how to thank you." She pointed to three sealed file boxes, similar in size to boxes that hold a ream of paper. "Those are yours, I believe."

Myra smiled. "Your giving those to us is thanks enough." She looked around. "Alexia?"

Her assistant came through a nearby door. "Yes?"

"Could you please move those to the car? Be careful. I need to talk with Oni in private for a moment."

As Alexia picked up the first box, Myra took Oni's arm and together they walked into the retreat's main office. "I have a concern and need you to be aware of something that happened in Taos ..."

After a brief stop in town at a local clothing store, Alexia drove them back to the motel. As they left the historic district of town, Myra began to sob. "You okay?"

"No."

"Can I ask –?"

"No. Please, g-give me a moment. I'll be okay. I-I don't know why I'm so emotional here." She lied.

"I know why."

Myra dried her eyes and looked at the young woman.

"The rental car thing, what happened to Diana. You're afraid something's going to happen to you, us, Oni, the others."

Myra didn't reply. She did have those concerns ... and a plan.

Nothing more was spoken until Alexia pulled up in front of the cabin.

"Would you please move those boxes into the living area? Let's take a survey of the contents before bed. I'll explain what I have in mind while we do that."

Over the next few hours, they discussed the day's turn of events while they indexed the contents and moved the diaries and other relevant material into two boxes, arranged chronologically. The third box held various mementoes. With hesitation, Myra discussed her concern about the potential danger they faced and her plan. Now, they were done and could only wait. Were they prepared well enough?

"What do you want to do with that stuff?" Alexia asked, pointing toward that third box. The clock read well past 1 a.m.

She yawned.

"Nothing at this time of night, that's for sure. I'll have to think about it." She stood and stretched. "Time for bed. No need to get up early, so let's sleep in." If they slept at all.

Alexia nodded. She didn't look like she would fall asleep any sooner than Myra would. She still couldn't fathom why she had become someone's target, but that someone meant business. She thought of Diana. Yet, Myra was fatigued. What if she failed to stay alert, failed to carry out her end of the plan. Would Alexia pay a price as she would?

"Don't forget what I told you to do."

"I won't." Alexia turned on her cell phone and clutched it to her chest.

Myra knew she wouldn't.

At first, Dewey stood there, stunned. It wasn't that Mitchell and the Hamilton girl had driven by him. He'd expected that. Well, hoped for that anyway. No, what had caught him totally off-guard was the car. He had memories of a yellow Mustang and a girl long gone. He'd thought the car belonged to someone helping the girl, who had been a threat because of what she'd witnessed. Yet, time passed and nothing ever came of it. She had disappeared from his radar, he never saw the car again, and life went on. Until now.

He now sat in his hotel room with his laptop opened in front of him. He'd spent thirty minutes searching until he found references to and a photo of Betsy Weston. That was the name on that cartoon he'd stolen from the dingy diner in Asheville. And one photo showed her next to a yellow Mustang. He'd thought she was there helping Alice search for that boy of hers. Was it the same car? What were the odds of that happening? He was amazed to learn that she had created one of his favorite comics. Why hadn't he ever put two and two together? Forty-plus years had passed. How well did he really remember Alice Cummings? Still, the girl in the car wasn't there helping Alice. She was Alice.

Next, he pulled up photos of Myra Mitchell, finding the current ones easily. Was there a resemblance? It took some surfing, but he finally retrieved some of her earliest publicity photos. The eyes seemed the same. Hair was easy for a woman to change. The nose? Maybe some work done there. Could it be true that fate had finally brought them back together? Was it some cosmic coincidence that led him to Eureka Springs? He had no doubts now. He was going to finally tie up a loose end that had been fluttering in the wind for decades.

Thirty-five

Dewey yawned, and yawned again as he sat just inside the edge of the forest, waiting. He'd spent a looong afternoon waiting for them to leave and followed them to Pond Mountain. Then he'd had his revelation and spent time preparing for his strike. He returned to the forest around the cabins at dusk and settled in for the right time to move in.

He'd hoped they would turn in right away, but no, he'd swatted mosquitoes for two hours before dense dark drove them into hiding. He'd fallen asleep at one point, only to wake up as he fell to the forest floor. He wasn't the young man who once could keep watch over his stills all night. He couldn't let that happen again. He focused on his newfound motivation to stay awake.

He wondered what time it could be. He could gauge the time during the day just by the position of the sun. But at night? He didn't know the North Star from the South Star. He didn't dare shine a light on his watch. The light might be seen, putting the women on alert and blowing his only opportunity so far at completing his mission.

He started at a rustling in the leaves to his right and impulsively shot a beam of light that direction. *Crap!* he thought as he doused the little Magnum flashlight. Had he just blown his cover? *Man, they better turn in soon.* He couldn't take much more of this.

As if they'd heard him, a few minutes later the light in the main room downstairs flickered off. Fifteen minutes later, the upstairs light went out, and moments later, the remaining first floor light went dark. He assumed these to be the two bedrooms as described in the resort's promotional brochure.

The main floor bedroom, occupied most likely by the Mitchell lady, would be his first target. Should he be discovered or heard, the top floor resident's only escape path would put her running right past him.

He checked the suppressor on the end of his Walther P22. On tight. After a fifteen-minute delay to allow them transit to dreamland, he eased into a crouch and cursed the tightness that had settled into his thighs and lower back. James Bond he wasn't. Hell, young he wasn't. He scuffled slowly at first, to work out those kinks, and crept up to the back door. Within a minute, he had the door unlocked and open, thankfully without a squeak. His eyes adjusted to the low light and he moved quietly toward the bedroom, where he found the door slightly ajar.

As planned, he pushed open the door and took three quick steps toward the bed as he raised his pistol toward the body in the bed. He quickly fired off three rounds, two to the chest area and one to the head. One for Alice, one for Betsy and one for Myra Mitchell. Finally, he had settled his score with Alice Cummings.

Albritton arose from bed to ease the urge of his bladder. The clock read 3 a.m. and although he'd come to accept these middle-of-the-night calls of nature, he'd had trouble returning to sleep afterwards for the past several weeks. In fact, sleep had become scarce in general and he often required a stiff nightcap plus a double dose of melatonin to fall asleep at all.

Not tonight. He fell asleep easily and soundly. He now had a true professional on the job. Two loose ends – Hamilton and Hastings – would soon be gone. He'd often thought about how to remove the latter problem, a plague since his schoolboy days, despite his usefulness in the early years of accumulating land.

He returned from the bathroom thinking all was well in his world again. Slumber reclaimed him as his head touched down onto the pillow.

Thirty-six

The man adjusted his night vision goggles as he followed the form of Dewey Hastings from the woods to the cottage. Once Dewey had dispatched the women, he would take care of Dewey. Hastings seemed old on his feet and took forever to approach the cottage. Precious time during which he could have been spotted. Still, he had to give the thug some credit. He picked the back door lock and entered the building in record time.

He knew of Hasting's preference for the Walther P22. Personally, he'd chosen a suppressed 9mm. That required only one quick headshot, whereas the .22 cal Walther, by necessity, would need at least three shots. Again, increasing the chance for discovery.

A moment after Hasting's entry to the building, a roar like two cannon blasts cracked the night silence and bright lights from the cottage and nearby buildings blinded the man. He threw off his night vision gear and blinked his eyes. Several figures from nearby buildings, including the office emerged onto the common grounds.

A young woman appeared at the cottage front door and yelled, "Someone call the police. Hurry!"

He eased deeper into the woods, keeping his eyes on the people from the resort. When he could no longer see them, they would not be able to see him either. At that point, he turned and made a hasty retreat to his vehicle. He needed to leave the area before police arrived. As he neared his car, two thoughts dominated his mind. First, the woman was armed and had anticipated the danger. The gun blasts he'd heard certainly weren't suppressed .22 shots. She must have taken Hastings out. That made her a more formidable target than the bumbling, overconfident Hastings himself. Second, his plan for a quick completion of his job lay tattered on the cottage bedroom floor. He'd had no Plan B, and now planning anything at all seemed unfeasible. He'd have no other chance for days, maybe weeks, with the expected police activity and the protective wall that would no doubt form around these women. He'd have to stick close by and take advantage of even the subtlest opportunity, improvising all the way.

He smiled. He enjoyed a challenge.

Myra waited for what seemed like hours before moving from the corner of the room where she'd been sitting, waiting. The form on the floor did not move. As lights came on in cabins around them, she gathered the courage to move. She flicked on a nearby floor lamp and watched. Still no movement. She thought about an episode early in her life. That man had continued with agonal breathing, a term she'd learned for her books.

She stood and walked over to the lifeless body. She didn't see a gun, but she knew he'd had one. A shattered mannequin head on the bed attested to that. She used her foot gently to turn the man's head so she could see his face. Her mind went numb. This was impossible. No. Her eyes fooled her. After forty years, could it be? The scar on the left side of his face seemed to say so.

Myra slowly moved to the main room and sat on the rustic couch there, her hands shaking. Angela, the resort manager, already stood at the door, cell phone in hand talking to someone. Alexia paced the hall outside the bedroom as if trying to muster up the fortitude to look at the bloody scene inside. Police sirens echoed through the hills in the distance, getting closer with every minute. To Myra, the incident seemed the surreal re-enactment of a scene from one of her books. Except that this man was Dewey Hastings. How was she going to reconcile this fact with her long-kept secret? How could she begin to tell the truth without revealing her preciously guarded past?

She'd retired to the bedroom with her fears. She'd coached Alexia to stuff the bed covers with pillows, like kids trying to fool their parents while they snuck out of the house for some truant tryst. She'd even secured two mannequin heads to add to the reality. She had hoped she would be proven foolish. She had hoped she'd never have to fire the 25th Anniversary Glock 17 she carried all the time in her purse.

Her heart began to race when the kitchen door opened. She knew a door had opened, not by any sound, but by the subtle change in air pressure in the cottage, and the bedroom door going ajar on its own. She sat tucked into the corner shadows as a dark figure pushed through the door and raised its arm to a shooting position. Three spits. Suppressed fire. By the third, she'd raised her arms, triggered the laser sight, and replied with two thunderous burps of her own. With the lights on, she saw her reward for hours of range training - two tight holes in the man's mid-sternum. He died before hitting the floor. And then she saw his face…

"Can I get you anything?"

Myra looked up when Alexia repeated her question. She shook her head. "Hardly the time for tea now, is it?"

Alexia frowned and wrapped her arms more tightly around her chest. Myra saw that the girl was shaking worse than she was. "Sorry. I … I … Tell you what, a glass of water would be nice. Thank you."

As Alexia returned with the drink, Myra noticed the first police officer approach the cottage with Angela talking and walking next to him. She stopped at the doorway while the officer entered.

Myra pointed toward the bedroom. "H-he's back there."

He returned to the living room a minute later.

"My gun's right there." She pointed to the coffee table in front of the couch. "Chamber's empty. The magazine still has 15 rounds. I removed it and laid it there." He reached for the pistol as if unsure how to pick it up. "I'm the only one who has fired it in months. Mine should be the only fingerprints. Use gloves to bag it." She smiled. Standard police protocols. She knew them by heart.

The constable left it in place on the table. Myra heard the crunch of gravel outside from another car's arrival. Rotating beacons of light filled the night like strobes at a rave. A tall, athletically built man in his mid-forties entered the building and the first officer deferred to him by stepping outside and standing at the door.

"I'm Detective Akers with the Carroll County Sheriff's Department." He handed her a business card. Myra nodded.

"He's in the back."

The detective followed the deputy's path to the bedroom and returned a moment later. To Myra, that made three confirmations that the man was indeed dead.

He pointed to the pistol on the table, but Myra anticipated his question.

"Glock 17. Chamber's empty and you can see the mag is out. It's mine. I fired it. I'm legally licensed for it in both California and Texas, with conceal carry permits in both states. Arkansas accepts the Texas permit in reciprocity."

"Why do you need a concealed weapon? You don't look

like –"

"Detective, do you know who I am? Did the manager here tell you?"

He shook his head noncommittally. "Myra Mitchell is the registered guest. That you?"

"Yes. Myra Mitchell."

He looked unfazed.

"New York Times bestselling author."

"Sorry, don't read much. I'm more of a video gamer myself. What have you written?"

She sighed and rolled her eyes. Of all the times to not be recognized. She threw out several names, mostly the books that became movies, and saw that something registered in him.

"You don't get to my level in writing the books I write without learning everything there is to know about handguns, assault rifles, and the like. They're part of our tradecraft, so to speak. Also, I've been advised by more than one security group that I should never travel without protection. I tried a bodyguard once. That didn't work, so that ..." She pointed to the Glock. "... is my security detail. It was, by the way, a gift from a friend. Perhaps you've heard of him? Ted Nugent?"

Now he seemed impressed. Nothing like name-dropping at the right time, with the right name.

"Those were two expertly grouped shots."

"You shouldn't own a gun unless you know to respect it and learn how to use it. I've spent hours on the range. That's what makes it such good security."

"We'll need to take it."

Myra nodded. "I assume I'll get it back at some point."

The man shrugged. "At some point, probably. So, tell me what happened?"

"Have a seat, detective." She began with her trip to Taos

and the assault on Diana there. She gave him the Taos detective's name and phone number. She followed with the trip to Eureka Springs, the suspicious call received by Maria at the Writer's Retreat, and a car that had followed her back to the resort. She outlined her fears and then the events of the past hour. She presented him with a narrative even a non-reader could appreciate and left nothing out, except that she knew the man.

By then, the county's crime scene team of two tired-looking men had arrived, as well as the county coroner. The detective nodded toward the gun and one man bagged it, and then placed the magazine in a separate bag. Myra could hear a local reporter, who knew to keep his distance from the scene, peppering the other guests with questions. An occasional camera flash popped through the open cottage door. Myra was glad to be hours away from the nearest paparazzi, and their mid-south wannabes.

"More water?"

Myra looked up to find Alexia hovering next to her chair. The detective and investigators busied themselves in the bedroom. Myra knew everything they would find would corroborate her story. She also anticipated having to stay in town longer than she planned. She shook her head. "I'm fine, thank you."

"You don't look well."

"Gee, thanks." Still, Myra had to admit she wasn't feeling so hot and her jaundice seemed to be worsening. "See if they'll let you talk with Angela. We'll need somewhere else to stay, and I might need to have my lab tests done somewhere around here."

Alexia went to the front door and talked with the constable, who allowed her to leave. A few minutes later, she returned to inform Myra the other cottage would become available later that morning. Myra laid back into the cushion. She hadn't felt this drained since her seventy-two hour binge following the release of the fourth book-turned-movie. At that time, though, she'd had ample reasons, all physical, for the exhaustion. Her current fatigue was purely emotional. She hoped. But then she noted the darkening color of the skin on her forearms.

Thirty minutes later, the detective emerged from the back and approached her.

"Looks pretty much like you described it. The gun was still in his hand. We found two .22 caliber rounds in the bed and one in the mannequin head. The Walther's magazine showed only three rounds fired. I'll have to present this to the prosecutor and we'll let you know his decision. You might get in trouble with some of our gun laws, but I can't see anything but self-defense on the killing."

"Getting in trouble I can deal with. Getting dead is something I'm trying to avoid." She stood up from the couch. "I'm told we can move to the other cottage later, if you'll let us move our stuff when it becomes available. How long do you think we'll need to stay in town?"

He shrugged again. "Up to the prosecutor. You do have copies of your licenses and permits, I take it?"

"I do. We might be able to make you copies at the office."

"I'll have the constable handle that for us." He sat down and motioned for Myra to do so. "So, do you know this guy?"

Myra hesitated and shook her head. He looked at Alexia. "You?"

"I've never seen him before." She sat down next to Myra.

"Your accent. The Carolinas?"

Alexia nodded. "Western North Carolina."

"Is Franklin in that part of the state?"

Alexia knitted her brow. "Yes, it is."

"The name 'Dewey Hastings' mean anything to you?"

She hesitated. "Noooo, I don't ... I don't think so."

"Ms. Mitchell, can you think of anyone who'd be out to kill you?"

Myra took a deep breath. *Yes, Dewey Hastings*, she thought, although a reason for his coming after her now eluded her. "No one I can think of. Unlike some of my peers who get death threats for degrading Islam, or speaking badly of some fringe group, my novels don't usually have much of a political message. I can't recall ever getting any threats. My publisher might know more."

The detective looked at Alexia. "Ms. Hamilton? Anyone?"

She looked puzzled. "Honestly, no, but before I received my graduate position at USC, I did some journalism back home. My apartment was burglarized once, about a week before I moved. Police thought it was a random event, kids looking for money or tech toys."

"Well, ladies, we might know more after looking into this guy, but I'd have to suggest that you, Ms. Mitchell, might not have been his primary target. I found this in his jacket pocket." He presented the women with a picture of Alexia, with details on her height, weight, and more noted in pencil on the back.

Thirty-seven

By first light, the body and related evidence had been removed from the cottage. The investigation moved outside where the team focused on one area in the adjacent woods. By noon, Angela and Alexia had moved all of their possessions to the nearby cottage. Alexia, in particular, appeared to be looking for tasks to keep her busy.

"Alexia!" Myra called upstairs looking for her assistant.

The young woman appeared from the kitchen. "I'm here."

"I need to go to town, but I'm not up to driving. Let's go."

"Right now? I …" She pointed to the kitchen.

Myra shook her head. "I'm not hungry and I'd rather not wait."

"No, that's not what I meant. I-I found something disturbing in one of the boxes." She pointed again to the kitchen. Myra followed her into the room. Letters and notebooks littered the table.

"I had to make myself busy, to, you know … so I started going through the first box. I found one of Betsy's earliest diaries. Angela was right; she had a rough life … and she mentioned a name that caught my attention. When I was a student in North Carolina, I volunteered with the Innocence Project. There was a man who was convicted of the murder of a girl in 1969. The teenager went missing. Blood was found at the man's home and a female body washed up on the shore of Thorpe Reservoir a few weeks later. The father identified it as his daughter. The convicted man has consistently claimed his innocence to this day, but after we worked the case, we found no DNA evidence we could use to exonerate him. To this day, I'm convinced he is innocent. Our whole team is."

Myra felt nauseated. She didn't want to hear anymore, but knew she had to.

"Why wasn't there any DNA if you had blood from the missing girl and a body?"

"We had the blood, which he claimed was indeed the girl's blood but that she had cut her arm and he stitched her up. We needed to compare that DNA with that of the girl found in the lake. We got an exhumation order and found the grave empty. Her body wasn't there."

Myra felt like she had at the restaurant with Samuel. She struggled to stay on her feet and maintain her composure, but her insides roiled. "Wh-what was the man's name?"

"Umfleet. Curt Umfleet."

"Oh, dear God," she whispered. In one fell swoop, her past was collapsing on top of her.

Alexia stepped up to support her. "Are you okay?"

A knock on the front door interrupted them. Myra took a deep breath, steadied herself, and walked to the door. She opened it to find two husky young men standing there in well-fitted chinos and polo shirts. Their crew cuts made a Marine look shabby, their upper torsos made Sasquatch look puny.

"Yes?"

"Ma'am, I'm Kenny and this is Gene. We're your protection detail."

"What? I didn't request a ..." She turned inside to Alexia, who shrugged her shoulders in denial.

"The man in New York said you might protest. He told us to ignore it, that he knew best."

Myra stood there dumbfounded. "Was this man's name Samuel?"

"Yes, Ma'am. DeMoss."

She threw her hands up in the air. "How in the world did he find out? Has he planted bugs in my luggage?"

"I believe, Ma'am, that someone in Taos, New Mexico called him. He mentioned an incident there. We're with a security firm out of Little Rock."

"One moment," Myra said and closed the door on them.

She turned to find Alexia already on the phone. A moment later, she nodded. Samuel had hired them. If Samuel had his way, soon she'd have an entourage the size of the President's. Yet, for once, she didn't have the energy to argue. She opened the door and stepped back to let them inside the cabin.

"Alexia, you're off the hook. Kenny, can you drive a stick?"

"Ma'am, I can drive anything on wheels, or treads for that matter. Also have fixed and rotary wing pilot's license. If it moves, I can pretty much handle it."

"That I can believe." She tossed him her car keys. "The Mustang outside. Your partner needs to stick with Alexia here."

"Sweeeet."

"What?"

"Sorry, Ma'am. That car's classic. I'll handle it with care."

"You sure will … and you might want to confer with the local sheriff's department. You guys are a day late." She wanted to add "and a dollar short," but she hated clichés.

"Ma'am?"

"Pleeease. Stop calling me Ma'am."

"Yes, Ma'am."

Alexia's chuckle ended with Myra's glare.

*　　*　　*

Fifteen minutes later, Myra and Alexia entered the Writer's Retreat while their "protective" detail stood guard outside. Myra admired their work ethic and devotion to details. Had she been younger she would have admired much more, but then, that's why her first and only other bodyguard hadn't worked out. Hers wasn't the body needing guarded.

And she felt guilty for her thoughts. She had a much more important mission now.

"I thought you didn't want to come," she whispered to Alexia once out of earshot of "the boys."

"I didn't want to be stuck in that cottage with Gonzo there either. Besides, I'm curious as to why you needed to come back here."

Myra held up an envelope. "We're on a new mission, dear." She lifted the flap and opened the envelope like a fish mouth. Inside was a key. "It was in the third box."

Oni appeared in the reception area as soon as they stepped inside. "Oh dear Lord." She rushed to Myra, crying, and smothered the author with a big hug. "Myra. Alexia. I am sooo glad you're okay." She paused. "You are okay, right?"

Myra nodded. Alexia shook her head.

"It's time, Oni." She held up the key. Alexia looked puzzled.

"Are you sure?"

Myra nodded again. "I owe a debt that I have to repay. I don't want to wait and maybe die before I can do that."

Oni turned and led them through a back door. Myra was impressed to find "Gonzo" Gene standing guard there, scanning the surroundings. He followed them to an adjacent building after activating some kind of device on his sleeve. Before entering the next building, Gene stopped them. "Please wait until Kenny gets here. We need to secure the building."

Oni whispered, "Is he for real?"

Myra nodded. "Very much so. Wait for Kenny."

Kenny arrived in seconds and entered the building. Three minutes later, he emerged. "Do you have a key for the locked room? Everything else is clear."

Myra handed him the key. A minute later, he gave them the 'all clear.'

The three women entered the building, one of the old homes that had been converted to rooms for retreat participants. Except for one room that had remained locked for decades. Myra heard a faint gasp from Alexia. She turned and saw the young woman's gaze fixed on the plaque above the door, "The Elise Kenwood Suite."

Myra entered first and Oni, waiting for Alexia to move, said. "Elise funded the creation of this retreat. I couldn't have done it without her."

Myra moved among the furnishings, gently sliding her fingers over the old drawing table and its worn stool. A nearby table held piles of papers that closer inspection revealed to be yellowed 'Sweetie and George' cartoons with a twist. Sweetie and George were younger and new parents of a baby named Jimmy Bob. Alexia thumbed through several sheets and a smile emerged.

"That would have been Betsy's next book," said Oni.

Myra had been remarkably silent since entering the room, but tears flowed freely as she moved from one piece of furniture to another, finally stopping at an antique roll-top desk. She reached around the back and retrieved a key to the desk's lock.

Oni motioned to Myra. "Alexia, meet Elise Kenwood, aka Betsy Weston."

Myra turned and faced her assistant with a chagrined look.

Alexia's demeanor flashed anger, and then became smug.

"Why? Why the big charade? You could have just told me."

Myra sat on the stool in front of her old drawing table. "As to why, well, I wanted you to experience something different. I wanted you to ferret out this story for yourself. I know we started off kinda rocky, but after a few days in Taos, I knew I wanted you to write my last book if I never got to. 'The Death of a Diva' was to be my life story. The ultimate rags to riches story, complete with sad ending. Plus, I didn't really want to come out of hiding just yet. Only Oni, my dearest friend ever, knew the whole truth and kept my secret, even from Angela and Tammie."

"So, why now?"

"I'm indebted forever to one man, a man who risked a lot to help me escape my miserable childhood home and alcoholic father. Curt Umfleet. He never killed Alice Cummings. His story is true. Here's the scar on my forearm that he sewed up. I am Alice Cummings, and I can prove it all." She started to cry. "All these years, I never knew. All these years, he's been in jail falsely because I cut out and ran and never looked back. I need to make amends for that."

She paused for a deep sigh. Oni stepped forward and put her arm around Myra.

"Tell me, what happened to his kids? Do you know?" asked Myra.

Alexia replied, "They live in their childhood home. He does odd jobs and she teaches Special Ed, I think. They barely get by. We did a fund raiser for them once, to fix the roof on that old house."

Myra furrowed her brow.

"Why? The Umfleet Family Trust owned thousands of

acres along Thorpe Reservoir. They could have sold that land to support themselves, to defend their father."

"What trust? And what land?" Alexia's eyes widened. "Omigosh, if the land you're talking about is what I think it is, it's been developed into multi-million dollar homes, a golf course, and more. It's one of the most fashionable gated vacation communities in the state." She became agitated and her mouth dropped open. "Th-that's why I'm a target. I was working on a story before I got my graduate position, on Curt's children and the family in general. I must have come close to discovering the truth."

Myra opened the roll-top and pulled out a thick manila envelope, overflowing with papers. "We need to get to North Carolina. ASAP"

Myra stuffed the envelope into her purse, carefully placed the 'Sweetie and George' materials into a nearby satchel, left the room, and walked toward the door. "Kenny! Gene! We need —"

She stopped in her tracks. The reflection on the door's glass window showed the two men lying on the ground next to each other, Taser probes and wires dangling from each of their backs.

Thirty-eight
❧◆◆❧

He sat behind a makeshift blind, adjusting his sight for the distance to the building's door. He'd been concerned about whatever protective wall would develop around the women, but now laughed at the two bumpkins lying on the ground. They had looked the part, probably did have military or police training, and had played the role well, covering the doors and securing the building. Yet, in reality, they did not truly believe there was a threat. Their vigilance waned when out of sight of their wards. He had simply walked down the sidewalk like any tourist, smiled and nodded at the two when they turned their attention toward him, and nailed them both in successive Taser shots when they turned back toward the house. For their bulk, they had fallen easily. Once down, he gave each a three-second buzz from his stun baton. That combination wouldn't kill them, unless they had some underlying heart condition, but it did guarantee him a minimum of ten minutes to get into position. More likely, they'd be down a full twenty minutes.

Now he held the high ground above the spring across the street. The building had two entries. The main front door, opening onto the street, appeared as if it hadn't been used in years. The women had used the side door. He had both covered. He would wait for the women to emerge and in their confusion over finding the bodies, he would quickly dispatch both women. Like the two guards, the third woman would live. He wasn't paid for collateral damage.

Myra's shaky hand stopped Alexia before she stepped through the door. Had she not seen the reflection, they would have simply walked outside to become instant targets.

"Get away from the door and avoid any windows," she said, pointing toward the reflection so the other women could see what she'd seen. She pulled out her cell phone, but the hills blocked the signals. The 'No Service' alert flashed.

Oni gasped, but rallied and took Alexia's hand. "This way."

Myra knew what was coming. She'd used this route on more than one occasion. In contrast to the common story, she'd stayed in Eureka Springs for over a week after discovering Nico's dalliances. Oni had hidden her in the very room that took on Elise Kenwood's name. "Alexia, you're about to see part of Eureka Springs the tourists never see. Remember what I told you about the city streets? Some of these streets have tunnels under them."

Oni grabbed a couple of jackets hanging on pegs in the hall. "Here. He probably knows what you're wearing … and it's pretty dirty in there."

"Where are we going? What do we need to do?" asked Alexia.

Myra paused. "She's right. We do need a plan."

"My car's at the bottom of the hill, where I usually park. Go that way past two houses and there's a door to the outside. You should be able to get to my car from behind the houses. There's a spare key under the passenger floor mat."

"What will you do?"

"I can get back to the office by going this way and call the police." She pointed the opposite way in the tunnel.

"But we need to leave town and our stuff is at Pond Mountain," protested Alexia.

Neither woman had an immediate reply.

"Tell you what, after the police arrive. I'll drive your car

341

back to the resort and get your things. Where should we meet up?"

Myra sought to control her shaking, but there was more to it than anxiety. "Silver Wings, and I hope he'll take on a charter flight." Myra took Oni's hand. "Please tell Angela that Betsy has missed her, too. You can tell her everything now." She handed her the key to the Mustang. "Oh, and when Dweedle-Dee and Dweedle-Dum wake up, tell them they're fired."

Thirty-nine
❧ ✦ ✦ ☙

Myra plopped into the hardback chair offered her. Her energy was waning. "Please, Captain. I saw it fly in two nights ago. I know it's airworthy."

"Myra, I know we go way back, but I can't accept the assignment."

"Why not? It's sitting right out there, and I know you'd love any excuse to fly it again."

Myra and Alexia sat in the office of the Aviation Cadet Museum. Their escape from Eureka Springs had not been without mishap, but Myra shook off the pain in her wrist after falling during their dash to Oni's car. She rationalized the weakness that led to the fall as being the result of exhaustion. She had heard from Oni that the perp had evaded the police, but they had discovered a temporary blind from where he undoubtedly planned to shoot.

"It's not the plane. I have no crew, and taking off from this grass field is quite different from landing. Thanks to the bastards who sued to stop this airfield from development, I have court ordered restrictions on the flight pattern."

Myra didn't have time to travel to Little Rock, or even Springdale, just west of Beaver Lake, for a charter. A plane might not be available and police protection could not be guaranteed for the length of either trip. More importantly, she felt her health swirling like the whirlpool encircling a drain. Her time was running out.

"Oh, c'mon. Years ago, when you helped me with my book research, you bragged about being able to land your C-130 on an aircraft carrier. Don't tell me a little tail wind and a short runway is going to ground you. Or are you just getting

343

too old for a little adventure?"

Captain Earl sighed. "You're baiting me now. Look, I-I still don't have a crew."

"Who flew in with you?"

"An old friend. He's gone home already."

"So, who do you need?"

"At a minimum, the 130J requires two pilots and for what you want, a loadmaster."

Myra rubbed her wrist as she thought. "Give me a minute." Her cell phone had full service on top of the hill where they sat. She dialed. "Oni, are the dweedles still there? We need a co-pilot and loadmaster for a C-130. Can they fill the bill?" She smiled at the answer, but even that smile did not come without effort. "Tell them they're forgiven and rehired. Bring them with you."

She turned back to the retired TWA and military pilot. "Got your crew. What else?"

"Well, I'll need to remove the old jeep that's strapped in for display. We'll put the Mustang there. We'll need to fuel up in Springfield, or maybe Memphis. I'll have to file my flight plan. You said Asheville, right?"

Myra nodded. Earl shrugged. "That should be it. I'll go start my pre-flight." He shook his head as he stood. "Never thought I'd be putting this baby to work again." Then he grinned.

"Oh, and here's your fee." She handed him a check. "Should cover expenses, that 2-acre field you want to buy next door, and a bit more."

His eyes widened as he saw the check in her hand for a quarter million dollars.

"This does give me a lifetime membership to the museum, too. Right?"

"Myra, that gives you an eternal membership. Thank you, thank you, thank you. I don't know what else to say." He stepped toward her and she started to back away from the expected hug, but gave in and let him physically express his thanks before he rushed from the building.

Alexia eyed Myra curiously. "What?" asked the author.

"Nothing."

"Oh no. Don't 'nothing' me. I've come to know that look. My generosity surprises you, doesn't it?"

Alexia replied with a wan smile. "Actually, you're right. My first impression of a selfish diva has been shattered these past two weeks."

"Then you'd be even more surprised to know that Elise Kenwood gave away pretty much everything Betsy Weston ever earned. When you get the chance to Google 'Elise Kenwood,' you'll find non-profits and schools all across this country with endowments in her name. I never needed it all, and I seemed blessed, to use your Christian term, with the ability to make money."

Alexia said nothing.

"What, no response?"

Alexia smiled. "Ever hear of the parable of the talents?"

"I may be a heathen, but I'm not Biblically illiterate. All good authors should know the stories of the Bible, Shakespeare, Dickens, and the like."

"Well, whether or not you believe, there are universal laws, or maybe 'principles' is a better word, that God set in motion that are valid for everyone. 'You reap what you sow' is an example. When the wealthy landowner gave each servant a set amount of money, the two who invested it wisely saw their returns multiply. The one who buried it was afraid to take a risk and wanted to make sure he could give the money back when called into account for it. He had his money taken away. You are reaping because you sow. I think Jesus' words to the religious teacher are good ones for you, too: 'You are not far from the Kingdom of God.'"

Myra remained silent.

"What, no response?" Alexia smiled.

Myra had no reply. Something inside her sensed a kernel of truth in what Alexia said. In addition, Alexia's "prophetic" words about God filling her deepest desire came back to mind. Did she actually have a glimmer of hope that Alexia would be right? Did she dare to resurrect a hope she'd given up for dead decades before?

"I'm not ready to die yet, thank you."

Alexia chuckled. "Knowing the stories of the Bible is one thing. Understanding the Bible is another. God's kingdom is not limited to the afterlife."

Again, Myra had no comeback.

"Ma'am?"

Myra grunted, as she turned to find Kenny standing near the office entrance.

"Ma'am, we're ready for you. Captain Earl said we should escort you to the plane. The Mustang is already secure and he's ready."

"Pleeease, don't call me Ma'am. Myra would be fine."

"Yes, sir, um, Ma'am. Let's roll. We, uh, won't get caught with our pants … um, we won't let you down this time, Ma'am. Promise."

Alexia frowned as Myra struggled to get up and leave the room. She assisted Myra, and for once, Myra gladly accepted the aid. At the main door, Kenny lifted one arm to block her way, and then preceded them from the building. Gene filed in close behind as they walked to Oni's car. The distance to the airstrip hardly seemed to warrant driving, but Myra knew she'd never make it on her own power. Plus, she had no desire to become a target in that wide-open space, so she put up no argument.

The car pulled right up to the cargo ramp of the huge transport plane and the men hurried the ladies into the cargo hold before Gene returned to the car and moved it to a parking area.

"Betsy?"

Myra, who was watching Gene jog back to the plane, turned to find Angela with tears in her eyes. "Hi, Angie." She held out her arms as the woman approached. "I'm so sorry, for so many things, and I ask you to forgive me." Angela embraced Myra.

Gene trotted up the ramp, and Kenny said, "Ready to go wheels up." He started toward the front of the plane.

Oni put her hand on Angela's shoulder. "C'mon honey, we need to get back."

Myra straightened up. "Oh no, you're both going. Gene, raise that gate and show us where to strap in."

Oni protested. "We can't go. We're not prepared –"

Myra stopped her. "You're going. We can buy you whatever you need when we get there. I am not leaving you behind to become targets like Diana in Taos. No way. Sit down and prepare to take off." Oni started to comment, but Myra raised her hand to cut her off. "NO! You're going. Gene!" With every ounce of strength she still had, she pointed to the lift button.

"Gene!" Alexia pointed toward a car careening off the county road toward them, as in some formulaic action flick.. The guard pulled his Beretta, rushed to the top of the ramp, and took a kneeling firing position. At that moment, flashing lights on the front grill and a burst of siren announced the car as an unmarked police sedan.

The auto swerved to a stop near the back of the plane, and two plain clothed men jumped out, identifying themselves as being from the Eureka Springs Police Department. Oni knew both and confirmed that to Myra. The older of the two waved for Myra to come down off the ramp.

"Alexia, Oni. Please go see what he wants. I just don't have the energy." Myra found her way to a nearby jump seat and collapsed into it. She had long ago realized there would be an emotional catharsis with the revelation of her secret, but that, combined with the physical stress of recent days and her illness, had dealt her a hand she wanted to fold on the flop.

Alexia came back to Myra while Oni continued talking with the officers.

"They're glad they caught up to us. Someone ransacked the old house with the Kenwood suite. The suite itself was torn up pretty good, but naturally, they, the police, have no idea what might have been taken and they'd like someone to inventory the place and give them a rundown on what's missing, damaged, and so forth. They did get a partial plate and car model. Preliminary investigation shows it to be a rental out of Springfield. The driver's license on file with the rental agency is bogus, but it's a fake North Carolina license. Seems that someone in our home state doesn't want either of us coming back there. Anyway, the police are trying to get security footage picturing the renter and they've alerted the police in Springfield and Little Rock."

Myra had little to say and found her thoughts a bit confused, which meant she must be sicker than she'd thought. Yet, now was not the time to say anything to anyone about her condition.

"Thera what not impo …" Why was Alexia looking at her so funny? Then she realized her words were not coming out properly. Was she now having a stroke, too? Wasn't liver failure bad enough on its own? Her heart began to jump at that worry. She started over, focusing on what she needed to say, speaking slowly, and enunciating each word. "There was nothing important or valuable left behind. My important papers are in that envelope in my bag. The Sweetie cartoons are in that satchel. The rest is old furniture and clothing. There was nothing to take."

"And nothing to point him in our direction?"

Myra shook her head as Oni walked up to them, and said, "They want me to stick around to go through the house. I told 'em I couldn't, but that I'd be back within the week. Not happy. Maria can inventory all of the rooms except the Elise Kenwood Suite."

"There's nothing in there worth anything. I was just telling Alexia that," said Myra.

"That's what I told them. Not happy, as I said."

Gene stood next to the gate mechanism, looking confused.

"Gene, roll it up! Let's go." Myra waved to the officers as the ramp rose into flight position. Her last glimpse of them was of their getting into the car. They couldn't hold them there, she thought, although the thought of an obstruction charge flitted through her mind. She dismissed that idea. With Oni's prominence in the community, they were unlikely to put up a fuss. They would all return soon enough to deal with the events of the past twelve hours.

Her head swooned as she buckled in for the takeoff. She caught Alexia grabbing hold of Oni's arm and leading her to the side. What was she whispering in Oni's ear?

Forty

Myra awoke in confusion, nauseated, but this time the strange sounds and smell of disinfectants brought back familiar and unpleasant memories. Where was she? What had happened? She last remembered the shuddering take-off of the C-130 transport plane on the grass runway.

She stirred in bed and immediately felt a hand on hers. She opened her eyes to a dimly lit room, but the nearby window told her it was nighttime. But, which night? As the furnishings and monitoring equipment came into focus, she recognized Oni and Alexia sitting next to her bed. The hand covering the top of hers belonged to Alexia.

"Welcome back," said Oni. "You had us worried." The smile on her face appeared forced.

"What ..." Myra's parched mouth had trouble releasing the words, but her mind seemed clearer. She recalled the confusion she felt as they boarded the plane.

"You fell asleep on the plane. At least we thought you had. When you didn't wake up in Memphis when we landed for refueling, we just thought it was exhaustion. When you didn't wake up in Asheville, we rushed you to the hospital. The ER doctor diagnosed you with hepatic encephalopathy. That's when –"

Myra waved her hand to stop her. "I know what it is," she whispered.

"Your ammonia level was one of the highest he'd ever seen. When we mentioned you were on the transplant list at USC, he calculated your MELD Score and contacted Doctor Kennison at UCLA. Together they arranged your transfer to Duke, so right now you're at the Duke Medical Center, scheduled for transplant in two days."

Myra had trouble absorbing this news. "Two days?" Then she remembered the purpose of her trip to North Carolina. "I can't. I need to —"

This time Oni put her hand up to stop Myra. "We're taking care of it. I still have your power of attorney, right?" Myra nodded. "And Alexia was quite efficient in contacting her friends at the Innocence Project, as well as the eighth division superior judge needed to handle the appeal. We asked that the matter be kept discreet because of the threats on your lives."

"Y-you did this all in one afternoon?"

Oni waggled her head. "Not exactly. You've been here three days."

Myra felt her spirits sag. She turned to face Alexia. "What else ..." She noticed for the first time that Alexia's attire matched her own 'haute couture' patient garb. "What's wrong with you?" Her first thought was that the assailant had found them and injured Alexia. "Did he find us? Did he hurt you?"

Alexia smiled. "No, actually, they somehow caught him in Little Rock trying to make flight reservations back here. His car rental had been tagged. So, as soon as he turned in the car, the airport police were notified and they actually got him. He hasn't talked, and they have nothing to hold him with in Arkansas, but seems he had outstanding warrants here in North Carolina, so ..."

"So, why are you, you know?" Myra waved her hand up and down highlighting the luxurious patient gown.

She smiled again. "Because God works in mysterious ways."

Myra furrowed her brow. "And that means what?"

"You're a Cummings. My great grandmother was a Cummings and if I'm right, she was your grandmother's sister.

We're family." Alexia snickered. "Just what you wanted to hear, I know. I should have mentioned that my interest in the Umfleet case was a little more involved than I led you to believe."

Myra didn't believe, couldn't believe, what she was hearing. The closeted skeletons began parading through her room.

"I volunteered to be tested, and as it ends up, I'm as close a match for you as they can find, short of a twin sibling."

That revelation took Myra's breath. The young woman she almost dismissed twice had volunteered to be her living donor. As Doctor Kennison had explained it, her priority on the transplant waiting list meant nothing if there was a living donor explicitly offering her the life-saving tissue she required. This young woman was personally responsible for the surgery she was about to undergo. Maybe there truly was a God who loved her.

Tears flashed down her cheeks.

"I-I don't know what to say."

"Well, that's a first," retorted Oni as Alexia laughed.

Myra wiped the tears from her cheeks. "I, uh, I promise it won't happen again," Myra replied, her voice cracking. She took Alexia's hand in hers and squeezed. "Thank you, from the bottom of my heart."

Alexia shook her head. "Hey, stop with the clichés."

"Look, I have an appointment tomorrow morning with Superior Court Judge Warren in Waynesville, about Curt Umfleet. So I need to get going. I have your papers. Don't worry, they're safe with me. He may want to meet and talk with you personally, but we'll work that around your surgery. I'll be back in the afternoon."

Oni rose and leaned over Myra to kiss her on the

forehead. "Believe it or not, I am so glad this is out in the open. It's one secret I'd grown tired of keeping, especially from Angela."

Myra took Oni's hand. "Speaking of which, where is she?"

Oni's face relayed her concern. "I don't know. She doesn't answer her cell and she was supposed to meet us here over an hour ago."

Forty-one
❦ ✦ ✦ ❧

Albritton paced in the small room, five steps up and five steps back. The monitor revealed an equally nervous woman in the adjacent room. He never "dirtied" his own hands. That's what he paid guys like Hastings to do, but Hastings had failed and would soon fertilize daisies somewhere. Wilkins had failed, too. Big time. He was in custody and could become trouble. Albritton felt like his back was against a cliff in some blind desert canyon. He could feel the heat.

He knew he had to give her time to worry, to let the anxiety build so she'd be more pliable. The problem was that same time delay worked on him as well. He could feel the sweat oozing into his armpits.

"Whachu want me to do?" asked "Little Hastings," as Ricky Lee was called behind his back. He had been a strong-arm guy along with Hastings and, being less intellectually endowed, seemed to mimic every move Dewey Hastings had made. He followed Dewey's orders without hesitation, to the point Dewey had always said the guy would jump off a building if told to. However, 'little' was far from descriptive of the man's bullish physique.

"We'll let her stew a bit longer, Ricky." Albritton hoped he could last that long.

An hour later, with a fresh shirt on, he motioned to Ricky to join him in the room next door. As he entered the room, he moved directly toward the comfortable couch facing the cabin's stone fireplace, while Ricky Lee stood guard at the door. The cabin belonged to a very helpful campaign donor and bordered Duke Forest immediately west of campus. Secluded but convenient, and far too luxurious to be really classified a cabin.

"Ms. Thoms, please have a seat." He pointed to a plush, nearby chair.

She glared at him, arms folded across her chest. She made no move to sit down.

"Can we get you something to drink?"

She remained still.

"Please. I have no intention of hurting you. I need some information, that's all." Her defiant stare gave him his answer. "Very well. I can come back tomorrow morning. There's a bathroom through that door." He pointed to a closed door. "The kitchen, through there, has a limited stock. Please make yourself at home, but my friend here will keep you company. You will be limited to these three rooms. Understood?"

No response. *Why couldn't she have made this easy?* Now he wouldn't get any more sleep than she would. Maybe less.

With a little cajoling, Myra convinced the nursing staff to allow Alexia to remain with her. Two hours after Oni left, they still had no contact with Angela. Campus security had been notified and informed of the earlier threats and events in Eureka Springs. Despite being demonstrably unhappy to have this trouble plop on their doorstep, they stationed an extra guard on the floor and contacted the Durham Police Department and, as an extra precaution, the SBI – the State Bureau of Investigation.

Myra's bedside phone rang. Alexia picked it up. "It's Oni." She held the receiver so both of them could hear.

"Has Angela shown up? I'm at the motel in Asheville and I'm safe, but I went by the motel in Durham and she wasn't there. The clerk said she thought she saw her leave in the presence of a big, burly man but she wasn't sure. I think we have a problem."

Myra motioned for ~~Angela~~ Alexia to hand her the phone.

"We already deduced that. We've talked with campus security and they've talked with other police agencies. The clerk gave them a description. There's nothing else we can do from here, even if I felt up to it." Oni didn't reply, but Myra was certain she heard a sob on the other end. "I promise to keep you posted if anything develops." Myra felt her own lip quiver as they said goodbye and she hung up the phone. She'd been right, but also wrong, to bring both women with them. If anything happened to Angela, she'd forego the transplant. She didn't deserve it.

Alexia sat up straight in the chair and looked sternly at Myra. "What do you mean, there's nothing we can do?"

Myra took offense. "I feel awful as it is about bringing Angela with us and putting her in danger. I don't need you lambasting me. Look at me. I can't even stand without an assistant. How am I going to get out there to help?"

"Who says we have to leave here?"

"What?"

"Why is she in danger? Because of us, well, me, actually. Why? We think it has to do with Curt Umfleet. Right? But why? Who has the most to gain by stopping us?" She paused. "I'll be right back."

Alexia arose and left Myra's room, returning a few minutes later with her laptop.

"While you were, um, comatose, I took the time to do some research." She pulled up a website of North Carolina's digital collections on one tab and a Google map of the western tip of the state on another. "You mentioned the land owned by the Umfleet Trust. I assumed it to be this area here." She pointed out the southwest end of Thorpe Reservoir. "Is this it?"

"Yes. As Curt explained it to me that night he drove to Cashiers, the family trust owned about two thousand acres there with miles of prime shoreline."

"Well, a lawyer named Emory Albritton gained control of that land and developed it into a gated community of million-plus-dollar homes. Millions of dollars were made, but I can't find any record of that money going into a family trust for the benefit of the Umfleet heirs. As I told you, Curt's two kids live in near-poverty conditions in the old family house in Frampton Corner. Albritton, on the other hand, lives in a mansion overlooking the lake, ran for the State legislature and then Senate, and ..." She stopped.

"And what?"

"He's running for the U.S. Senate now. What would happen if this story came out?"

Myra nodded. "Plenty of motive for murder. Couldn't have plotted it better myself. With their mother dead and no other relatives, I would have made him the guardian of the children when Curt went to prison. That would have put him in the position to pull this off."

Alexia suddenly looked deflated. "Did you already know this?"

"Know what?"

"All of this. What I just told you." Myra shook her head. "He *was* named their guardian. I found the original court records. Plus, it looks like there are dozens of other shady deals involving land around Cashiers and the lake."

Myra suddenly saw how it all went down. The young woman she had seen murdered in her home's drive had somehow become Alice Cummings, the fact bolstered by her pa's testimony. He and Dewey held a grudge against Curt and used the opportunity, and the body, to frame him. How had Albritton figured into it all? There had to be a connection between Albritton and Hastings. That was the only logical explanation.

"So, what now? We have a suspect. We have motive. Can we connect the two men, this Albritton and Hastings? Or Albritton and the guy they have in Little Rock, for that matter."

"No, I can't. And I can't prove my theory."

"So, plot it out. Let's pretend this is a novel. You're this far along in the story, the middle's beginning to sag, and the protagonists – that's you and me – are physically incapacitated, or about to be. Where does the story go next?"

"Hire a PI."

Myra winced. "You could, but you don't have time to bring that person up to speed, and they'd have to dance through hoops to get the information. It could take weeks to make a case that they'd then have to turn over to the authorities, who in turn would have to verify everything, take it to a Grand Jury... You get my drift. Me? I'd go straight to the cavalry, the police."

Alexia smiled as if she finally had one up on Myra. "You could, but that would take time, too. They'd focus on building a solid case, dotting all the "i's," to be clichéd. They would take weeks, if not months, to convene a Grand Jury. Can we implicate a senatorial candidate without solid evidence? How do we accomplish all this and get Angela back quickly? I was thinking more in terms of the PI staking out the Senator and trailing him. Letting him lead us, the PI, anyway, right to Angela. In the meantime, we could call the authorities tomorrow and lay out our case. If the PI finds Angela with the senator, then we have him. If not, we could still drift off into anesthetic sleep the following morning knowing we'd done everything we could."

"Damn, you're going to make one fine suspense author."

Minutes later, Alexia was on the phone with a sleepy investigator, a man who had worked with the Innocence Project. He walked into the room within the hour, after hearing what his retainer would be and of the healthy bonus he would earn, if he found Angela before the transplant surgery. He needed no coffee to stimulate him after that and Myra preferred being gassed knowing that all was well.

Forty-two

Myra awoke early, despite the late night of brainstorming with Alexia. Together they had laid out a roadmap for authorities to use to investigate what they now saw as a long history of fraud and theft by a prominent politico. State Senator Albritton's personal wealth, and the rise to power it had funded, had been borne from over a dozen land swindles, the largest of which was the outright theft of the land owned by the Umfleet Family Trust.

Myra's brain simmered in anger at this man who had robbed the family of the man who had once helped her to a new life. Combined with her angst about the upcoming surgeries, for her and Alexia, she was surprised she slept at all.

"Good morning," said Alexia as she poked her head into the room. "Looks like you slept about as much as I did." She eased into the room and sat in the chair at Myra's bedside.

Myra nodded. "I could have used the anesthetist last night about 3 am."

"I took the liberty of contacting the SBI directly," said Alexia. "I hope you don't mind."

"I don't, but it'll be a few days before we can talk with them."

Alexia rolled her eyes and turned toward the window. "Umm, actually, they're sending someone over this morning. They should be here in about an hour, after breakfast. I asked the nursing staff to hold them at the nurses' station until I come to get them. I've been told there's a conference room down the hall where we can meet privately."

Myra sat there silently. Did she have the stamina? She could let Alexia lay out their case to the agents. She no longer held any reservations about the young woman's capabilities. No. This had become too personal. She wanted to be there.

"Could you wheel me there? I hate to ask, but I don't think I have the strength to walk to the room on my own."

Alexia smiled. "What? No grand entrance?"

Myra replied with a wan smile. "No, the diva is dead. A diagnosis of terminal disease tends to hammer reality back into even the densest mind. I, uh ... I humbly ask for your assistance."

"No clichés? No 'staring death in the face,' 'one foot on a banana peel and the other in the grave?' No 'buying the farm' or 'cashing in the chips?'"

Myra laughed. "It's not over 'til the pumpkin-colored lady sings."

Alexia stood and stepped outside the room for a moment. She rolled a wheelchair into the room. "I commandeered this on my way over. To make sure we had one when you needed it."

Myra looked up at Alexia and beckoned her back to her bedside. She took the woman's hand. "Thank you, Alexia. For everything." A tear formed in the corner of her eye.

"God loves you," said Alexia as she leaned over and kissed Myra on the forehead. "And you're growing on me, too. I'll be back to get you when they arrive. I have one more phone call to make. Remember my wanting to see Justice Hoglund in Santa Fe? Well, looks like he was the judge in the Umfleet trial. He might have some valuable testimony against Albritton."

Myra reflected on that comment and realized she, too, had someone to track down.

Myra took a deep breath and straightened up in the wheelchair as Alexia rolled her into the conference room. Two men sat at the table and both rose as the women entered. Myra took the lead.

"Gentlemen, good morning. I'm Myra Mitchell and this is Alexia Hamilton." She put her hand forward.

The older of the two men shook her hand. He appeared to be late thirties, trim, with conservative grooming. His dark grey suit was well tailored and pricey, more expensive than Myra would have anticipated for a state investigator. The second man was a few years younger and dressed more to her expectations.

"I'm Agent Albritton, of the Professional Standards Division of the State Bureau of Investigation. This is Agent Barrows. I understand you have some information about possible crimes by one of our state legislators."

"Pleasure to meet you, Ms. Mitchell. I'm a fan," said Barrows as he extended his hand.

The two women exchanged glances.

"Excuse me, Agent Albritton, but are you related to Senator Emory Albritton?"

The agent's demeanor showed a subtle change. "Yes, ma'am. He's my uncle. May I ask why?"

Myra turned to the second man. "Agent Barrows, we have a conflict of interest issue here. I think we need to talk with you alone."

Albritton arose and dressed early, and was surprised to find Misty already dressed and in the kitchen. The aroma of brewing coffee began to permeate the room. Over the past two weeks she had seemed cold and indifferent. Was it his anxiety? Or was it her? On reflection, her aloofness seemed heightened over the previous week. Or was that just how he interpreted her behavior?

"Something wrong? Is there something bothering you?" he asked, as he grabbed a travel mug and filled it with coffee.

"I'm fine." She sipped her coffee. "You'd better get going. I'll be leaving right behind you to meet Teri for tennis."

He stepped up to kiss her and she backed away.

"Hey."

"Sorry, I think I'm getting a cold sore."

He shook it off, picked up his briefcase, and walked out to the garage. True to her word, he noticed her SUV following him a minute later. Their local home overlooking Jordan Lake put him almost equidistant from Raleigh, and his office at the State Capitol, and Durham, where Duke University sat. As much as he needed to go to the house near Duke Forest, he actually had to meet someone else at the Capitol Building before going to the office.

Several hours later, not having heard from Misty, he worked through the lunch hour and headed to his campaign office where he met briefly with his manager and strategist.

"Emory, this race is yours to lose. Don't do something stupid." His manager's words echoed through his mind as he left the meeting. He'd already done it by kidnapping the Thoms lady. How could he have been so brainless? His bigger quandary ... how could he undo it? His gut churned.

He picked up his cell and dialed his wife. No one at home. He tried her cell and got her voicemail. "Honey, I've got to run over to the Greensboro campaign office for a brief interview. I'll call you as I leave. Maybe we can go to Bin 54 for dinner. If that works for you, please call and make a reservation for seven o'clock. Thanks. Love you."

He hated lying to Misty, but this would give him time to question the Thoms lady and get home within her time expectations. Twenty minutes later, he pulled into the drive of the house. Little Hastings' car remained parked in the same place. He entered the home and Ricky Lee greeted him.

"Wondered if you was coming back." He grinned, as if jesting with a peer.

Albritton ignored the man's attempt at camaraderie. "How is she?"

"Last I checked, she found a book and was reading. She did check all the windows like you figured, but they held. She's made no escape attempts. Hasn't eaten much, either."

Albritton entered the room and found Angela sitting in a comfortable chair, a recent Myra Mitchell book in her lap. Even now, he couldn't get away from that Mitchell lady. The woman looked calm, but he had never felt so anxious.

"I hope you've been comfortable."

She made no comment or moves that might reflect her thoughts.

"Did you get enough to eat?"

No reply. For a second, he thought she was about to ignore him and resume reading.

"Look, like I said last night, I don't want to hurt you. I just need some information."

Suddenly, there was a commotion in the front of the house. He heard a scuffle and Ricky saying, "Don't go in there. Stay here and I'll get him." An instant later, Misty burst through the door.

"You cheating son-of-a-bitch! I knew it! I knew it. I could tell something was up, but I didn't really think you'd cheat on me after all these years."

Ricky came charging in. "I tried to stop her. I knew you wouldn't want me to hurt her."

That's when Albritton noticed the handgun in his wife's

hand.

"Is this her? Is she the reason for all these late evening campaign meetings? Damn, Emory, why?"

"Misty, it's not what —"

Unexpectedly, the Thoms woman stood up, put her hands on her hips in feigned indignation, and faced her captor. "Didn't you tell her, Emory? I thought you said you were getting a divorce."

Albritton couldn't believe what he'd just heard. Was this Thoms lady crazy enough to want them both dead?

The senator's wife began to raise the gun toward Albritton, but Ricky Lee ran at her. She must have sensed his movement because at the last moment, she turned toward the man and pulled the trigger. A look of horror flashed across Ricky Lee's face as a bloody flower blossomed across his chest. Just as quickly, Misty dropped the gun and put her hand to her mouth in realization of what she'd just done.

In that moment, Angela dashed for the door. Albritton tried to detain her, but she broke free just as another man, a stranger, appeared in the door. Angela tried to push past him as well, but he said something to her that got her attention. Albritton couldn't hear the words, but watched as the woman joined the man willingly and together fled from the house.

Albritton's mind was in chaos. Should he go after them? Misty sat sobbing on the floor, her hand unsteady as she kept pointing toward Ricky Lee. Should he try to comfort her? Should he call 911? Try to tend to Ricky's wound? The gun. Where was the gun? His campaign. The press. Stunned by the turn of events, he stumbled toward the front door and exited the house in time to see the Thoms woman and the stranger climb into a car and speed off.

Forty-three

Myra sat in bed flipping through channels on the TV. Nothing caught her interest. Nothing was capable of claiming her attention. Her mind focused on two things – Angela and the next day – and nothing on earth would displace those from her thoughts.

Dinner came and went. She had no appetite. It didn't matter whether that was the result of her illness or of her preoccupation. The tasteless chicken broth and green gelatin held no appeal. She sipped the tea in a fruitless attempt to ease her parched mouth.

Her nurse entered the room with a small paper pill cup in one hand and a Styrofoam cup of water in the other. She extended it toward Myra. "Here. Something to help you sleep."

Myra took both and placed them on the stand positioned across her. "Thank you."

"You sure you don't want to eat a little something? It might be days before you get to eat after the surgery."

Myra shook her head. "Even Surf and Turf from Harris's Steakhouse in San Francisco wouldn't interest me tonight. Thank you, though, again."

The phone rang and the nurse picked up the receiver to hand it to Myra. Myra listened, and smiled. Alexia's plan had indeed worked. Angela was safe, and the authorities were preparing their case against Albritton. Now, she could take that sleeping pill.

Forty-four
❧❧ ✦ ✦ ❧❧

How he got home remained a mystery, but Albritton had somehow managed to return safely to his Jordan Lake home. He held a vague memory of tracking down a trusted aide to come get his wife's car while he drove her home. He didn't remember driving or undressing Misty and putting her to bed. Unfortunately, he vividly recalled the events preceding that and the brisk walk he took with their dogs during which he heaved the gun as far into the lake as he could. He was now guilty of not only kidnapping and unlawful restraint, but of leaving the scene of a crime, failing to report a fatal shooting, tampering with evidence and obstruction.

Life had spiraled out of control ... because he had been stupid. He had allowed himself to become so emotional, so worried and preoccupied about what the Hamilton girl may have discovered that his common sense evaporated. Now, it seemed obvious that she never got so far as to connect him to the Curt Umfleet trial. His actions had now resulted in multiple people being injured, two dead, and his whole life being sucked into an inescapable black hole.

Misty had been catatonic. He'd given her a sedative to help her sleep and could only hope that she'd be able and willing to talk with him upon waking. It was too late to flee the country and only a matter of time before the police arrived. He could have turned themselves in, but the thought of Misty in a jail cell nauseated him. With luck, she would have this one last night in their home, in her own bed. No matter what happened, he wanted her to understand that he loved her, and would never cheat on her and never had.

Now he sat in his study with three fingers of scotch,

feeling three sheets to the wind. His hope for one last night together, in their own bed, faded. The police would come for them any time now. He was sure of it.

Absentmindedly, he flipped on the television at the beginning of the evening news. The anchor came on after the lead-in.

"Our top story tonight is a report of an alleged kidnapping and murder in a luxury home bordering Duke Forest. Police received a call from an Arkansas woman stating she had been held against her will at the home for the past thirty-six hours and had witnessed another woman shoot the kidnapper, who apparently worked for that woman's husband. Details are sketchy, but the story is being corroborated by a local private investigator well known for his work with the Innocence Project. How this might be related to the Innocence Project is not known at this time. As an added twist, a prominent politician appears to be involved and his wife may have been the shooter. We'll have more on this story as it develops."

The phone on his desk rang for the sixth time since he settled into his chair. He ignored it. His cell chimed with the receipt of a text message. He glanced at the text. His campaign manager was going ballistic. He needed to talk with him ASAP.

Albritton didn't have the strength. He'd gone beyond stupid. Maybe he shouldn't have tossed the gun. At that moment, he felt like eating the barrel.

Forty-five
❧ ✦ ✦ ❧

Myra floated as if she was in a dream, half-awake but
unable to open her eyes or talk. She became aware of
something in her throat but it didn't gag her. She sensed air
being forced into her lungs. She tried to take a deep breath but
couldn't.

"She's coming out of it."

The voice sounded distant. She realized she was indeed
coming "out of it" remembering she'd gone to surgery early
that morning. A sense of elation overcame the fuzziness. She
had survived the surgery. Her greatest fear became a worry of
the past.

"I'm Jean. You're in the recovery area. Try not to fight
the ventilator. You still need it to help you breathe."

Myra felt the desire to fight the machine, but she hadn't
the strength. She relaxed and listened to regular whoosh of the
ventilator, it's timing corresponding to the filling of her chest.
She drifted back to sleep.

"Is she okay?"

Myra again began to sense her surroundings. The thing in
her throat was gone. The whoosh of the ventilator was gone,
but that now familiar tick of the IV infuser came from her left
side. A mask covered her face, but she could take a deep
breath, almost.

"Yes, she's doing quite well. She's starting to wake up."

"Can she hear me?"

The voice was Alexia's.

"She can, but I'm not sure how easily she'll be able to

respond."

The male voice was familiar, too, but she couldn't put a name to it. That was her doctor, wasn't it?

"Myra, it's me, Alexia. Can you hear me? Here's my finger. Squeeze it if you can understand me."

Myra felt warm flesh in her right hand. She tried to squeeze but wasn't sure if she'd succeeded.

"Good. You're about to go to the ICU and I'll be going to the post-op floor, but they'll let me visit. I just wanted you to know that everyone is safe. You can rest comfortably. We're all safe. Do you hear me?"

Myra squeezed the finger in her hand, a little stronger this time.

Albritton awoke to the repeated ringing of the doorbell, his mind groggy and his gut churning. He glanced at the empty bottle of Glenfiddich lying on its side on his desk. His mouth felt like a freshly graveled road. His back ached. He had passed out at his desk.

The doorbell rang multiple times again and he heard a muffled yell from outside. The events of the last evening flooded into his mind and his heart began to race. Misty! He needed to check on Misty, first and foremost.

He raced upstairs to the master bedroom to find her sleeping peacefully on top of the covers. He remembered tucking her in, under the covers. He approached the bed.

"Honey?" he whispered. He didn't want to wake her, but knew he had to.

He sat down next to her and touched her forehead. She felt cold. He stared at her. "You're cold. You should have stayed under the covers."

He tried to move her, to pull the covers over her and realized she wasn't breathing. Her arms were stiff. Her color, pale. Panic covered him and the mental fuzziness evaporated. He glanced around and saw the sedative pill bottle, cap off, on the floor. Empty.

"Oh dear God! Nooooo!" he screamed.

"Uncle Emory! It's Mike! Uncle Emory!"

Albritton rushed to the top of the stairs. He hadn't heard the door open, but his nephew stood in the foyer.

"Mike! Please! Call an ambulance! Misty … Oh dear God."

He crumbled to the floor, sobbing. What had he done? Why had this happened? How had things gone so badly?

He recognized Mike at his side. "Uncle Emory, I've called for EMS. Where is she?"

Albritton pointed toward the bedroom and watched his nephew race to the room, only to emerge slowly, head down.

"I'm sorry, Uncle Emory. I don't think EMS can help."

Another man walked up the stairs. "Sir, I'm Agent Barrows. I work with your nephew. We have warrants —"

Mike waved him off. "Give us a minute, Rod. Please."

Albritton felt his nephew's arms envelope him.

"So sorry, Uncle Emory."

Albritton noticed tears in his nephew's eyes. He took a deep breath and straightened up, trying to regain his composure. That's when he noticed half a dozen men in the foyer below. He knew why they were there. He pointed toward them.

"Sorry, Uncle Emory. We have warrants to search the house, and your office, and the house in Cashiers. They're all being searched as we speak."

Albritton nodded. He knew they'd be coming. It was that

girl's fault … and that Mitchell woman. His life was shattered. The love of his life, dead … because of them. The tears stopped. His heart raced but not in fear. Anger grew inside. He patted his pocket. His car keys were still there.

He stood and slowly descended the stairs. He watched the agent named Barrows give instructions to the men.

"I'm going to have to show them the safe room, too, Uncle Emory. Sorry, but since I know about it, I'm bound to let them search it, too."

Albritton knew what that meant. His wealth and prominence made him a target. They had designed the safe room as a secure place to hide should his family be in danger. No one could enter the property without triggering security monitors and alerting anyone in residence. Such a warning wouldn't, couldn't, prevent a home invasion by anyone intent on harm. The warning only gave the family time to find safety inside. When Mike was a child, he had loved the secret room and the ability to "spy" on others with the monitoring system within – all done in play with his uncle's permission. In recent times, Albritton had used the secure room to store sensitive documents. Those documents would etch the final line on his tombstone.

He walked up to Agent Barrows and asked, "Am I under arrest?"

"No Sir. But please remain on the premises."

He headed for the front door.

"Uncle Emory, don't. Please stay here."

Albritton ignored his nephew and walked out the door. He shoved aside an officer who stepped in to intercede and ran for the car. By the time the officer was back on his feet, he was halfway down the drive. His life was over. He wasn't going alone.

Forty-six
❧◆◆❧

Myra eased off the bedpan but left it under the sheet. She didn't have the strength to lift it onto the side table. She grabbed the bed control and raised the head of her bed so she could watch the activity around her. Large glass windows between her room and the central work area of the Intensive Care Unit gave her an unobstructed view of the nurses at work, as well as giving the nurses an unobstructed view of her on the bedpan. Oh, for a little privacy. Still, nothing in life was wasted on a writer, and a writer she would always be.

She took a sip of water and marveled that no nausea followed. For weeks, nausea had been her constant companion. She didn't miss it. Even the green Jell-O looked good.

"Hey! How'd you get in here?"

"You can't be in here!"

A man rushed past the nurses' station. He looked disheveled and angry ... and he was heading right for Myra's room.

"Security!"

"Someone call security!"

Two nurses scrambled after the man, but he threw them both off and onto the floor. Within seconds, he entered Myra's room, scowling and breathing hard.

"YOU have destroyed my life!" He pointed toward Myra. "You and that miserable Hamilton girl."

He stepped closer to the bed. Myra could see he was unarmed, but she had no strength to fight him off.

"My wife is now dead, thanks to you two."

He walked to the edge of her bed and yanked the pillow

from under her head. In a split second she couldn't breathe, her face smothered by the pillow. She scratched and clawed at the bed. She tried to grab and lift the bedpan. Pain rained through her abdomen.

"Get off of her!"

Suddenly the pillow was gone and she gasped for air as she saw Alexia on the man's back, her arm around his neck in a tight stranglehold. The man fought back, pushing off the bed and throwing himself and Alexia backward against the nearby wall. She heard a thud and groan, and saw the man arise without Alexia. Abruptly, his back arched and his eyes bulged. He shook violently and fell to the floor, writhing.

Three security officers piled on top of him, pulling his hands behind him, and attaching flexi-cuffs. A fourth officer removed the probes from Albritton and holstered his Taser X2. As they dragged the man from the room, several nurses rushed into the room. Two attended to Myra while two more bent over Alexia.

One of Alexia's attendants straightened up and yelled to the nurses' station. "Get me a stretcher and call the surgeon STAT. I think she's bleeding internally."

Myra found the strength to push her nurses aside. She raised herself up in the bed so she could see Alexia. Once again, the young woman had voluntarily sacrificed herself for Myra. Tears eroded her cheeks as she watched them rush Alexia out of the ICU to the OR.

Forty-seven
❧◆◆❧

Myra sat on the edge of her bed, looking out the window over the Duke campus. She'd been moved to a regular med/surg bed on the transplant floor two days earlier. Alexia's donor site incision had broken open in the scuffle, but the surgeons had been able to repair it easily and she, too, was back in a regular bed recovering. Myra had not been able to see her and longed for the opportunity.

She stood slowly and moved to the nearby sink. The mirror above the sink reflected the marked improvement she had made since receiving part of Alexia's liver. Her skin color, while still a shade of ochre, no longer placed her in the Great Pumpkin's family.

She heard a knock at the door and turned to see two elderly gentlemen in the doorway. She quickly made sure her derriere wasn't exposed through her patient gown.

"Yes?"

The two men stared at her and she returned the glare, scrutinizing first the scrawny white-haired man in the wheelchair. Her eyes widened. Could it really be?

"Betsy?"

The voice, though frail, took her back decades.

"Jim?" It had to be him, Jim Fleming.

He nodded and she hobbled over to give him a hug.

"Or should I say, it's me, George." He grinned. "You made me famous."

"Same old smile. Goodness, I never thought I'd see you again."

"Good genes. Aiming to hit the century mark next year."

"You certainly have come a long way, young lady," the

375

other man said. He looked roughly twenty years younger than Jim but stout and nearly bald. A long scar graced his scalp.

"Sir?"

"You don't recognize me, do you?"

"No, Sir, I'm afraid I don't."

He extended his hand. "Thomas Mathews."

"Esquire," added Jim.

Myra took a deep breath and gasped. "I-I thought you died in a car accident. I ..."

"First, Judge Warren asked me to confirm you're you." He smiled. "So, what do you remember most about our very first meeting?"

"The look on your face when I told you my story about my baby being taken by my father and sold."

"And ..."

"I was still lactating and you had your secretary check me to confirm that."

"Betsy Weston is back aka Myra Mitchell. As I said, you've come a long way. Backwoods Carolina to bestselling author. I feel honored to have played a part."

"But you ... You were in a coma and I thought you died."

"As I recall, you had to leave town suddenly. And I didn't even think of it when you came to Sally's funeral. That week was such a blur," said Jim.

"I was nearly killed. Spent four months in a coma ..." He pointed to the scar across his scalp. "... and another three months in physical rehab. It took me over a year after that to get back to work, and by then, the Umfleet trial was such old news I never heard or knew about it until now, with this story about you breaking all over the news. When I read about the old case, I was able to put the pieces together and I contacted Judge Warren."

Myra stepped around the wheelchair and hugged the aged attorney.

"Please. Please come in and have a seat. I could use some company right now."

The next two weeks in the hospital evolved into a homecoming of sorts for Myra. Jim Fleming returned off and on with several of the "girls" from the Rest Stop that Betsy had known. The women had done Sally 'Sweetie' Fleming justice by becoming successful businesswomen, lawyers, and one, a gynecologist. All left the trade and never looked back. Those meetings were bittersweet in their memorials to Billie and Jennie.

Judge Warren and a court stenographer came to visit and take Myra's deposition. With Counselor Mathews' testimony to back up Myra's, she was assured that Curt Umfleet's freedom was but days away.

True to that assurance, Curt Umfleet's conviction was overturned and his release date set. Myra sweet-talked, cajoled, threatened, and cried to get her doctor to release her for Curt's prison release. Her doctors relented only enough to give her a day pass to attend the event. Alexia, now free of her hospital gown and staying with Oni and Angela at the motel, joined her roommates in picking up Myra at the hospital and driving her to the prison.

As Curt emerged to a cheering crowd of Innocence Project volunteers and a strong press contingent, Myra stood from her wheelchair and walked up to him. Tears streamed from her eyes as she hugged him.

"I'm so, so sorry this took so long. Can you ever forgive me?"

"Never held it against ya. God allowed Joseph to go to prison and he became the second ruler of Egypt. Silas and Paul went to prison and God made the earth quake. The jailer and his guards came to know the Lord that day. I just figured He had a job for me there, so I made the best of it. I knew He'd take care of the needs of my children. Never had a doubt."

Curt's son and daughter joined Myra and she held all three until the son tired of it and pushed away.

"Curt, I'm forever indebted to you. I'll make sure things are right for you," said Myra.

"Not necessary. God's got everything under control."

Forty-eight

❧✦✦❧

"I'm nervous as a long-tailed cat in a room full of rocking chairs."

Alexia laughed. "Cliché. You must be feeling better; you're baiting me now."

Curt Umfleet's homecoming party had been delayed until Myra's discharge from the hospital. Oni and Angela had returned to Arkansas after Myra promised not to delay her return to Eureka Springs. Alexia had the wheel of the Mustang and played her role as chauffer.

"I haven't been back to Frampton Corner since I left North Carolina."

"Then this trip is past due." Alexia turned off U. S. Highway 64 at Cashiers and headed toward Frampton Corner. "So, this adventure is almost finished. Has God met your deepest desire?"

Myra looked ahead down the road and didn't answer.

"On my last trip here, in this car, I almost turned back at this point." Myra gripped the door handle tightly as she remembered that trip.

A mile down the road, Myra suddenly said, "Next right. Take the next right."

Alexia jammed the brakes and slowed enough to make the turn safely. A sign said, "Frampton Cemetery – 1 mile."

Myra racked her brain to recall the directions to her mother's grave. As they entered the gate, she noticed a new sign and directory listing family plots. "Here. Stop here." She pointed to the directory. "Be a good girl and check the directory for the Cummings family plot. Elizabeth Cummings to be precise."

379

Alexia started to say something, but stopped and did as requested. A moment later, she maneuvered the car along the cemetery's narrow lanes until she found the right spot.

"Do you need any help?"

"No. Thank you."

Myra exited the car and walked slowly toward her mother's grave. She stood there silently for several minutes, fondling her great, great grandmother's necklace that adorned her neck and trying to remember what her mother looked like. She couldn't and that disturbed her. She started to turn away, but stopped to stare at the adjacent grave. "Rest in Peace ... Amos Lloyd Cummings." She was surprised to see that he'd died just two years earlier. *The alcohol must have pickled him*, she thought.

Alexia joined her. "Your parents?"

Myra nodded. "My mother died when I was a child." She sighed. "You asked a while ago about my deepest desire. Well, for years all I thought about was having the chance to piss on my father's grave for what he did to me. But I knew that unladylike act of public indecency would likely land me in jail. I settled for spitting on his grave when I got the chance. Now ... I can't bring myself to do it. Maybe I've finally forgiven him. In a way, he gave me a new life by letting me go and by saving my mother's small inheritance for me. He could have spent it on drink. Probably wanted to, but he didn't, and he made sure I got it."

"That was your deepest desire?" Alexia looked deflated as if she'd expected something grander.

"No, but it was a desire."

Myra turned abruptly and walked back to the car. Alexia hustled to catch up. They drove past the old Post Office, the Sheriff's office, and the local courthouse. No different, but the old home across from the Sheriff had been "remuddled" to someone's idea of Victorian. A yard sign advertised antiques, but it looked as if the "Closed" sign had been permanently affixed to it. Hoping to capitalize on tourists' love of the local scenery, several of the old homes were now boutiques, one a wine bar. Only the latter showed any signs of life, but it offered no temptation to Myra now. The changes failed to give the town any allure and Myra gave the revitalization effort a weak D-plus. Minutes later, they turned up that all-too-familiar road to the top of the mountain.

Myra was surprised to see scaffolding surrounding the Umfleet home. Repairs had already been started. The new steel roof glistened in the sun as it awaited painting. A backhoe sat parked behind the house where a trench had been dug and footers poured for what appeared to be a new addition. Alexia parked near that backhoe.

Curt was the first to greet them.

"Looks mighty different, don't it?" He hugged the women and took Myra by the hand. As they walked toward the house, he raised her arm and glanced at the forearm. "See, Mary told ya I did good work. Not much of a scar to be seen." He smiled.

Myra raised her other hand and swept it across from one end of the house to the other. Before she could say anything, Curt spoke up as if reading her mind.

"House needed fixin' up and with my comin' home, we needed to expand."

Myra gave him a quizzical look.

"The judge awarded me over a million dollars for wrongful incarceration. Gonna fix my house and get a couple of new cars. Then we'll see who the Lord wants me to help next."

"Don't forget, you got a strong civil case against Emory Albritton. He stole your land and –"

Curt interrupted. "We'll cross that bridge soon enough."

Myra and Alexia shot each other a glance that said, "cliché," without having to verbalize the word. Myra smiled at her friend, a young woman who had become one of her dearest friends. She was literally a part of her now, Myra had joked. As usual, Alexia had put it biblically. Jesus said it, prior to being crucified, "Greater love has no one than this, that one lay down his life for his friends."

As Alexia had put it, her Lord had laid down his life for everyone, even Myra. If only she could believe that. Her deepest desire had not been fulfilled.

Forty-nine
❧ ◆ ◆ ❧

On the drive up to the Umfleet's, Myra had closed her eyes as they passed her father's house. After fleeing all those years ago, she could never come to accept it as *her* old home, too. She didn't want to relive anything that had gone on in that house. Yet, after an hour at the party, she felt an inexplicable curiosity to see the home. She approached Alexia.

"Dear, would you be willing to leave this gaiety to help me walk down the hill?"

Alexia furrowed her brow. Myra had shared some of what had happened to her at her father's hand. These were stories even Oni and Diana had never heard.

"Are you sure?"

"Of course. It's only a building, right? An inanimate object. The monster no longer hides in the closet."

"Tell you what, I'll pull the car around and drive you down. That'll make it easier to come back up here afterwards. You're not to exert yourself, remember?"

Myra nodded. That made sense.

The first thing Myra noticed was the old shed, and all the junk, was gone. Only its foundation remained. The house was brightly painted like some Victorian "painted lady." The color scheme wasn't quite architecturally correct, but it sure livened up the old place. Myra climbed out of the car and looked up at the old kitchen window where she saw the face of a man staring out at her. She moved toward the front porch and she realized he was still staring, at her car.

Myra climbed the two steps to the front porch and paused to stroke the wood railing and look about. The sun had started its descent behind the distant mountain and she stood as she often had as a teen, mesmerized by the beauty of the sunset. Only when the front door opened did the spell break.

The front door opened and a man cleared his throat, but Myra continued to gaze westward. "Can we help you?" he asked.

At that, Myra started and turned to face him. "Oh, oh ... I am sooo sorry. I'm trespassing, aren't I?" She turned back toward the valley. "Isn't it beautiful?" She paused, soaking in the beauty. "Oh ..." She faced them again. "I'm sorry. My name's Myra. I-I didn't mean to disturb you folks."

A woman had joined the man on the porch and Myra overheard her whisper in his ear. "Be right back." She assumed them to be husband and wife.

"You're right about that. Probably the best view in the whole county." He joined her for the dénouement. Dark would quickly follow. The woman emerged from the house holding something.

As twilight lost ground to the night, Myra faced them. "Thank you for sharing your view. I should get going."

"Would you like to have tea with us?" The man stared at his wife, apparently confounded by her invitation. "I mean, these roads are treacherous in the dark and --"

"Thank you, but I've imposed enough." Myra turned to leave the porch. "I have someone driving for me, and we need to get back to the Umfleet's.

"Ms. Mitchell, please, we'd be honored." She held up the book in her hands. "We love your writing."

The man snatched the book from his wife and compared the jacket photo with the woman standing before them.

Myra stopped and edged back onto the wooden porch, unsure what to do. "I know. Not much of a resemblance, but the past few months have been rough." She had a good vibe about this young couple, but did she want to go inside that house? Most memories from inside remained on the unpleasant list.

She took the book and pulled a pen from her jacket pocket. "Umm, I don't usually –"

"We understand," interrupted the man. The woman's eyes cast down.

Myra looked at them. "Your names?"

"I'm Jared Hilsing and this is my wife, Amy."

Myra noted for the first time that the young woman was pregnant, and well along with her pregnancy at that. Myra autographed the inside of the book and handed it back to Amy. "I started to say, I don't make it a habit of accepting invitations from complete strangers. But, Amy, Jared, I guess we're no longer *complete* strangers. If it really isn't an imposition, I'll take you up on that offer."

Amy's smile illuminated the gathering shadow. She elbowed her husband. "Go get her friend and I'll set the table."

Amy opened the front door and motioned for Myra to enter. Myra hesitated. In her mind, her father waited inside. Would he be drunk and abusive or sober and tame? She forced herself through the doorway and, in that first glance of unfamiliar furnishings, remembered what she'd told Alexia just minutes before. The house itself held no negative energy, only the memory of a long dead past inhabitant. The interior was remarkably pleasant and bright, the furniture, homey and comfortable. No pretentious electronics. A floor to ceiling bookshelf, filled with a variety of authors, dominated one wall. She scanned the titles and found all of her books as well as those of many good friends.

Jared and Alexia joined them and Myra introduced Alexia to Amy. Alexia eyed Myra nervously.

"You've turned this place into a lovely home. Very cozy," Myra stated as she sat down to her cup of green tea.

"So, you were at the Umfleets?" asked Jared.

Myra nodded.

"We heard that he'd been exonerated and freed. What a shame he had to spend those years in jail," said Amy. "We aren't aware of any details, but I figure we'll hear about them sooner or later, with them living so close and all."

Myra felt no need to say any more. She stood and looked up the stairs toward her old room. "This is the kind of house that needs a big brass bed and antiques. Do you like antiques?"

"I guess." Amy shrugged. "We already have a big brass bed. It came with the house 'cause no one could dismantle it without destroying it, and no one had the heart to do that."

"May I see it?"

A look of anxiety crossed the young woman's face, but she finally said, "Uh, sure, I guess. The upstairs is kinda messy. Please don't look too closely."

Jared led Myra up the stairs and seemed surprised when she forgot to wait for him to lead the way and walked right to her old room. Other than a new mattress, new linens and a colorful wedding knot quilt, the bed had not changed. She looked at the side of that bed and recalled the day she awoke to find Jimmy Bob gone. She rushed from the room and down the stairs before her emotions broke free.

"I'm sorry, Amy, but we need to go. Alexia."

"But, I ..."

"Your home is lovely dear and I am honored to be a guest, but I'm suddenly not feeling well and we need to go."

Alexia stood without saying a word, but her look was all too clear – *"I didn't think this was a good idea."*

Fifty
❧❦◆◆❦❧

The following morning Myra picked at her food in the motel's breakfast room. She'd been silent all the way back from Frampton Corner, and Alexia hadn't pushed it. This morning, however, Alexia wouldn't let it go.

"So, what was that all about last night? You accept their invitation to tea and then we leave abruptly before finishing the first cup? Why?"

Myra looked at the young woman, her heir apparent, destined to write her biography, and realized she hadn't given her all the pieces. "I shouldn't have gone up to my old bedroom. It proved too painful." She then told Alexia the rest of her story, about Jimmy, her flight from Frampton Corner, her stay at the Rest Stop.

"I've spent a quarter of a million dollars trying to find my son. I even had an attorney offer my father $100,000 to give up the information. He refused, still insisted that baby was stillborn, that he had no grandchildren. There were times I thought I was crazy, that I had indeed imagined bringing Jimmy home with me. That usually led to a binge, but the wine never erased the memory. The only thing I have left of him is a photo buried in a box, and it's probably rotted away by now."

Alexia sat silently soaking it in for several minutes and finally said, "I think that would have driven *me* crazy. Look, we have to go back. You need to see if that chest is still there, if the photo is still in it."

Myra knew she was right.

After eating, they climbed back into the Mustang and made the trip again to Frampton Corner. Alexia needed no directions this time and drove directly to the old house. Myra

387

walked to the front door and rang the bell. No answer. As she stepped off the porch, Jared and Amy pulled into the drive in their car. They caught up to Myra as she reached the Mustang.

"We were in town and saw you go down Main Street," said Jared.

"I want to apologize for last night."

"That's okay," replied Amy. "If you weren't feeling well —"

"I wasn't being totally honest." Myra paused. She didn't want to continue but saw Alexia nodding her head in encouragement. "I grew up in this house. That was my old room and my old bed. Something happened to me in that room, something terrible, and the memory of it overwhelmed me. I hadn't expected it to after all these years, but it did."

Jared and Amy looked at each other and Jared spoke first. "Are you the one Mr. Umfleet was accused of killing? Is that why he's free now, because you came back?"

Myra nodded.

Both let out a long sigh. "Wow."

"We came back this morning to apologize and to, uh, ask for one thing, a favor."

"Sure," said Amy. Jared didn't look so enthusiastic.

"Do you have a shovel?"

Jared shrugged and nodded.

"Meet me by the old foundation." She pointed toward the area of the old shed.

Jared walked off to get his tool and Myra walked to the foundation, took ten paces along the western side, and stood waiting for him. Was it even possible that the chest would still be there? Five minutes later, Jared pulled a metal box wrapped in old rubberized canvas from the ground. Myra trembled as he unwrapped it. All those years and never unearthed, was everything still in there? Would the contents be intact?

Jared carried the case to the home's front porch and placed it on a small table. "Would you like to do this alone?"

Myra smiled nervously. "Not on your life. You own the property now; this box is yours. There's only one thing I want from the box." Amy started to protest, but Myra held up her hand. "Just one item. The rest is yours."

Using a sturdy screwdriver and hammer, Myra tried to pry the box open to no avail. Jared took the hammer and with one solid whack, broke open the lock. Myra opened the lid. Its contents remained in remarkable condition. She removed a small manila envelope and opened it. Tears welled up in her eyes as she clutched the faded 3-by-5 photo and a tattered birth "certificate" to her chest. She held it out to Alexia.

"The final piece. My proof, after all these years."

She pushed the box toward Amy. The young woman opened the lid, gasped, and grabbed her husband. Jared stared at the contents.

"All yours. Railroad gold that my grandfather once gave me for a rainy day. If I recall correctly, it's probably worth over $50,000 in today's market. Maybe more to collectors."

"We can't take this!" Amy protested.

"What do you mean, *take* it? It's yours. Salvage rights on *your* property. I'm sure you can find a good use for the money. Your family is about to expand by fifty percent."

Jared started to stammer, but Amy cut him short. "We'll discuss it later."

Myra chuckled. Leave it to the wife to use common sense.

Amy turned back to Myra. "Thank you. Actually, it's going to double. We're expecting twins. What's that?"

Myra hesitated, but turned the crackled photo to show her. "My only photo of my baby. Two days old in bed with me.

Two weeks later, he was gone, taken while I slept ... to God knows where."

Amy burst into tears and rushed from the porch. Myra sat back, unsure as to what just happened. Even Jared looked surprised by his wife's action ... until he saw the photo and his face blanched. A moment later, Amy returned and thrust something into Jared's hand. Now as teary-eyed as his wife, Jared said, "My biologic mother," and gave Myra a matching photo.

ABOUT THE AUTHOR

Braxton can't lay claim to wanting to be a writer all his life, although his mother and seventh grade English teacher were convinced he had what it would take. He went to Duke University, earned a Bachelor's Degree of Science in Engineering with a major in Bio-Medical Engineering, and found his way into medical school at the University of Cincinnati. Following a residency in Emergency Medicine at Madigan Army Medical Center, he served tours as the Chief, Emergency Medical Services at Fort Campbell, KY and as a research Flight Surgeon at Fort Rucker, AL. Who had time to write?

By the late 1990's, his professional and family life had settled down, somewhat, and his mother once again took up her mantra, "Write a book. You're a good writer." Yet, with no experience in writing anything other than technical articles, he hesitated to try his hand at fiction. That changed in 1997 when the local newspaper held a writing contest for Valentine's Day. Out of 1100 entries, he made it to the top five finalists and realized that maybe he could write fiction after all.

The next ten years saw him learning the craft of writing through local writers' groups, seminars, critique groups and more. "Indebted" (©January 2013) marks his second formal publication.

Fifteen years after that first hesitant start, he can't find enough time to write as much as he'd like. He now lives in Missouri with his wife, Paula. Their two children are grown and with three grandchildren nearby, "Papa" wears a number of hats.

Other books by Braxton DeGarmo:
The Militant Genome (July 2012)

Made in the USA
Lexington, KY
12 November 2013